Past Crimes

An Alexis Parker novel

G.K. Parks

This is a work of fiction. Names, characters, places, events, and other concepts are the product of the author's imagination or are used fictitiously. Any resemblance to actual persons, living or dead, places, establishments, events, and locations is entirely coincidental.

Copyright © 2021 G.K. Parks

A Modus Operandi imprint

ISBN: 1942710291
ISBN-13: 978-1-942710-29-5

For my mom, who reads all my books.

BOOKS IN THE LIV DEMARCO SERIES:

Dangerous Stakes
Operation Stakeout
Unforeseen Danger
Deadly Dealings
High Risk
Fatal Mistake

BOOKS IN THE ALEXIS PARKER SERIES:

Likely Suspects
The Warhol Incident
Mimicry of Banshees
Suspicion of Murder
Racing Through Darkness
Camels and Corpses
Lack of Jurisdiction
Dying for a Fix
Intended Target
Muffled Echoes
Crisis of Conscience
Misplaced Trust
Whitewashed Lies
On Tilt
Purview of Flashbulbs
The Long Game
Burning Embers
Thick Fog
Warning Signs
Past Crimes
Sinister Secret

BOOKS IN THE JULIAN MERCER SERIES:

Condemned
Betrayal
Subversion
Reparation
Retaliation
Hunting Grounds

BOOKS IN THE CROSS SECURITY INVESTIGATIONS SERIES:

Fallen Angel
Calculated Risk

ONE

"I told you to wait in the car," Detective Derek Heathcliff whispered while the medical examiner went to grab the files.

"You forgot to crack the window," I said.

He dug the car keys out of his pocket and shoved them into my hand. "Go wait in the car."

"But you might need my help. I can consult." I looked at him with big puppy dog eyes. "Please, Derek. My skills will get rusty if I don't put them to use."

"I doubt that. You work cases all the time for Cross Security."

"It's not the same."

"You should have thought about that before you resigned from the FBI."

"I didn't have a choice." I'd been having a lot of second thoughts about the path my life had taken after recent events. "Resigning was the right decision. Going back to the OIO is the mistake I'm paying for, that everyone's paying for."

He watched me from the corner of his eye. "Is that what you got out of the meeting we just left? Because that wasn't the point."

"What was the point? To make me cry? Every time someone shares during these little group therapy sessions of ours, I nearly lose it."

"It's not group therapy. It's a support group."

"Yeah, for those of us dealing with survivor's guilt. News flash, the meetings make me feel worse. Working will take my mind off of it and make me feel better."

"Are you sure? I know you don't like bodies, and this one's not pretty."

"I can handle it."

"I don't have authorization to hire you as a consultant. That would require Lt. Moretti's signature and paperwork. Lots of paperwork. The last thing you need—"

"Is to sit alone in your car and dwell on everything discussed in group. Let me focus on something else. Work's always a good distraction. I'll consult unofficially."

"Fine, you can stay, but you can't examine the body. Don't say or touch anything. As far as everyone else is concerned, you're not here."

I held up my palms and took a step back. "Hey, I'm invisible."

The look in his eyes told me he regretted not dropping me off before coming here, but he didn't want to ditch me after the meeting. We both needed moral support. He scanned the log sheet on the desk while we waited.

"All right, Detective Heathcliff, the medical examiner is ready for you." The lab tech handed him a copy of the preliminary report.

Heathcliff flipped the pages, reading as he went. "Thanks." He headed toward the door in the back, and I followed at his heels.

"Uh, Detective, your date can wait out here," she said.

I turned to her. "I'm not his date."

"Okay," she checked the sign-in sheet, but I hadn't signed in, "who are you?"

"She's no one," Heathcliff said. "She's invisible, and she's going to wait right here and not say a word." He gave me a hard look. "Right, Alex?"

"What if someone sneezes? Can't I say bless you?"

Rolling his eyes, he headed for the door. "I won't be

long."

"Fine."

When he opened the glass door, the smell of decay and industrial strength cleaner grew stronger and lingered even after the door shut. I studied the room. I'd been here a couple of times before. Frankly, I didn't need to see an autopsy in progress or a body butterflied open on a table. The last time I did, I scrubbed my skin raw and even that didn't get the smell off of me. Hopefully, being in the outer office would save me from such a fate. Heathcliff, on the other hand, was a goner.

The lab tech retook her seat, working on a report while glancing in my direction every few seconds. "Sorry, I know you're invisible and not supposed to speak, but can I get you anything while you wait? A coffee or soda?"

"No, thanks." I couldn't see much through the hanging blinds, except for Heathcliff's back and an occasional glimpse of a white lab coat or sheet. From this angle, it was hard to tell what the white fabric was. "Does Detective Heathcliff bring dates here often?"

"No, but a few of the guys in the department have tried it a time or two."

"Badge bunnies," I murmured.

"Most likely, unless they're just into that whole death-goth scene."

"Oh, the movies in the cemetery crowd. I know the type. It's just another trend I don't understand."

"Me neither." She stopped what she was doing. "I didn't mean to offend you. But you didn't sign-in, and I don't see a badge hanging around your neck or from your belt. I figured since Heathcliff's off-the-clock, maybe he was actually enjoying some off duty companionship. The guy's always so buttoned-up and serious about his job. I didn't think he had any friends outside of work. I'm glad he was out, enjoying himself."

"Enjoy would be the wrong word."

"Well, whatever it was, I'm sorry it got interrupted."

"I'm not." The last place I wanted to be was stuck in a church basement. I moved closer to the desk, so I could glimpse the report she was working on. "Who's the DB?"

"No idea. We're hoping dental records will give us a match. Prints were beyond the realm of possibility, and DNA hasn't gotten us anywhere yet."

"But you're already running it. When did the body come in?"

"Yesterday."

"Cause of death?" I asked.

"We weren't sure at first since there were so many options, but it looks like a fatal gunshot wound to the chest."

"Why couldn't you pull prints?"

"His fingertips were damaged, a combination of perimortem injury and degradation after being in the ground for so long."

"In the ground?"

"Yeah," she quirked an eyebrow, "he got dug up accidentally."

"From where?"

"You're inquisitive."

I tried another approach. "How long do you think he's been in the ground?"

"Are you sure you aren't one of those death-obsessed freaks?"

"I'm sure." I wasn't obsessed with death, but it followed me around like a stray dog.

"Okay, who are you? You're not a cop. You're not the detective's girlfriend or date. So why do you want to know these details? You're not a reporter, are you?"

"No, just a police consultant."

"I didn't know the police hired a consultant for this case. We don't even have the victim's name yet."

"They didn't. I just happened to be with Heathcliff when he got the call, so he let me tag along."

"I see." She turned back to her report. Her attitude toward me had become less friendly in the last two seconds, though I wasn't sure why.

"How long was the guy in the ground?" I asked again.

"Our best guess, based on the rate of decomp, is seven to ten years."

"Wow, no wonder fingerprints aren't viable. That's a

long time to be dead. Why the urgency?" DNA analysis usually took time because of the backlog. Why would a cold case get bumped to the top of the list?

"I don't know. You'd have to ask the detective that question."

I didn't recall any high-profile unsolved murders from ten years ago, but around that time, I was just starting law school. I wasn't paying attention to such things. Still, Heathcliff wouldn't have come here immediately after our group therapy session if this wasn't important.

While I waited for him to finish speaking to the medical examiner, I looked around the office. Unfortunately, I couldn't see inside the lab, and the tech had stopped answering my questions. Maybe if I'd told her I was a private investigator or former federal agent, she would have been more forthcoming. It was hard to say for certain, but no matter my title, I had no authority to be here or request information. Those days ended the moment I handed in my badge.

"Sorry about that," Heathcliff said as he stepped out of the lab, the door automatically closing behind him. He tapped the edge of the folder a few times against his palm. "Are you ready to get that drink now? I know I am."

"Sure."

We returned to the car, and he locked the folder in the trunk. I gave him a suspicious look when he got behind the wheel, but he pretended not to notice. "Do you need to call Martin?" He pointed to the clock on the dash. "We're usually at the bar by now. You don't want him to worry if he gets there before we do."

"It's Monday night. There's not a chance in hell Martin's even left the office yet. If you need to check-in at the precinct, we have time."

"No, I already called Moretti and passed along John Doe's COD. The ME sent the slugs to the lab, so ballistics should be back by morning. Hopefully, we'll have an ID by then."

"In that case, it looks like the rest of our night is free. We could go to a different bar. One that's closer. I just have to let Martin know where to pick me up."

"Nah, I like our usual bar. It's quiet. I don't know anyone there."

I wondered if he was embarrassed to go to a cop bar with a security consultant or if he just didn't want his brothers-in-blue to see us together. After all, I'd nearly gotten him killed not too long ago, and then I bungled a case with another police detective not too long after that, resulting in an innocent man's murder. The police department probably figured I was a jinx.

The dust had barely settled when one afternoon Heathcliff barged into my office and forced me to go with him to a support group meeting. He'd been dragging me to these things every Monday and Thursday for the last four weeks. Tonight was the first time we broke from our routine of heading straight to a bar afterward to get sloshed.

"Not that I mind, but why did you have to rush down here after our meeting? I thought you were off duty," I said.

"I'm a major crimes detective. There is no off duty."

"I guess not." I paused, but he remained tight-lipped. "This case must be really important. We could have ducked out of the meeting early."

"The guy's dead. He's not going anywhere, but since the ME texted me that he finished the preliminary examination and determined COD, I figured it'd be best to find out what else he might have learned about John Doe."

"Isn't this a cold case?"

He glanced at me from the corner of his eye. "Didn't you promise not to speak or ask questions?"

"I don't recall."

He let out a displeased humph. "If we're right about who the victim is, this is an eight-year-old case."

"I didn't think John Doe had been IDed."

"Not officially, but the LT has a theory who he might be."

"Why?"

"I don't know."

"Where was the body found?"

"Near the airport. They just started clearing that spare field to expand the parking lot, and a backhoe dug him up."

Heathcliff remained facing forward, but his tone and body language stiffened. "Why are you so curious?"

"It's in my nature. Do you want me to tell you the story of the scorpion and the frog?"

"Parker, you are not the scorpion. The scorpion couldn't resist inflicting harm. That's not you." And just like that, he'd changed topics.

"You wanna bet?"

He hit the brakes, and I jerked forward in the seat. "Stop that right now. Agents Lucca and Jablonsky getting attacked and Cooper getting killed weren't your fault."

"What about you?"

"What about me?"

"You're not okay. And I'm the one who dragged you into that mess."

He hit the gas, waving at the motorists behind us who had honked at our abrupt stop. "Don't start. You didn't get me involved in anything."

"Derek, you stepped in to save me. You've done it more than once, and every time, it's cost you."

"This last time it didn't. I walked away, and you barely survived."

"You didn't walk. You set yourself up as bait. If that psycho hadn't taken Lucca, he would have come for you."

"I failed, and you were shot. He nearly killed you."

This kind of thinking was the reason Heathcliff needed group therapy. Admittedly, I exhibited the same self-loathing and blame for the role I played in others' suffering, which is probably why he made me endure these sessions with him. "Good thing scorpions are hard to kill."

He slammed on the brakes again. The seatbelt caught me just before my face collided with the dashboard or the windshield. "Alex Parker, you are the biggest pain in the ass I know, and you're also one of my closest friends. I care about you, which means I will do everything in my power to make sure nothing happens to you. I lost one partner. I won't stand by and wait to lose another one. The entire point of these sessions is so you figure out this isn't your fault and recover from this ordeal. But somehow, you seem to be missing the point."

I ignored the angry beeping coming from behind us. "It seems you missed the point too."

"No. I accept that I can't control everything. I accept that I didn't pull the trigger or hand my partner the razor blades. That's not my fault. Sure, I wish I'd seen the warning signs, but she took time off. She didn't want me to see her downward spiral. She didn't want me to stop her. And there wasn't a damn thing I could have done about that. I've learned to let that go, just like Gwen when she left the safe house. I could have kept her safe, but she didn't let me. Now I'm working on letting go of the shit that just went down with you."

"Derek—"

"That doesn't mean I'm going to turn a blind eye to someone in trouble. I won't step away when there's something I can do, some action I can take, to prevent a tragedy or stop an offender or save you if I can. You're the same way. That's why we fought. It's why we're fighting now."

"We're not fighting." I held up my palms. "All I meant by my comment was that I have an inquisitive nature. I can't help it."

"Uh-huh." Again, he waved off the annoyed drivers and continued to the bar. We didn't speak again until he parked a block away.

"I hate how well you know me," I said. "Not many people know where my thoughts will go, especially before I do. Honestly, I thought we could just talk about your case."

"We've spent a lot of time together under tense conditions. I know how you operate."

"I also know how you operate." He'd intentionally changed the subject and put me on the defensive to avoid answering my questions about John Doe. "Why did you put the folder in the trunk? Why don't you want me to read it? If you don't think I pose a danger to you by getting involved, why are you afraid of me poking around in your case?"

"It's not that."

"What is it?"

His expression shifted to an unreadable mask, a trick he

perfected from years spent undercover. "We go inside. We drink. We talk about the meeting. That's what we do every Monday and Thursday. Let's not break from tradition."

"Screw tradition. Something's going on. What am I missing?"

"You don't want to know." He opened his car door. "Let's go inside. I really need that drink."

TWO

"The call came in yesterday afternoon." Heathcliff sipped his beer. "Since I was next up, I went to see what the fuss was about. Most of the injuries could have been inflicted prior to the man's death."

"What kinds of injuries?"

"His fingertips were removed, which could be accidental, but the four bullets in his torso were not."

"Would you like another?" the bartender asked, gesturing to my glass.

"Sure, thanks." I slid it closer for him to refill.

"Still light on the rum, miss?" he asked.

"Super light," I said.

Heathcliff watched as the bartender filled the glass with cola and added just a splash of rum. "That's a travesty. At this rate, you might as well stick with a straight-up coke. It would save you five bucks on every refill." The detective glanced around the room, but no one crowded us. "Don't tell me you have to go back to the office after this."

"No, but this way, I don't notice the rum, so I can drink more. It's ingenious."

He eyed the glass for a moment, shook his head, and took another sip of his beer. "I didn't mean for this case to upset our routine."

"No problem. It's not like I look forward to these sessions." I blinked, feeling my throat tighten as I recalled the choked back tears of members of the support group. "You know what these meetings have taught me? That this shit isn't isolated, and a part of me is relieved this doesn't just happen to me. But at the same time, it breaks my heart that so many other people have to go through this. That you're going through this." I gulped down my drink, barely tasting the rum. "It's not fair. I don't want other people to feel the way I do."

"They might feel worse."

That sentiment made my already aching stomach tighten into knots. "I hate that. I hate this feeling of helplessness."

"Despair," he corrected.

"That too." I curled the edge of my napkin around the bottom of the glass. "No matter what we do, how many people we arrest or try to save, it doesn't make a bit of difference."

"It does to the ones who survive."

"Surviving isn't easy either. You were in that room. You heard the stories."

"No one said surviving isn't hard, but it makes a world of difference. By living, we can still make things better."

"Or worse."

"Only if we stop trying."

I turned to him, wondering if he actually believed it. "Unless we keep failing, over and over again."

"The human brain focuses on the negatives, not the positives. It's how we're wired. It's probably a survival instinct." He snorted, finding the thought amusing. "You've done good. You've helped more people than you realize. The few names you remember, the ones you failed, that's just the universe's way of balancing the scales."

"I don't like it."

He drank some beer. "You don't have to. That's just life. Take comfort in knowing that's how we all feel."

"That makes it worse."

"Because you take comfort in knowing you aren't alone

in your grief? I get that. Believe me, I do." He exhaled slowly. "Did Cal say anything to you?"

"Cal?"

"The guy who runs the group."

"Oh, Sergeant Pain-in-the-Ass."

Heathcliff chuckled. "He's not a bad guy."

"He tried to get me to open up, but I don't want to." I turned to face the bar, placing both arms on the counter while I spun the glass around and around.

Heathcliff put his hand on my forearm. "You don't have to share with the group. I told you that. There's no pressure."

"It doesn't feel like it. He cornered me after last Thursday's meeting. I'm just glad you stepped in to save me. I appreciated that."

"Cal's just worried. He wasn't giving you the third degree. He talks to everyone who attends the meetings, in case you haven't noticed."

I hadn't. The only thing I ever wanted to do once a meeting was over was escape so I could lick my wounds. "When you first started going to these meetings, how long did it take before you decided to share?"

"Alex, we're all different. Some people have been going for years and never say a thing."

"I don't want to be there that long."

He moved his hand up to my shoulder and gave it a squeeze. "When I'd been stuck in mandated therapy, it took me two months before I said a word to anyone. But my progress was monitored by the department shrink. I didn't have much of a choice. You're not on a deadline. I'll go with you as long as it takes."

"You don't have to. Isn't your attendance voluntary?"

"It is. Until last month, I hadn't been to a meeting in years, but lately, I feel like I could use some help. I think you can too." He dropped his hand and finished his beer. "You know, if you don't want to talk to the group, you can talk to me. You can always talk to me."

"I'm talking to you right now."

He smiled. "I know."

Admittedly, I'd opened up to him more after these

sessions than I had to anyone. Perhaps it wasn't group therapy that was helping. It might have been Derek.

We sat in silence for what felt like an eternity, contemplating everything that had been said during today's meeting. Eventually, my mind went back to the mysterious body, and I cursed Heathcliff for distracting me again. "Why is Moretti so obsessed with John Doe?"

"I'm not sure he is."

"Our trip to the ME's office tonight says otherwise. The LT told you to stay on top of this. Tell me why."

"I already told you. He thinks he knows who the victim is."

"And you want the suspense to kill me?"

"Fine, but you didn't hear this from me." Heathcliff waited for me to nod before continuing. "Moretti worked a case eight years ago. A guy vanished off the face of the earth. He left almost everything behind and never touched his bank accounts."

"Any sign of foul play?"

Heathcliff popped a handful of pretzels into his mouth and chewed, possibly to buy time or to clue me in that he didn't want to talk about this. Too bad I was determined to remain distracted. "The front door to the guy's house was left open. His security system had been turned off, and the hard drives taken. His blood was found in the shower drain. Moretti figured he'd been killed, but he could never find the body. Until now."

"How does he know John Doe's the same guy? Did John Doe have a wallet or any personal effects with him?"

Heathcliff reached for more pretzels. "That would make this easier, wouldn't it?" I didn't know if that was a yes or no, but I could tell from his interest in the bowl of pretzels that he had no intention of answering my question. "Search teams are scouring the area for additional forensic evidence."

"The lab tech said they're running DNA and dental records."

"They're doing what they can. John Doe was missing a few back molars, so dental records might be a bust."

"Do you think he was tortured?" I asked.

"Possibly."

"The victim's fingertips are gone, and he's missing a few teeth. It sounds like whoever killed him wanted to make sure he'd never be identified. Why didn't he take a brick to the guy's face?"

"Who says he didn't?"

"Are you serious?"

"I don't know." He gestured to the bartender for another beer. "The remains were badly damaged. It's hard to say for certain when it happened, but the ME's working on it."

"Too bad the guy didn't have his driver's license with him."

"No license. No wallet. That would have made my job too easy."

"But he had something with him that Moretti recognized." I hoped Heathcliff was drunk enough to answer my questions if I danced around them.

The look on Heathcliff's face indicated I was right, but he didn't tell me what they found with the body. "Let's talk about more pleasant things." He jerked his chin up, just as a hand slid across my back.

"I'm sorry I'm late." James Martin took a seat on the empty stool beside mine and leaned over to kiss my cheek. "How are you tonight, gorgeous?"

"We could be worse," I said.

Martin tightened his grip on my waist. "Is that the consensus, Detective?"

"No, I'm good. Though, I was threatened with forcible removal from the Cross Security offices by a spunky receptionist when I went to pick up Alex."

"She told you I wasn't there," I reminded him.

"But you were." Heathcliff chuckled. "In other words, Alex tried to pull a disappearing act again."

"She does that."

"It's called self-preservation," I said.

Martin leaned in closer. "Are you okay?"

"I will be."

The bartender returned. "What can I get you, sir?"

"Another round for my friends," Martin gestured to our nearly empty glasses, "and I'll take a Macallan, neat. Also, a cheeseburger, two orders of fries, boneless honey barbeque wings, and whatever the gentleman will have."

"Actually, I'm going to take off. It's been a long day." Heathcliff slid off the stool. "I'll see you Thursday, Alex."

"I might be busy."

"Thursday," he insisted, leaning down to give me a quick hug before shaking hands with Martin. "Take care of her."

"Always," Martin said.

"I don't appreciate the sentiment. I am capable of taking care of myself." But the men ignored me. Shaking it off, I tried to clear away the melancholia that had only gotten worse in the last few seconds since Heathcliff's case was no longer distracting me.

"What were you talking about?" Martin asked. "You shut up pretty quickly when I sat down."

"A case." I changed the subject. "You must be starving. You ordered enough food to feed a small army."

"I've been in meetings all day. I didn't even have time to grab coffee, let alone lunch. Plus, you ought to eat something." He eyed the glass in front of me. "How many of those have you had?"

"Two." I squinted. "No, three." The bartender returned with a refill. I picked it up and sucked on the straw. "Make that four."

"Yeah, you definitely need to eat."

"I'm not hungry." I swiveled around to face him, propping my head up with my hand. "Is that why you didn't bother to ask what I wanted? You knew I didn't want anything."

"That, and while I find it adorable how you steal my fries, I thought you could use a plate of your own."

"Am I really this predictable? First, Heathcliff, and now you. I give up." I dropped my head to the bar, tired of fighting to remain functional.

"Did you want something besides wings? They have nachos. You like nachos."

"I'm already a little queasy. The spiciness will rip my stomach apart." I glanced at him from the corner of my eye. "That's why you ordered honey barbeque instead of buffalo. Damn you."

He laughed. "Do you want to take off? We can skip dinner and just go home."

"No, you're hungry. You should eat." His order played through my mind. "What happened at work today? You only order cheeseburgers when shit happens."

"Nothing happened. I like cheeseburgers."

"Yes, but you rarely eat them. They're your comfort food."

"I'm fine." He trailed his fingers up my back and gently massaged my neck. "I'm just worried about you. Did you share in group today?"

"No."

He frowned, continuing to rub my neck. "Do you think you might one of these days?"

"I don't know. Everyone's been through the same thing. It'll just be more of the same. I don't want to unload on anyone else."

"But they unload on you."

"They unload on everyone in the room. That's the point."

"That is the point," Martin said.

"Subtle."

He chuckled just as the bartender returned with two plates. "Can I get you another scotch?" the bartender asked.

"Please." Martin slid the fries closer to me.

I sat up and looked at the food, and he pushed a cup of ranch dressing closer. "Fine, but if I spend the night with my head in the toilet and end up developing an aversion to the wonder that is the French fry and boneless wing, I'm holding you personally responsible."

"Deal." He snagged one of the wings out of the basket.

We ate in silence. Well, Martin ate. He hadn't been joking. He inhaled his burger and fries, followed by most of my fries and three quarters of the wings. I switched to regular cola and sipped the fizzy liquid while the emotions roiled around inside of me and my mind fought to remain focused on Heathcliff's case and my list of things to do in the morning, but as usual, my thoughts drifted to the stories I'd heard earlier tonight.

"Are you ready to go home?" Martin asked as he waited for the bartender to return his credit card.

"Are you? Or do you want to stop somewhere for dessert?"

"I'm stuffed." He shrugged into his jacket. "I'll have to double up on my workout tomorrow."

"Why? Afraid your eight pack abs might turn into only six or four?"

"Says the woman who kills herself every morning with pilates and barre routines."

"Not true."

"It is true." He put his arm around me as we headed for the door. "Don't think I haven't noticed the bruises on your legs and the damage to your feet."

"I'll stop going en pointe."

"Alex, barre workouts were meant to be rehab. They weren't supposed to turn into an obsession. Is this what it was like when you were a kid? Two hours a day working on routines?"

"No, back then, it was at least three."

"Jesus. Someone should have reported your parents."

I cocked an eyebrow at him. "For what?"

"Child abuse." He opened the car door. I got in and slid across the seat, so he could climb in next to me. "Marcal, home, please."

"Yes, sir." Marcal, Martin's driver, offered me a smile, which I automatically returned.

"That's not abuse. Most ballerinas train just as hard or harder. My parents were never abusive," I said.

"Maybe not physically, but withholding love, affection, and just being assholes did a number on you."

I stared at him. "I'd expect Mark Jablonsky to be that blunt. I'm not used to you doing it."

"I'm sorry. I just see how much you're hurting now, and I can't help but think if they'd been decent and treated you the way children are supposed to be treated—"

"I'd be better at coping."

He pressed his lips together, realizing this might cause an argument. "Yeah."

"You're probably right. I'd also have been a functional member of society and gone into some other profession, and none of this would have ever happened." I turned to stare out the window, and he reached for my hand, rubbing his thumb in gentle circles against my wrist.

THREE

As usual, things never seemed as bleak in the morning. In fact, I felt better. It didn't make any sense to me, but after grief counseling, I always felt better. Lighter. More at ease, even though the session itself made me miserable and ruined the rest of my evening. But in the light of day, it was little more than an afterthought, just like Heathcliff's case.

The alarm sounded again. Martin switched it off, rolled over, and kissed me. "How are you feeling today, beautiful?"

"I'm okay." My eyelashes were stuck together and I was congested from crying myself to sleep, but it was the truth.

He kissed me again. "Do you want to join me for a swim?"

"No."

"How about a run?"

"I could go for a run."

"Good. Give me an hour in the pool first. You can go back to sleep until then."

I closed my eyes, listening to the sounds of him getting ready before disappearing from the bedroom. Once I heard the alarm beep, indicating he deactivated it in order to go outside, I climbed out of bed and peered out the French doors.

That man didn't waste a second. He was already

splashing around in the pool. The muscles in his back and shoulders rippled as he glided through the water.

Watching him took my breath away and filled my insides with a pang of longing. I loved him more than anything. It's why I let Heathcliff manipulate me into going to grief counseling. It's what Martin wanted. He wanted me to bounce back, and I'd do anything I could to give him what he wanted. He always did the same for me. Some people called that love. Others called it unhealthy codependence. But for us, it worked, even if I'd spent a good portion of my time fighting against it.

While he was outside, I put on some leggings, a baggy tank top, and tied my long brown hair into a knot. Then I went into the kitchen, drank a glass of water to combat the hangover, and went downstairs to the home gym to stretch and work through one of my old barre routines before we went for our run.

When Martin came inside, he wasn't surprised to find me working out. Instead of trying to force me out of the dance studio, he took to the heavy bag while keeping an eye on me. By the time I finished executing several jumps in a row and wondering if I'd broken a toe in the process, he was doing push-ups while in a full handstand. Every muscle in his torso was taut and pronounced.

"And you say I push myself too hard," I said.

"If you're going to push, so am I." He finished his set and got back on his feet. "Ready for that run?"

"Where do you get the energy?"

"It must have been the cheeseburger." He gave me a sexy grin. "I hate that you're killing yourself, but my god, you're hot as hell."

"Stop that."

"You first." He tossed a towel to me, so I could wipe my face.

I laced up my sneakers and met him at the door. My legs were already shaky, but I wouldn't let that stop me. We ran around the perimeter of his estate twice, through the gardens and around the pool, before sprinting down the long and winding private road. Once we reached the main connection, we turned and raced back. By the time we made it inside, I thought my legs would fall off.

We showered together, Martin supporting my weight between his body and the wall when my muscles gave out. Afterward, he went to make breakfast while I sat on the floor and dried my hair. By the time I got downstairs, he was on the phone with someone from the office. I ate alone at the table, wondering what Lucien Cross, my boss, would have in store for me today.

Ten minutes later, we were in the car on our way to work. I picked up the newspaper from where it sat on the seat between us. Below the fold on one of the interior pages, the headline caught my attention.

Grave Uncovered at Construction Site. Not many details were included, but that had to be Heathcliff's case. Police personnel didn't usually come out in droves for ancient burial sites or unearthed cemeteries, so the number of investigators at the scene worried me. This wasn't good. Who was John Doe?

Putting the paper down, I slumped against the seat and closed my eyes. At least I wasn't a cop, so I didn't have to deal with any of that. It was one of the few perks of being a private detective. For the most part, I chose my own cases. But this one had my attention, and I couldn't quite shake it.

Martin hung up and nudged me. "Tired?"

I opened one eye and looked at him. "What do you think?"

"You didn't have to get up when I did."

"I'll remember that next time."

"Maybe we should try to get to bed earlier." He scooted closer and stroked my cheek. "What are your plans tonight?"

"I have no idea."

"My last meeting should be finished by 8:30, nine o'clock at the latest." His phone buzzed, and he dug it out of his pocket and read the message. "Well, I hope nine o'clock will be the latest. It could be ten."

"How about you call me when you're done for the night? I'll let you know where I am and what I'm doing." Sliding down in the seat, I rested my head against his shoulder and entwined my fingers with his.

With his free hand, Martin picked up the paper and unfolded it over his lap. I'd almost drifted off when the car came to a stop. Peering out the window, I hoped to see a traffic light. Instead, the town car had stopped in front of the office building that housed Cross Security.

Martin dropped the paper, grasped my face with his free hand, and kissed me a bit more passionately than he did most mornings. When he pulled away, a contented sigh passed between my lips, and he smiled.

"Hold on to that thought." His green eyes sparkled.

"The only thoughts I have are about sleep."

"Perfect since mine are about sleeping with you."

"You need to work on your material."

"You always say that, but these lines work perfectly every time." He gave me a quick kiss. "I'll see you after work. I hope you'll still be feeling good tonight."

"Yeah, me too." I always got introspective as the day wore on. "I'm tired of being sad."

"That's why you need grief counseling, Alexis."

"I know, but that doesn't mean I have to like it." I opened the car door. "Have a good day, handsome."

"Stay safe, sweetheart. I love you. Remember that."

My hand went to the rings hanging around my neck, and I clutched them in my fist. "Ditto."

The town car didn't pull away until after I made it inside the building. While I waited for the elevator, along with several accountants, realtors, and possibly a stray lawyer or two, my mind drifted to the day ahead. I had a few open investigations in the works, but Cross probably had more assignments to dole out. If he didn't, I might swing by the precinct and see what Heathcliff was up to.

"Good morning, Ms. Parker." The receptionist handed me a blue folder as I stepped out of the elevator. "Mr. Cross wants you to take a look at the proposal he's drafted. He wants your input concerning the established timetable."

"Fine." I tucked the folder underneath my arm without opening it. "Does this mean no morning meeting?" Hopefully, I'd missed it.

"No, ma'am." She didn't seem to notice when I cringed

at the word, which always brought back bad memories. Psychologists referred to it as a trigger word. "The morning meeting will start promptly at eight."

"Did Cross do that intentionally just so I couldn't skip out?"

The receptionist didn't understand it was a joke. "No, I don't think so. Eight is common, unless Mr. Cross has other things on the agenda for the day."

"Yeah, I got it." I raised the folder. "Thanks." I went down the hall and let myself into my office. "Hey, Kellan."

My associate's office was across from mine, and since he had his door open, I figured he'd be able to hear me despite the hum of another bustling morning at Cross Security.

"Are you talking to me today?" he asked.

"I'm considering it."

"That's nice. I never know when you're talking to me and when you're not."

"That's on you, buddy. Spying is a no-no."

"Yeah, I got the memo," he mumbled.

"Do you know what Cross has been up to all morning?" I flipped open the folder and scanned the details. Our boss wanted to know if I could perform an evaluation and a potential overhaul of a new client's thirty-three story office building and internet protocols in less than two weeks. That would require full-time commitment. I'd have to give up pesky habits like sleeping, eating, and bathing to get it finished in time.

"No idea. He's holed up upstairs. The assistants have been scurrying around, so it must be big."

"Of course, it's big." I closed the folder and stuck it beneath the tray at the edge of my desk before turning on my computer. "Everything Lucien does is big."

"That's what she said."

I turned to look at Kellan.

He grinned, letting out a snort. "Hey, it's just a guess. It's not like I've seen him with any supermodels lately."

"I have. Well, she wasn't a supermodel, but she was beautiful."

"Seriously?"

Gossiping with Kellan was asking for trouble, but I

missed talking to him. "It was during our trip to Vegas."

"They're all gorgeous in Vegas. Was she a showgirl?"

"I don't think so." I turned back to the notes and files on my desk.

"Stripper? Prostitute?"

"You're talking about our boss."

"Dominatrix, then?"

I stifled my laugh, pushing the thoughts out of my mind. Cross had a large tattoo on his back. He must have some tolerance for pain. He might even enjoy it. "Any idea why he delayed this morning's meeting?"

"Eight a.m. is not a delay. You're just usually not here this early." Kellan stepped into my office with two mugs. He put one of them down on my desk and studied me closely. "Puffy eyes." He cocked his head to the side, waiting for an explanation, but I silently sipped my coffee and browsed the Lopez file. "Are you still having trouble sleeping? Or is it something else? Is everything okay?"

"I'm fine. I just don't like mornings."

"Me neither."

"At least I got up." Plenty of people who knew me no longer had that luxury. Again, morbid thoughts and flashes from brutal crime scenes filled my mind. Closing my eyes, I took a deep breath and slowly exhaled. I couldn't do anything to change it. I could only move on and do better next time. When I opened my eyes, Kellan was staring at me. "What?" I asked.

"Nothing. I'll meet you in the conference room." He tapped his watch. "Two minute warning."

I clicked the icon and checked my e-mail. Cross had left me half a dozen messages regarding two of my investigations and the new assignment he just gave me. Aside from that, I didn't see anything pressing.

Again, my thoughts returned to Heathcliff's case and the mysterious John Doe. Based on the photo in the paper, it looked like the police could use the help, and I'd much rather look into that matter than the assignments Cross had given me.

With a few minutes to spare, I searched the internet for any updates on the story. The news outlets didn't have an

ID. From the way the articles read, the media knew less about the situation than I did. But that kind of police presence meant something. I just didn't know what.

Shaking off the realization that I'd come full circle in my musings this morning, I grabbed a blank legal pad and my cup of coffee and headed down the hall to the conference room. To my surprise, the morning meeting hadn't started yet.

Kellan pointed to the empty chair across from him. "I saved you a seat."

"You hate me that much?"

Bennett Renner, another Cross Security investigator, chuckled and pulled it out for me as I rounded the table. "Have you spoken to Lucien this morning?" he asked.

"No, but he left me a whopper of an assignment." The clock on the wall said 8:04. Cross was always punctual. Something was up. I looked around at the dozen investigators assembled. "Has anyone seen Cross this morning?"

"He's here," someone said. "He's been on the phone since he got in."

"He must have a big fish on the hook," Renner said.

"Let's hope not," I mumbled. That would mean more busy work for us.

Just then, Lucien Cross entered the conference room with a stack of folders. He handed them out and took a seat at the head of the table. Despite my recent avoidance of these meetings, I'd been to enough of them to know something had Cross stressed. I just didn't know what.

FOUR

Cross went around the table, asking for updates on our cases before doling out additional assignments. As usual, I was the only one without a folder. I liked to believe it was because I was technically a private contractor, which is why I failed to see any reason for attending these morning meetings. However, the boss didn't agree. He had just turned to face me when the door to the conference room opened.

Two police officers stood in the doorway. The receptionist flitted around them, doing her best to get them to leave. But they ignored her, much the same way Heathcliff had the previous night.

The taller one held out a folded piece of paper. "Lucien Cross," he said, "we have a warrant for your arrest."

"This has to be a joke," Renner said. "C'mon, Frank, what's the punchline?" He stared at the shorter cop.

"Leave it alone, Bennett. This matter doesn't concern you," Frank warned.

"This is Lucien Cross. You must have made a mistake." Renner moved to stand, but Cross gave him a sharp look. Amusement and annoyance played over Renner's chiseled features. "What are the charges? Showing the police department what they're doing wrong?"

Renner had been a homicide detective, forced off the job due to an injury. After he recovered, Cross hired him as an investigator. That had been four or five years ago. Maybe more. But Renner still knew plenty of cops, including one of the men who'd come to arrest our boss.

"Murder," the cop said.

Cross cocked his head to the side, as if the words rang a bell. "Is the paperwork in order? I'm not going anywhere if it's not."

"See for yourself, sir." The lead officer held out the warrant, and Cross read it carefully.

"I'd like to contact my attorney, so he can meet us at the precinct. I'm sure Mr. Almeada will want to contest this." Cross waited, but the police didn't give him the go-ahead to remove his phone or make the call.

"Stand up, Mr. Cross. Keep your hands where we can see them," Frank said.

"Kellan, make sure Justin is made aware of the situation and have him contact Mr. Almeada," Cross instructed.

"No problem, boss." Kellan kept his hands on the table. Since most of us were former law enforcement, we knew the drill.

The lead cop looked around the crowded conference room, realizing most of us were armed. "We don't want any trouble. We're just doing our jobs," the taller cop said.

"And I was doing mine until you interrupted." Cross's expression soured. "We're in the middle of a meeting. This can't wait until we're finished?"

"Your meeting just ended," the cop said.

"Fine. In the meantime, you have your assignments. Everyone, get back to work." Cross turned to look at me. My eyes had been glued to him since the moment the police announced he was under arrest. "Alex, take the morning to clear your schedule. I need you to handle a case for me. Whatever else you're working on, finish up or pass it off. Got it?"

"Is this about the assignment you left for me?"

"No, this is something else. Understand?"

"Not at all."

He stared at me, his eyes narrowing ever so slightly. "Justin will brief you."

"Sir," the police officer said, growing even more impatient, "stand up."

Cross complied, holding his hands out to the sides while they removed the handgun nestled against his hip. Then they waited for him to put his jacket on before turning him around, cuffing him, and walking him out of the conference room.

"What the hell just happened?" Renner asked.

Several of the other investigators shrugged, as if things like this occurred every morning, collected their case files, and returned to their offices without another word. Even with Cross gone, they'd do their jobs and follow orders.

Kellan looked at me. He knew I rarely fell into line like a good soldier, and given the circumstances, I was even less inclined to comply with our boss's request.

"Do you know what's going on?" he asked.

"Why would I?"

"You came in this morning asking about Cross. You have friends who are cops. You must know something."

"I don't."

"Are you sure?" Kellan asked.

"Take it easy," Renner interrupted. "Alex isn't the enemy. If Cross trusts her, so should we."

"Fine." Kellan gave me a final look and headed for the door.

"Crazy morning." Renner pushed his chair beneath the table. "Can you believe they just arrested Lucien for murder? That's ridiculous."

"Is it?" I'd seen the look on Cross's face. He wasn't surprised he'd been arrested. The thoughts ran rampant through my mind, processing dozens of scenarios at lightning speed.

"You think our boss actually killed someone?" Renner asked.

"I spent the last several minutes observing him. Not once did he deny it. And when the officers told him the charge, he didn't appear shocked or surprised. He looked resigned. You used to be a homicide detective. What do you think?"

"I'm going to make some calls and find out what's going on." Renner collected the files in front of him and stopped in the doorway. "Do you need me to take over any of your cases? I have some room on my plate."

"Can l let you know in a couple of hours?"

"Sure, no problem."

I grabbed my legal pad off the table. "Let me know what you find out from your cop buddies and if I should start the job search. If so, I'd like to do it before the rest of Cross Security snatches up all the best positions."

"Aren't you going to make a few calls yourself?" Renner asked. "You have friends in major crimes. They might know something."

"I'm sure they do." My gut said this tied directly to Heathcliff's case. That would explain his caginess. But after what just happened, I wasn't sure I wanted to know the details. "Cross has made it abundantly clear he doesn't like people in his business. I don't want to piss him off."

"Who are you kidding? You piss him off all the time."

"This is different."

"You realize you're the only one around here who thinks he's guilty."

"You were a cop. You know how it works. They wouldn't serve a warrant unless they had evidence."

"If Lucien killed someone, he didn't have a choice. I'm guessing almost every Cross Security employee has killed someone at some point during his or her career. It doesn't mean any of us should be arrested for murder."

"You have a lot more faith in people than I do."

Renner studied me closely. "How can you be sure he's guilty? We don't have any facts or details. We don't even know who he's accused of killing."

"I know what guilt looks like. I've seen it in the mirror plenty of times, and I saw it on Lucien's face when the cops handed him the warrant. He did whatever they think he did, and if he didn't, he sure as hell feels guilty enough not to deny the charges."

"Are you sure you're not projecting? After your last assignment, it'd be natural—"

"This isn't about me."

Renner held up his palms. "Okay." But from his tone, he only said it to pacify me.

I stepped into my office and closed the door. I had a lot to think about. The first thing I did was pull out my phone and call Martin.

"Hey, beautiful, miss me already?" he asked. "I know I told you to hold on to that thought, but I'm going to need you to wait until tonight."

"James, I have to tell you something."

"That can't be good." His tone shifted. "Is everything okay? Are you okay?"

"I'm fine. You might not be. Lucien Cross was just arrested for murder."

"What?"

"I don't know any of the details. I have no idea what's going on, but since you're working with him on that R&D project, I figured this could negatively impact you and MT when the news breaks."

"Shit."

"Tell me about it."

"This is the last thing I need right now."

"I'm sorry."

"It's not your fault. Thanks for telling me. I'll notify legal and our PR department and have something drafted and waiting. Do you know who they think he killed?"

"Not yet. I'm going to call Heathcliff as soon as we hang up."

"Okay, let me know what you find out."

"I will."

FIVE

"I can't talk about this with you," Heathcliff said.

"Cross just got perp-walked out of our morning meeting. At least tell me if I should be looking for a new job."

"It wouldn't hurt."

"Really? It's that bad?"

"Dammit, Parker, I'm not supposed to discuss this with you."

"Fine, can you put Detective O'Connell on the phone?"

Heathcliff sighed. "He can't talk to you either. Moretti's orders."

That meant Cross's case was being investigated by major crimes and not homicide, even though the two departments often overlapped. My gut had been right. John Doe and Cross's arrest were connected. They had to be. I'd been taught to never believe in coincidences. "Did you get an ID on your John Doe?"

"Uh-huh."

"At least give me his name."

Heathcliff hesitated, torn between following orders and honoring our friendship. Finally, he whispered, "Trey Knox."

"Is that name supposed to mean something to me?"

"You have resources. Look it up."

Martin wasn't the only one who could read between the lines. "Is that the man Cross is accused of murdering?"

"Parker, I have to go. Do yourself a favor and stay out of this."

"I can't do that."

"Why am I not surprised? Just be careful. I'll see you Thursday."

Before I could reply, he hung up. Since the phone call hadn't gotten me very far, I'd have to do my own research. At least I had a name, and since Heathcliff mentioned my resources, I started with the Cross Security database.

Eight years ago, Trey Knox hired Lucien Cross to work an asset retrieval. Knox's home had been burglarized and his priceless sports memorabilia had been stolen. The police didn't have any solid leads, so Knox went to the private investigator, hoping to increase his chances of a recovery.

According to the file, the case had been closed. I checked records, but Knox's account balance had never been paid. It'd been written off. Granted, Knox was one of Cross's first non-corporate clients, so the Cross Security filing and billing system might not have been as streamlined as it was today. But I found that odd.

I noted the date Knox signed a contract with Cross Security, figuring that might come in handy. I'd need the police reports of the original break-in and any subsequent reports the police department had on file concerning Trey Knox. Heathcliff said the man had vanished eight years ago, and Moretti had been assigned to investigate his disappearance.

Given the date of the contract, I had to assume it was around the same time Cross had taken Knox on as a client. That might explain why Knox never paid for services rendered. It could also be part of the reason Cross had been arrested this morning. He might have been one of the last people to see Knox alive.

Cross Security had access to a lot of law enforcement databases, but the Knox files were inaccessible. The police department might have sealed them or moved them behind a firewall of some sort. Cross had an illegal back door into their system, which might explain why they'd taken extra precautions with this case. Of course, that would mean they knew about his illicit access.

"That's another problem for another day," I reminded myself. Instead, I'd have to get the police files another way.

I called the precinct to see if I could find out what was going on, but I was told the public wasn't allowed access to open cases.

"I'm not the public. I work for," I skimmed the details Knox had provided to Cross, "Home Insurance Inc. We're conducting a review on home invasion claims made in the last decade and need access to the police reports to compare them to our records." The lie sounded hollow even to my ears, but I hadn't been prepared. Today had me off-kilter.

"You can come by the precinct and pick up a copy." The desk sergeant gave me the address, in case I didn't have it, and hung up. So much for plan A.

Pulling out my cell phone, I moved on to plan B. After three rings, SSA Mark Jablonsky answered my call.

"Why are you calling so early?" he asked. "Shouldn't you be at work?"

"I am at work." I waited, figuring if the supervisory special agent had heard the news, he'd let me know. But Mark didn't say anything. "I need a favor."

"Doesn't Cross Security have enough fancy tools and tech that you don't need to annoy the federal government with your requests anymore?"

"Not when it comes to law enforcement issues."

"What do you want, Parker?"

I debated telling Mark, my former boss and mentor, that Cross had been arrested. That would just lead to a lecture on why taking this job was such a bad idea. Instead, I started by asking about Trey Knox. "Have you heard about the body that got dug up at the airport?"

"It's all over the news."

"The dead guy is Trey Knox. Does his name ring any bells?"

"Should it?"

"It didn't for me either, but eight years ago, he vanished. Until now, no one had any idea what happened to him. I was hoping you could get access to the police files and find out if they had any leads back then or if those leads are panning out now."

"Why do you care? You work private security. *Private.* Ongoing criminal cases have nothing to do with you, especially murder cases."

"Please." But I knew he wouldn't budge until I gave him a reasonable answer. "Knox had been a Cross Security client. I'd like to know what happened."

"Ah, I see. So this is about avoiding scandal and keeping any dirt off of Cross Security."

"Something like that." His guess had been on the nose, except it was already too late to avoid scandal and dirt.

"Normally, I'd tell you this isn't my problem. But since Lucien Cross did play a small part in keeping me alive when I was shot, I guess I owe him one. I'm in the middle of something, but when I have a few free minutes, I'll make some calls and see what I can find out."

"Thanks, I owe you."

"Drop by the federal building after hours, and we'll go over the details. Dinner's on you."

"You got it."

"And none of that healthy shit. The doc said I'm fully recovered, so don't try to feed me rabbit food or that gelatin crap. I want real food or the deal's off."

"Fine."

Unsure where to go from here, I reread the sparse Cross Security file on Trey Knox's case. Eight years ago, Lucien Cross was the only investigator at the company. But his assistant, Justin, was still around. Maybe he knew something. I needed to talk to him. After all, Cross told me to clear my plate, pass off my cases, and take on a new assignment. Since Justin was supposed to brief me, I could kill two birds with one stone.

Grabbing the file Cross left for me at reception, I brought it down the hall to Renner's office and asked him to handle it. Then I took the elevator upstairs. During the short ride, I wondered what case Cross wanted me to take care of.

I had no idea why he chose me. I wasn't exactly a team player. No one would find me waving a "Go Cross Security" banner. Frankly, Renner, Kellan, and the rest had demonstrated their willingness to drink the Kool-Aid on more than one occasion. Any one of them would have been a better choice, which led me to believe whatever this was, it wouldn't be easy or pleasant.

Could it have something to do with Martin or MT? Cross had made me sign on the dotted line that any work I did for Martin Technologies would fall under the Cross Security umbrella, but that was because he knew Martin would never hire him, even though the two were currently partnered together on a project.

I thought about the doozies Cross had assigned me in the past, but there had been a vast array. This could be anything. Since it would be a waste of time to ponder this for another moment, I decided I'd use it as leverage to convince Justin to tell me everything there was about Cross's connection to Trey Knox.

The elevator doors opened, and I strode down the hall. The large conference room on my right was packed with members of our in-house counsel, public relations department, and a few receptionists. Cross's arrest had the rest of the staff freaked out, even if the investigators didn't seem to take this seriously.

"Ms. Parker," Justin spotted me heading his way, "I was just about to call you."

"Sorry, it took me so long. I had to clear my schedule."

"Yes, I understand." He opened the door to Cross's office. "Let's speak in here."

"Are you sure Lucien won't mind?"

Justin gave me a look and entered the lavish office ahead of me. He took a seat behind Cross's desk, causing me to wonder if he snuck in here and sat in the big man's chair whenever the boss was out. "As I'm sure you're aware, we have a situation."

"Don't tell me we're out of coffee."

"No." Justin stared at me. "Lucien was arrested this

morning."

"I vaguely remember that." Obviously, he hadn't gotten my joke. So much for breaking the tension.

"Sit down." He gestured at the client chair in front of Cross's desk.

"I have a few questions."

"We'll get to them. But let me go first. Suffice it to say, Lucien has left specific instructions with his attorney per your role in what's about to happen."

"What's that?"

"I just said—" Justin began.

I held up my palm. "I know. I heard you. But I don't understand what's going on. Cross got dragged away in handcuffs. The cops are saying he killed someone. He didn't exactly deny it either, but everyone's acting like this is just another Tuesday. I know I don't go to a lot of morning meetings, but this isn't a normal Tuesday. Shouldn't helping him be our priority?"

"I'm glad to hear you say that." He deflated, sinking deeper into the chair.

"You're worried about him."

"Of course. I've been with Lucien since the beginning, since before the beginning. This isn't good. He doesn't deserve this."

"Did he do it?"

Justin didn't answer. Not a single muscle twitched. "Do you think he did?"

"It doesn't matter what I think."

"Good. Personal feelings won't help matters. He believes you can be objective. You've made your dislike of him known."

"I don't dislike him."

"Really?"

"I don't trust him, but the man has saved my life on at least three occasions. Maybe four. It's hard to keep count." Granted, if Lucien hadn't assigned me those cases, I never would have been in harm's way in the first place, but that was neither here nor there. The job was the job, regardless of who pulled the strings. I couldn't blame him for the potential peril. "He's gone out on a limb for me. I'd like to get to the bottom of this."

"Does that mean you're willing to return the favor?"

I couldn't be sure what that would require since I had no reason to think my boss was wrongly accused, but Justin was loyal. If I didn't agree, he'd shut me out of the investigation. "What does Cross want me to do?"

"He has a case for you."

"I know. He said that before he left. What case?"

"His."

I felt as if we were performing our own version of *Who's on First*. "I know. Which one?"

"His."

"His?" The word didn't compute. "Doesn't he work multiple cases at a time?"

"No, Ms. Parker, you're not taking over one of his cases. You're taking over his case. He suspected things might turn out this way. That's why he chose you to work the murder investigation."

I nearly choked. I'd expected to have to coax the info out of Justin. Instead, I was being offered the keys to the kingdom on a silver platter. This had to be a trick. Cross always planned his moves three steps ahead. Did that mean he was guilty and wanted to use my skills and favorable status with the police department as a get out of jail free card?

"What's wrong?" Justin asked.

"Cross Security has a strict policy against working homicides. Those fall under the purview of police jurisdiction. We do not get involved in police matters."

"I see you finally got around to reading the employee handbook."

"Right, so is this some kind of joke?"

"No." He sat up straight. "Look, I know you've had difficulties with Lucien in the past. His whole obsession with James Martin didn't help matters. But that's water under the bridge. They're working on a joint project. Lucien's arrest could negatively impact that partnership. You don't want that. I don't want that either."

"Now you're resorting to blackmail?" He stole my move before I could use it.

"I want you to realize it's in everyone's best interest for you to take this on." He stared into my eyes. "Lucien is my oldest and best friend. He needs help. Your help."

"Why me? Renner's a former homicide detective. He's better equipped to handle this. If nothing else, he's better prepared and has a lot more contacts."

"The look of impropriety would be enormous." There was something he wasn't saying.

"Is this because I have friends in the department?"

"That and several other reasons. Namely, the police allow you to consult for them. Bennett Renner doesn't hold that special designation. Furthermore, you're not a Cross Security employee."

"Again with the handbook?"

"Technically, if an employee investigates on Lucien's behalf, he would be in breach of contract."

"Cross would fire someone for helping him?"

"Lucien doesn't always do things that will benefit him, but he tries to do what's right."

I choked back my snort. From what I knew of my boss, he'd take whatever actions benefitted his agenda. As far as I could tell, there was no moral or ethical element to them. Everything was just business, like hiring me and then spying on me to gain access to Martin.

"What happens if I say no? Do I get fired on the spot?"

"You have the right to refuse per the terms of your contract. I just hope you won't."

"Can I think about it?"

"Sure, take some time. Mr. Almeada should be arriving in the next few minutes. He'll want an answer before we proceed."

"But no pressure, right?"

"Maybe a little." He went to the door. "Make yourself comfortable. Would you like me to get you some coffee?"

"You don't have to do that."

"It's not a problem. The espresso maker's right outside." He didn't wait for me to answer before slipping out the door and gently pulling it closed behind him. I wondered if he left me unattended so I could snoop through our boss's files, but that didn't feel like the case. He must have left me in here so I could think, except I had no idea what to think.

Two minutes later, he returned with a tiny mug and saucer. He placed it on the coffee table near the couch. I picked it up and moved to stand in front of the window. Justin knew our boss pretty damn well, and he thought Cross deserved my help. But the one thing Justin hadn't said was Cross didn't do it.

Could I defend a murderer? Was it even up to me to decide? The police must have plenty of evidence. They wouldn't have gotten an arrest warrant otherwise.

"Justin," I turned around to face him, "what can you tell me about Trey Knox?"

"How do you know that name?"

"Answer my question."

"Knox was a client. One of the first. Cross agreed to help him, traced his stolen property to a storage unit, and called in a tip to the police. After that, the situation went off the rails, and Knox vanished. The police came by, asked some questions, and kept tabs on us for a while."

"They suspected Cross was involved in Knox's disappearance?"

"That'd be my guess, but I don't know anything for sure."

"Did Cross try to find him after he disappeared?"

"Yes."

"Great. Tell me everything. Start at the beginning."

SIX

Justin went to the filing cabinet and pulled out the hard copy of the Trey Knox file. Inside were pages of Cross's handwritten notes and theories. None of this had been on the company's servers. I turned a page and found a copy of the police report Knox had filed concerning the burglary.

"Did you ever meet Trey Knox?" I glanced at him while I skimmed the details.

"Several times."

"And?"

"He was a difficult client."

"Difficult how?"

"He withheld vital details which proved detrimental to Lucien's well-being."

"I need you to elaborate."

"Like I told you before, Ms. Parker, I don't know much about what happened. All I know is Lucien had his nose broken, a contact of his was attacked, and there were threats."

"What kinds of threats?"

"I don't know."

If he said those three words one more time, I would scream. "Then how do you know Cross received threats?"

"He beefed up security and assigned a detail to follow me and Gloria, our receptionist."

"Does she still work here?"

"No, she quit six years ago, right after she got married. I don't think she was aware a detail was following her."

"Does she know anything about the situation with Knox?"

Justin shook his head. "Lucien did his best to keep me out of the loop. Gloria had no idea what was going on. She just answered phones and scheduled meetings."

That meant she wouldn't be able to help me piece this together. "What else can you tell me about Knox?"

"Everything's in the file." He nodded at the folder in my hand. "If you have any other questions after reading that, you'll have to ask Lucien." The intercom beeped. "Excuse me for a second. Mr. Almeada's here. He'll want to speak to you."

While Justin was gone, I read the background information Cross had compiled on Knox, hoping to identify the party responsible for the break-in. According to the police report, the security system had been dismantled, indicating a professional team had been behind it. However, Knox didn't do much outside of work and sports collecting. His collection had some expensive pieces, namely a championship ring, but robbing Knox wouldn't lead to a big score without a fence. A pro probably wouldn't waste his time on this, which meant the break-in had to be personal, just like the murder.

Before I could get any further, Mr. Almeada barged into the office. He looked pensive. "You shouldn't be reading that."

"Why not? Cross wants me to work the case."

"He does, but you haven't signed yet. We need to get the formalities out of the way before you begin work." He placed his briefcase on the glass coffee table and popped open the lid. Removing a contract, which had tabbed signature boxes, he placed it on the edge of the table and put a pen on top. "We need to go over the terms."

"Doesn't that sound official?" I abandoned the file on Cross's desk and crossed the room. Picking up the contract,

I skimmed it for any hidden gotchas. But it looked like a run-of-the-mill agreement. "This says I'm working for you and not Cross."

"That's correct. I'll be hiring you to investigate my client's case and report back. Do you have a law license?" Almeada loomed above me, watching as I reviewed the paperwork.

"No."

"But you graduated from law school."

"Practicing law was never my intent." I put the pen down. "Why? Are you having trouble finding lawyers at Reeves, Almeada, and Stockton who are willing to work on Cross's case? I don't want to sit second chair."

Almeada rubbed a hand over his mouth to hide his snort. He found my comment amusing. "I'm handling Lucien's case personally. Hiring you to do some digging into the matter counts as work-product. It'll be privileged, which is why I need you to sign the contract."

Justin entered the office and closed the door. He eyed me from across the room, silently encouraging me to sign.

"Do you know who Cross is accused of killing?" I asked the attorney.

"I have all the details." Almeada checked the time. "I have to get back to the precinct soon. They plan to continue the interview after lunch. I'd like you to come with me. I can brief you in the car if you're fuzzy on the details."

I could refuse, but I didn't know what would happen if I did. A lot was riding on this—my livelihood, Martin's business, and Cross's freedom. "I have doubts concerning Cross's innocence. I won't conceal a crime. Are you sure you want me to sign this? The other investigators in this office would be a much better fit. Bennett Renner would be perfect."

"Renner can't be involved. In fact, you'll have to operate solo while you investigate. Anything you discover is not to be shared with anyone outside of Cross's legal team." Almeada picked the pen up and slipped it back into my hand. "You'll understand why soon enough. Just sign. We have to get going."

"Did he do it?" I asked.

Almeada swallowed. "I don't know. It'll be your job to find out."

"What if I come up with an answer you don't like? Then what? We hide it? Bury it? Cover it up?"

"That'll be my problem, not yours."

"How is it not my problem? I swore an oath—"

"You're no longer a federal agent, Ms. Parker. Your oath is worthless."

Before I could respond, Justin crossed the room and grasped my forearm. "He didn't do it." The conviction in his eyes told me he believed it. "Lucien wouldn't have insisted on assigning you this case if he had anything to hide. He knows you won't stop until you get the truth. He does a lot of questionable things, but he wouldn't self-destruct like this."

Almeada choked a little on his next inhale.

Justin glared at him. "He wouldn't."

"I hope you're right." I signed and initialed all the tabs and handed the contract back to Almeada. "Now what?"

The attorney double-checked everything and tucked it into his briefcase. "Let's go speak to our client." He strode out of the office and straight to the elevator. "You've had a few run-ins with the law yourself," he said when we reached the lobby.

"Comes with the territory."

"Does it?" He glanced at me as we made our way out of the building. "You realize Cross Security has rules and regulations in place to prevent that from happening. Yet, I recall coming to your assistance a time or two."

"Do you have a point? I'm not the one staring down a murder rap. Cross should have obeyed his own rules."

Almeada waited until we were inside the car before he said, "Lucien came up with those guidelines for a reason. When he started out, things didn't always go his way. He learned a lot of tough lessons."

"I know about the settlement, how Cross killed a cop to protect a young woman."

"How?"

"Don't worry. Cross didn't violate the gag order. I ran into Jade McNamara in Las Vegas several months ago. She told James Martin what happened, and he told me." Apparently, Cross hadn't bothered to disclose this information to his attorney.

"I see. That'll make the rest of this easier. You know Cross and the police have always had a tumultuous relationship. That's never changed. In the past year, things have gotten better. I'm guessing you had something to do with that. That's why word of Lucien's arrest this morning came out of left field. I didn't see it coming. I don't think he did either."

"I doubt anyone expected Trey Knox's body to surface."

"Good point."

The news about the airport expansion had been announced months ago. Details on the new parking lot, along with maps and drawings, had been in the papers. Perhaps, Cross did have time to prepare for this. Had he gone to the airport to move the body and gotten caught?

"Why do you think the police arrested him?" I asked.

"When Knox disappeared, Lucien got bumped to the top of the suspect list. He was the only person they could place inside Knox's house the day of his disappearance. Since they never had any other solid leads, Lucien remained their prime suspect."

"Surely, they must have more to go on than that."

"Cross had a forensic expert on his payroll at the time, and he'd also gone through the police academy. He had the knowledge and know-how necessary to pull off a nearly perfect murder. The police found a few drops of blood in Knox's house and a broken shower door, but no other indications of a struggle or abduction. Knox's car was parked at his place of business, but he never reported to work. Security cam footage saw someone walk away from the car. It could have been Lucien, but a positive ID couldn't be made."

"Still, that's circumstantial," I said. "Have they found the murder weapon?"

"Not that I'm aware."

"Then none of this makes any sense. Just because Cross was the last person to see Knox alive, that doesn't explain why the cops think he did it. Did an eyewitness place him at the scene? Do the police think the bullets will match his gun?" I couldn't imagine that would be the case. "Don't tell me Cross went to the airport to move the body."

"Don't be ridiculous."

I shrugged. "Y'never know."

"The police have found a few things, which might appear flimsy on the outset, but when combined, add up to a convincing narrative. That's why I need an investigator to find logical reasons to explain everything away and find out what actually happened to Trey Knox."

"Does Cross have an alibi?"

"The murder took place too long ago. The police can't pin it down to an exact time and date, which will make supplying an alibi difficult, if not impossible."

"That will also make it harder for the prosecutor to make a case."

"Theoretically."

"What about the injuries Knox sustained? His missing molars and fingertips, do the police believe Cross did that?"

"Probably, since those are the steps one might take to commit the perfect murder."

I didn't buy it. "The police have something else. Something irrefutable. A smoking gun, so to speak."

"If they do, they haven't brought it up yet. Until they decide to use it against Lucien, they don't have to tell me about it." Almeada studied me from the corner of his eye. "Are you speculating, or do you know something I don't?"

"All I know is what they have isn't enough to charge him."

"You're probably right, which is why the police are running the clock while they collect more evidence and build their case."

"Why won't you loop Renner in? He can help."

"If the circumstances were different, I would. But Renner worked the Knox disappearance, along with Lt. Moretti. I can't have him working for me. It'll muddy the waters and open up anything he finds to extreme scrutiny. I'm not giving the DA's office a slam dunk case."

"Is that why Cross hired Renner?"

"What do you mean?"

"Just what I said. Did Cross hire Renner to insulate himself in the event Knox's body surfaced?"

"You should ask Lucien that question?"

SEVEN

I slipped into the observation room, hoping no one would notice. The police were in a rush to get things underway. As soon as we entered the precinct, they brought us to the interrogation room. Cross was waiting inside. But I hung back, figuring I might learn more from the other side of the glass.

"Ma'am, you can't be in here," the tech said as he checked the recording equipment.

"I'm part of Lucien Cross's counsel," I said.

The tech plugged in the audio cables. "His attorney's right there."

"I didn't say I was his attorney."

The tech checked the monitor, making sure the green light was on. Then he tapped on the glass to let Lt. Moretti know he could get started with the interrogation. "The fun's over. Let's go, lady." He grabbed my elbow and dragged me out of the room.

"Whoa." Heathcliff almost collided with us. "What's going on here?"

"This woman was trying to sit in on the interrogation."

Heathcliff eyed me. "Is Moretti in there?"

"Yes, sir," the tech said.

"All right. She can stay."

"But, Detective—" the tech began.

"Save it. This is my case. My decision." He looked past me at the two-way mirror. "My ass."

The tech released his grip on my elbow. "Make sure the lieutenant knows that."

"Will do." Heathcliff slipped past us. "You coming, Parker?"

Satisfied, I slunk back into the room. After making sure the recording equipment was working, Heathcliff moved beside me, resting his shoulder and hip against the wall in order to keep an eye on me and the goings-on inside the interrogation.

"Thanks," I said.

"Yep."

Moretti sifted through the police file. "Let's not waste any time, Mr. Cross. You and I have done this dance before."

"It's been years. Refresh my memory," Cross said.

"Trey Knox, remember him?"

"Vaguely."

Moretti nearly laughed. "Have there been that many?"

"That many what?" Cross asked. Almeada leaned forward a few inches, ready to intervene. But this wasn't a court of law. The only real power the attorney had was to keep his client from incriminating himself.

"Clients." Moretti's eyebrows raised a quarter of an inch. "Did you think I was going to say victims?"

"That's enough," Almeada warned.

Moretti ignored the attorney, his focus on Cross. "Trey Knox was one of your clients. He hired you to work a recovery roughly eight years ago. Didn't Detective Heathcliff go over these facts with you earlier today?"

"Did you?" I asked.

"I do my job, Parker."

Cross used his cuffed hands to rub his chin. "That's right. It must have slipped my mind. Low blood sugar. My breakfast was interrupted, and lunch, well, that was a joke."

"Can I get you a sandwich? A salad? Chips?" Moretti asked.

"You could remove the cuffs to start," Almeada said.

Moretti leaned over, unhooking the bracelets from Lucien's wrists. "What else can I get for you?"

"I'd like you to cut the bullshit and let me go," Cross said.

Almeada nudged him with his knee, but Cross's expression didn't shift. He wanted the police lieutenant to know just how annoyed he was.

Moretti slammed the folder closed. "Fine. I'll cut to the chase. Did you murder Trey Knox?"

"Knox is dead?" Lucien asked, a smug expression on his face. The look made my insides ache. Again, he failed to deny the claim.

Heathcliff's gaze remained glued to my face. "You think he did it."

I swallowed. "Watch the interrogation."

"I'll learn more by watching you."

"I don't know anything."

"Would you tell me if you did?"

I jerked my chin at the glass, just as Moretti said, "His remains were uncovered at a construction site."

Lucien didn't even flinch. "The bastard got what he deserved."

"Why would you say that?" Moretti asked. "Eight years ago, when I questioned you about Knox's disappearance, you thought he was a swell guy. Did something change?"

"Knox was a conniving son of a bitch. Your investigation into the man should have uncovered a few truths."

"Really?"

Almeada leaned over to whisper in Cross's ear.

"Your boss has a hell of a poker face," Heathcliff said. "Yours, on the other hand, could use some work."

"What do you want me to say?" I glanced at him before returning my focus to the interrogation. "Last night I offered you my help, but you shot me down."

"You didn't have to volunteer to help the other side," Heathcliff said.

"I didn't volunteer."

"Either way, we're working different sides of the street."

"Derek, that was not my intent. We have the same goal in mind. We want to find a killer."

"No, Parker, I want to put a killer behind bars. You want to protect him."

"I wouldn't do that," I said, unsure how true it was.

Almeada continued to whisper in Cross's ear, acknowledging the subtle nods and headshakes. Finally, the attorney said, "This is harassment. You tried to pin Knox's disappearance on my client eight years ago, but you didn't have anything then. And as far as I can tell, you don't have anything now. This is a waste of our time."

"A lot's changed in eight years. Now I have Knox's body and plenty of evidence. Right now, your client still has a chance to come clean. If he tells me what happened, I'll make sure mitigating circumstances are factored in. Things will go a lot easier on him, but only if he cooperates."

"Fuck you," Cross said.

Almeada nudged him again, a little harder this time. "I need time to confer with my client in private."

Moretti stared at Cross. "Do the smart thing. Do what your father would want you to do."

Cross didn't move, but his eyes burned with a hatred that I'd never seen before. Moretti had cracked the indifferent façade, even if Cross's words had been far from apathetic. Moretti remained unfazed as he scooped up the file and headed for the door.

"Who's Cross's father?" I asked.

Heathcliff chuckled. "Like I said, you need to work on your poker face."

"Derek, I'm serious. Who is he? What does he have to do with any of this?"

He narrowed his eyes, not believing that I didn't possess that knowledge. But when his unwavering gaze was met by nothing but confusion, he said, "Police Commissioner Cross."

I stumbled backward, glad the wall caught me because the news nearly knocked me over. "You're joking."

"Nope."

The words didn't compute. "What? How?"

"Forty years ago, a man and woman met, fell in love, and—"

"Shut up." This situation was beyond screwed up. "Does the commissioner know his son's been arrested?"

"I'm sure he does. But the mayor's running for reelection. He's promoting that whole crackdown on crime thing. Don't you keep up with the news?"

"I try to avoid politics."

Heathcliff snorted. "Good luck with that."

"When I woke up this morning, I didn't realize I'd be living in a soap opera."

"It's not a soap opera." Lt. Moretti entered the room, unplugged the microphone, and turned off the camera to give Almeada and Cross their privacy. "You shouldn't be here." He stared at Heathcliff. "Did you let her in?"

"She wandered in on her own."

"Remind me to talk to the desk sergeant about that."

"Lieutenant, I'm here to help," I said.

"Help who? According to what Almeada said, you're working for him."

"Technically," I admitted.

He ran a hand over his face, elongating his jowls. "What can you tell me?"

"About what?"

"Knox. Cross. What went down between the two?"

"I don't know. I haven't had a chance to talk to Cross yet." I folded my arms over my chest and matched Moretti's dead-eye stare. "Maybe after you let me speak to him, I'll be able to answer that question."

Moretti ignored me and spoke to Heathcliff. "I want to wipe the smug look off that bastard's face. Did you hear what he said? He despised Knox and hasn't shown even the slightest hint of compassion or remorse over the man's death. Dollars to donuts, he killed him."

"Probably." Heathcliff remained professional, but inside, he was squirming, stuck between duty and friendship.

"Once we serve the search warrant, he'll be singing a different tune." Moretti shifted his focus back to me. "You're supposed to be working on Cross's behalf. It'd be in his best interest to come clean now. Once I lay my cards on the table, the case will be solid. He won't have any room to negotiate. I'm trying to do him a favor. I'm giving him a chance to get ahead of this. You need to convince him to cooperate."

"Cooperate? You're hoping for a confession," I said. "That'll never happen. He's not an idiot."

"He messed up, Parker. He's probably spent the last eight years thinking he got away with it, but he didn't. It came back to bite him in the ass. I'm offering him an olive branch. There's only so much I can do."

"How stupid do you think I am?" I looked from one man to the other. "If you had anything, you would have charged him by now."

"Do you want to know what we have?" Moretti opened the door. "Let me show you." He nodded to Heathcliff. "Give Cross five more minutes with his counsel. Then you and Parker can get situated in the interrogation room. I'll have the techs set up our little show and tell."

"Yes, sir." Heathcliff gestured that I go ahead of him.

We stood in the hallway, an unfamiliar tension between us. "I don't like this," I said. "You knew what was going on last night, and you didn't tell me."

"I couldn't."

"It's me."

"I know, but Moretti gave me strict instructions. I shouldn't have taken you to the ME's office."

"That's why you left the file in the trunk." I stared at him. "But the details you gave me, those were real."

"I didn't lie to you."

I bit my lip, working through what I knew. "Four shots to the chest, resulting in a fatal gunshot wound to the heart. Shots like that could indicate an emotional trigger."

"Overkill. Anger," Heathcliff suggested, "which goes along with the animosity Cross has displayed toward Trey Knox."

"Actually, he didn't display much emotion." Cross didn't seem to care Knox was dead and had no problem showing that to the police. "A grouping like that would rule out a professional. Don't you think Cross would be a better shot?"

"It depends. We are talking eight years ago. He was just starting out."

"But he went through academy training. Surely, cops learn to shoot better than that."

"I've seen plenty of cops who couldn't hit the broad side of a barn, who barely qualify."

"What about torture? Cross isn't a sadist."

"You work for him. You'd know better than anyone, but he does know a thing or two about forensics and how bodies are identified. That could explain it."

"You also thought Martin was guilty when he was suspected of murder, but you were wrong."

Heathcliff smiled. "Nine times out of ten, I would have been right. Lightning doesn't strike twice. This time, I am right." He checked his watch and knocked on the interrogation room door. "Take it from me, Parker. Lucien Cross is a killer, and from the look on your face, you know it's true."

"My face doesn't say a damn thing."

He raised one eyebrow but kept his mouth shut as he slowly opened the door. "Time's up, gentlemen."

EIGHT

A police tech placed a laptop on the table, inserted a USB drive, which he'd removed from an evidence bag, and hit play. The laptop screen filled with footage from a beach resort. Waves crashed in the background while Cross threatened a man I assumed to be Trey Knox.

"If I ever see your face again, I will end you," Cross hissed.

"Now you're threatening me?"

"It's not a threat. It's a promise."

"What are you going to do, Lucien? Take care of me the same way you took care of the Russians?"

Cross snorted. "You can't extort me. I'll expose you for what you are. You don't know what I've found on you or the info I have on your various aliases, so I suggest you do us both a favor and stay away."

"Lucien, you're no angel. You can't do anything to me and still come out smelling like a rose. It'd be a shame if your actions were to come back and bite you in the ass."

"If they do, you're getting bit too."

"This is a non-extradition country."

"You should keep in mind, Mr. Knox, I have dozens of Special Ops trained mercenaries on my payroll who know a thing or two about international travel. They won't have a problem grabbing you in the middle of the night and *taking care of the situation. Understand?"*

The video reached the end, and Moretti shut the laptop lid. He let out a noisy exhale. "Now that you and your counsel have had time to converse, I'm hoping you've reconsidered."

Cross stared at the screen.

"Where did you get that?" Almeada asked.

"We found it inside a safe deposit box." Moretti removed the USB drive, placed it back in the evidence bag, and slid it closer to Almeada.

Almeada read the label and attached chain of custody form. "Has it been authenticated? It's easy for footage to be doctored or faked. I'll want a third-party lab to verify the results you've reached."

"It's real." Moretti smiled at Cross. "Isn't it?"

"That doesn't prove anything." Cross leaned back in the chair, finding a spot on the wall to stare at. I'd conducted enough interrogations to be familiar with that behavior. No matter how tough or indifferent Cross acted, the footage had gotten to him. This was his 'oh shit' moment.

It was time I stepped in. "A safe deposit box? Surely, you would have conducted a thorough search of Knox's property when he went missing. Have you been sitting on that recording for eight years?"

"No, Parker," Moretti scowled at me, "we located the box after we found Knox's remains."

"How?"

"The key was hidden inside the man's shoe. The one place the killer didn't think to look."

"Didn't you check his bank records prior to that? Wouldn't you have discovered its existence years ago?"

If looks could kill, Moretti would be facing homicide charges of his own. "The box wasn't registered in Knox's name. It was opened under an alias, probably one of the aliases Cross knew about."

"What alias?" I asked.

Moretti didn't want to answer, but since he'd opened this can of worms, he didn't have much of a choice. The recording was his smoking gun—his ace in the hole—it amounted to a deathbed declaration and probably gave enough credence to the police department's request for a search warrant. "Thomas Gunn."

"Are you sure that isn't a real person?" Almeada asked. "It sounds like a real person to me."

"What do you think, Mr. Cross?" Heathcliff asked. "Is that one of Knox's aliases?"

"I am unaware of Mr. Knox using any aliases or nicknames."

"That's not what you admitted on the recording." Heathcliff jerked his chin at the USB.

Unsure how to respond, Cross held his tongue.

"Have you investigated the possibility that Mr. Gunn exists?" Almeada asked.

"We take our cases seriously around here. We perform our due diligence," Moretti said. "The bank had a photo ID on file of the man who opened the box. His photo matches Trey Knox."

"When was the box opened?" I asked.

"Eight years ago." Moretti slid into the seat and stared at Cross. "Do you want to tell me what went down between you and Knox? The man tried to blackmail you. That'd piss me off. No one would blame you for threatening to kill him."

Cross took care to select his words. "People make idle threats all the time."

"Where were you when that footage was taken?" Moretti asked. "The sand and crystal clear water looked rather nice."

"I don't remember."

Almeada nudged him again. The police would use the topographical features in the distance to determine the geographical location. They'd also subpoena Cross's passport records and travel history.

"When was the footage taken?" Cross asked.

"It had a timestamp on it," I said. "Have you determined if that's accurate?"

Heathcliff nodded to me. "It is."

"In that case, it might have been Vanuatu. I can't be sure. It's been eight years." Cross emphasized the length of time. "I've traveled a lot this decade. It all blends together."

"That was right after Knox disappeared. About three weeks after his disappearance, if I'm not mistaken. How did you find him?" Moretti asked.

This changed everything. Knox didn't disappear because he'd been murdered. Knox had fled. "Vanuatu is a non-extradition country," I said.

"Yeah, he mentioned that on the recording." Moretti glared at me for disrupting his flow. But what did he expect? There were too many cooks in the kitchen.

"Was Knox involved in any illegal activity?" I asked. Perhaps Cross had helped hide his client. The threats he made might have been meant to keep them both safe, though I wasn't sure how.

Cross quietly cleared his throat. I'd worked for him long enough to know I'd done something to piss him off. Moretti sensed the shift in the room, as did Heathcliff.

"An officer will be right outside. You change your mind and want to talk, let us know. If not, you have the room to talk things over with your counsel." Moretti nodded to us. "For your sake, Lucien, you should talk. There's a deal to be made here. You just have to tell me what happened. Maybe we could discuss what Knox meant about the Russians in more detail. That intel might be worth something. Or you could tell us about Knox's aliases and whatever crimes he was involved in. I want to help you, but you have to give me something."

Cross didn't move or blink.

"Just think about it." Moretti ushered the cops out of the room and pulled the door closed behind him.

"That could have gone worse," Almeada said. "The first thing we'll do is challenge the recording and its discovery."

"That's a waste of time," I said.

Cross gave the two-way mirror a dirty look.

"It's safe to talk," I said. But he didn't believe me, so I opened the door, made sure the attached observation room was locked, and stepped back inside. "The cops aren't spying on you."

The unreadable mask he'd put in place slipped, and he turned his anger and frustration on me. "What the hell are you doing, Alex?"

"My job."

"Interrogating me isn't your job."

But I didn't let him distract me. "The footage wasn't faked. You knew what would be on the recording, where it took place, and when. That means you knew Knox was alive after he disappeared. Did you give him a new identity and send him away?"

"I did more than enough for that lying prick," Cross said.

With just the three of us in the room, Cross wasn't nearly as guarded. But I still couldn't get a clear read on him. He was hiding something. I just didn't know what. "Tell me about him," I instructed. "How did you track him down after he disappeared?"

"Knox was obsessed with sports. When he took off, he left a championship ring behind. It's the only piece of his collection he couldn't bear to part with. The morning of his disappearance, I'd gone to his house to return it, but he was gone. I left the ring in his desk drawer. But since I'd spent so long trying to track it and the rest of his collection down, I had feelers everywhere. When Knox finally made some inquiries, word got back to me. I tracked his internet handle and took a little trip." Cross stared at the mirror, not fully believing the conversation was private. "Knox was alive and well when I left him."

"You threatened to kill him. Shit, Lucien, you threatened to have black ops guys abduct him in the middle of the night."

"Your point?"

"Did you kill Trey Knox?"

"Do you really have to ask me that, Alex? Isn't it obvious?"

"You've yet to deny it." I waited, wondering if he would.

"I didn't kill him." Cross studied my expression. "But it doesn't matter what I say because you don't believe me."

"I'm not sure."

"I wouldn't have asked you to investigate if I were responsible. That'd be suicide. I know you won't stop until you figure out what happened. Right now, that's exactly what I need. Eventually, you'll believe me. You'll have to.

And once you do, so will they." He nodded at the glass.

"Is that why you chose me? To manipulate the situation?" It wouldn't be the first time my connections made me the ideal pawn in one of Cross's games.

He reached for a glass of water and took a sip.

"Did you hire Bennett Renner for the same reason?"

Cross quirked his head to the side. "You think I hired a detective because he tried to put the screws to me and failed?"

"It depends. Did you ask Renner to throw the case or look the other way? Is that why it took the police this long to find Knox?"

His confused look turned into a glare. "No, that had nothing to do with Renner getting a job at Cross Security. Frankly, that's the number one reason why I almost didn't hire him. I don't believe in rewarding incompetence."

"What changed your mind?"

"He needed a job."

"That was it? You hired him just like that?" I didn't believe it, especially after all the hoops Cross had made me jump through when he first considered hiring me.

"Pretty much."

"Lucien," Almeada said, "we need to focus here. Knox mentioned what you did to the Russians on the recording."

"That's inconsequential."

"Are you sure?" Almeada sighed. "It could turn problematic real fast."

"It won't."

"Regardless, you shouldn't give them anything," Almeada cautioned.

"I don't intend to," Cross said.

"What did you do to the Russians?" I asked. Whatever it was had Moretti interested.

Cross gave Almeada a hard look, silently communicating that the attorney ought to keep his mouth shut. "It'd be best if you let that one lie, Ms. Parker." The sudden formality meant I'd struck a nerve. At this point, several. "Do the police have the murder weapon yet?"

"No," I said.

"I've seen the autopsy report. Knox was shot in the

chest." Almeada reached for his briefcase. "Four times."

"Have you seen the report?" Cross asked me, and I nodded. "Do you think he was killed by a professional hitter?"

"A pro wouldn't have shot him in the chest. It would have been a headshot, possibly execution style. Four to the chest is sloppy, emotional, especially after..."

"After what?" Cross asked.

"After he'd been tortured."

"Tortured?" Something flickered behind Cross's eyes.

"His molars were removed and his fingertips burned off."

"Dammit." Cross blinked hard. "Knox was a real piece of work. I knew it'd catch up to him, but I never thought I'd be blamed." He tapped his pointer finger on the table, unaware he was even doing it. "That doesn't make any sense. We didn't overlap. He worked for arms dealers and cartels."

"What was Knox involved in?" I asked.

"Smuggling."

"Do you have proof?"

"Rumors of a ledger, but nothing solid. I never investigated."

"Why not?"

"It's complicated." Cross went back to staring at the wall. "Just get me out of here. I'll figure the rest out, but I can't do that from a holding cell."

"That's easier said than done. They plan on executing a search warrant," I said.

Almeada cursed. "We expected as much. Any surprises I should prepare for, Lucien?"

"Nothing."

"I'll do my best to slow them down and run whatever damage control might be necessary. What about Justin? They'll want to bring him in for questioning," Almeada said.

"He knows how to handle the situation, but make sure he's okay," Cross said.

Almeada didn't seem nearly as optimistic on this point. "Given who your father is, I think it's time we loop him in.

He has plenty of clout. We can use that to our advantage."

"No. I didn't want his help then, and I sure as hell don't want it now. He doesn't know anything about this, and even if he did, I doubt he'd care."

"Regardless, a phone call could work wonders," Almeada said. "You could be home by dinner."

"No." Cross folded his arms across his chest and sat back in the chair. He'd always said and done what he wanted, but this was nothing more than sheer stubbornness.

"Lucien—" Almeada began.

"I pay you to act on my behalf. I said my father stays out of this, so he stays out of this. Got it?"

Almeada met my eyes. "You might as well get to work since our job has gotten exponentially harder."

"I'll see what I can do, but don't hold your breath."

NINE

After walking out of the interrogation room, I tried to gather as much intel as I could from my buddies in blue, but no one would talk to me. Moretti made sure a cone of silence surrounded the Knox murder. Heathcliff kept a watchful eye on me, keeping me away from anything of use. Unfortunately, he knew all my tricks and exactly where I'd go for my intel.

"Parker, do you think he'll talk?" Heathcliff asked.

"Only if hell turns into a ski resort."

"You should leave this alone."

"I said I'd look into it, so I'm going to look into it."

"But you think he's guilty."

"I might have changed my mind."

"Why? What did he say to you?"

"He told me he didn't kill Knox." Cross had also said a lot of other things which didn't bear repeating to the detective assigned to the case.

"The evidence says otherwise."

"Does it? What do you have besides an eight-year-old tape and circumstantial evidence? Someone broke into Knox's house and stole his property. Whoever did that could just as easily have killed him. Obviously, Knox had enemies. I need to find out who they are. Knox might have been involved in some shady shit."

"Did Bennett Renner tell you that?" Something flickered behind Heathcliff's eyes.

"No, but I'll be sure to ask him about it."

"Do that." He led me to the door. "I have to get back to work. But you're okay, right? After last night's meeting, I just wanted to touch base."

"I'm fine, Derek." I'd be better if everyone stopped acting like I was on the verge of a nervous breakdown.

"All right. If you need to talk to someone, I'm around, case or no case. We just can't talk about this."

"I get it. I don't want to get you in trouble."

"That'd be a first." He smiled and tapped my arm with the folder in his hand. "Don't forget to call Renner."

Did the no-nonsense detective just give me a lead? I went outside and dialed. Renner answered on the second ring. "Hey, I have a favor to ask."

"Sure, do you need me to take over more of your cases?"

"Not at the moment." The last thing I wanted to do was tip him off to the situation given his complicated history with the case and Mr. Almeada's instructions. But Heathcliff told me to talk to him, so I had to find out why. "Do you remember working with Lt. Moretti eight years ago?"

"Moretti was only a sergeant then. We worked one case together. That was it."

"Do you remember anything about it?"

"Oh, shit. Is that why Cross was taken out of the conference room in handcuffs?"

"Possibly. I'm hoping you might have some copies of your notes or a few files on hand."

"Let me see what I can dig up."

"Thanks, Bennett."

"No problem."

Since it would take time for Renner to get the files together, I headed to the construction site where Knox's body had been found. The photo in this morning's newspaper didn't do it justice. Crime scene tape roped off an area roughly the size of a football field. Cadaver dogs were being led up and down the field while a group of forensic experts scanned the giant mountain of dirt which had already been cleared away with scanners and other X-ray devices.

Patrol officers guarded the perimeter. The two closest to me noticed when I stepped out of the silver sedan. Since Cross Security had a fleet of these cars, I wondered if the cops recognized it. But they only appeared mildly interested in my arrival.

A few bored reporters hovered near three news vans. The heat and humidity had wilted their perfect hair and made their makeup melt and run, leaving trails of clumpy foundation on their faces. By the time the six o'clock news started, they'd have to endure a thorough touchup.

Realizing the police wouldn't talk to me and the reporters were more likely to question me than answer my questions, I searched the area for anyone who might be more compliant. A few trailers sat off to the side with the construction company's signage stuck in the ground next to the door. Bingo.

I zigzagged around the crime scene markers, noting the collection of items placed on a tarp near the mountain of dirt. More than likely, those items meant nothing. But they could be evidence or more of Knox's remains.

Going up the steps, I knocked on the door. "It's open," someone yelled.

I twisted the knob and stepped inside. An oscillating fan clicked as it blew the warm air around the room. Plans hung on the wall beside a calendar.

"What do you want?" a man asked, not looking up from the papers on his desk.

"Did you find the remains?" I asked.

"No, Christian did." He tore his eyes from the page. "You a reporter?"

"No, sir."

"Cop, then." He snorted, noticing the gun resting beneath my jacket in my shoulder holster. "I already told you people everything I know. We got hired to build a new parking garage. The plans are right there." He pointed to the blueprints tacked to the wall. "I got the permits here.

City signed off on it. Airport wanted it done. Now I got to wait for you to say it's okay to continue. Meanwhile, my guys aren't getting paid."

"I'm sorry about that."

"If we're going to be delayed too long, we'll have to move to another job site. I don't know when we'll finish there or when we'll get back to this. You want to give me a ballpark figure on the situation?"

"That depends on what you can tell me." I grabbed a folding chair and sat down. "Start at the beginning."

"Jeez." He wiped the sweat off his face with a stained bandana. "We were leveling the ground. We'd just dumped the latest pile when Christian spotted something odd poking through the dirt. He went to see what it was, and that's when he found the dead guy."

"Was it like an arm here and a leg there?"

The contractor stared at me like I was insane. "No. What the hell's wrong with you?"

"Plenty, but my current problem is no one on the force wants to tell me anything."

"Yeah, I hear that. Most of the dead guy was wrapped up in a tarp. It got torn when we scooped him up. It's not like he was a skeleton or anything when we found him."

"Mummified?"

"Nah, just...like not a lot left to him, like in those old zombie movies where they come up from the ground."

The thought made my stomach turn, but this guy seemed excited to discuss it. This was probably the craziest thing that happened on one of his construction sites. Sure, he hated the delay, but at least he had something to tell his pals when they were sitting down for a cold one.

"Did you take any photos?" I asked.

"I...uh..."

"I won't tell." The police would confiscate them. "I'm just curious."

"We called 9-1-1 as soon as it happened and shut down for the night. It's been two days. We're still shut down. I wanted to make sure I had proof to back up the shutdown in case anyone questions my decision, y'know."

"Sure. I just want to see the photos."

Reluctantly, he pulled his phone out of his pocket, unlocked it with his pointer finger, and tapped the screen a few times. He slid it across the desk and nodded down at it. "There ya go."

"Have you shown these to anyone else?"

"No one's asked."

"Not even the reporters outside?"

He snorted. "They want something exclusive like this, they better be willing to pay for it."

The photo didn't show much. The tarp had been duct-taped around the body. The tape had aged and curled. Forensics would have checked for fingerprints, fibers, and other trace evidence. From the ripped opening in the side of the tarp, Knox's arm and hand were visible. A shiny championship ring hung from his bony knuckles. The fingers curled into claws that ended prematurely just above the upper joint. The ragged cuts and blackened tips must have been excruciating, or so I imagined. For Knox's sake, I hoped it happened after he was dead.

"Gruesome, isn't it?" The contractor held out his hand, and I returned his phone. "I heard some reporters talking. They said he's been here a good, long while."

"Eight years. You didn't happen to find anything else, like a wallet or keys?"

He shook his head. "Once the police showed up, they took over everything." He leaned forward and peered out the window. "What are they even looking for?"

"Evidence."

"Good luck with that."

Taking the hint, I went out the door. Members of the crime scene unit were sifting through a pile of dirt, as if panning for gold. They must have been looking for bone fragments or bullet casings. I took a few steps toward them, noticing the patrol officers at the perimeter sidestepping until they were in front of me.

Instead of trying to charm my way beneath the tape, I nodded to them and set out for the news vans, but it'd be best to avoid the reporters for now. Lucien didn't need his arrest broadcast to the world, and neither did Martin.

A group of construction workers sat on a bench beneath

a makeshift tent where they were drinking beer and watching the cadaver dogs. One of them whistled at me. "Hey, baby."

"Yo," I slid my sunglasses up until they rested on top of my head, "have you seen Christian?"

The one who whistled looked disappointed. "What you want is a real man."

"Shut up, Tom." Another guy gave him a shove. "What can I do for you, lady?"

I sauntered over to the tent, noticing the patrolmen had taken an interest. This might have been the most fascinating thing that had happened all day. "If it isn't the man of the hour."

He looked confused.

"You found the body," I said.

"Oh, yeah, I guess." He took off his cap and scratched his head before putting it back on.

"Which is why we're sitting around like a bunch of morons with our thumbs up our asses." Tom took another swig of beer. "You wanna sit down, honey? I'll make room." He swung one leg around, straddling the bench before patting the seat in front of him.

Ignoring him, I asked a few more questions about the body, but none of the construction crew knew what happened. "The cops haven't told you anything yet?"

"Nothing," Christian said.

"Have they found anything else?"

"Not that we can tell," Tom chimed in. "It's just one body. They cleared him out. It's done. We get back to work. I don't see what the big deal is. It's like they're digging for diamonds or something."

One of the dogs barked. A tech went to that location with a scanner in hand. A few minutes later, they dug up what appeared to be a cardboard bucket. "Excuse me." I moved away from the tent, noticing the reporters had also caught on to the action. The cops opened the container, finding a dozen, discarded chicken bones.

"That's why littering is frowned upon," someone muttered.

I spun to see who had said it, catching a glimpse of a

man in coveralls walking away. He moved swiftly and with purpose, wearing a solid black jumpsuit with little blue booties over his shoes to keep from leaving shoeprints, like the rest of the police techs. His hands were clad in matching blue latex gloves.

But something about his appearance was off. I turned to study the techs near the pile of dirt. The backs of their coveralls were also solid black, but they didn't have belts on the outside. And they didn't have guns.

I turned back around, but the man had vanished. Setting out in the direction he traveled, I kept my eyes peeled for him, but I couldn't find him. After circling the entire perimeter and not spotting any other techs or police personnel dressed in a similar fashion, I returned to my car.

Beneath the wiper blade was a note. *Back off, unless you want to get hurt.*

TEN

I didn't know who left the note. The construction site didn't have any surveillance cameras. The reporters and police personnel had been too distracted by the chicken bucket to notice anyone lurking near the parking lot.

The man dressed as a tech but armed to the teeth must have been the bastard who left the note. Based on the way he was dressed, he might have been a cop. After all, the police wanted Cross to hang for this. They wouldn't want me investigating on his behalf. They might have recognized the company car or run the plate and found that it was registered to Cross Security. Scaring me off was just a way to break up the monotony of the day, or so I told myself.

The note was probably more bark than bite, but my senses went on high alert. My gut said this was a lot more than some baseless threat. I couldn't shake the mental image I had of the guy walking away. Where did he go? Why wasn't I able to find him? I only looked away for a few seconds. How could anyone disappear that quickly?

Before I started the engine, I checked my surroundings for signs of danger, dropped to my belly, and searched beneath the car for trackers or other devices. I felt around the front and rear bumpers, the tire wells, and the tailpipe. Nothing.

Just to be on the safe side, I returned to Cross Security and asked the techs to scan the car. While I was there, I gave them the note and asked if they could run prints. Since the person who left it might have been a cop, I didn't want to hand it over to law enforcement until I knew for sure. Cross's paranoia had rubbed off on me, but if a cop threatened me, I wanted to know before I turned him in, just in case someone wanted to get cute or creative and brush this under the rug.

"I'll be in my office. Let me know what you find."

"Yes, Ms. Parker." The tech nodded to me. "We should know something within the hour." He studied the paper carefully. The guy wore gloves, which probably meant they wouldn't find prints or DNA, but I had to try. Maybe the bastard hadn't worn gloves when he'd written the note and only put them on when he stuck it underneath my windshield wiper.

I'd just made it to my door when Renner snuck up behind me. I jumped back, my right leg almost giving out, a side effect of this morning's workout. I wobbled, and Renner reached out to steady me. "What's going on, Parker? You don't look so good."

"I don't feel so good."

He pushed open my office door and led me to the couch. "Is your leg acting up again? They tend to do that from time to time." He slapped the side of his where it was held together by pins.

"It's not that." But I shook the question away, nodding down at the thick stack of files tucked beneath his arm. "What have you got there?"

"Everything I could find." He took a seat beside me. "Have they charged Lucien with anything yet?"

"No, they're running the clock. They want to hold him as long as they can so they can collect more evidence."

"Don't they know who he is? Who his dad is?"

"They don't care. His dad does the mayor's bidding. The city wants to push the investigation."

"Oh, that's right. The crackdown on crime. Is that why they're coming after Lucien now?"

"They're coming after him because a body surfaced." I

reminded myself not to say too much. I had to ask questions, not answer them. "You have to tell me everything you remember about the Trey Knox disappearance."

"Have you seen the official report?"

"No, Moretti's keeping me in the dark."

He grinned. "Good thing I've got my copy right here."

I took it from him and removed the rubber band. Aside from details and notes from witnesses, there wasn't much to go on. "What made Cross the prime suspect in Knox's disappearance?"

"He was our only suspect. Well, the only suspect left standing."

"What does that mean?"

"This all started when Knox reported a break-in at his house. Soon after, his belongings were found inside a storage unit, amongst crates of guns and drugs. Whoever stole from him was into some serious shit. The thief would have been our prime suspect, except that storage rental traced back to a Russian gangster. Vasili Petrov." Renner looked at me. "Ring any bells?"

"No."

"Petrov hoped to make it big. He lacked family support, so he ran his own show. He was a cruel son of a bitch. He operated a few strip joints and ran drugs and girls out of them. The usual shit you'd expect. Since Knox's stuff was found in Petrov's storage unit, we figured the two must connect."

"Why wasn't Petrov a suspect in Knox's disappearance?"

"The night before Knox fell off the face of the Earth, Petrov got killed in a drug deal gone wrong."

Could that be the Russian Knox had referenced in the recording? My skin erupted in gooseflesh. "Still, this was a good lead." I flipped pages. "Anyone who worked for Petrov could have been involved."

"That's what I thought, but it never panned out. The Russian connection turned into a dead end."

"How?"

"After Petrov's death, the Russians went to war with the bangers who killed him. Gangs and OCU had eyes all over the Russians. We would have known if they'd taken Knox."

On the coffee table, Justin had left Cross's files. I picked them up and read the police report on the break-in before comparing it to the items the police recovered during the raid of Petrov's storage unit. "Trey Knox's stolen possessions weren't the only stolen items found inside that unit."

"Which is why we figured maybe Petrov or one of his guys was involved in a burglary ring. The big Russian had ties to an area pawn shop. We figured it might have been an additional revenue stream or a way to launder money. Petrov could have had a crew steal stuff from people's houses, pawn it off, and use the revenue to clean the cash from the strip joints, or vice versa. Gangs was looking into that, but the investigation hit a wall. Petrov's death caused his illegal enterprises and legit businesses to crumble."

"No one moved in to fill his shoes?"

"Not that I know of."

"All right. Fine." But it wasn't, and I made a note to investigate further. If Cross had done something to piss off the Russians, he'd need help from an agency equipped to deal with the problem.

"Are you sure you're okay?" Renner squinted at me. "You look really pale."

"It's nothing. That's just my skin tone—ghostly."

Renner got up and grabbed a bottle of water from the cart in the corner. "At least drink this." He twisted off the top and handed it to me.

I hated that I couldn't tell him the truth, but it was for the best. "So if Petrov and the Russians are out, what about other people in Knox's life? I'm sure he had enemies. Everyone does."

"We looked into everyone, but Knox wasn't close with many people. The only family we found was a half-sister he hadn't spoken to in eighteen months."

"Who reported him missing?"

"His boss." Renner pointed to a section of his notes. "Knox called in sick the day before he disappeared. But when he didn't call or show up the next day, his boss got worried. A couple of officers went to his house to perform a wellness check, and that's when they found his front door open."

I read Renner's notes. "Since you didn't know when Knox went missing, how could you rule out his coworkers?"

"They were at work. We did our best to ascertain where they'd been that morning and the previous night. But everyone's story checked out. Sure, it's possible someone could have slipped away for an hour and done something to Knox, but he lived in a gated community. The only person who went to Knox's house during the window in which he disappeared was Lucien."

"What about the security guards at the gate?" The details weren't included in Renner's notes. "Did anyone check into them?"

"The guards were clean, even Lucien said so."

I switched to Cross's file. He'd performed background checks on the guards when he was determining who was responsible for the prior break-in. But they were clean. Cross believed that even though the main entrance had a gate, the wall around the rest of the neighborhood was easily penetrable. Anyone could jump the wall and get in and out undetected. And since the stuff taken from Knox's house wasn't large or heavy enough to require a van or truck, the thieves probably shoved it into a few backpacks and slipped out.

"The evidence of foul play isn't clear," I said, returning to Renner's notes. "The broken glass and blood drops might not have been from a struggle. It could have been from an injury."

"Cross said the same thing. He suggested Knox had cut himself on the broken door and left his house to seek medical attention, but since we found his car parked in the garage at his office with a small bloodstain in the trunk, that theory never sat right with anyone in the department. We believed the killer used Knox's car to transport the man's body."

"Which would have meant Knox was already dead when he disappeared."

"That's what we figured."

I knew that wasn't true, but I didn't want to correct Renner. "Okay, what about Knox's last known whereabouts? Where's the last place anyone saw him alive?"

"The night before he disappeared, Knox stopped for takeout on his way home from Cross Security. It was after midnight." Renner found something about that disconcerting. He took the files from my hands and flipped the pages again.

"Knox was a client. That's not that odd," I said, hoping it was true. "What about his cell phone? Did you ping it?"

"It was off, so we couldn't track it."

"Did you follow up with the restaurant?"

"Yeah, right here." He pointed to the shorthand he'd written. "Knox was alone. No one followed him when he left."

"Let's say Knox was alive when he vanished. How does that change your impression of the scene?"

Renner scratched at the greying patch near his temple. "It's been so long. But if I were to walk into a scene like this today, knowing the guy was alive, I'd think he tried to stage his own death."

That was the same conclusion I'd reached. "Did Moretti reopen the home invasion investigation?"

"It never officially closed. We found Knox's belongings, but we never IDed the actual thieves."

"They must have worked for Petrov."

Renner nodded. "I'm sure of it, but Moretti got it in his head that whoever broke in to Knox's place had intimate knowledge of the security system and had disassembled it, like the way a professional installer would do it."

"Like Cross?"

"Now you're starting to see why he was the prime suspect. It didn't help matters that Lucien lied to us repeatedly."

"About what?"

"Stupid things, but if he'd lie about them, why wouldn't he lie about where he was and what he was doing?" That was the cop in Renner. Even though he was on our boss's side, he realized the story didn't make sense.

"What did he lie about?"

"When we questioned him the day Knox disappeared, Lucien had two black eyes and a broken nose. He said it was from kickboxing class, but his gym didn't offer kickboxing classes. We checked."

"Of course, you did."

"Yeah," Renner's brows knit together, "so how did he get beaten up?"

"Another case?"

"Possibly." He glanced at the file Justin had left. "Was Cross working on another case?"

"Bennett, you know I can't answer that."

"Yeah." He turned to another page of notes. "We tailed Cross for a couple of weeks after Knox vanished, but he never did anything out of the ordinary. But as soon as we stopped following him, he got on a plane and flew straight to a non-extradition country."

"How long was he gone?"

"According to passport records, four days. But he stayed gone for almost two weeks. Moretti was sure he wouldn't come back to the city. He figured Cross killed Knox, realized what he'd done, and decided it'd be wise to get out of Dodge. We were surprised when he returned."

"Did anything ever surface after that?"

"That was it. The department did its best to keep tabs on Cross, but too many other cases came up."

"What about Commissioner Cross? What did he have to say about that? I wouldn't think he'd want officers harassing his son."

"He always told us to follow the evidence. If Lucien was guilty, I don't think he would have protected him."

ELEVEN

I had to start over and look at this with fresh eyes, without any preconceived notions. Truthfully, I didn't know what happened eight years ago. All I could do was work the case like I would any other. Even though Moretti had worked the Knox disappearance and already had a starting point, Knox being alive after his initial disappearance had thrown a wrench into Moretti's theory. He'd have to start fresh or close to it. I should have time to catch up. I just couldn't do it in this office with Cross loyalists peering over my shoulder and asking for updates.

After collecting all of the files and facts, I went upstairs to speak to the forensic experts to see if they had made any progress on the note I'd left. They weren't able to pull prints or find any DNA. The note had been written on a sheet of blank copy paper. They scanned it in, but without another handwriting sample to compare it to, it was useless.

"Here." The tech placed it in an envelope to avoid contamination and handed it back to me.

"Great." I gave it a wary look and tucked it into the top folder. "What about my car?"

"We didn't find anything, except your oil's a bit low."

I had no intention of using the company car again until after the case was resolved. In the event Cross got sentenced for Knox's murder, there would be no more Cross Security or company perks anyway. I might as well get used to it now. Plus, I didn't want any more weirdos leaving vague threats on my windshield. I shook my head when he offered me the keys back. "My car's downstairs. I'll use that for now."

"Yes, ma'am."

"Call me whatever you want, just not that."

After thanking him for his help, I went to see Justin. Mr. Almeada had beat me to the punch and was speaking in hushed tones to Cross's executive assistant. I cleared my throat as I headed for them.

"Thanks for the file, Justin," I said. "Is there anything else I should know?"

Almeada looked at me. "I take it you haven't come up with anything yet."

"I'm working on it. These things take time." I resisted the urge to show him the threatening note. Almeada would blame the cops and file a harassment complaint. Right now, it'd be better to play nice. Honey and vinegar and all that. "Do you want to clue me in on the Russian thing?" I asked, paying close attention to see if Justin reacted to the comment. But my question didn't faze him in the least.

"Let's deal with one problem at a time." Almeada told Justin to get everything together, and then the attorney led me into Cross's office and closed the door. "Let me remind you it's not safe to discuss these matters with anyone else."

"Justin knows what's going on."

"Yes, and the police will question him about what happened eight years ago. We do not need them asking about what we're doing now. Understand?"

"Fine." I held the stack of files a little closer to my chest. "In that case, it'd be best if I don't work from the office for the next few days."

"I agree. In fact, I was just about to suggest it. But while I have you here, what do you think about the recording?"

"It means Knox didn't vanish because he'd been killed. He fled. According to Cross, it's because he was involved in illegal activity."

"Can you prove that?"

"I'll see what I can do. But there is a second possibility."

Almeada folded his arms over his chest. "Don't tell me Lucien could be lying."

"That's a third possibility. The second possibility is Cross helped Knox disappear."

"Like an accomplice?"

"From what I heard and saw, it sounded like they had a falling out. They might have even thrown a few punches. Mutually assured destruction typically means both parties are involved in the same shady shit." I let that sink in before adding, "You know what they say. The only way for two people to keep a secret is if one of them is dead."

"Just find out who killed Knox."

"I have a question for you. Do you think Knox's killer set things in motion so Cross would take the fall?"

"The overlap." Almeada stared at me. "Lucien doesn't think they have any enemies in common. It's probably a waste of time."

"Let me determine that."

Almeada smiled, despite the situation. "I'm glad to hear you're finally onboard. What do you plan to do now?"

"Go through all of this," I indicated the stack of files, "and figure out what's what. It's too late to make a trip to the bank, but I'll do that first thing tomorrow."

"Let me know if you need any help."

"If I do, it won't be from you. It'll be from Justin. Is that okay?"

"Only ask him about the past. Don't give him info on the present."

"Gotcha."

Deciding I needed to find some place neutral to think, I went to the Martin Technologies building. During the short drive, I wondered if Knox's killer would have been willing to wait nearly a decade before pinning the crime on Lucien Cross. Perhaps setting Cross up to take the fall had been a contingency and not the main goal.

That was possible. It was also possible I was reading the entire situation wrong. Despite everything I'd been trained to believe, coincidences occasionally happened and mistakes were often made. The killer might have overlooked the key in Knox's shoe. Perhaps, he'd even left the ring on the man's finger on purpose to make some sort of statement. From what I'd read about Knox, whose entire life revolved around work and sports, the ring could have been left as a big *screw you*, but I wasn't sure how.

As I pushed my way through the monogrammed glass doors, Martin's head of security reached into the drawer and held out a pass. "Mr. Martin had a feeling you'd be stopping by today." Jeffrey sent me upstairs to Martin's office.

Since Martin was in a meeting, I settled onto the couch and spread everything out on the coffee table. My beloved knew I'd show up. He wouldn't mind if I worked from here.

Somewhere between reviewing Cross's notes and referencing Renner's copy of the police report, Martin returned. He didn't say anything, preoccupied with his own work crisis. There was a good chance he hadn't even noticed me.

After forty-five minutes of reading and research, I dropped the files onto the table. "I can't believe this is happening." Resting my head in my hands, I stared down at the eight-year-old case file.

Martin looked up from his spot behind his desk. "What's the verdict?"

"I don't know. The files are lacking."

"Why do you think Cross killed him?" Martin asked.

"Originally, the police believed Cross was the last person to see Knox alive. Cross went to his house the morning he disappeared, allegedly found the door unlocked and the security system disarmed, but he never reported the disturbance to the police. That raised their suspicions, along with several other factors."

Martin stopped what he was doing and focused entirely on me. "Like what?"

"Cross had recently been in a fight."

"With Knox?"

"Jury's out on that one." I wondered if that might explain the broken shower door and blood drops found at

Knox's home. "But it turns out none of that matters. Knox didn't die that day. He died at least three weeks later. The exact TOD is yet to be determined."

"Don't you need to figure that out?"

"It's on the list." I stared at my note to check into Knox's aliases and travel arrangements. "Maybe if I figure out how Knox slipped out of the country, I can figure out how he slipped back in, assuming Cross didn't send a team of mercenaries to extract him."

"What?"

"You don't want to know."

"Unfortunately, I need to." Martin got up from behind his desk and took a seat beside me. "What have you found so far?"

I gave him the abbreviated version of everything I'd learned today, including the conversation Cross and Knox had on the tropical island.

"Do you think Cross hired someone to kill Knox?"

"My gut says no. It's too risky. But I don't know for sure."

"I trust you." He tucked a strand of hair behind my ear and leaned in for a kiss. "Is anything else going on? You seem off."

Martin had enough on his plate. The last thing I wanted to do was tell him about the threat left on my windshield. "Nothing for you to worry about."

"Aside from Cross getting charged, going to prison, and having his reputation take my company down with him."

I looked away, afraid he'd see something else in my eyes. My notepad stared up at me. "Cross said Knox had been a smuggler, but his official job title was acquisitions manager. He shipped items in and out of the country all the time. Maybe he used his contacts to stow away or slip past customs."

"Where did you say the police found Knox's car?" Martin asked.

"At the parking garage near his office."

"What about surveillance cameras? If Knox caught a cab to the airport, the trail might start there."

"The police checked. A man exited the vehicle, but they

couldn't make a positive ID from the footage. After he left the garage, cameras lost sight of him. The police had no idea where he went or if that's when Knox disappeared." I flipped to Renner's notes and pointed out the detective's theory. "They thought Cross killed Knox, put the body in the trunk, dumped the body somewhere else, and then abandoned the car in the parking garage."

"But the recording disproves that." Martin read a few lines of Renner's notes. His brows knit together in consternation. "All right, I'll leave this up to you." He climbed off the couch and grabbed his tablet. "I have a meeting. If you leave before I get back, stick a note on my desk and let me know what I should do regarding a press release."

"I have no idea. Lucien wants his PR guys to get together with your PR guys to discuss things."

"I know. They've been on the phone for the last thirty minutes, not like that's going to salvage this situation." He sighed. "My problem, not yours." He went to the door. "I'll see you later."

The police had studied Knox's phone records, but he hadn't used his phone the day of his disappearance or ever since. His browser history hadn't popped up anything related to travel. From the looks of it, Knox didn't plan to leave. He simply escaped. Did he intend for his departure to be a one-way trip? Or did he always intend to return?

I skimmed his call logs and text messages for any overseas calls. But I found nothing. The last call he received had been from work the prior morning. Aside from work calls, the only person who had spoken to Knox before he disappeared was Cross.

Knox's financials were also a dead end. He didn't use his debit or credit card to book a flight or boat trip. The last charge on his card had been when he picked up takeout the night before.

That was it. Nothing after. His accounts contained a few thousand dollars, and since his salary was automatically deposited, his account grew while he was gone. If Knox planned to leave his life behind, why wouldn't he take his money? The man must have been afraid he'd be tracked.

Everything pointed to him faking his own death, which meant someone wanted him dead.

Since Cross had tracked him down, someone else must have too. Did the killer lure Knox back to the city using the championship ring? Again, all fingers pointed to Cross.

A cold chill traveled through me. How did the ring get from Knox's house to his finger? Did he return home to get it? Or did the killer take it from Knox's desk drawer? Could there be two rings?

I had to find out if it was the same ring. If so, that would limit the possibilities. However, no matter the answer, it wouldn't remove Cross from the suspect list.

Hitting speed dial, I waited, phrasing and rephrasing the question in my head. "Tell me about Knox's ring. Did the police ever recover it?" I asked when Justin answered the phone.

"They found it in Knox's desk drawer when they searched his house."

"Do you know if the police took the ring into custody?"

"I doubt it. They searched the house for clues to Knox's whereabouts. But since his home was never deemed an active crime scene, they left everything where they found it."

"What happened to Knox's house when he didn't return?"

"Hang on," Justin said. A moment later, he came back on the line. "According to property records, his half-sister took over the mortgage payments when the bank notified her of the potential foreclosure. Last year, she had Knox declared dead. All of his property was then transferred to her."

"Do you have anything on her?"

"Until now, I didn't know Knox had any family. Lucien never made any mention of it."

"Can you run a full workup on her?"

"Sure, no problem. I'll call you when it's ready."

"Thanks, just don't tell anyone about this." Almeada would not be happy.

TWELVE

I stood in front of the floor-to-ceiling windows in Martin's office. From up here, the city looked peaceful, but I knew the closer I got to ground level, the more chaotic things would be. Instead, I stared straight ahead, enjoying the view of the skyline. Then the phone rang.

It was Justin. "Knox's half-sister, Emily Kane, moved into his house six months after he disappeared. She took over his mortgage payments since she had co-signed his loan. But I don't think they were close. I haven't found any photos on her social media that include Knox, and there's no mention of her half-brother disappearing." Renner had said the same thing.

"That's family."

"Last year, she had him declared dead. His house is now in her name, along with the rest of his assets."

"Knox didn't have any other relatives or a will?"

"No."

I double-checked Cross's files, but Emily's name didn't show up anywhere. According to Renner, the police had spoken to her, but at the time, she didn't live locally and had an airtight alibi. "Can you send me the intel you've gathered?"

"I've already uploaded it to your dropbox."

I hung up and printed hard copies from Martin's printer.

Emily was married with two kids, both under the age of four. She had no criminal record. She'd been a corporate lawyer before becoming a stay-at-home mom who did freelance work from home. Her husband was a plumber. Neither of them had exorbitant means, but since Knox's house was partially paid for, it made sense why they moved in.

On a whim, I gave her a call. The police had already given her the news of her half-brother's demise. But she didn't seem particularly distraught.

"You two weren't close?" I asked.

"No. When Trey's dad married my mom, we functioned like two separate families. Me and my parents, and Trey and his mom. Aside from the occasional birthday or Christmas card, I rarely heard from Trey. Once every few years, he'd pop up for a visit, but that was it. When I turned twenty-one, he took me to Atlantic City. He thought it'd be a nice, get-to-know-you sibling trip, but he spent the entire time in the casinos."

"He was a gambler?" I'd come across that in Cross's notes.

"Sportsbook mostly. That's why he needed someone to co-sign the loan on his house. Trey made more than enough money, but he had debts due to his sports addiction." She shook it off. "Who did you say you were?"

"Alexis Parker. I'm investigating Trey's death."

"I already told the cops everything when they first told me he disappeared and again when they found his body. Nothing's changed since yesterday."

"Do you still live in his house?"

"Yes," she said slowly.

"Since you're his only known relative, you inherited his possessions."

"That's correct."

"Do you remember coming across a championship ring?" I shuffled through the pages until I found the description Knox had given when he filed the original police report and read it to her.

"No, I never found anything like that."

"Are you sure? The police searched Trey's house after he disappeared and said it was in his desk drawer."

"They must be mistaken. I would have remembered finding something like that. Frankly, my husband and I would have been thrilled. Trey had credit card debt, which I had to pay off when I took control of his assets."

"What about Trey's bank accounts? Didn't they cover it?"

"Not entirely. Interest rates are sky-high."

"Do you know if Trey's gambling ever got out of hand? Did he owe anyone money?"

"Just the credit card companies."

I thanked her for her time and hung up. Before I could figure out my next course of action, the door opened, and Martin stepped inside.

"I see you made yourself at home behind my desk."

"I wanted to see what it felt like to be in charge." I climbed out of his chair. "It sucks."

"Tell me about it."

I grabbed the stack of pages. "I should go. I don't want to get in the way."

"Nonsense." He went behind his desk, pulling files out of one of the cabinets before sliding into the chair I just vacated. "You don't bother me. You can always just sit on my lap or pull up a chair." He winked before entering his password and clicking through the info on the screen. "We could try sharing power."

"Neither of us will get anything done that way."

"Any updates?"

"I just spoke to Knox's half-sister. It looks like the ring found on the body was the same one Knox hired Cross to recover."

"Shit. I should get ahead of this before news breaks on his arrest."

"That'll probably happen as soon as he's charged. Moretti's serving a search warrant tomorrow morning. It'll happen after that."

"That gives me a little time, I guess." He stared into my eyes.

"I won't be able to get him released before that happens. This is too complicated a case, especially with so many factors working against him."

"And you're not entirely convinced he's innocent." Martin's phone rang, and he held up a finger while he spoke to one of the secretaries. After he hung up, he muttered a few expletives.

"You have a lot going on. I'm gonna go so you can work without the distraction."

"I do enjoy the distraction. I just wish it didn't involve your boss and my business partner being behind bars."

"If you have any sway, maybe you should call his dad or convince Cross to do it himself."

"Do I know his dad?"

"Cross's father is the police commissioner."

"Oh." He thought about it for a moment. "It makes sense, I guess. They have the same last name. Why didn't you tell me this sooner?"

"I just found out. There are a million Crosses in this city. How was I supposed to know the man hell-bent on thumbing his nose at the cops and proving he could do their jobs better and more efficiently was the commissioner's son?"

"Well, you are an investigator, and Cross has a giant chip on his shoulder. He gets that from living in his father's shadow. I can relate." He snickered. "At least we know you don't have daddy issues, like the rest of us."

"No, I just have abandonment issues and a blind spot when it comes to the men who employ me." I leaned down and kissed him gently. "Do whatever is best for your company. Wait, don't wait, it's up to you. Cross might not have killed Knox, but he's not innocent. People in my line of work have blood on their hands." In Cross's case, it might be Russian blood.

*   *   *

SSA Mark Jablonsky opened the bottom drawer of his desk and pulled out a bottle of scotch. "Did you find anything new in the police report that you didn't already know about?"

"No."

Jablonsky had gotten the files pertaining to Knox. Renner's notes read more like a narrative, but the facts remained the same. The official reports were inconclusive, but they provided one thing I didn't have before—a list of cops involved in the case. Aside from Moretti and Renner, I didn't know any of the officers and detectives who worked the original investigation. But I'd make it a point to get to know them, starting with Officer Joe Gallo.

"Detective Heathcliff wouldn't let you see it?" Jablonsky poured a hefty splash into a coffee mug and slid it toward me before grabbing a second cup from the top of his filing cabinet.

"Heathcliff does his best to follow the rules."

"Tough to do around you."

"I've warned him about that." I picked up the scotch and took a sip, enjoying the warming sensation as it slid down my throat and spread through my chest. Flipping the report around, I pointed to the section which addressed Vasili Petrov's connection to the storage unit. "Did you see this?"

"Uh-huh." He knocked back the scotch and poured himself another, his eyes never leaving my face. "Interfering with organized crime never ends well."

"No kidding."

"At least you finally learned your lesson."

"That's why I need your opinion. The risk appears minimal, but if it's not, I'll have to drop the case. I won't risk pissing off another crime boss."

"What did Moretti have to say?"

"Every cop I've spoken to says the same thing. The Russians didn't kill Knox."

"But you're afraid they have it wrong."

I didn't want to think about how close I'd come to losing Martin and my ability to look my reflection in the eye after pissing off a mobster, and thinking about the casualties would only trigger a panic attack. "Heathcliff lost someone because of me and that stupid decision. He wouldn't tell me the Russians weren't involved if he didn't believe it. I just have to be sure."

"He doesn't blame you for Gwen."

"I blame me."

"I know. It's why you sacrificed your career." He shook his head. "We're not getting into this. The point is, you know better than to fuck with organized crime. Italians, Russians, punks on street corners, it doesn't matter. You stay the fuck away. End of story."

I sucked in a shaky breath. "Yep, but the cops also said Cross killed Knox. And I don't buy that, not after this." I nodded down at the threat I received.

He slowly sipped from his mug. "You've lost sight of the obvious. This is Cross's problem. Let him deal with it."

"It's not that simple. I've signed a contract with his attorney."

"Break it. Marty knows good lawyers, and no contract is enforceable if it requires you to violate the law."

"I'm not sure it does."

"It puts you in danger." He placed his index finger on top of the threatening note. "Here's your proof."

"It's not about the contract," I admitted.

"No shit." Mark sighed. "This is about your misguided need to save everyone."

"I wonder where I learned that."

"It couldn't have been from me. I trained you to keep your head down and do what you're told. We all know how well you listened to those lessons."

"But what if Cross didn't kill Knox? What if this is a frame-up? Doesn't he deserve the benefit of the doubt?"

"This morning, you thought he killed someone."

"I still think that. I just don't think it was Knox."

"You think Cross had something to do with Vasili Petrov's murder."

"Knox alluded to the possibility on the recording."

"That could have meant anything. Honestly, Alex, I don't think Cross has the balls to do something like that." He moved the keyboard over and entered a few things. "According to official accounts, Vasili Petrov was killed by the KXDs when he failed to deliver the drugs he promised. That led to the Russians retaliating and taking out several bangers. The cops stepped in and put a stop to it."

"And everyone was under surveillance and it had nothing to do with Knox or Cross."

"Bingo."

"So what do you think happened?"

"Let me take a look." Mark reached for the stack of files I'd placed on his desk. Despite what he might have wanted me to believe, he already had a theory and knew just as much as I did about what was going on, possibly more since he had the FBI databases to consult. "If I had to guess, I'd say Cross found the storage unit, ran down the name on the rental, and found the connection to Petrov. Since Cross has several ins with the police department, he heard about Petrov's demise and decided to tell Knox the Russians would no longer be a problem. His client probably saw the headline in the paper and jumped to the wrong conclusion. Cross must be regretting that now, along with the threat he made on tape. Now that was fucking stupid."

"People say things like that all the time. It doesn't mean anything. I threaten to kill Martin on an hourly basis, but I'd never actually do it."

"This is different. Knox is dead. Cross is in custody. It looks like he made good on his threat."

"Why haven't the police charged him yet?"

"Do I need to remind you about my stance regarding police incompetence?"

"Moretti's your friend."

"Still, he's not the brightest crayon in the box. Case in point, he likes you."

"You like me too."

"You're more like family. I have to like you." He leaned back, gingerly stretching. I stared at his flat stomach, a side effect of nearly dying due to another of my screwups. Mark caught my gaze, rocked forward in the chair, and let out a grunt. "I'm fine. Better than fine."

"So you're going to help me help him?"

"Maybe." He grabbed another file out of the drawer. "The police haven't charged him yet because they are hoping to find the murder weapon. If they can't, the next best thing would be to determine the exact time of Knox's death. They want to find out when he got back to town. They won't risk charging Cross with murder unless they know the case is airtight. Right now, it still has holes, but they're running out of time."

Which meant I was too. "I have to go," I said.

"Alex, it's noble to want to help. I know Lucien Cross has saved your life a time or two, but, keep in mind, your life wouldn't have needed saving if he hadn't put you in that position in the first place. You don't owe him anything."

"Maybe not. But if he goes down, Cross Security does too." A lot of the investigators were former law enforcement officers who'd messed up. I often referred to us as broken toys. Cross gave us jobs, purpose, and a paycheck that did a decent job compensating for the hazards we faced. "This will impact Martin Technologies because they partnered together on that biotextiles R&D thing. I don't want to think about what the ramifications will be for the people I care about if Cross is convicted of murder."

"Cross made his bed. That has nothing to do with you. That was his decision. His mistake."

"I've made plenty of my own." I lost track of how many second and third chances I'd been given.

Mark blew out a breath and pointed a finger in my face. "Fine. You want to work this, we'll work it. But I'm calling the shots. And for once in your life, you are going to do everything I tell you, when I tell you, and how I tell you. Do you understand?"

I nodded, resisting the urge to say something sarcastic or inappropriate. Now was not the time for jokes.

"I don't like that some weirdo in a jumpsuit left a threat on your car, so we're going to pull everything the Bureau has on Vasili Petrov, get the head of OCU in here, and perform a threat assessment. We need to know who's in charge of the Russians now, if they're loyal to Petrov, and if they've made any noise about getting revenge. If this has even the slightest hint of caviar or vodka about it, you're walking. Got it?"

"Yes, sir."

He pointed to the tiny couch pressed against the wall in his cramped office. "Sit down and get comfortable. We'll probably be here all night."

THIRTEEN

The hours went by while we researched and reviewed. The vast FBI files and dossiers on the Russian mafia left little to the imagination. By the time we were finished, I knew all the major players, their wives, their kids, their mistresses, and the hired muscle. I knew what clubs they went to, what crimes they were suspected of committing, and what time they walked their dogs.

One thing was clear. They had no interest in Lucien Cross, which meant either Cross had nothing to do with Vasili Petrov's murder or the Russians had been too busy focusing on the rival gang who shot their comrade to waste their time on some corporate gumshoe.

"It's not the Russians. They didn't kill Knox," Mark said, watching as I crossed a few points off my list.

"The police had access to Knox's home. The ring had been there, but according to Emily Kane, Knox's half-sister, there was no ring."

"Of course not. It's on the dead guy's finger."

"Yeah." I waited for Mark to reach the same conclusion I had.

Sighing, he let out a low whistle. "Someone could have stolen it. Knox's house had been burglarized once before.

G.K. Parks

The news of his disappearance was widespread. The thieves could have returned for a second pass, or someone else figured it'd be an easy score. Knox was an avid collector. According to Cross's files, a lot of people knew that. Any one of them could have taken it."

"The killer might have taken it to lure Knox back to town."

"Or Knox went back to his house to get it. Either way, you have to figure out who his enemies are."

"That's the thing. No one knows. Cross insists Knox was involved in smuggling, but he doesn't have any details."

"Smuggling what specifically?"

I shrugged.

"Find out." Mark jotted something down and stuck the sticky note to the corner of his monitor. "I'll do some digging. We'll discuss it tomorrow at lunch."

"We're having lunch?"

"After everything I've done for you, the least you can do is take me to lunch."

"Deal."

He pointed at the clock. "Moretti's working late tonight. If you hurry, you can probably still catch him and ask about cops who might have a bone to pick with your boss."

"Moretti won't talk to me. He threatened to arrest me for interfering."

"He won't. He likes you."

"I don't think that'll stop him."

"Tell him what you found." Mark handed me the threatening note. "And tell him about this. I want to make sure he knows someone's screwing with you. If it is a cop, he'll take care of it. Dominic's one of the good ones."

"Fine." I collected my things and grabbed the note off the desk. "Keep your phone on. If I get tossed in a cell, you're my one call."

"My battery's low."

I narrowed my eyes at him. "Charge it."

* * *

It was after midnight. Shift change happened an hour ago,

- 93 -

but since Moretti was determined to make this case, he'd be burning the midnight oil. I just hoped he was taking the phrase literally.

I parked in the nearest space, debating if I should go inside. But something told me it'd be better to have this conversation outside of the hallowed halls of the precinct. Instead, I settled in behind the wheel, knowing he'd have to come out eventually.

While I waited, I called Martin. He hadn't left work yet either and wasn't sure when he'd get home. He and his projects manager were crunching numbers.

When the wait got to be too much, I got out of the car. Pain shot through the backs of my calves, up my hamstrings, and along my quads. The hours spent researching had caused my overworked muscles to tighten up to the point that I could barely walk. The only way to fix that was to move around and stretch.

Stupid, I thought. Working out was supposed to improve my performance, not hinder it. What would I do if someone jumped out of the shadows and attacked me? I couldn't exactly fight him off.

My mind recalled one of the gruesome stories a survivor had shared in group during last Thursday's session. My imagination turned on, and I squinted through the darkness. Did I see someone lurking near the side of the building?

"You're losing it," I muttered to myself, but I took out my flashlight, palmed my gun, and poked around in the dark corner of the parking lot. A door slammed, and I jumped, spinning toward the source of the sound. But I didn't see anything. "Hello?"

Silence.

Slowly, I edged around the corner of the building. A couple of cops who'd come off shift were hanging out on the front steps, joking about something. That must have been what I heard. They nodded to me.

"Do you need some help, lady?" one of them asked.

"No, I'm waiting for someone."

"You want me to relay a message? I can tell whoever it is to get his ass in gear." He jerked his thumb at the entrance.

"No, that's okay."

He nodded and went back to talking to the two other cops.

Unlike the rear parking lot, the front of the precinct was well-lit. The rear entrance only had two small lights at the door and a couple of lampposts placed near the center of the parking lot. So when I trudged back to my car, everything suddenly seemed darker and a lot more sinister.

I bounced gently on the balls of my feet, loosening up my muscles. At least my legs didn't hurt anymore. But I felt eyes on me. Watching. Waiting.

My thoughts returned to the case. Did a cop kill Trey Knox?

I couldn't stay out here with my imagination running rampant. So I headed for the door. Just then, it swung open.

"Jesus, Parker, you know better than to sneak up on a cop. Are you trying to get yourself shot?" Moretti clutched his chest. "Put that thing away before someone gets killed." He nodded down at my gun. "Drawing on a cop is a death sentence. What's up with you? You know better than that."

I shoved the gun into my holster, hoping my rapidly beating heart would slow. "We need to talk."

"Is this about Cross?" Moretti unlocked his car door.

"Lucien didn't kill Knox."

Moretti gripped the roof of the car with one hand, internally debating whether to hear me out. "You weren't around eight years ago. You don't know what happened."

"Why don't you tell me?"

"Jablonsky requested the files. I'm sure you're already up to speed."

"I didn't see any proof. Sure, I get why you thought Cross might have done it. Wrong place, wrong time. But you watched the recording. Knox was alive and kicking three weeks after you thought he'd been killed. That means you were wrong. Cross didn't do it."

Letting out a laugh, he turned to me. "Cross said he'd kill Knox if he ever came back to town. Guess what, he came back to town. And he ended up dead. That's pretty open and shut if you ask me." He looked around the dark parking lot, but we were alone. "I know I'm going to regret asking, but what makes you so sure Cross is innocent?"

"Cross wouldn't kill a client."

"Didn't you shoot a client not too long ago?"

"First of all, he lived. Second, he was a serial killer. And third, I didn't say I wouldn't kill a client. I said Cross wouldn't."

"I'm going home."

I grabbed the edge of the car door before he could slam it shut. "You offered him a deal if he told you about the Russians or Knox's illegal activities. How do you think they fit into this?"

"I'm not sure they do. But Knox implied otherwise, so I'm willing to explore it." He scrutinized me. "The best thing for Cross to do is cooperate. If he didn't kill Knox, whatever he tells me might lead us to the actual killer. Talking can only help him, but he won't say a damn thing. In my book, that makes him guilty. Since you want to help him, tell him to talk."

"He doesn't listen to me."

"In that case, I'll see you later."

"Lieutenant, wait." I folded my arms over my chest and rested my hip against the inside of his door. "There's something else you need to know."

"What is it?"

I pulled the note out of my pocket and held it out to him. "I already had it checked for prints and DNA. It's clean. The bastard who left it on my windshield wore coveralls, like the crime techs assigned to the airport construction site. But he had a belt and gun. No one else did."

Unfolding the note, he read the words carefully. "You saw him?"

"Only briefly from the back."

"Can you describe him?"

"Buzzcut, dark hair. I already told you what he was wearing."

Moretti rubbed his eyes. "When did this happen?"

"About an hour after I left the precinct."

"Did you report it to the police on scene?"

"Mark said I should bring it straight to you."

"Ten hours later? Did you get lost on your way here?"

I reached for the note. "Just forget it."

He kept a firm grasp on it. "Do you think the man who threatened you is a cop?"

"I wouldn't be surprised, given the circumstances."

"Meaning?"

"Knox's killer went to great lengths to conceal his victim's identity, but then he leaves a collector's item dangling from the man's mutilated fingertip. That doesn't make a damn bit of sense. Everyone who ever met Knox knew the significance of that ring. It's why you put a rush on the ID and how you knew what DNA sample to use as a comparison. As far as I know, the ring was tucked safely away in Knox's desk drawer. The police found it when they searched his house the day he went missing. They knew where it was. It wouldn't have been hard for one of them to stick it on Knox's finger after the body was discovered."

"We don't know how or when the ring ended up on Knox's body, but Knox could have retrieved it himself as soon as he returned. Leaving the ring on his finger could have been an oversight."

"What about the safe deposit box key which just so happened to lead to a recording that points you to the perfect suspect? Isn't that a little too convenient?"

"It was in the guy's shoe. Who kills someone and takes their victim's shoes?"

"Plenty of kids get murdered because someone wants to steal their Air Jordans or whatever the hottest new kick is."

"We both know that's not the case here."

"No, but I watched the recording. That wasn't from a surveillance camera. The angle was wrong. Someone hid a camera somewhere inside that private cabana and filmed Knox's exchange with Cross. Everything about this screams setup."

"Knox might have made the recording. He probably figured he could use it as an insurance policy. No cop I know has the time or money to waste on a trip across the world."

"Even if Knox set up the camera, how could he know

Cross would show up? Cross had no idea what happened to Knox. It's why he kept investigating after the man disappeared. He wouldn't have done that if he wanted him gone."

"He might if he wanted to make sure Knox never returned. People lie, Parker, especially your boss. How do you know he kept investigating?"

I closed my mouth and shook my head.

"It's in a Cross Security report somewhere." Moretti gave me a look. "Right?"

"Maybe."

He sighed. "You're biased."

"Just listen to what I'm saying. You trust my judgment. So hear me out."

"Fine, Knox didn't plan to record Cross. So what? It doesn't change anything else. The video is damning. Cross hasn't even tried to defend it other than to say he didn't mean what he said."

"It changes the parameters of the recording. Either Knox set up a camera to record someone else, or a third party spied on them and planted the recording in the safe deposit box just so you would find it."

"That's how you plan to clear Cross's name? By claiming this is an elaborate frame job created by a third party?"

I pointed at the note in Moretti's hand. "There is a third man. There's your proof."

He rubbed a hand over his mouth. "All right. Let's go back inside so I can take your statement. After that, I want you to sit with a sketch artist."

FOURTEEN

The sketch artist flipped his pad around so I could see it. "Any identifying features? A mole? A scar? Freckles on his neck? Anything like that?"

"No."

He put his pencil down and handed the sketchpad to Moretti. "Here's the suspect."

Moretti glowered at it and rubbed his eyes. "What the fuck am I supposed to do with this?"

"I told you I saw him from the back."

"This description fits half the cops in the department and ninety percent of the assholes behind bars." Moretti passed orders along to the watch commander that second shift should question the reporters and construction personnel at the scene to see if they noticed anyone suspicious. When he hung up the phone, he sighed. "I'll look into it, but we both know this isn't going anywhere. Just keep an eye out and watch your back. That's all I can tell you for now." He thanked the sketch artist and logged off his computer. "Now if you don't mind, I'd like to go home and get some sleep."

"You're not listening."

"Parker, it's late. I'm tired. We'll deal with this in the

morning. C'mon, I'll walk you out."

We didn't even make it to the double doors before an alarm sounded. The lights dimmed, the emergency lights creating a trail to the door. "What is that?" I asked.

"Fire alarm." Moretti barked orders to the men in the bullpen to log out, secure any evidence or weapons, and to evacuate the area. "Get out of here, Parker. I'm sure I'll see you tomorrow."

"What about the holding cells?" I couldn't just let my boss remain trapped in a burning building.

"We have evacuation procedures in place. We got this." He shoved me toward the doors. "Now go."

The stairwells were crowded with dozens of police personnel who were evacuating the building. I got swept into the group descending the staircase. But I didn't smell smoke. On the main level, the desk sergeant directed officers to perform tasks. In the chaos, I ducked back into the stairwell and headed downstairs to the holding cells to make sure the police didn't forget about their captives.

Halfway down the steps, thick, white smoke obscured my vision. Automatically, I covered my nose and mouth with the collar of my shirt. Clutching the railing, I moved blindly into the white abyss. I couldn't see the lights through the impenetrable white sheet.

When I reached the bottom of the steps, I nearly tripped when the handrail abruptly stopped. I'd been here several times before, but blind, it felt like unfamiliar terrain. Everything was a grey-white. A shadow moved to my left.

"Hello?" I stuck an arm out in that direction, but I met nothing but air. Creeping forward, I knocked into the side of the desk. Righting myself, I kept one hand on the furniture. Despite the smoke, the room wasn't warm. The smoke wasn't due to a fire. So what caused it? "Is anyone in here?"

I stopped to listen, hearing nothing but a constant whooshing, like air releasing from a balloon, and then footsteps. Heading in the direction they'd come from, I used my arms to feel my way across the room. When my left hand banged against the metal bars, I ran my fingertips along the edge, not surprised when I found the cage open.

Moving on to the next holding cell, I heard the door squeak when my hand came into contact with it. Another one open. The police must have already cleared the room. By the time I reached the fourth door, the fire alarm stopped. There was no fire.

The whooshing sound continued, but I couldn't determine precisely where it was coming from. Perhaps behind me and to the right. Footsteps sounded again, padded thuds on the tile floor as if from felt-soled boots. Focusing on the sound, I stopped moving and held my breath, straining to determine the exact location. That's when the metal bars directly in front of me violently clanged.

Surprised, I jumped back, my hand knocking against the open cage door to my left. A strangled gasp sounded, and the metal clanged again. Despite the smoke, I sensed movement in front of me. The shadows danced, and I strained to see through the dense cloud of white.

The footsteps were beside me now, quiet squeaks against the tile. The smell of aftershave overpowered the chemical scent of the smoke. He was beside me. Pivoting on the ball of my foot, I searched for him through the fog. The shadows were darker. Just as I reached out to grab him, he barreled into me with his shoulder, knocking me into the holding cell door.

It clanged shut, the sound reverberating throughout the room. And then he ran. I raced toward the stairs, tripping on something along the way. Keeping one arm in front of me, I slammed into the wall, feeling for the opening before chasing him up the stairs.

I stumbled, unable to see and judge the distance. Cracking my shins against the edge of the step, I grabbed the banister and hauled myself up. His muffled footfalls weren't that far ahead of me, but he kept charging up the steps. I had to catch him.

Just as the smoke started to thin, he stopped. I was almost on him. Another few steps and I'd have him.

He could be a cop. But every cop I knew would have announced himself, and they sure as shit wouldn't knock me into the holding cell door. So who the hell was this guy?

And what was he doing downstairs during the evacuation?

He turned around, placing one hand on the railing and the other on the wall, and swung both of his legs up and kicked me in the sternum. The force of the hit broke my grip on the handrail, and I flailed, hoping to grab onto something even as I fell backward down the steps.

I screamed out of surprise. My low back impacted against the edge of the step, followed by my upper back hitting the next step. The momentum made me roll in a diagonal, sideways motion, tumbling backward into the white abyss, my lower legs dragged against the wall while my elbow and shoulder scraped along the other side, catching on the metal hook of the railing, until I finally came to a stop in a heap at the bottom of the steps.

The adrenaline had me on my feet, and I ran shakily back up the stairs. As soon as I cleared the smoke line, I caught a glimpse of a man in tactical gear with close-cropped dark hair exiting the stairwell on the main level.

Shouldering my way through the double doors, I skidded to a stop near the front desk, searching for any sign of him. The desk sergeant was still barking orders, but she stopped when she caught sight of me. "Ma'am, are you okay?"

"The man in full tac armor, where did he go?"

"The team's outside."

I burst out the front door to find a bomb squad unit getting briefed. All of the men wore the same tactical armor. The soles of their boots were thick rubber. Which of these bastards just knocked me down the steps? Another thought sprang to mind. What was he doing down in the holding cells?

The desk sergeant appeared behind me. "Ma'am, what happened? You're bleeding."

"One of those assholes just threw me down the stairs. Tell Lt. Moretti what happened and make sure he detains them." She reached for my arm, but I brushed past her. "The holding cells were evacuated. Where are the prisoners being detained?"

Before she could answer, I spotted patrol officers guarding several men in handcuffs in a roped off area in the parking lot. Another area had been set up for the women detainees. From the top of the steps, I scanned the crowd, but Cross wasn't there.

"Shit."

"Lady, stop." One hand rested on the butt of her side arm.

"He's not here." That could only mean one thing. Turning around, I ran as fast as my legs could carry me. The desk sergeant and two patrol officers were at my heels, but they'd have to shoot me if they wanted me to stop.

Running downstairs, I raced into the cloud of smoke. By now, the whooshing noise had stopped, but the smoke had yet to clear. Banging into the desk again, I jerked backward and moved forward, counting my steps as I went. When I reached the end, I placed my hand on the back wall, maneuvering around until I found the door for the last holding cell.

It was open, and I crouched down. The strangled gasp I'd heard earlier could only mean one thing. Was I too late? My fingers brushed against a piece of cloth. Crouching down, I wished the smoke would clear so I could see. But I didn't have time to wait. "Lucien?" I asked.

Whoever was on the floor didn't move.

My fingers followed the sleeve of his shirt to his collar. Once I touched skin, I felt for a pulse. I had to reposition my fingers three times before I found it, but it was there. Letting out a breath, I lifted my hand toward his mouth and nose, but I couldn't tell if he was breathing.

"Lucien," I said again, convinced the shirt had to belong to my boss. How many suspects were wearing Armani when they were arrested? "Wake up." I gave him a slight shake, but he didn't respond. "Help. I need some help over here," I bellowed.

The yellow beam of a flashlight cut through some of the smoke, but it did little more than headlights in fog. Someone knelt beside me, and when she spoke, I realized it was the desk sergeant. "Get those windows open. We need the air cleared out now. And get the EMTs down here." Her elbow knocked against mine as she felt for his pulse. "Who is he?" she asked.

"I can't be positive, but I think it's Lucien Cross."

"Shit." A cool breeze came from somewhere, and the thick clouds began to thin. Through the haze, she felt around his head and neck for any injuries. "Where's this blood coming from?" She pointed to the stains on his shirt.

"Me." I noticed it dripping from a gash on my upper arm. Until now, I'd been numb to the pain, but it hit me like a brick. My arms, my back, my chest, and my legs all competed for my attention, but I ignored it. "I don't see any obvious injuries on him."

"What the hell happened?"

"I don't know. I came down here to make sure he got out okay. The smoke was too thick to see, but I heard someone. He shoved me and ran for the stairs. Before I could get a good look at him, he knocked me back down here."

"The guy in tac armor?"

"Yes."

"Who are you?"

"Alexis Parker. I work for him."

"Cross?" she asked.

"Yes."

Before she could ask anything else, the EMTs arrived. Visibility had improved to the point where I could see a few feet in front of me. The paramedics cleared me away. Within a matter of seconds, Cross was awake, confused and agitated, but awake.

"Thank god." I watched as they took his vitals and checked him for signs of a concussion. But they couldn't determine why he'd blacked out. Near the desk, I spotted a metal canister. Grabbing a latex glove out of the EMT's bag, I reached down to pick it up, yanking my hand away when I realized how hot it was.

"Don't touch that. It's evidence," Lt. Moretti said, appearing in the doorway. He jerked his chin at me, and a female medic entered the room. "Make sure you patch her up. This one's trouble, so don't take any of her gruff."

"Yes, sir," the medic said.

"Parker, why do you always have to make my life so damn complicated?" he asked.

"Do you believe me now?"

Moretti eyed me. "We'll see." He headed toward the stretcher the EMTs had wheeled in for Cross. One of the officers had handcuffed him to it. "Any idea what's going on, Mr. Cross?"

Cross sneered at him. "I'm pretty sure one of your guys just tried to kill me."

"Are you sure about that?" Moretti asked. "What do you remember?"

"An attack, but I'm not saying another word without my attorney. You're not going to twist this around on me. I won't let you."

"Someone just attacked you and you still won't cooperate? I didn't realize you had shit for brains."

"Whoever attacked me was one of yours. For all I know, it could have been you." Cross glared at him, the heart monitor beeping a warning. I watched the exchange, but I kept my trap shut. Cross rubbed his throat with his free hand. "I require medical attention. You can't deny me that." He stared daggers at Moretti.

"Fine." The lieutenant raised his palms and stepped back. "Go with him," he said to the two officers.

"I'll go," the desk sergeant volunteered.

"Okay." Moretti came back to the desk just as the EMT finished wrapping the bandage around my arm. "Since he won't cooperate, you're going to tell me what happened."

Cross looked surprised to see me. "Why are you here?"

"She might have saved your life, numbnuts," Moretti mumbled.

A stern warning replaced the surprised look on Cross's face. "Careful what you say, Ms. Parker. The sharks always smell blood in the water."

FIFTEEN

After I told Moretti everything that happened, he had the canister from the smoke grenade taken to evidence collection. No one from the bomb squad had strayed off course. Every single member had been present and accounted for. The same was true of the few ESU members who'd been assigned to secure the armory.

The sergeant who'd been keeping an eye on the holding cells had supervised the evacuation of the prisoners until he'd been told to go outside. The man who'd taken over had lieutenant bars, but the sergeant didn't recognize him. When asked, he couldn't remember the man's name either. So much for taking precautions.

Moretti promised he'd check the CCTV feeds. Since the precinct was lousy with them, he was positive the bastard must have gotten caught on camera. I didn't share his optimism, but there was little I could do.

Before leaving, I thoroughly checked my car, but it hadn't been tampered with. As I climbed off the ground, I could feel every bruise and cut. My shins had several welts, and I dreaded the thought of how my back would look by morning. But I was okay. I just didn't know if Cross could say the same.

On my way home, I called Almeada. Tonight, the attorney was earning his overtime. He assured me Cross was irate but otherwise fine. The doctors wanted to observe him overnight, but a light bruise had appeared on his neck. They believed the unsub had locked him in a chokehold, resulting in his loss of consciousness.

Every piece of evidence pointed to someone in the department being involved. I just didn't know why. No matter how I manipulated the facts, I couldn't fathom how Knox's murder connected to any of this, but Cross must have the answers. Despite the fact I was supposed to clear his name, I was more interested in finding out who wanted to murder him.

But it was late and I was tired and sore, so I headed to our apartment instead of commuting back to Martin's estate. Martin and I agreed earlier it'd be best to remain close to our respective offices given the Cross debacle. But I dreaded having to tell Martin what happened.

"Honey, I'm home," I called, but he didn't answer. I dropped the files on the kitchen counter, made sure the balcony door was locked, even though we were twenty-one stories high, and changed into yoga pants and a long-sleeved t-shirt, to hide as much of the damage as I could.

Even though I was hurt and exhausted, I forced myself to stretch. My muscle fibers needed to relax. Hell, I needed to relax. But the stretching only made the pain worse and did nothing to calm my mind. Instead, my synapses fired on all cylinders.

I lifted back into downward dog before pulling my left leg through and folding forward into pigeon. The killer can't be a cop. But I had to assume the man who left the threat on my car and the one who attacked Cross in the precinct were one and the same. Both times, he wore police garb. He was in a police station and at an active crime scene. He had to be a cop.

So how did this factor into Knox's murder? Did this guy kill Trey Knox? Or was he just taking advantage of the situation by framing Cross for murder, only to try and kill him before the truth could come out?

Exhaling, I came out of pigeon, flipped around, and

stretched my legs out in front of me, flexed my feet, and folded forward. Fortunately, my hamstrings didn't snap, even though they felt like they wanted to. My back, on the other hand, wasn't happy with the movement. After breathing into it as long as I could stand, I moved into a lunge to stretch my quads, switched sides, and decided that better suffice.

Despite the stretching, something told me I'd feel even worse in the morning. So I poured myself a glass of water, popped a few pain relievers, and rummaged through the cabinets while I replayed my conversation with Moretti. Who could have recorded Cross threatening Knox?

The only people who even knew Cross had left the country after Knox's disappearance were the cops, who'd been keeping tabs on him, and Justin. Could Cross's executive assistant be involved? After a moment of careful consideration, I ruled him out. Moretti checked alibis, and Justin never made the suspect list. Still, it wouldn't hurt to ask.

Dialing the office, I wondered if anyone would answer. A skeleton crew of techs and medics were always on call, but the office staff kept normal business hours. Most of the investigators did too.

No one answered the main line, so I tried Justin's office number. When he didn't answer, I considered heading back to work and digging through the filing cabinets and servers until I found what I wanted, but that thought held little appeal.

A few seconds later, my phone rang. "Did you just call?" Justin asked.

"Yes. I have a few questions."

"What's going on?"

From his tone, he hadn't heard what happened, and I wasn't about to tell him. "I thought I'd tackle this mess from a different angle and wondered what you know about the trip Cross took a few weeks after Knox disappeared. Do you know where he went? Did you go with him?"

Justin laughed. "I wasn't invited. Lucien took off after things calmed down. His back was acting up, and he'd just gotten his nose fixed. He wanted to go somewhere warm to rest and recover."

"His passport records indicate he left the country for four days, but the police said he was gone for two weeks."

"He went to work things out with his ex-girlfriend. They ended up in Las Vegas for a week and a half, until the tables cooled down."

"Jade McNamara?"

Justin hesitated for a moment. "Yes. How do you—"

"Did she go with him on his excursion out of the country?"

"I'm not sure. He didn't mention it."

"Did Cross tell you what he was planning to do or who he was going to see before he left?"

"I don't think so."

"Okay." I opened the fridge and stared at the nearly empty shelves. We hadn't stayed at the apartment lately, so aside from a few condiments, the fridge was empty. I thought about ordering from one of the late night delivery places, but I didn't have much of an appetite. Instead, I grabbed a box of sugary cereal from the pantry. "What did you do while Cross was gone?"

"We were in the midst of moving offices. I had to oversee the construction, make sure the phone lines and internet got connected, and set everything up. I was supposed to have that time off, but it never happened."

"Are the contracts and installation receipts you signed in records?"

"Yes, Cross Security has copies of everything."

"Just checking."

"You think the police will want these details?"

"Probably." I pulled out a spoon and filled my bowl. No milk. Oh well, at least it wouldn't get soggy if I got distracted, even though I enjoyed soggy cereal.

"Let me know if there's anything else I can do."

"Get some sleep," I said. "Tomorrow's another day."

I considered working at the counter, but my body would have none of that, so I sprawled out on the couch and picked at my bowl of cereal while making a list of police personnel who could be involved in Knox's murder. Cross always said the police hated him and the feeling was mutual. Until tonight, I hadn't witnessed anything firsthand. Now, I wasn't so sure.

The settlement the police department paid Cross came with an NDA. He couldn't give me any gruesome details, and neither could the department. Is that what caused the animosity between them? Cross killed one of their brothers-in-blue. Even if it couldn't be talked about, the rumors must have spread. Could this be retaliation for that?

A key scraped in the lock, and I reached for my gun. A moment later, the door swung open. I jumped but didn't aim. Martin entered, looking as tired as I felt.

"Hey, sweetheart." He came over for a kiss, noticing my firearm. "Expecting company?"

"Sorry, I'm just..."

"Freaked out?"

"Yeah."

He tugged on his tie. "Want to tell me why?"

That was the last thing I wanted to do. "This case has me twisted around. I think a cop might be involved."

He winced as he took off his jacket. "A cop?"

"Whoever killed Knox must have known about the recording, or someone else stumbled upon it." I wondered if Knox or the killer had sent it to a cop, who waited for the right time to make it resurface. I'd have to get the information on the safe deposit box from the bank in the morning. Until then, all I could do was speculate. "The killer might have even filmed it. The ring found on Knox's body had been inside his house, but the police had access to it. A cop could have planted it on the body."

"I hate to play devil's advocate," Martin said, moving into the kitchen to wash his hands before pouring himself a bowl of cereal, "but couldn't Knox have gotten the ring and done everything else himself?"

"He didn't shoot himself four times in the chest."

"Not that, but he could have made the recording, decided that was enough of an insurance policy, returned home, stuck the tape in the safe deposit box, and picked up his ring."

"Knox lived in a gated community. No one went to his

house except for the police and eventually Knox's sister and her family. Sure, someone could have found another way in besides the front entrance, but if Knox planned to return to his life, why wouldn't he go through the front?"

"Good point. Maybe Knox didn't want anyone to know he was back. Maybe he avoided the security guards for a reason." Martin dug into the cereal, crunching loudly. When he swallowed, he said, "Why do you think a cop's involved?"

"Cross always says the police hate him. He has enemies. Believe me."

Martin assessed me, his eyebrows raising slightly. "What am I missing?"

It was my turn to take a bite in order to buy time.

He slid onto the sofa. "Alex, just tell me whatever it is."

"Someone left a note on my windshield warning me to back off."

He put his bowl on the coffee table and took mine off my lap. "Do you know who did it?"

"Not yet. I had Cross's people run it. Then I showed it to Mark and gave it to Moretti."

"All right. Good." He entwined his fingers with mine. "Are you okay?" He cocked his head at the long sleeves. "You look a little stiff."

"Someone attacked Cross in his holding cell. I was there when it happened, but I didn't get a good look at the guy. I'm fine. Don't freak out."

"I won't, if you won't." He glanced at my gun.

"Deal."

"Is that why you think a cop killed Trey Knox and is framing Lucien for his murder?" Martin asked.

"The man who attacked Cross dressed like a cop, just like the guy who left the note on my windshield."

"Cross and the police department have a history of bad blood, according to the story I was told."

"Speaking of, do you still have Jade McNamara's contact info?"

"Lucien's girlfriend?"

"That's the one."

"Let me check." Martin scrolled through his list of

contacts. "You know, if I hadn't run into her at the tech conference and she hadn't told me about how she and Lucien met, I never would have agreed to partner with him to create body armor from biotextiles."

"I'm fairly certain that's why Cross made sure she was there and why the two of you happened to meet." Cross manipulated every situation to his advantage. I just wondered if he could be doing the same thing now. "I told you he always has ulterior motives."

"I'll try to listen next time." Martin handed me his phone and stole a kiss. "Do you want me to call her?"

"No."

He grinned. "You're so damn sexy when you're jealous."

"I'm not jealous. But I dare you to say that again when I'm armed and angry."

"You're always armed and angry, but you're still damn sexy."

I entered the number into my phone and handed him back his when it buzzed with an incoming message. He went into the other room, giving me some privacy to talk to Jade. Luckily, she lived in Colorado. Even though it was late, it wasn't nearly as late as it was here. Good thing the time difference worked in my favor.

The women's shelter Jade McNamara ran had someone manning the phones twenty-four seven. When I said I was calling on behalf of Cross Security, the call was immediately redirected to Jade.

"Hello?" The worried tone told me this woman cared a great deal about Cross.

"Hi, Ms. McNamara, this is Alexis Parker. We met briefly several months ago at the tech convention. I work for Lucien Cross."

She thought carefully. "Lucien spoke to you at the pool. Blue bikini, right?"

"Yes."

"I remember. Is he okay?"

"Um...well..."

"Oh god, what happened?"

"He was arrested."

She didn't say anything right away. I wasn't sure how to

take the silence. "What for?"

"Murder."

"What?" she squeaked. "Does this have anything to do with Scott?"

"Scott?"

"My ex. The cop."

"No, sorry. He's accused of murdering Trey Knox."

Again, silence.

"Is that name familiar to you?" I asked.

"No."

More silence, so I said, "He didn't do it."

"I didn't think he did."

"Are you sure you don't know Trey Knox?"

"I don't think so."

"Eight years ago, Lucien came to visit you. You spent some time together in Las Vegas."

"Most of our time is spent there. You'll have to be more specific."

"Most?"

"We meet up every few months. Vegas works year round and is perfect for a weekend here or there without wasting too much time on travel. It's how we manage. We don't have a normal relationship or any relationship. You can't even call it open. It's just...when we're unattached, we see each other when we can."

I sifted through the files and gave her the exact date that coordinated with Cross's trip.

"That must have been our first trip together," she said.

"Did you go somewhere else before Vegas?"

"No. Lucien left me a message and asked if I'd meet him there."

"Do you know where he was before that?"

"I'd imagine at home."

"Do you recall him talking about clients or encountering any problems?"

"Nothing stands out. But that was so long ago. What does this have to do with Lucien's arrest?"

"The man he's accused of killing died around the same time Lucien took that trip."

"I wish I could tell you something that would help. Tell

me what I can do. Is he okay?"

"He will be."

"But he's in custody. They arrested him, so he's in jail, right? Has he been hurt?"

"Why would you ask that?"

"Since you work for him, you must have been law enforcement at some point. You know how they are. They band together. It's like a cult or a gang. They protect one another. Lucien killed one of theirs. He didn't have a choice." She sniffed. "Scott was going to kill us both. But his friends on the force don't know that. No one does. They didn't see what Scott was like at home, what he became."

"Do you know any cops who might have an axe to grind? I could use some names."

"That damn settlement. I knew he never should have taken it."

"But you didn't. You can tell me what I need to know."

She exhaled slowly. "I haven't thought about this in some time. Give me your e-mail address. I'll think about it and send you some names."

"That'd be great."

"Alex, despite what I just said, Lucien grew up around cops. He probably has just as many friends as enemies. One of them might be able to help you more than I can."

Cross never struck me as the type to have friends, let alone friends with badges. "Who?"

"Do you know KC's?"

"The cop bar?"

"Yeah. The guy who runs it came to see me in the hospital after the shooting and apologized. He came by a lot to see Lucien while he was recovering. Maybe you should talk to him. He could probably tell you which cops might cause trouble."

"Do you remember his name?"

"No." She sighed. "Dammit, what was it?"

"Don't worry. I'll figure it out. I can always ask Lucien." I just couldn't ask him about anything pertaining to the settlement.

"But he's okay, right?"

I didn't want to tell her about tonight. "Yeah, he's fine."

"Get him out of there. If he stays behind bars too long, he won't be."

I'd witnessed that firsthand. The voice in my head warned me not to make promises I couldn't keep, but after spending these last few weeks in group therapy, listening to people share similar experiences and tales of grief, I knew what I would want someone to say to me if I were in her position. "I'll get him out of this. He'll be fine. Pissed at the department for the inconvenience, but otherwise fine."

She let out a shaky sigh. "Okay."

SIXTEEN

The phone didn't wake me, but the sound of Martin groaning in pain did. "Son of a bitch." He flattened onto the mattress, reaching across with his left hand to grab the phone off the nightstand.

I turned to see if he was okay, regretting the movement almost immediately. "Are you all right?"

"Fine," he grumbled. "I just tweaked my shoulder." He handed me the phone. "It's for you."

"Thanks."

After rubbing his eyes, he sat up and stretched his arm, slowly circling it a few times before reversing direction. Then he threw off the covers with his left hand and swung his legs over the side.

"Are you sure you're okay?" I asked.

"I'm fine. Answer your phone. Whoever's calling at this time of morning probably isn't."

"Hello?"

"Morning, Ms. Parker." It was Almeada. "I just thought I'd update you on the situation."

"Is Cross okay?"

"Medically speaking, he's fine. The police have taken him back to the precinct. I've also been informed search warrants have been issued. You should avoid Cross Security for the time being. The police are in the process of confiscating files, weapons, and computers, as we speak."

"I knew they would."

"Tell me you found something. The attack last night should be a game-changer."

"I'm working on it. I spoke to Moretti before and after the incident. He agreed to look into an alternate theory."

"Do you have another suspect for Knox's murder?"

"Sort of."

"What does that mean?"

"It means I don't have anything solid yet. I'll let you know when I do."

"I don't like surprises." Almeada didn't sound like he was in the mood. Then again, at just past six a.m., neither was I.

"None of us do. What did Cross say happened last night?"

"Lucien said a cop attacked him. He gave his statement, but his recollection is limited. They were clearing out the holding cells, one at a time. By the time they got to his cell, someone else took over."

"Did he get a look at him?"

"No, the bastard remained at the desk until the room cleared. Then he set off the smoke grenade. Lucien tried to evade him, but he couldn't see anything. He's not sure if the guy had thermal vision or what, but he opened the cell and snuck up behind him. The next thing he remembers is waking up after the smoke cleared." Almeada sounded suspicious. "Is that the way you remember it?"

"By the time I got to the holding cells, they were empty, but the attacker was still there. I couldn't see him, but I could hear him. He ran past me." I glanced at Martin who had stepped into the closet to select a suit. "He got away before I got a good look at him. Moretti knows. He's scrubbing the precinct's CCTV feeds."

"What about the officer in charge of the holding cells?"

"From what I heard last night, he didn't remember much about the guy. No name or badge number. I'm sure Moretti will get a description." At least, I hoped he would.

"Is there any evidence to corroborate Cross's version of events? I wouldn't put it past the police to say this was a failed escape attempt."

"The metal canister, but I don't know if they pulled prints. You sound just as paranoid as your client."

"I'll look into it, just as soon as I'm done supervising the execution of the warrants."

"Are they searching Cross's apartment too?"

"Yes," Almeada raised his voice, "even though this is a complete and utter waste of everyone's time since there is nothing to find."

"They're just doing their jobs."

"And I'm doing mine. Make sure you do yours."

"Meaning?"

"In case you haven't realized it, Ms. Parker, Lucien's life is in danger every second he remains behind bars. Figure out what happened to Trey Knox. The clock's ticking."

I hung up, wondering why someone attacked Cross last night. Was the attack meant to silence my boss? Again, thoughts of Knox's attempt at blackmail came to mind. What did Cross know? Why was he attacked? For revenge? Or to silence him before he could share Knox's secrets? Would the attacker have choked the life out of Cross had I not intervened?

I didn't know the answer to any of those questions, but I had to find out. I just didn't know how much time I had. The bastard warned me to stay away once. He came after Cross several hours later. At this rate, he'd try again soon. But his one failed attempt would make a second attempt harder, unless he already had access. "Dammit."

Martin glanced over his shoulder. "Are you all right?"

"I have to get Cross out of that holding cell."

"If the man who attacked him isn't a cop, won't he be safer on the inside than the outside?" Martin asked.

"I'm not sure, but the attack isn't enough on its own to get Cross released. I'm sorry. I know you were hoping he'd get out of this predicament before it bounced back on your company."

"I'm not just worried about that. I'm worried about him. I don't want to see him get hurt, but you said he has blood on his hands. If he is guilty of something heinous and knows more than what he's letting on, what's to stop him from taking care of the problem once he's released?"

"I can't think about that. Right now, everything indicates Cross is being framed." This felt like one of those dilemmas that had been discussed during group therapy. "I have to follow that theory until it's disproven." Biting my bottom lip, I knew there was far more to it than that, but I couldn't let someone kill Cross.

Satisfied, Martin pulled out a slick, black suit and a nice white shirt. He hung them from the hook on the door and analyzed his ties. "Color or monochrome?"

"Since when do you let me dress you?" I climbed out of bed, nearly toppling over on my sore legs. My back pinched, and it took several deep breaths before I was able to stand up straight. Thankfully, he didn't notice. I moved closer and ran my palms gently over his shoulders, clavicle, and chest. "Go with the silver."

"That's what I was thinking." He hung the tie next to his shirt and brushed a strand of hair out of my face. "Who was on the phone?"

"Cross's attorney."

"Truthfully, how bad is it?"

"It's bad. The police are searching Cross Security and Lucien's apartment for the murder weapon and whatever other evidence they can find." I massaged his shoulders, retracting my fingers when he winced. "I can't remember the last time the scar tissue gave you problems."

Martin shook his head. "It's fine. I'm fine."

"Don't lie to me. You aggravated it doing those ridiculous handstand push-ups yesterday morning, didn't you?"

"It's not from push-ups. It's just tension from everything going on. Work, mostly."

Stress and long hours behind a desk, I surmised. "The extreme workout didn't help."

"Probably not." He stared into my eyes. "What are we doing this morning? Running stairs?"

"I did enough of that last night."

He grabbed his clothes. "If you're skipping the workout,

so will I. I should get to the office and figure out what to do. The entire project is falling apart. Cross's name on it is sure to be a PR nightmare."

"So let it fall apart. Who cares? Cross wanted to diversify. You never wanted this."

"Body armor wasn't my thing, but the research into biotextiles was. I diverted most of my research to Cross's project, thinking it wouldn't make much of a difference, but now, I could lose it all. We hired researchers to do the extra work. If that gets scrapped, people will lose their jobs. I can't let that happen. They have families to feed and bills to pay. It's not their fault Cross fucked up. I want to switch them over to my original R&D project, but we don't have the budget after everything we've spent on this." He blinked a few times. "I have to find more capital—a new backer or personally invest."

"Could you do that?"

"Personally invest?"

"Yes."

"I will if there are no other options, but my accountant strongly discourages it. It's not a smart decision, not on something this unstable with a partner who might be spending the next decade in prison. The bad publicity will draw additional scrutiny to whatever techniques we develop and make it harder to apply the research to other applications later on." He swore. "As it is, MT's stocks are projected to take a hit once the news spreads about Cross. We're holding back on issuing a statement until charges are filed, but I have to make a decision soon. When this becomes official, it's going to hurt. I have to find a way to mitigate the damage."

"You need me to clear his name."

He grabbed my sides with both hands. "Alex, listen to me. I don't need Cross to walk if he's guilty. What I need, sweetheart, is for you to be safe. Someone threatened you yesterday." He gently rubbed his hands up and down my ribcage. "I saw the bruises on your back while you were sleeping. What happened?"

"I fell down the stairs."

He pressed his lips to my forehead. "May I see?"

Reluctantly, I turned around and pulled the shirt over my head. Martin let out a hissing sound before pressing his lips against the nape of my neck. He stepped into the bathroom, only to return with some supplies. He changed the bandage on my arm and gently rubbed arnica over the horizontal bruises on my back.

"I'm okay," I said. "You can stop."

He put a bottle of pain relievers on the dresser. "I'd like to say the same to you."

"I'll be careful," I promised.

"You always say that. But your scars say otherwise."

"Do you really want me to step away from this case?"

Martin let out an exasperated sigh and pressed his forehead against mine. "I'm in no condition to have this conversation. I'm functioning on less than three hours of sleep. The last thing I want is to fight with you."

I nodded and kissed him. "Thank you."

"For what?"

"Everything."

"I'd like to do more. All you have to do is ask."

"In that case, there is something."

"What's that?"

"When things calm down, get rid of the ballet studio you made for me. I love it, but..."

"You're going to kill yourself on the routines."

I touched his right shoulder. "And apparently you're along for the ride."

"I'll have the floor picked up and the barre taken down. We can move the mirrors around and use them elsewhere."

"I hate to ask. I know how much trouble you went to for me. But if I hadn't worn myself out on the barre, maybe I would have been able to chase down the attacker before he knocked me down the stairs." My thoughts went to the time I wasted in the dark parking lot waiting for Moretti. Did I actually see someone lurking in the shadows?

"I wanted to rip it apart as soon as I had it installed, but you wouldn't let me."

"I just needed a good reason," I said. "Now I have one."

SEVENTEEN

The first thing I did was call Moretti. He didn't answer, so I left him a message, asking if he'd check the footage from the precinct parking lot. I gave him the approximate time, hoping the exterior cameras might have caught sight of the bastard entering the building. After that, I reviewed my notes and files. Jade hadn't e-mailed me the list of names yet, so the only ones I had were the cops who originally worked the Knox break-in and disappearance.

I ran backgrounds on each of them, but I didn't find any suspicious money transfers into any of their accounts. That didn't mean anything. Motive wasn't always financial. Cross was hard to get along with. No one would have to be bribed to take a swing at him, metaphorically or otherwise, especially if it was a cop with a vendetta.

Until now, my biggest question had been whether Cross was guilty of murder. Now the question was whether the person who attacked him in the holding cell had anything to do with Trey Knox. Depending on how the pieces fell, the man from last night could have killed Knox and wanted to silence Cross before he divulged details on Knox's illegal enterprises, not that my boss knew anything, but I had to assume the killer might not know that after seeing the recording.

Conversely, Cross could be getting shafted by a vindictive cop, either in the form of a frame job or the attack that occurred in the holding cell. It was also possible the two weren't connected, but again, I had to defer to Jablonsky's infinite wisdom on these matters. Coincidences didn't exist.

This was getting ridiculous. I could speculate all day, but it wouldn't get me any closer to finding the truth or nailing the bastard who'd done a stellar job of pissing me off. Regardless of Cross's guilt or innocence, no one had the luxury of choking out my boss and kicking me down the stairs and getting away with it. I'd make sure of that.

I arrived at the bank as soon as they opened, but parking was next to impossible. After going down several side streets, I found an empty space two blocks from the bank. The morning sun nearly blinded me, but I did my best to count the number of security cameras I passed along the way. The closer I got to the building, the more surveillance equipment I spotted. Like most banks, this one didn't scrimp on surveillance.

When I entered, I spotted an armed guard lingering near the teller windows. He looked to be in his late forties or early fifties with a wispy salt and pepper goatee and wiry eyebrows. His shoes, belt, and holster had been polished to a shine. He kept a watchful eye on the doors and every person who entered. At the moment, his focus was on me.

From the way his stance shifted, his hand moving closer to his gun, he realized I was armed. But I didn't let that deter me. I had my carry permit and credentials. I also had a lunch date with Mark, so he'd get me out of trouble if it came down to it.

To my right were offices and cubicles. To my left were several stations filled with withdrawal slips and other common banking forms. The bank manager's office was pressed into the rear corner, near the row of teller windows. A staircase, hidden at the end of a narrow hallway, led up and down, probably to the safe deposit box room, the vault, and more administrative offices. I'd done a stint undercover in a bank, so I had a general idea of how things worked.

The guard kept an eye on me while he scanned the rest of the room to see if I was alone. When he made his approach, I decided it'd be best to avoid a scene, so I went to one of the empty stations, picked up a pen, which was chained to the desk, and scanned the cubbies to see what types of forms they kept stocked.

A man and woman exited from the bank manager's office. They each shook hands with her, a petite woman in a power suit who had her hair pulled back in a tight bun.

"Do you need some help?" the guard asked from behind me. He stood just out of striking distance. He must have been a professional. From the spit-shine, possibly former military, but the goatee and unruly eyebrows made me think otherwise. Either way, security was tight.

"How long have you worked here?" I asked.

"What?" He knew I was casing the place. He just didn't know why, but he wouldn't let my question distract him.

I turned slowly, keeping my hands on the counter. "I need to speak to someone about a safe deposit box, specifically a box that was opened eight years ago."

"What is this about?"

"Police business," I said, hoping that'd be enough to satisfy him.

"Take a seat in the waiting area." He jerked his chin toward the couches and armchairs arranged around a coffee table which held a stack of creased and dog-eared magazines. "Someone should be available soon."

"Right over there?" I replaced the pen in the cup and pointed.

"Yes."

"Is the coffee free?"

He gave me a funny look. "Help yourself."

"Wonderful." I checked his name tag. "Thanks, Novak."

"Do I know you?"

I winked at him and headed for the couch. That move only agitated him further. Given how seriously he took his job, my behavior would not be tolerated, especially if I were here for nefarious reasons.

He kept an eye on me while I poured coffee into a paper

cup and took a careful sip. Once I settled into an armchair with a magazine, he knocked on the bank manager's door, watching me while he spoke to her. He nodded and returned to his post near the teller windows. A moment later, she came out of her office.

"Miss," she said, "come with me, please."

The six other customers who'd been waiting, glanced up, making sure she wasn't talking to any of them before returning to their devices and magazines. I tossed the greasy *New Yorker* onto the pile, took my cup, and followed her back to her office. Novak clocked my every move.

Once we were in the privacy of her office, she took a seat behind her desk, her hand clutching the edge, probably inches away from the silent alarm. "What can I do for you today?"

"Like I told the chatty Mr. Novak, I'm hoping to gather some information concerning a safe deposit box. Until the police opened it yesterday morning, no one had accessed it in eight years, or so I was told."

"Who are you?"

I offered her my winning smile. "Alex Parker. I'm an investigator. The safe deposit box in question is box 243. The man who rented that box registered it under the name Thomas Gunn, which we believe to be an alias for Trey Knox. You have a photo ID of Mr. Gunn on record, which facial rec has confirmed matches Trey Knox." I threw out a lot of details and jargon in the hopes she'd assume I was a detective assigned to the case.

"That box has been emptied."

"Yes, ma'am, I'm aware. The evidence is in police custody. We just had a few questions concerning the owner, how it was paid for, and how often it had been accessed and by whom."

"I already handed over those records."

"I'm just following up."

"Gunn?" She reached for her keyboard.

"Thomas Gunn. G-U-N-N."

"He opened a checking account with our bank roughly eight years ago with a starting balance of one thousand dollars. The monthly fee came out of that account. At the present, the account has a balance of $422 remaining."

"Has there been any activity on the account?"

"Just the rental fees for the box."

"Do you recall the last time anyone accessed the box?"

The skin around her lips crinkled as she frowned. "Tuesday morning."

"You mean when the police opened it?"

"Yes."

"What about prior to that? How often did Mr. Gunn access his box? Do you know?"

"Of course, I know. We take our customers' security seriously. Customers must fill out the form and present their key before we allow them into the vault room."

"Did anyone besides Mr. Gunn try to access the box?"

"No."

I was getting the distinct impression she was stalling. "Theoretically, anyone with the proper safe deposit box key could have gotten access to it, though."

"It's possible, but there is only one key. The only person who possessed it would have to be the owner."

Or whoever took it from him. Another thought occurred to me. Since Knox was such an avid sports collector, why wouldn't he keep his priceless sports memorabilia in the bank vault? "What's the exact date the box was opened?"

She clicked a few keys, debating with herself whether to answer. Finally, she told me. The box was opened after Knox disappeared and after Cross had returned from his Las Vegas vacation. I cursed. This didn't help matters.

"What's wrong?" Her hand inched closer to the alarm.

I shook my head. "It's been a long, few days. Everyone's overworked. We don't know if we're coming or going. It's not every day a cold case turns hot." I smiled, sensing she had realized I didn't introduce myself as a detective or show her my badge. Any minute, she'd have her guard remove me or the building surrounded. It'd be best to avoid that if I could. "You wouldn't happen to have security footage from eight years ago, would you?"

"Certainly not."

"In that case, I'll need Mr. Gunn's contact information

in order to follow up."

She stared at me. "I'll need to see some paperwork or identification first."

"Sure, no problem." Slowly, I pulled out my P.I. license and slid it over to her.

"You're not a cop?"

"No, ma'am. I'm an investigator. I've consulted with the police on several cases." Which was not a lie. "A man was murdered. His body was found near the airport. You might have seen the story in the paper. It's rather high-profile. The police could use as much help as they can get. As you can imagine, they're slammed. The safe deposit box key was found with his remains, which is how we found out about it. I'm just doing my part to follow up on a potential lead. Gunn's obviously an alias." I rolled my eyes. "I mean, really, Tommy Gun, you'd think criminals would get a bit more creative than that."

She laughed, but her face remained pinched. "I'm sorry, but I can't just hand over private information without a court order or the customer's consent."

"He's dead. I don't think he consented to that either."

"Why don't you speak to Mr. Novak? He's been with this branch for seventeen years. Perhaps he can help you. He has a photographic memory. Maybe he'll recall something useful." She called to Novak, who looked disappointed when she asked him to speak to me while she dealt with some other business.

"Thank you," I said.

From the look on her face, she didn't trust me but had decided it'd be safer to appease me than risk refusing to assist a police consultant.

EIGHTEEN

"Do you remember Thomas Gunn?" I asked.

The guard stared blankly at me. "Is that even a real name?"

"No." I glanced around the security room, which was a tiny reinforced office upstairs. Two other guards were on the floor while Novak spoke to me. However, he'd shut the door and took a seat in front of it, effectively blocking me in. "It's an alias. I would have hoped someone at the bank might have caught on. You're a smart guy. It seems like that should have been in your wheelhouse."

"I have nothing to do with the customers."

"What about the unruly ones?"

He stroked his goatee the way villains often do in movies. "So you're a private eye?"

"Uh-huh."

"Is that why you carry a nine millimeter in a shoulder holster?"

"I used to be on the job," I said, hoping to find some common ground with this guy. Novak had no intention of cooperating. As far as I could tell, the reason he was humoring me was to keep me detained while the other security guards made sure my appearance wasn't part of a heist. Or I'd seen one too many bank robbery movies.

"Police?"

"Federal."

He nodded but didn't offer up his resume for comparison. "I didn't think private eyes worked police investigations."

"It depends on the case. Sometimes, there's overlap. Other times, I get asked to consult."

"You have friends in the department?"

"Yes, sir."

He nodded a few times, glancing at the security monitors while maintaining his focus on me. "What box did you say?"

"243. The police showed up with the key. They had a court order and cleared it out. Did you supervise that?"

"I might have been there."

"They found a USB drive. Do you remember what else they pulled out of the box?"

He shrugged.

"The bank manager said you have a photographic memory," I wheedled.

"I wasn't paying that much attention. It's none of my business what someone keeps hidden away."

"You can stop watching the cameras. I'm not here to rob the place. Actually, if I wanted to get the layout or a look at your security, this would be the way I'd do it. Y'see, I actually worked undercover in a bank once. Do you remember a few years back when ATMs were getting knocked over?" Thoughts of Michael Carver, my late partner, came to mind, which made me smile and want to cry at the same time. Damn grief counseling was making me insane. Whoever said experiencing feelings was a good thing was an idiot. "I helped catch them."

"Good for you." Novak didn't appreciate my attempt to build a rapport. Most men I'd encountered would share a story to top mine. But this guy didn't say a word.

"Why don't you tell me how long you plan on holding me? Are we waiting for the police to arrive? I can make a call and get them here faster. I have work to do. And while I'm thoroughly enjoying getting to know you better, this is a waste of time, unless you plan on answering my questions."

He gave me a hard look. "Why would it be a bad idea to bring you up here if you were planning a robbery?"

"For starters, you have to remain with me. That means there's one less guard available to respond. Second, these monitors cover the entire bank. If I were to overpower you, I'd have access to everything, and assuming I had accomplices, I could guide them in and out without getting caught."

"But you'd be stuck here."

"I'd be stuck inside but not necessarily in here."

His hand rested on the butt of his gun. "Bad plan, huh?"

"Not the best. I actually work for a private security firm. We evaluate a lot of corporate security, which doesn't have to meet the same standards set by the FDIC, but billion dollar industries worry a great deal about security, so I have a bit of experience."

"Where do you work?"

I didn't want to answer that question, but it might be the only way to get me out of the room, even if the banking staff and security guards realized I was working in opposition to the police department. "Cross Security and Investigations."

"Cross?"

"Yeah, have you heard of us?"

"Those are the big leagues. In fact, Mr. Cross was just here Monday."

"As in two days ago?"

"Uh-huh."

"Does he bank here often?"

"No, first time." Novak rubbed his free hand over his mouth. "Funny thing, seeing as how he asked for a brief tour and rundown of our security features before filling out forms to open a safe deposit box. And now you're asking questions about a box and telling me how you'd rob the place."

My chest constricted. Why did Cross come here the day before he was arrested? How did he know? Did he try to break into Knox's safe deposit box? More importantly, did he succeed, remove whatever had been inside, and overlook the USB drive in his haste? "That's not what I was saying. I was just suggesting in the future you shouldn't detain anyone in the security office."

"Right."

"I thought you didn't deal with customers. Why do you remember Cross stopping by?"

"Like I said, he wanted to assess our security system. Most of it is confidential, but I gave him the five cent tour. He mentioned he was in the business and introduced himself. That's the only reason I interacted with him."

"Did he offer you a job?"

Novak stared at me. "Is that supposed to be a bribe?"

"No, sir. I just wondered." I swallowed. "The surveillance footage should still be saved. Would you mind showing me the footage from Monday?"

"You don't believe me?"

"Please."

He surreptitiously glanced at his watch and then the bottom right monitor, which showed the bank manager on the phone. He was stalling, which meant he might just give me what I wanted. "Fine."

He dialed it up and pressed play. While I stared in horror at Lucien Cross entering the bank, Novak's phone rang. He answered, grunted a response, and hung up.

"Am I free to go?" I asked, my eyes glued to the screen. "The police department vouched for me, didn't they? If not, I have SSA Jablonsky's business card in my wallet. You can always give him a call."

"That won't be necessary. Lt. Moretti said to tell you whatever you want to know."

That must mean Moretti was starting to believe me. "What do you have on Thomas Gunn?"

Novak shook his head. "Copies of the access logs for box 243 are downstairs, but no one's asked to access that box since it was opened."

"Do you remember anything about Mr. Gunn? Did he look like his photo ID?"

"I can't be certain, but if he didn't, it would have raised a few red flags."

On the screen, Cross was led down to the vault. The cameras caught him from all different angles. There was no denying it was him. "What are you doing, Lucien?" I mumbled. He stopped, peered into the vault room, nodded to the security guard, and returned upstairs to fill out the paperwork. After that, he was taken back to the safe deposit boxes inside the vault room. No cameras were inside to ensure the customer's privacy. After the bank manager inserted her key and opened the box, she left him alone in the room. I didn't know if the police knew about any of this, but I didn't want to tell them. Twenty minutes later, Cross left the bank. "Do you know where he went after this?"

Novak flipped through a few different camera feeds until he found one of the exterior. Cross got into a town car and drove away. I made a note of the timestamp to compare to his calendar. As far as I knew, Cross had meetings all afternoon. Going to the bank hadn't been on the agenda. Did anyone at the office even know about this?

"Did the police check anything else while they were here? Perhaps they missed something."

"They just asked about Thomas Gunn and Trey Knox. They opened the box and collected the documentation we had on him. That was it."

"Thanks." I stood, and Novak did the same, twisting the knob and letting me out of the office. "You run a tight ship, Mr. Novak. Just remember, bank robbers tend to work in teams. They'll keep hostages together, but when it comes to guards, they'll divide and conquer."

"Whatever you say, lady."

The bank manager met me at the bottom of the stairs. She held out a photocopy of the safe deposit box records. "I'm sorry for the inconvenience. We can't be too careful. I'm sure you understand."

"Not a problem." I glanced down at it. "Mr. Novak mentioned Lucien Cross opened a safe deposit box on Monday. Does he have an account with the bank?"

"No, he doesn't. He paid cash for a year's rental. Not many banks offer safe deposit boxes anymore. He wanted to try it out in order to see if his clients could benefit from it. What does Mr. Cross have to do with this?"

"Nothing." I hoped. "I was just curious."

Cross's visit couldn't have been a coincidence, but Moretti hadn't mentioned it. Either he was holding back, or he didn't know. My money was on the latter.

How did Cross know about Knox's safe deposit box? The police hadn't even made a positive ID of the remains until Monday night. Cross went to the bank five hours before Heathcliff received the call. None of this made a damn bit of sense.

As I headed back to my car, I called Almeada and told him what I discovered. "Did you know about this?" I asked.

"No."

"Cross didn't tell you?"

"No."

"How did he know Knox's remains had been found and the key was on his body if he didn't kill him eight years ago and bury him behind the fucking airport? No one knew any of this until Knox had been IDed late Monday night. Explain to me how Cross knew five hours before anyone else."

"I don't know."

"Self-preservation," I muttered, recalling what I'd been told by Justin and Almeada when they convinced me to work this case. "Tell me that bastard isn't using me." He could have set everything up, including the attack in the holding cells. At the moment, I felt duped. Cross Security had trackers on all company vehicles. Everyone at the office knew where I was yesterday. A fellow employee could have left the threat on my windshield and drove off. The weird guy in the jumpsuit might have been a patrol officer who'd been asked to assist the crime techs and had nothing to do with any of it. "Is this just a trick to confuse the cops?"

"Ms. Parker, I don't know anything about this. I'll speak to Lucien and find out what's going on. Just stay the course. Continue to investigate. I'll deal with your findings, whatever they may be. I'm sure if Lucien did something, he had his reasons."

Unfortunately, that's what worried me.

NINETEEN

Cross had me so twisted around, I wanted to scream. *Stick with your gut, Parker,* my internal voice berated. First impressions were usually correct, and my first thought had been Cross is guilty. But I let him and what I thought was logic dictate otherwise. Now I had no idea what to think. Cross knew a lot more than he let on.

I thought about calling Martin, but he wouldn't want to hear I'd just pulled a complete one-eighty. Regardless of my indecisiveness, he'd act in the best interest of his company and his employees. I didn't believe the same about Cross, and I wondered if he'd just hung my reputation on a lie. Why did I let him manipulate me again?

Just then, clanging metal caught my attention. It sounded just off to my right. I was a block and a half from my car. The streets were crowded. Several other people turned at the noise, giving the alleyway a wide berth.

In broad daylight, muggings were less common, but they still happened. I reached into my jacket and removed my gun, keeping it concealed. There was no reason to cause a panic. Slowly, I peered around the corner. Several metal trash cans stood side by side. The clang sounded from behind them, causing two of them to tremble and shake.

"Is someone there?" I took half a step forward. "Come out. Keep your hands where I can see them."

The cans rumbled again, and this time, I heard a squeal. The can on the end crashed to the ground. The squeal sounded again as more of a scream, as an alley cat trapped a rat in its mouth. The feline stared up at me, pleased with its kill, stuck its tail in the air, and headed deeper into the alley.

Disturbed by the image, I holstered my gun and stepped back onto the sidewalk. Damn, if I didn't feel like that rat. As I turned down a side street and headed for my car, I heard more rattling. Not another cat. I didn't have the stomach to see that a second time this morning.

As I headed down the next block toward my car, the skin on my arms prickled. Something wasn't right. I glanced around. This street wasn't as busy as the one I'd just left. I didn't spot anyone immediately, but I felt as if I were being observed. The rattling had stopped, but now I wondered if I should have taken a moment to investigate the source of the sound.

Turning around, I watched the few people who'd been behind me walk past. No one paid me any heed. They had no interest in me.

Glancing at the other side of the street, I didn't notice anyone tailing me. When I got close to another set of trash cans, I slipped my hand into my jacket and took a deep breath. These were pulled up against the curb. Trash day. One lid hung off to the side. Another lid remained on the ground, and three of the other cans were covered. Could the rattling have been the wind banging the loose lid?

Despite my better judgment, I checked the three closed cans and the one with the loose cover. But I didn't find anything inside. *Parker, you're losing it.*

Shaking it off, I hurried toward my car. A man was crouched down on the sidewalk next to my front tire. There was something familiar about him. At first, he appeared to be tying his shoe, but I knew better.

"Hey," I yelled, "what are you doing to my car?"

He stood, turning away from me. He didn't appear to be

in a hurry, but something about his stance wasn't quite right. A black baseball cap obscured most of his features. And with his jogging suit, I couldn't quite tell if he was armed.

The street and sidewalk around my car sparkled in the morning sun. When I was ten feet away, he pivoted, lurching toward me while swinging an empty metal trash can at my head. I threw up an arm. The impact propelled me backward, and I crashed into the empty cans hard enough to leave me dazed.

He darted away, picking up speed as he ran. I shoved the cans out of my way and ran after him, clutching my gun by my side. He had half a block head start.

I pumped my legs as hard and fast as I could. My thigh cramped from exertion and overuse, but I pushed on. Every bruised muscle in my back lit on fire, but I ignored it. I'd nearly closed the distance between us when he grabbed another empty trash can from the side of the road and hurled it at me.

I tried to dodge, but it was too large. It sideswiped me with enough force to knock me off balance. Regaining my footing, I stumbled around the trash can, avoiding the other two he knocked over in his attempt to slow me down, and raced around the corner in pursuit.

As I rounded the corner, he kicked me in the stomach, grabbed my shoulders, and kneed me hard in the solar plexus, where he'd hit me last night, knocking the air out of my lungs and sending me sprawling to the ground.

Twisting around, I swept my leg out, knocking his feet out from beneath him. He landed and rolled until he was next to me. The lower portion of his face was concealed beneath a bandana.

He pinned my arm with his shoulder and knocked the gun out of my hand. I grabbed for him, but he slid off of me and kicked me a few times while I gasped to get my lungs working. I threw up my arms to block and curled into a ball to protect my midsection while I inched toward my gun.

Once I was close enough, I stretched out and grabbed it. The moment he spotted the gun in my hand, he slammed another trash can down on top of me and ran. By the time I knocked it off, he'd vanished.

This can hadn't been as thoroughly emptied. A busted bag of trash had spewed all over me. "Ugh. Disgusting." I picked my way through the mess, keeping an eye on the direction he'd escaped.

"Are you okay?" A woman ran across the street toward me. "I saw what happened."

"Did you see who did this? Or where he went?" I tucked my gun away, afraid it would frighten her.

"Not really." She picked a piece of rotten banana peel off my arm. "I already called 9-1-1." The gash on my arm had started to bleed again. "You look like you took quite the beating."

"I'm okay." I could feel every place my body collided with the stairs, but I couldn't let that stop me. I'd been through far worse than some scrapes and bruises.

"Are you sure?" She stared down at the mess.

"Yeah."

"Why did he attack you?"

The better question was how did he know I'd be here. "He seems fond of trash. Maybe he hates that I recycle."

She laughed nervously, picking bits of who knew what out of my hair. She reached for the metal trash can, but I stopped her.

"There might be evidence on that. I'm hoping he left a few fingerprints behind."

"Oh, I hadn't thought of that." She gave me an odd look. "Are you sure you're okay?"

"Would you mind hanging around until help arrives, just in case." I didn't need the help, but I might need a witness statement. I didn't know how much she'd seen, but I didn't get a good look at the guy. That damn bandana and cap had made determining his identity impossible.

Three minutes later, a police cruiser pulled up. An uneasiness spread through me. That was fast. Too fast. Was the attacker one of these cops?

"What's going on here? We got reports of an assault in progress. Did one of you call it in?" one of the officers asked.

"I did." The woman pointed to a spot on the other side

of the street. "I just came out of the nail salon when I saw this woman getting beaten with a trash can."

The officer led her across the street, asking questions, and entering the nail salon to see if anyone else had seen what happened, while his partner assessed the damage and checked me out.

"Is that what happened?" the other officer asked me.

"More or less." I wondered how he'd look with a bandana. The jogging suit could have been on over his uniform. The cruiser could have been parked a block away. But was he too short to have attacked me?

He shined a flashlight in my eyes. "Paramedics should be here soon." He tucked it away and tore open a packet and blotted the scrape on my chin with antiseptic he'd taken out of the first aid kit. "Are you dizzy or nauseous?"

"I'm nauseous from the smell of trash."

"What were you doing when he attacked you?"

"I was heading back to my car." I'd forgotten all about it. "I have to check something. You might want to come with me."

The bastard hadn't vandalized the company car, but he vandalized my car. Driving my personal vehicle was supposed to make it more difficult for someone to link me to Cross Security and for my coworkers to track my movements. But apparently what I drove made little difference to this asshole. Again, I couldn't help but wonder how he knew I'd be here. I'd told Almeada what I planned to do, but who else had I mentioned it to?

"Where were you when the call came over the radio?" I asked suspiciously. I'd been stuck in the bank for a long time. The manager had called the precinct to verify my identity. All a cop would have to do is search DMV records for the make, model, and color of my car, show up, run a few plates, and bam, he'd know exactly what windshield to break.

"We were performing our normal patrol."

"So you were in the area?"

He smiled. "Yes, ma'am." That was supposed to reassure me. Instead, it made me even more uneasy.

At the sight of the damage, I stopped dead in my tracks.

Besides the smashed windshield, the unsub had keyed a message into the side of my car in large, unmistakable letters. *You've been warned.*

"Is this your car?" the cop asked, hitting his radio and requesting a support unit.

"Uh-huh."

"Do you have any idea who did this?"

"I know exactly who did it."

"Who?" The officer looked unsure, possibly even a little apprehensive.

"I don't know his name." I pointed to the various garbage cans scattered around the sidewalk. "Those need to be printed. He touched them, especially the one I pointed out earlier. The one you put beside your patrol car."

"But you said you know him."

"The man who did this threatened me yesterday. He's going to get caught. I'll make sure of it."

The officer sighed. "How about we start with a few basics? Height, weight, skin color."

His partner came to meet us. The woman who he'd spoken to must have finished giving her statement and left. I hoped he had taken down her details. If I'd been thinking clearly, I would have asked for her name so I could follow up on my own if necessary.

The second cop whistled. "The offender did this too?"

"Yeah." I studied the other cop, but he was too lanky to have attacked me. Still, his partner fit the bill. "When did you guys last take a break?"

"Don't worry about us, we're fine," the officer I'd been speaking to said. "Let's get some basic info while we wait for the ambulance to show up. How about we start with your name?"

"Alexis Parker." I wondered if they might have a jogging suit and baseball cap hidden somewhere in their vehicle. The trunk would be a good place to hide it. "Would it be okay if I made a call first?" I waited for him to nod before I reached into my pocket and pulled out my phone. By some miracle, it wasn't broken.

I tried Heathcliff, but it went to voicemail. A 9-1-1 text

from me with the address and details would get a response, but I wasn't feeling too keen on the police department. I must have caught that condition from Cross. Instead, I decided to use my phone-a-friend.

After dialing Mark Jablonsky, I told him I might be late for lunch and gave him an abbreviated version of what happened and where I was. We hung up just as the ambulance arrived.

I didn't need one, but I let them check me out anyway. Luckily, nothing appeared broken. While they cleaned my scrapes, I answered the officers' questions. By the time we were done, a government-issued SUV double-parked beside my car. The flashing lights would keep the annoyed motorists from becoming too belligerent.

Mark stepped out and came around the side. "Are you okay?"

"Just pissed off."

He lowered his sunglasses so he could stare over the rim at the two cops. "Did you canvass the area and see if anyone spotted the offender?"

"Not yet. We're waiting for backup."

"What did I tell you?" Mark mumbled to me. Before he could tear them each a new one, a second police cruiser pulled up. "Amazing timing." He watched the two men shut their doors and join us on the sidewalk. Now we had a party.

In short order, crime scene collection was called to fingerprint the trash cans. The mobile scanner didn't turn up anything but useless smudges.

Under Jablonsky's unyielding gaze, the four officers took to knocking on doors and questioning people on the street. Several surveillance cameras covered the area, but since the attack happened two blocks from the bank, their security would be useless. Luckily, the area was teeming with other businesses and plenty of cameras.

"At least we won't have a shortage of footage," I said.

"The next time I say we should meet for lunch, let's make it breakfast instead." He surveyed the area, noting the relevant cameras and jotting down the addresses. "That might have kept you out of trouble."

"I'm not even sure why I'm in trouble."

He nodded at the side of my car. "You've been warned."

"Apparently, which means it's the same asshole from yesterday."

"Unless we're dealing with multiple assholes who are working together." Mark asked the cops to pop their trunks. Despite their confusion with his request, they complied. Not a single jogging suit or bandana was in sight. "Satisfied, Parker?"

"Not really." At least that ruled out four patrol officers from the list of thousands. The nagging thought returned. Who knew I'd be here? Almeada knew, which meant Cross knew. And he'd visited the bank Monday afternoon, before the police had any idea what was going on. A sick feeling came over me, and I wasn't sure it was from the smell of trash.

Mark reached for his phone. "An assault isn't Bureau jurisdiction, but police corruption is. After everything you've told me about the incident inside the precinct last night and the attack on you today, I think it'd be best if we opened an investigation. Don't you agree?"

"I don't want you getting roped into anything dangerous."

He snorted. "This wouldn't be the first time you dragged me into one of these."

"Don't remind me."

He relayed the information and hung up. "We'll perform our own investigation in addition to whatever the cops decide to do. I doubt this is a top priority for them." He stared at the side of my car. "You'll need a new paint job. I'll have it towed to the lot so we can check it for evidence."

"And trackers."

He put on a pair of gloves and felt around the front and rear bumper, but he didn't find anything. "I'll have one of the techs go over it with a fine-tooth comb. You really think someone's tracking you?"

My hand went to the charm hanging from the chain around my neck. Martin kept a tracker on me as part of his acceptance of my career. It was supposed to be something only he could access. But Cross had given it to him, which meant the techs at Cross Security could get the data. "I'm an idiot." The police served a warrant this morning. They had all the Cross Security data at their disposal.

"Don't jump to conclusions." He peered inside my car. "Do you have anything sensitive inside? He could have smashed your windshield to get something off the dash or seat."

"Everything's in the trunk."

"Pop it." Mark reached in and pulled out the stack of files I had with me. "Is this everything?"

I read over his shoulder. "That's it."

He put them in the back of his SUV and grabbed my go-bag. It contained a change of clothes, some emergency cash, makeup, and extra bullets, along with whatever random items I thought I might need. "Glad to see you're always prepared."

"You taught me that."

"And it actually stuck. Amazing."

"I've already had a shitty enough day. I don't need to hear remarks from the peanut gallery."

After stowing my bag next to the files, Mark took a blanket out of his trunk, covered the passenger seat, and gestured for me to sit inside. "Try not to stink everything up."

"I'll do my best." I climbed in, my back and stomach aching from the assault. My hands shook a little from the adrenaline as I massaged the painful knot out of my thigh.

A few minutes later, two other government vehicles pulled up. Mark briefed the agents and climbed behind the wheel. "You still owe me lunch. Originally, I figured we'd grab takeout and go over your case in my office, but now, I'm thinking a fancy steakhouse and some kind of flaming dessert. But first, you need to shower."

"I need to go to the precinct. I have to speak to Moretti."

"Shower first," he insisted.

TWENTY

"Why didn't you call me?" Heathcliff grabbed my chin and turned my face from side to side, checking out my scrape.

"I did, but you didn't answer. I guess you were busy."

"Last night. Why didn't you call me last night?"

"And tell you what? That some asshole pulled the precinct's fire alarm, choked out my boss, and kicked me down the stairs?"

He rolled his eyes and reached into his desk drawer for a first aid kit. He pulled on a pair of latex gloves and uncapped a tube of ointment. "Why didn't the paramedics bandage you up?"

"They did, but I had to detour to the FBI locker room and shower before coming here. So the bandages had to go." I'd left my necklace there, figuring if the asshole wanted to make another attempt, he could explain himself to a room full of FBI agents. I'd taken my rings off the chain and had them in my pocket, figuring leaving expensive jewelry behind wasn't a good idea.

"And the FBI doesn't have first aid kits or a medic on staff?"

"I didn't want to bother anyone. They don't like me over

there."

He applied the ointment to my scraped chin, examining the rest of my face for other signs of injury. "Are you sure you didn't break anything? Stairs are dangerous, and you took quite the fall."

"You saw the footage?"

"What I could make out through the smoke."

"Have you IDed the guy?"

"Not yet." He wrapped a bandage around the gash on my arm. "Are you sure you don't need stitches?"

I'd forgotten just how much he liked to play doctor. "Were you and Martin separated at birth?"

"What?"

"He patched me up this morning. Now you're doing it. I don't like it."

"Neither do I." He reached back into the first aid kit. "Do you want a band-aid for that?"

"Only if it's pink or has cartoon characters on it."

He ignored me, unwrapped the bandage, and stuck it to my face. "You don't want it to get infected."

"It's just a scrape."

Ignoring my protest, he closed the first aid kit, tossed the gloves in the trash, and put the box back in his drawer. "The LT has the full report, but we couldn't pull prints off the smoke grenade we found next to the sergeant's desk. He wore tactical gear, but it wasn't ours. It looked high-end, private sector."

"The cop guarding the holding cells said the man who ordered him to evacuate had lieutenant bars. Why didn't he notice the discrepancy?"

"I dunno, but the unsub had a nameplate and Velcro identifiers. Maybe that's why." Heathcliff glanced around the bullpen, but no one seemed interested in us. "He grabbed them out of Lieutenant Avery's bag."

"How?"

"Avery stowed his gear in his car but found another way home. The man who attacked you broke into Avery's car and stole his gear about an hour before the alarm was pulled."

I didn't imagine it. I had seen someone lurking in the

shadows. I should have said something the night before, but it was too late now. "Did the unsub take Avery's body armor too?"

"No, Avery doesn't have a personal set he keeps in his car. What he has is provided by the department, which is kept in the squad cars and armory."

"That doesn't mean the man who attacked me isn't a cop."

Heathcliff ran a hand over his mouth. "I understand you didn't get a good look at this guy last night. What about today?"

"He wore a bandana. All I could see were his eyes. They were dark."

"Brown?"

"Probably."

"That's not much to go on."

"Have the sketch artist add it to the list." I gingerly sat back in the chair. "What did the sergeant say? He must have gotten a better look at the guy. He should be able to give you a more accurate description."

"He didn't recall much. Short, close-cropped hair, brown eyes, medium build, and average height. Nothing remarkable about him."

"Had he ever seen him before?" Last night, Moretti said he hadn't, but I hoped that might have changed.

"No." Heathcliff's gaze shifted to the computer screen. "I'm not sure if I can pull up the footage, but maybe you might recognize him." He worked the mouse, growing frustrated. Finally, he found the footage. "These aren't good angles."

I leaned in, but the camera only caught the top of the unsub's head, a bit of his forehead, and his prominent brow line. "This is the best you can do?"

"We're working on it." From his tone, the attack at the precinct had the police on edge. He closed the window. "The warning on your car, what was that about?"

"Apparently, I don't listen."

Heathcliff snorted. "No shit, really?"

I gave his arm a shove. "Obviously, someone isn't happy I'm poking around in Knox's murder. The fact that he attacked Cross must mean he doesn't want my boss to talk either, unless he figures killing Cross would close the case. Knox's killer dies in lockup. The Knox murder is solved, and given how much the police department loathes Lucien Cross, the rest just gets swept under the rug."

"Watch your mouth," Heathcliff warned. "You know I wouldn't do that. Neither would Moretti nor any of the cops you know."

"Sorry," I said. His expression eased. "IAD must be riding everyone's ass."

"You could say that. It's only gotten worse now that they've heard the FBI is getting involved." He leaned in. "How sure are you this asshole's a cop?"

The bullpen was practically empty, but to be on the safe side, I lowered my voice. "Fifty-fifty."

"Walk me through your logic."

"The only people who even knew I'd be at the bank this morning were Almeada, possibly Cross, and the police. I didn't use the company car because of trackers, but someone still could have tracked my movements. Cross Security probably records the data on that lowjack Martin saddled me with, and the police were there this morning confiscating everything. The man who vandalized my car could have figured out where I was that way, or he found out when the bank called the precinct to verify my story."

"Do you think he planned to hurt you?"

I hadn't thought about that. "Probably not. I surprised him. I'm guessing he would have just carved up my car and left. Thinking back, the unsub didn't attack me outside the holding cells either. He just wanted to escape. As far as I can tell, the only person he intended to hurt was Cross."

"If he wanted to hurt him."

"What is that supposed to mean?"

"I'm just speculating."

But it was more than that. "The precinct has tons of cameras. He must have gotten caught on one of them."

"We analyzed the CCTV feeds, but they're inconclusive. The man who attacked you never looked up at the cameras."

"Like he knew where they were?"

"Possibly."

"See?"

Heathcliff worked his jaw. "I'm not supposed to tell you any of this, but since Jablonsky's involved, you'll hear it anyway." He took a folder off the stack and laid it open in front of me. "You want some coffee?"

"Sure." While he was gone, I skimmed the file. The same brand and lot number of smoke grenades used during last night's attack was kept in the munitions cabinet at Cross Security.

A moment later, Heathcliff placed a steaming mug in front of me, closed the folder, and put it back on the stack. He didn't say a word, but his eyes spoke volumes. After blowing on the steam, he took a careful sip and waited for me to say something.

"You think the unsub works for Cross?"

"You mean one of your coworkers?" Heathcliff shifted in his chair, forcing me to look at him. "Or do you think Cross hired someone else?"

"Like a fixer?"

"Or a hitter. After all, he hired you to fix this, right? So you're the fixer. What better way to convince you of his innocence than by hiring someone to scare you and maybe beat you up a little." Heathcliff glanced at the report. "You said you didn't think the man today was armed, but the one you thought might have left the note on your car was. It stands to reason Cross doesn't want you dead, just freaked out enough to believe someone is framing him. The man who allegedly attacked him last night could have snapped his neck, stabbed him, shot him, or killed him a million other ways. But he didn't. Have you asked yourself why?"

"Cross might have gotten lucky. If I hadn't shown up, he might have had the life choked out of him."

"Possibly, but it's something to think about."

"I've already thought about it."

"And?"

"I won't know anything until I speak to Cross." I turned at the sound of Jablonsky's booming voice reverberating through the bullpen despite Moretti's office door being closed. "We should probably do something about that."

"Agreed."

Heathcliff followed me to Moretti's office, where I knocked softly on the door and entered without waiting for an invitation. Heathcliff stepped into the cramped room and pulled the door shut.

Moretti glared at Jablonsky. "I'd forgotten just how cantankerous you are. Shouldn't your near-death experience have given you a new lease on life? You should be grateful for my help."

"I am," Jablonsky shouted, too teed up to control his volume, "but if one of yours is threatening Parker, I have a big problem with that. The entire Bureau has a problem with it. And you, of all people, should have a problem with it."

"I'm looking into it," Moretti said. "I told her that last night."

"And today, the situation escalated."

"These things take time."

"The bank manager called. The police knew where I was," I said.

"I'm aware." Moretti retook his seat and read the info on his screen. "No viable prints were found on the trash cans. I'd say we should check your car, but apparently, the Bureau has already towed it away."

"We'll let you know what we find," Jablonsky said.

"Was it the same man you saw at the airport?" Moretti asked me. "The same man from last night?"

"I can't say with one hundred percent certainty, but I think so."

Moretti zeroed in on Heathcliff. "Officers already canvassed the area, but take a ride and see what you can find out. Flash your badge and collect as much surveillance footage as possible. This guy must have gotten spotted somewhere. I want to know who he is."

"Yes, sir." Heathcliff ducked out of the office.

"Sit down, Jabber. You shouldn't get this worked up. You'll give yourself an aneurysm." Moretti gestured to the chair beside where Jablonsky stood. "You've known me long enough. You ought to know by now I won't tolerate a cop abusing his position, taking the law into his own hands, or retaliating against anyone, especially Parker."

Jablonsky sunk into the chair. "Have you heard any whispers?"

Moretti stared up at me. "I can't discuss this in front of a civilian, especially one hired by a suspect's attorney."

"Didn't you want to speak to Cross?" Mark asked me.

"Has Mr. Almeada arrived yet?" I asked.

Moretti shook his head. "He's at Cross's apartment. He'll be here once we've completed the search. Cross is back in his cell if you want to see him." He picked up his phone, dialed an extension, told the guys in holding to tell Cross to expect a visitor, and hung up.

Nodding my thanks, I let myself out of his office and headed down the stairs. Lucien barely spoke when we were alone inside an interrogation room. I doubted he'd speak to me while in a holding cell, but I had questions that needed answering.

TWENTY-ONE

Cross remained segregated in his own private holding cell. He had gotten a blue rubber ball from somewhere and was bouncing it off the wall. From the expression on his face, his thoughts must have rivaled those of escape artists and mass murderers.

"Planning to take out the entire precinct with that blue ball of yours?"

He caught it on the return bounce. "Where's Almeada?"

"Supervising the police while they search your apartment."

"It's a waste of time. There's nothing for them to find." He put it down on the bench and tapped a spot on his chin while eyeing me. "Is that from last night?"

"No, this a remnant from my morning trip to the bank."

"What happened? Did you trip on the sidewalk?" Cross turned to look at the three uniformed cops positioned at the desk.

"Funny." I moved closer to the bars. "How are you doing? What did the doctors say?"

"They don't know why I passed out, but I'm guessing this," he indicated the bruise on his neck, "had something to do with it."

"Why didn't he kill you?"

Cross cleared his throat. Based on the dark circles beneath his eyes and the red around his irises, he hadn't slept. Was that due to fear or guilt? "Is that your way of asking for a thank you?"

"You need to tell me what's going on."

"How should I know?"

"You went to the bank. How did you know about the safe deposit box?"

"Lower your voice," he hissed.

"Answer the question."

"Get me out of here, and I will."

"That's not how this works."

"You work for me. This works the way I say it does."

I let out a huff, cycling through a long list of retorts. But verbally sparring with him was a waste of time. We'd end up irritated, and neither of us would be satisfied. "Where'd you get the ball?"

"What?"

"Who gave you the blue ball?"

He narrowed his eyes. "Are you enjoying saying that?"

"Tell me where you got it."

"Who cares?"

"Did you bribe an orderly?"

"Ms. Parker, what do you want from me?"

"Either tell me about the bank or tell me about that." I pointed at the rubber ball which might pop under the pressure of his closed fist. "It's your choice."

"Have the police searched my office yet?"

"Answer my question first."

He grumbled, stuffing his fists into his pockets. After clearing his throat, he said, "One of the desk sergeants gave it to me. She thought I looked bored."

"I need her name." The only desk sergeant I could think of was the one who volunteered to accompany him to the hospital. Jade said he had friends in the department. I wanted to know who they were, and this might be the quickest way to find out.

"Why does it matter?"

"It could be important."

"It isn't."

"Fine. How did you know about Knox's safe deposit box?"

His eyes went wide, warning me to back off. "Not here."

"You have to tell me something, Lucien. I can't help you if I don't know what's going on." I paced in front of his cell. Moretti didn't need DNA to know Knox's body had been found. The ring gave it away. Cross wouldn't have needed DNA to know that was Knox either, which meant plenty of cops knew Knox's body had been found near the airport before the DNA results came back. As soon as the ME finished photographing the remains, Knox's shoes and clothing were passed along to evidence collection. That's when the police would have found the key. Safe deposit box keys looked unique, and the bank's initials were etched onto it, just beneath the box number. "You have friends who are cops. Tell me about them."

"What?"

"I'm guessing someone tipped you off. That person had to be a cop." I didn't know if the same person gave him the ball, but it was possible. "Jade mentioned you've gone to KC's on occasion. In case you didn't realize it, that's a cop bar."

"Jade?" His voice was so low I could barely hear him, but his tone made my skin crawl. From the crazed look in his eye, he'd physically rip me apart if he could. "She has nothing to do with any of this. Leave her alone."

"I would, but you won't answer my questions. You refuse to help yourself." I inhaled which caused a sharp stabbing pain in my chest and back. "Who attacked you?"

He lunged toward the bars, stopping just short of hitting them. "I don't know," he spat.

"The bastard kicked me down the steps when I chased after him. He used a smoke grenade to conceal his presence, the same kind of smoke grenades the security teams at Cross Security keep on hand. Do you want to explain that to me?"

"What's to explain?" He cleared his throat, growing more agitated. "It's a smoke grenade."

"The bastard left a note on my car yesterday. The

company car, for clarification. And this morning, he keyed my car and broke the windshield. I'm gonna need you to fix that."

He squinted. "You think I did this?"

"I don't know what to think. You won't tell me what's going on. You have secrets. A lot of things don't make sense. The police arrested you due to the circumstances and the recording, but then I find out you were at the bank before the body had even been positively identified. What do you expect me to think?"

"I expect you to believe me when I say I didn't kill Knox. He had enemies. Surely, one of them is responsible."

"I agree. Right now, the man who's repeatedly threatened me to back off this case and went through all that elaborate planning to attack you inside the precinct's holding cell should be on the top of the suspect list, but he's not, at least as far as the police are concerned."

"What do you think?"

"If the unsub from last night killed Knox, why didn't he try harder to kill you and me?"

"He tried." Cross jerked his chin at the bandage on my arm. "It looks like he tried to silence you too."

"Did he? He could have shot us. Stabbed us. Snapped your neck like a twig."

"According to what I was told, you intervened in the nick of time. Next time, show up two minutes later, and maybe you'll get the outcome you want."

"I don't want you dead, Lucien. I just want to know what's going on."

"It's obvious. The police are framing me. One of them went to a lot of effort to attack me while I'm vulnerable."

"You think the unsub's a cop?"

"Don't you?" He stared daggers at me. "Isn't that the point of your questions?"

"The unsub could be a cop, the killer, one of his associates, or someone you hired."

"You better hope I never get out of here."

I snorted, even though his words triggered the warning bells in my brain. "You won't, unless you help me help you. And after the morning I've had, I'm reconsidering everything. So I'm giving you five seconds to tell me how you knew about the safe deposit box, or I'm walking away. And you can rot in here."

He held the glare. "My father's career police. I grew up around cops. I may have a friend or two, but if I tell you who they are, they won't be my friends anymore."

"I'm lovely. The life of the party. They won't mind a quick meet and greet."

"You'll drag their names through the mud. You'll tarnish their reputations. It's best if you leave them alone. Find another way."

"They can help you."

"No."

I still didn't know if he was playing me. This could all be manufactured, background to feed into the theory his arrest was a frame job. "Did Knox tell you about the safe deposit box?"

He closed his eyes, fighting with himself over answering or telling me to fuck off. In the end, self-preservation kicked in, like I knew it would. "No. I had no idea it existed."

"Who told you about the safe deposit box key?"

Returning to the bench, he sat down and bounced the ball against the wall, catching it on the return. "Sgt. Rostokowski gave me the ball. She knew I wouldn't be able to sleep after the attack. She's done this job for over thirty years. Don't jeopardize her pension, or so help you. Watch what you say and who you say it to. This is a police station. It's not safe for you to speak freely, not with me. Not with anyone."

I stepped closer to the bars. "Do you have any other friends I should know about?"

"The sergeant will help you with whatever you want."

"Okay." I sighed. "Jade said she'd e-mail me a list of cops with a bone to pick with you. If your friend can't help, a list of your enemies might."

"Let it lie." He threw the ball so hard it bounced off the wall, pinging back and forth until it finally lost momentum. Until today, I never feared Cross, but he'd never been this desperate. And desperate often led to terrible decisions.

"Digging up the past is how I ended up in this situation." His right eye twitched. "She's finally free. I won't let anything drag her back there, not even my life or my freedom. She's been through enough. I've put her through enough. Jade is off limits. Is that clear?"

I ignored the question. "Cross Security has plenty of employees who believe in you. Loyal, dedicated, hardworking men and women who love their jobs and appreciate the second chance you've given them. But you didn't ask any of them to work your case. Instead, you asked me. I want to know why."

He laughed bitterly. "You're the only one I trust."

"That's a lie. You don't trust me. Try again."

"No, Alex, that's the truth. But more importantly, the police trust you. They'll value your findings."

I held up my palms. "All right."

He picked up the ball, tossed it against the wall, and caught it. "Tell Almeada to stay close. Once the police finish cataloging whatever evidence they believe they've found, they'll move me to central booking for processing. I'll need him to make sure my arraignment is expedited."

"Okay. Stay safe, boss."

He snorted. "Easier said than done." He didn't turn to acknowledge me, but he no longer appeared to be planning an escape that required murdering every cop in the building. Instead, the wheels were turning in another direction. I just couldn't tell what he was thinking.

"Hey, Lucien, for what it's worth, she loves you. The thought of anything happening to you scares her."

"She shouldn't be scared. I want her to feel safe. That's all I've ever wanted."

TWENTY-TWO

Sgt. Sara Rostokowski was the woman I encountered last night, the one who'd gone with Lucien to the hospital. According to her personnel record, she'd received several commendations. She was ten years past her required twenty for a full pension, which told me she loved her job. And from the things she'd said last night, she cared a great deal about my boss.

After thanking Detective Jacobs for helping me out on what I told him was my attempt to identify the sergeant who'd assisted me last night, I made my way to the empty desk across from Heathcliff's and took a seat. He hadn't returned yet, but he'd be back soon.

While I waited, I went over everything I knew about the man who attacked me. The threats told me the unsub connected to Knox's murder. I just didn't know how.

The condition of Knox's body indicated his death had been brutal. But the unsub hadn't been nearly as vicious. Maybe he'd mellowed in the last eight years, but that didn't make sense either. Nothing did.

"Hey, Parker." Heathcliff slid into his chair. "What are you still doing here?"

"I was just asking myself the same question. Did you get

anything off the cameras?"

"No. The asshole got lucky. We didn't get a look at his face. The techs are playing around with reflective surfaces, hoping the manipulations might yield better results, but I wouldn't hold my breath." Heathcliff checked for updates on his caseload.

"I wasn't planning on it. Even if you find an angle that works, he still wore that stupid bandana. What about tracking his movements?"

"He got into a white sedan. The plates were masked, so we can't find out who it's registered to, but I assigned several officers to scrub DOT cams. We might find out where he went or where he came from. Either one could lead us to him."

"Forgive me if I'm not that optimistic."

"Neither am I." He clicked a few keys, mesmerized by the data on the screen.

Scooting my chair closer, I leaned over so I could see the screen. "I have to wait for Almeada to finish speaking to Cross, so we can discuss the search warrant, unless you'd like to tell me what the cops found instead."

"What else is on your itinerary?"

"Once Jablonsky's done with Moretti and the guys over in internal affairs, he and I are going to lunch."

"You mean you're going to bash the department and gain access to information you aren't supposed to possess?"

"Yes, but we'll be eating steak while we do it."

He scanned the screen, his forehead creasing as he read. "Then what?"

"Then I have something else to take care of."

"Like what?" Normally, he wasn't this inquisitive.

"It's Wednesday. Our meeting's tomorrow. Why do you care what I'm doing?"

"Quid pro quo?" He took a sip of coffee, waiting for me to nod. "Cross will be charged in a few hours. An unregistered weapon was found on Cross's property, which is being tested and compared to the slugs we pulled from Knox's body."

"Unregistered?"

"It was hidden inside Cross's vehicle. It's the same caliber as the gun used to kill Knox. More than likely, it's the murder weapon."

"That's a stretch."

"No, it's not. It's an illegal firearm. Either way, Cross has some explaining to do."

"Great," I said sarcastically. "Where was it found?"

"Hidden in a compartment beneath the spare tire in the trunk."

"Cross drives a Porsche. He doesn't have a trunk with a spare tire."

"Not that car."

"He has another car?"

"Technically, it's a sports utility vehicle." He gave me an incredulous look, but before he could say anything, my phone chimed. Almeada was outside.

"I have to go."

"Not yet. Where's my quo?"

"You ever go to KC's? It's a cop bar."

"I know. I've been a few times. It's quiet and a little depressing, not really my scene. If I want to drink alone at a bar, I'll go somewhere people don't know me, so they won't bother me. Or I'll pick up a six-pack on my way home. Why do you ask?"

"I just thought it might be worth checking out. That's what I'm doing later tonight."

Heathcliff gave me a confused look. "Does this have something to do with our standing bi-weekly appointments?"

"Nope." I climbed out of the chair, trying not to wince.

"This conversation is not over."

"I already told you everything you need to know." I winked and headed down the stairs. As soon as I stepped foot outside, I spotted Almeada's car parked in a reserved space. He waved me over, unlocking the doors as I approached.

Sliding into the front seat, I knew from the look on the attorney's face things weren't going well. "What did Cross say when you asked him about the bank?" I asked.

"He said he was there Monday afternoon. He had

meetings with clients all day. One of them inquired about placing sensitive materials in a safe place and thought a bank vault would be the best idea. Cross went to a few banks to determine which one offered the most protection and superior insurance options."

"How many banks did he visit?"

"Three."

"Did you verify this?"

Almeada handed me the list. "That's why I hired you."

I read the names and the approximate times Cross said he'd visited. "This is bullshit. He went to that bank because he found out about Knox's safe deposit box." I studied the attorney. "What he tells you is confidential. Doesn't that extend to me?"

"It does."

"So why are you lying about this?"

"I'm not. That's what Cross said."

"Bullshit."

"It doesn't look like bullshit. It looks like a professional performed his duties to the fullest extent of his capabilities."

"In other words, he's covering his ass." I knew Cross was paranoid about discussing his case and defense in the precinct, but this was insane.

Almeada disagreed, but since we were on a time crunch, he didn't waste any more of our precious seconds arguing with me. "This morning's search is catastrophic to our case. Have the police said anything to you?"

"Pretend they didn't. What did they tell you?"

"They're charging Lucien with Knox's murder. They're confident they found the murder weapon. It was concealed in a hidden compartment inside his SUV."

"When did he get an SUV?"

"He bought it after he returned from his trip eight years ago."

I didn't say anything while the facts sunk in. After all, Cross couldn't exactly transport a body inside a sports car. But was he stupid enough to forget where he stashed the murder weapon? "Who else has access to his SUV?"

"He keeps it parked at the office for use when security is

of the utmost importance. Since it's armored, it's the ideal transport vehicle. Any of his employees could have accessed it."

I thought about the vehicles I spotted every morning when I went to work. A few armored SUVs always remained in the corner. The navy blue one was parked in a designated spot—one of Cross's spots. The logs would show who used the vehicle and when. But the facts were adding up to just one conclusion. Lucien Cross was a killer.

The man who attacked me threw a monkey wrench into the works, but he could be a distraction, possibly working for Cross, or just a cop with misplaced intentions. "Has Cross mentioned any of his contacts in the police department to you?" I asked.

"I'm not sure what you mean."

"Friends, acquaintances, anyone who would stick their neck out for him."

"Why do you want to know?"

"What about Sgt. Rostokowski? Does that name ring any bells? She went with him to the hospital last night."

Almeada shrugged. "Again, this would be the reason I hired you."

"I understand that, but Cross refuses to cooperate, so I figured I'd ask you."

"Give Justin a call. He'd know better than anyone."

"You don't think it'll hurt Cross's case?"

"At this point, I'm willing to risk it. The police have means and motive. If you think you're on to something, explore away."

I studied the attorney. Despite what he'd said, he'd hoped Cross would be released before charges were filed. "What's our plan now?"

"I'll request the police keep him isolated. The commissioner's son getting shivved while in lockup wouldn't play well in the press."

Cross didn't just have to worry about the asshole from last night. He had to worry about every criminal his father ever arrested. "They'll kill him."

Almeada inhaled sharply. "Let's make sure no one has time to find out who he is or who his father is. The sooner the arraignment happens, the better. I'm nearly certain I can get him released on bail. After that, we'll have access to the evidence. We'll rip the case apart from there. I'll try to get it kicked before it goes to trial, but if we go to trial, we'll be prepared."

"Even if he did it?"

"I told you to let me worry about that." Almeada opened his car door. "Just find out as much as you can and bring the facts back to me. Whoever attacked Cross last night is probably a good place to start."

"I agree. I'm just not sure Cross does."

As I got out of the car, I wondered what Cross would do once he was released on bail. After our earlier exchange, I wasn't sure I wanted to know. Hopefully, he'd calm down between now and then. When I left, he seemed a bit more hopeful than when I'd arrived. I just didn't know if that was enough to keep the desperation at bay.

* * *

"Now that the police have the murder weapon, it's game over." Mark dabbed at the steak sauce that had fallen onto his tie. "I don't care who Cross's attorney is. There's too much evidence against him."

I stared at my plate, too anxious to eat. "What about the bastard who keyed my car and used me as a garbage dump? What does Moretti have to say about him?"

"Not much, I'm afraid." Mark took a roll out of the basket and buttered it. "Internal affairs is looking into the matter. Cross has a reputation. Half the department reveres him. The other half wants him in the ground."

"That's what Almeada said. Do we know why?"

"Everyone has a different answer. Did you know Cross wanted to be a cop? He went through academy training but flunked out right before graduation. Apparently, he had issues with one of his instructors. Something about violating common practices. Cross followed the chain of command and went to the sergeant. When that didn't work, he went above the guy's head, but no one listened. Eventually, Cross went to his dad, who told him not to question authority. The next thing you know, Cross fails an exam and gets booted from the program. That's probably when the bad blood first started."

"It got worse when Cross went up against Jade's abusive ex-boyfriend, who happened to be a police sergeant."

"Look, I'm the farthest thing from a fan of Lucien Cross. The smug bastard doesn't listen to anyone and is driven by the bottom line. He makes stupid mistakes that are going to get people killed. I didn't like him when we first met at that symposium several years ago, and I still don't like him. But I wouldn't destroy his life over it."

"You think someone in the police department's trying to do that?"

Mark finished his roll and tossed his napkin onto his plate. "They are rushing this case ahead. Moretti's got this thing fast-tracked, but that's only because he's getting pressure from on high."

"The commissioner?"

"That'd be my guess. Commissioner Cross has been taking a lot of flak lately. The mayor's adamant about equal treatment under the law and fairly administering justice. Officially, the commissioner has recused himself from this case, but it's still too scandalous. From what I can tell, he wants it solved as quickly as possible. Knox was killed eight years ago. It's a cold case. The remains should have been left on a slab in the morgue for a few weeks before DNA even came back. But some schmuck points out the ring, gets major crimes involved, and makes sure Moretti knows about it. That was orchestrated."

"It doesn't hurt that the former commissioner's son is the prime suspect and the case was never solved under dear, old dad's watch." I swallowed. "At the risk of piling on, you should know Cross went to the bank Monday afternoon. He claims it was for a client, but..."

"You think he tried to break into Knox's safe deposit box and steal the evidence."

"The thought may have crossed my mind."

"How'd he know about the box?"

"He won't say, but when I asked about the cops he knows, he got defensive."

"One of them must have tipped him off."

"That's what I'm thinking. I plan to drop by this cop bar Jade told me about. She said the guy who owns the place worked with Cross's dad and cares a great deal about Lucien. He might be able to tell me something. If not, I'll swing by the precinct and speak to Sgt. Rostokowski since she's pulling graveyard this week."

"Do you think she requested that shift just so she could keep an eye on Cross?"

"You mean to keep him safe?"

"Maybe." Mark's phone rang. "Hold that thought." He checked the display before answering. I listened in on his end of the conversation. From what I could tell, Agent Lawson and several other FBI techs finished examining my car. They didn't find any tracking devices, fingerprints, or other evidence that would point them to the man who attacked me. "What about surveillance footage?" Mark paused. "Yeah, that's the same thing the police said. Just keep at it, and let me know. I want to know where that white sedan went." He chuckled. "She's pissed off, but what else is new?"

When he hung up, I asked, "Was that about me?"

"Of course. Who else do I know who's always pissed off?"

"Besides you?"

"Touché." He sobered. "I have no idea who this asshole is who attacked you, but he's clever enough not to get caught."

"If he tries something again, I'll be prepared." No more insane workouts would get in my way, but the bruises might be another story. Stabbing a piece of steak, I popped it into my mouth and chewed. "What do you think? Did Cross kill Knox?"

"The evidence is pretty clear. Ballistics doesn't lie. The unregistered gun hidden in Cross's SUV was used to kill Trey Knox."

"But it's been eight freaking years. Why would Cross keep the gun? And why hide it in a vehicle designated for company use? None of that makes a damn bit of sense."

"He went to the bank. Don't you find that suspicious?"

"Yes."

"So what's your current theory? Vindictive cop or disgruntled Cross Security employee?" Mark asked.

"Either one's possible, unless Cross is right, and Knox's killer is someone Knox pissed off. But the gun makes no sense. You've visited Cross Security enough to know how that place operates. There's no way a gun remained hidden in a company car for eight years without anyone noticing. Someone put it there. Recently." Cross's words about trusting me played through my head as I picked up my phone and read the copy of the report Mark had forwarded to me, which he'd received from Moretti. "The police didn't find any prints on the weapon. I'd say it was planted. The unsub could be doing all of this just to keep us distracted."

"Possibly. Playing defense means you don't have much time to work on offense."

"That's why I asked for your help." The check arrived, and I picked it up. "I just worry about the ramifications down the road. Right now, the unsub is targeting me, but the second that changes..."

"Alex, stop. I'm okay. Whatever happens, it's not your fault. It never was, and it never will be. Frankly, I'm amazed you even asked for a favor."

"You hate when I ask for favors. As I recall, you have a tendency to remind me the federal government has better things to do with its time."

"It does, but I can squeeze you in if it's something important."

"Like giving me a ride back to my car?"

"I guess that can be arranged, but let's not make this favor thing a habit."

TWENTY-THREE

After contacting Justin and getting a copy of Lucien's schedule from Monday, I did my best to retrace my boss's steps. Cross had four meetings that day and didn't miss any of them. He managed to squeeze in the bank trips around his meetings.

I spoke to the two other bank managers. They recalled Lucien touring their vaults and safe deposit rooms, asking questions, and writing down the information concerning pricing and insurance fees. But he didn't open a box with either of them.

His story checked out. Almeada would play that aspect up to a jury. I could already hear the violin music in the background.

Regardless, I didn't buy it. I doubted the prosecutor would either. Sure, I was cynical and jaded. Perhaps, with enough time, Cross could convince me a client set him up, so I made some calls to be proactive.

Mr. Rathbone had asked about alternative options for stashing sensitive materials. He didn't tell me what those materials were, and I didn't ask. But that backed up Cross's story. However, Rathbone was a long-time client and personal friend of Lucien's, which made their interaction suspect in my mind. Rathbone would probably cover for Cross, not the other way around.

Cross used his normal car service to go to the banks. His driver didn't remember Cross toting around any suspicious items or hardware. And since the USB had been left inside the safe deposit box, I figured Cross hadn't been able to break in. The two-key lock was supposed to be nearly impenetrable. But all locks weren't created equal, and I'd seen someone jimmy boxes open without wasting much time on the locks. But maybe Knox had picked a better bank with stronger security measures in place.

Since I'd never figure out the truth behind Cross's visit to the bank or what he gained from accessing the safe deposit box room, I moved on to other issues. By now, Cross Security was back to normal. Well, as normal as it could be with its leader behind bars.

"Hey, Justin." I leaned against the counter, watching the hustle and bustle going on inside the nearby conference room. "Busy day?"

"You're not funny."

"Next time, I'll wear a big rubber nose."

"What happened to your face?"

I rubbed the bandage. "I slipped on a banana peel."

"Fine, don't tell me."

Jerking my head toward Cross's office, I asked, "Can we talk in there?"

"Sure."

The room looked a lot different. All the drawers in the filing cabinets had been emptied. Cross's computer was gone. And the closet had been searched.

"Who's Sgt. Rostokowski?" I asked.

"Sara?"

"That's her name?"

Justin nodded. "She's always looked out for Lucien. When we get stuck on something or need to see some files we can't access, he calls her. He's fond of her."

That would explain the ball. "Did she tip him off about Knox's body being discovered?"

"No."

I could kick myself for not questioning Justin sooner.

"Who did?"

"No one."

I scrutinized him, but I didn't see the lie. "What about incoming calls and Cross's phone records?"

"You already looked, remember?"

"Someone tipped him. Tuesday morning before the police came to arrest him, he knew what was about to happen."

Justin rubbed his eyes. "He didn't run. Doesn't that mean anything? Guilty people run."

"He's too smart to run." The problem with running is once you start, you can't stop.

Reaching into his pocket, Justin pulled out his phone, thumbed past several screens, and handed it to me. "That's what you want."

Monday afternoon, Justin received a call from the precinct. "Who called you?"

"Officer Joe Gallo."

Gallo. That name was on my list. He worked the Knox break-in. "Why would he call you about this?"

"He and Lucien are friends, sort of. When Lucien found Knox's belongings inside the storage unit, he called in the anonymous tip to Officer Gallo. Gallo had been first on scene. They shared intel on Knox. I guess you can say Cross trusts him."

"The feeling must be mutual."

"I guess. Every once in a while, when a client gets into some minor trouble, Gallo gives us the heads-up."

"Us?"

"Lucien isn't always reachable. I am. Gallo tells me what's going on, and I assess the situation and contact whoever can handle the issues our clients are facing."

"How long has this been going on?"

"For the last six or seven years."

How could so much have been going on at Cross Security that I never knew about? "Do the police know about this? Have they checked your phone records?"

"No."

"Gallo called you because he didn't want anyone to know what he'd done. Who else trades favors with Lucien?"

"A few other officers and civilian staff, but not on a regular basis. Occasionally, Lucien will go to KC's if he gets desperate."

"Jade mentioned it to me. Who's the proprietor?"

"Jim Harrelson. He worked with Lucien's old man. They were partners back in the day."

"I take it Jim watches out for Lucien."

Justin snorted. "I'd call it more of a love-hate relationship."

"Ah, family obligation."

"They aren't related," Justin said.

"Not by blood, by the badge." Justin seemed confused, but I shook off his question. I couldn't explain it, but I lived it. "When's the last time Lucien stopped by KC's for a drink?"

"I'm not sure."

"Okay." I stared at him, hoping whatever else he might be hiding would shake loose, but he didn't say anything. "I need to see the logs of who used Cross's SUV."

"Lucien doesn't have an SUV."

"The navy blue armored truck in the garage is registered in his name, not in the company's."

"That must have been an oversight. It's strictly for company use."

"Regardless, I need the logs." Going with my gut, I added, "The police found the gun used to kill Trey Knox hidden inside the SUV when they searched it this morning."

"What? That's not possible." He appeared genuinely shaken. "Let me get them."

I followed him out of Cross's office and down the hall. Records was housed in a small alcove. The room was in disarray. The police had taken the files and computers. But Justin had downloaded a copy onto a separate hard drive from the cloud, so Cross Security could continue to function. He plugged the drive into his personal laptop and clicked a few keys. The printer whirred to life, and I grabbed the warm sheet of paper before it landed in the tray.

In the last year, the SUV had been used at least once by

every security team Cross employed. Everyone had access. The gun could have been placed in the compartment beneath the tire at any time, but the teams always checked everything before they picked up a client. The last time the SUV had been used was a month ago. After that, it had collected dust in the garage. "Do we have security footage of the garage?"

"Yes." Justin brought it up. "How far back do you want me to go?"

I gave him the date the SUV was returned and scanned the screen. "You've got to be kidding. Aren't there any other cameras in that area?" Only the driver's side of the vehicle was fully caught on screen. From the angle of the parking spaces, I couldn't even see the rear gate.

"Let me check." He clicked the links to the other feeds, but nothing covered that area. "That's all we have."

"What's the next closest camera that someone would have to pass in order to get to the SUV?"

Justin brought up the footage. "I'm not sure how this helps."

"That makes two of us, but make me a copy anyway."

He did as I asked and handed me a thumb drive. "We need to prove the gun isn't his."

"Possession is nine tenths of the law. The SUV is his, which doesn't help matters. Not to mention, Cross basically threatened to send a kill squad to eliminate Knox. This won't exonerate him. Honestly, I don't think anything will."

"He didn't do it," Justin insisted.

"Look at the evidence. What do you see?"

"One hell of a frame job. Lucien wouldn't be stupid enough to do the things he did if he killed Knox."

That's exactly what I thought. "Why didn't you tell me about Gallo? You can't conceal things from me. It only hurts Cross and implicates you. If you believe he's innocent and you want me to prove it, you have to tell me the truth, the whole truth, and nothing but the truth."

"I don't see how that phone call was relevant."

Sighing, I collected the copies and left the records room. I went downstairs and spoke to the members of the security team who'd last used the SUV. None of them recalled finding a handgun hidden beneath the spare tire or anywhere else inside the vehicle. When they finished escorting our celebrity client around town, they made sure to clear out all the gear.

"We checked everywhere and returned our equipment. It's in the logs. Didn't you see them?"

"Yes," I said, "but I wanted to be thorough." After ascertaining their alibis for the previous night and this morning, I returned to my office, pulled each of their personnel records, cross-referenced them to Trey Knox, and ran their financials, but they were clean. Whoever put the gun inside Cross's SUV had done so within the last four weeks.

Plugging in the drive, I scanned the surveillance footage, marking down possible suspects. Unfortunately, every single member of Cross Security traipsed right past that SUV on a regular basis, even Lucien himself. Without footage of someone accessing the SUV, I had nothing. Maybe my luck would improve at KC's bar.

TWENTY-FOUR

The bartender poured a lemon drop martini and placed it on a napkin in front of me. From the look of disdain on his face, I could tell he didn't approve of such a girly cocktail. Normally, I wouldn't imbibe while at work, but the pain relievers from earlier had worn off. I'd have to stop by the store on my way home to pick up more. But for now, this would have to suffice.

I took a sip. "That hits the spot."

"You looking for someone, sweetheart?" He wiped the bar and tossed the rag over his left shoulder.

"The only person who calls me sweetheart is my boyfriend."

"Does your boyfriend come here a lot?"

"I'd be surprised if he did."

The bartender filled a pitcher from the tap and slid it down the bar before the guy approaching could even ask. Ah, the benefits of being a regular. "So why are you darkening my doorstep?"

"Do you talk to all of your customers like this?"

"Just the ones I don't know." He scowled at the martini. "I'm guessing this isn't the kind of place a lady like you normally goes."

"You'd be surprised." I spun on the seat. A dartboard

hung from the wall. Aside from that, I didn't see much in the way of entertainment. "This is the kind of place people go to drink away their troubles before they bring 'em home, right?"

"Something like that."

I took another sip and smiled up at him. "Just my kind of place." Too bad Heathcliff wouldn't let us hang out here for an hour every Monday and Thursday night. I'd rather do this than spend it in a church basement. "What do the initials stand for?"

"Hell if I know. When I bought this place, the sign was already out front. I thought about changing it but saw how much that would cost and figured it's as good a name as any."

"You're Jim?"

"That depends. Are you looking to serve him papers?"

"I'm just looking for some information. When's the last time you saw Lucien Cross?"

He swallowed. "Who are you?"

"A concerned citizen."

"Get out of my bar."

I lowered my voice and leaned closer. "You don't want me to go. I was hired by his attorney to investigate the crime he's accused of committing." I placed my business card on the counter in front of him. "I work for Lucien."

He picked up the card, holding it up to the light and flicking the cardstock. "Well, I'll be damned. The kid's at least done one thing right in his life." He put my card down.

"Do you know what's going on?"

"I'm not on the job anymore. I don't hear all the comings and goings, but when Lucien Cross gets arrested for murder, that causes a buzz. Who do they say he killed?"

"Trey Knox."

Jim sucked something loose from his back teeth and made a face. "Name rings a bell, but I can't quite place it. Memory's not what it used to be. Wanna help me out with that?"

"Knox was one of Lucien's first clients. He hired him to work a recovery. His house had been burglarized."

"That's right. What can I tell you that you don't already know?"

"Plenty, I'm sure. What do you remember from eight years ago?"

"Not much, except Lucien started coming around a lot more. He only does that when he's doing something he shouldn't. The first time he set foot in this place was when he decided to stalk a cop. Don't get me wrong, the bastard had it coming. He was an abusive son of a bitch with a drinking problem. But still, I warned Lucien to watch his step. He didn't listen and nearly ended up dead."

"Did you warn him about working the Knox investigation?"

"No, but there was something weird about it. If there wasn't, he wouldn't have shown up as often as he did. He told me it was so he could speak to the cop who caught the case."

"Joe Gallo?"

"Yeah. He's a beat cop through and through. Real boots on the ground type. He does the job and knows his shit. He knows not to overstep even when the detectives are running themselves in circles for no reason. Gallo thought there was something weird about the Knox break-in. He and Lucien talked about it a few times."

"Did you know Lucien called in the anonymous tip which led the police to the stolen merch?"

"I suspected, but Lucien never said. That was weird too. That kid, smart as a whip with real potential, but a chip on his shoulder the size of the Grand Canyon. If he does anything right, anything that'll show up his pops, he'll shout it from the rooftops. That's why I never understood why he kept that one quiet."

"Drugs and guns were found in the same storage unit. They belonged to the Russian mafia."

"Jesus." He ran a hand over his face. "At least his brains override his pride on occasion. Do you think the Russians offed Knox?"

"No."

"But you don't know who did. And I'm guessing for you to come all the way here, you're thinking Lucien did him in." He waited, but I refused to answer. "How much evidence is against him?"

"Lucien knew Knox was dead before anyone else did. Want to tell me how he might know something like that?"

Jim wiped the bar again and offered me a refill. "Someone tipped him."

"Like Joe Gallo?"

"Could be."

"Any other cops you can think of who might warn Lucien?"

"Plenty, I'm sure."

I sipped my martini, wondering how much Jim knew about the situation. "According to Lucien, the police hate him."

"He's delusional. They don't hate him, not exactly. Sure, seventy-five percent of the people who frequent this bar wouldn't mind knocking his teeth in, but he has friends in the department too. His pops is beloved. Out of loyalty, they'd help out his kid. Still, if it has to do with Knox, I'd start with Gallo."

"What about Sgt. Rostokowski?"

He smiled. "She'd knock Lucien's teeth in for even thinking something stupid. But that's just Sara." He assessed me. "You ever been on the job?"

"If I answer that, you'll definitely throw me out."

"Fed?"

"Not for some time."

"You've seen some shit. I can see it in your eyes. Lucien's seen shit too. He was never a cop, but he could have been a damn good one. His pops didn't want that life for him. He didn't want this life for him either. But he's damn proud. Don't tell Lucien that. He'd never believe it anyway."

The bell chimed, and I turned to see a tired looking cop enter. By the time he reached the bar, Jim had a mojito waiting for him. "Thanks, man," the officer said.

"Hey, Joe. I want you to meet someone," Jim said. "This is..."

"Alex Parker," I said. "You're Joe Gallo?"

"Sure am." He tucked his left hand into his pocket,

hoping I wouldn't see his wedding ring. "What can I do for you?"

"Do you mind if we talk in the back?" I nodded toward an empty booth in the corner.

"No problem."

I thanked Jim and led Gallo to the booth. I hated having my back to the door, but I wanted to box him in. More than likely, he wouldn't want to answer my questions. So I had to make sure he couldn't easily escape.

"What can I do for you, Ms. Parker?"

"Why did you call Lucien to tell him Trey Knox was dead?"

His cheeks flushed. "You're confused."

"Don't deny it. Justin showed me the message. I know who you are. I know about your connection to the break-in at Knox's house."

"It sounds like you already know everything." He moved to stand.

"Why did you tell Cross about the body?"

"Knox had been his client. The man disappeared. No one ever knew what happened to him. It drove me a little crazy. I'm sure it did the same to Lucien. I wanted him to know we finally found Knox."

"Did you ever investigate Knox's disappearance?"

"A little."

"And?"

"And what? I'm a beat cop, not a homicide detective. As far as I can tell, Knox pissed someone off. They killed him and buried him in the field near the airport. It's pretty open and shut."

"Do you know who killed him?"

"Of course not."

"The police arrested Cross for the murder. I'm sure you heard about that."

"He didn't do it."

"How do you know?"

"Knox had secrets. He wasn't a good guy. I don't know what he's involved with, but he had gambling debts and must have gotten mixed up with organized crime. That's probably why he got killed."

"Did Cross tell you any of that?"

"Why do you want to know?"

"I work for him." I showed him my business card. "I'm trying to clear his name."

"Really? It sounds like you're building a case against him and anyone who might have helped him."

"Do you know how Knox's stolen ring ended up back on his finger? That's how you recognized him, isn't it?"

"It is, but I don't know how that happened."

"Doesn't it strike you as strange that an item found in Knox's house after his disappearance ended up back on his finger?"

"He must have come back for it."

"So you knew Knox didn't die the day he disappeared?" Gallo had just contradicted himself, which made me wonder what else he might be lying about.

"I don't know what happened. No body, no crime. Everyone knows that. Cross took off a few weeks later. He didn't say where he was going, but he must have had a lead. When he returned, he seemed more relaxed, like he could finally put the whole Knox situation behind him."

"Did he say anything to you when he got back?"

"He showed up for a drink one night and told me Knox wasn't worth our time or energy anymore."

"How did you interpret that?"

"Considering Cross had flown halfway across the world, I figured either Knox skipped town before his problems got worse or Cross's vacation had made him reassess his priorities. Apparently, he met a girl while he was away."

"Did he tell you about her?"

"Not really, but I could tell. That dumb grin and no interest in bedding a badge bunny. That's got to be love, right?"

"Or herpes."

Gallo scowled. "Like I said, Knox had pissed off some powerful people. But if he fled, maybe the ring's the reason he came back. He was a fanatic. Crazy obsessed. He'd rather die than live without his precious collection. He's like that freaky little dude in those movies with the gold ring."

"You never thought Cross killed him?"

"Why would he? He did everything for that guy. Between you and me, he couldn't stand him. He was happy to be free of him." He cocked his head to the side, reading my thoughts. "Again, not in a rest in peace kind of way, but a he's someone else's problem kind of way."

"If Cross washed his hands of this and was glad to not have to think about Knox, why did you call him on Monday and tell him Knox's body had been discovered?"

"I already told you I thought he'd want to know."

"You could get in a lot of trouble for that. Why didn't you wait?"

"Cross had been the prime suspect when Knox disappeared. I knew they'd bring him in for questioning."

"The police arrested him for murder. Do you know why?"

Gallo gulped down his drink. He thought long and hard, unsure if he should answer. "You were at the precinct last night, weren't you? You work for him, so you already know the answer to all these questions. Why are you wasting my time asking?"

"I'd like to hear it from you."

"You want me to incriminate myself, but I won't."

"I just need to know if you told Cross about the safe deposit box key they found with the body."

"Screw you." He picked up his drink and walked away. At least now I had my answer.

TWENTY-FIVE

I arrived at the precinct a few minutes before shift change. Moretti hadn't left his office. From the open files on his desk, I couldn't tell what he was working on. But I could guess. Gently, I knocked on the door.

He looked up. "Cross has been charged. He's no longer with us."

"I know. I wanted to talk to you, off the record."

"What about?"

"I spent a good portion of my day looking into the murder weapon. I don't think it's Cross's. It's not registered to him. His prints aren't on it, and according to Cross Security records, which I verified by watching the security footage, Cross hasn't used that SUV in years. The last security team assigned to it made sure they cleaned everything out. The gun wasn't inside a month ago." I gave him the exact date.

"Okay, so who could have put it inside?"

"Anyone."

"Narrow it down for me."

"Anyone who works for Cross Security or has access to the garage. That would be everyone else in the building—building security, the police who conducted the search, janitors, repairmen, et cetera."

He narrowed his eyes. "You said you scanned security footage. What did it show?"

"Nothing. The camera angle doesn't cover the rear of the vehicle."

"So Cross could have panicked and stowed the gun in there."

"Why would he panic after eight years? Why would anyone keep a murder weapon that long? Cross is a giant pain in the ass, but he's not an idiot. Don't you agree?"

"This case smells like yesterday's catch, but it's out of my hands."

"It's your case," I argued.

"I turned in my report, including my recommendation that we hold off on filing charges until we know more about who's behind last night's assault, but I got overruled. DA's office went ahead with it. Evidence supports the conclusion that Lucien Cross is a killer. The murder weapon was found in his vehicle. Cross was caught on tape threatening Trey Knox. Pair that with Cross being one of the last people to see Knox alive, the visit to Knox's house the morning he disappeared, and his mysterious trip out of the country three weeks later, and that's that. Cross is getting arraigned in the morning." Moretti went back to reading the files on his desk. "Go home and get some sleep. You look like death warmed over."

"You have to do something."

He stared down at the papers on his desk. "Like what?"

"Put a stop to this."

"Isn't that your job?"

Taking that as my cue to leave, I grabbed two cups of coffee before heading down to the front desk. A thin woman with a starched shirt and grey hair pulled back in a twist stepped up to the desk. She must have recognized me from last night but didn't let on. Once she settled into her chair, she asked, "How are you tonight?"

"Sgt. Rostokowski?" I needed to make sure.

"In the flesh."

"I'm Alexis Parker." I pushed one of the cups toward her. "I thought you might like some coffee."

She gave it a suspicious look. "Thanks." But she didn't touch it. Obviously, she was wary of strangers with gifts.

"I have a question to ask."

"All right."

"Did you give Lucien Cross a rubber ball?"

"That's not what I expected you to say. Would you mind showing me some ID?"

I took out my wallet and handed it to her. She carefully examined my P.I. license before picking up the business card I placed on the counter next to the cup. "You saved his life last night. What can I do for you?"

Now that I was here, I wasn't sure what to say. Her straightforward demeanor had caught me off guard. "Did you know he was going to be arrested?"

Her face fell. "No."

I believed her. "Are you privy to any of the details of his case?"

She glanced around, but since shift change had just happened, most cops were too busy getting situated to pay attention to us. "Just the basics." The look on her face told me that was the end of the conversation.

"Why the ball?"

"The benches in the holding cells are hard on his back. He won't complain, but I've known him since he was a little kid. I can tell when he's in pain. He's just too proud to ask for anything. I offered to get him a blanket or see if I could find a pillow, but he refused." She looked at me. "Don't tell him I said this. He'd deny it anyway. But he's scared."

"And angry."

"Wouldn't you be if you were framed for murder?"

"Extremely."

She raised an eyebrow, seeing the look in my eyes. "Why do I get the impression you've had some experience with this?"

Could that be the reason Cross wanted me on this case? I hadn't considered it. No one knew about that. No charges were ever filed. The police who'd been hunting me ended up helping me. But Cross knew a lot about the inner workings of the police department, more than I ever realized.

"Is there anything you can tell me about Cross or Knox that might help?"

The sergeant shook her head. "I'm sorry. I wish I could, but I just cover the desk."

"No problem. Thanks for your time."

"Alex, wait." She swallowed. "I'm sure he couldn't be bothered to say it, but thanks for helping him last night."

"I was just doing my job."

By the time I made it home, Martin was already in bed. Relieved that I didn't have to explain the fresh bruises and scrapes, I found his watch on top of the dresser and took it into the kitchen. Carefully, I removed the back and pulled out the tracking chip from the inside and replaced the cover. In case that asshole used Cross's tech to follow me, I didn't want to risk the same fate befalling Martin.

After that was done, I covered the chip in foil and placed it in a small metal case which was supposed to block radio signals. I didn't know how well it worked, but it'd suffice for tonight. Once I was satisfied I'd minimized the potential threat, I changed into one of Martin's shirts and crawled under the covers. He shifted in bed but didn't rouse. Gently resting my hand on his chest, I closed my eyes, too tired to think and too confused to know where to begin.

When I woke up the next morning, Martin had already left for work. Rolling onto my back, I regretted the move immediately. But the longer I remained, the less I ached. My mind wandered and dread filled me. Did Lucien Cross survive the night?

Corrupt cops who were caught often died in prison. A lot never even made it to trial. Cross wasn't a cop, but his father was top cop. Any repeat offenders Cross encountered would have served their first stint under his father's command. Hopefully, the offenders Cross encountered were as clueless as I'd been, except most of the cops on the force knew Cross. And since a good percentage wanted to mop the floor with him, they'd make his identity known. I had to get him out of there. I just didn't know how.

Dragging myself out of bed, I popped a few pain

relievers, took a hot shower, and slathered on the arnica. After that, I grabbed my notes and studied the case against my boss. The look on his face couldn't be quantified, but he was guilty of something. I saw it in his eyes. Even desperate and losing it in a holding cell, a part of him believed he deserved to be punished.

"Did you do it?" I stared at the paper, hoping it would answer me. But it didn't.

He wouldn't have hired you if he did. Justin's words came back to haunt me.

Ripping the top sheet off my pad, I balled it up and tossed it onto the table. The only way to catch the killer would be to determine who wanted Knox dead. Except I'd already spent hour upon hour digging through the man's background and coming up blank. The police had years to do the same, but they never found anything damning.

Knox had no criminal record. But Cross thought he was involved in smuggling. And since Knox managed to disappear to a tropical island, he must have had already established identities. I just didn't know what they were.

Thomas Gunn, the name ripped through my brain like lightning. That was the alias Knox had used to open the safe deposit box. Back then, banks didn't require as many steps to verify a person's identity, but the man had to provide at least two forms of ID, like a birth certificate, driver's license, or passport.

During my career, I'd come across several expert forgers and paper guys. To fool a bank, the fakes would have to be pristine. I'd have to run the name.

Grabbing my computer, I searched for Thomas Gunn. Several existed, but I couldn't find much on them. I needed resources. Since the police already executed the search warrant, I could use Cross Security resources without issue, so I grabbed the tracking chip from Martin's watch and headed to the office.

Thomas Gunn never traveled to Vanuatu, which meant Knox must have had more than one alias. He must have gotten his papers from a pro, and only so many operated at the level necessary to trick customs. So I called my contacts.

It took the entire morning and most of the afternoon, but I finally tracked down the man who created Thomas Gunn—Barry Chessin. I'd run up against him a few times while working at the OIO. He was an excellent forger. He specialized in fake IDs but dabbled in counterfeiting wine. That's how he'd gotten on the OIO's radar. The best thing about Barry was he kept copies of everything. He liked to admire his art.

When I arrived at the tiny shop, Barry wasn't pleased to see me. But I had enough proof of his illegal activities that he couldn't deny it.

"What other IDs did you make for Trey Knox?" I asked.

"C'mon, Alex, you know me. I'm on the straight and narrow now. Let's not talk about the before times."

"You're right. I do know you." I looked around his shop. "Unless you want me to call my friends and have them examine that printer you have in the back and those inks you have hidden under the counter, I suggest you answer my question."

"I'm not a narc."

"I'm not asking you to narc. Knox is dead."

"Well, no kidding. Why do you think he needed the IDs?"

"Whose idea was Thomas Gunn? That doesn't sound like one of yours."

"It wasn't." He watched anxiously as I moved around his store, which specialized in tie-dye and screen print t-shirts. He should have come up with a better cover for his illegal activities. "Give me some credit."

"Gunn's burned now," I said. "I just want to know what other names this guy might have used. Winchester? Colt? Smith or Wesson?" He rocked on the stool where he had perched. "I'm not on the job anymore. I work private security. We play in the grey too. I bet some of our clients could use a good paper guy. What do you say?"

"It sounds like entrapment."

"Does it? I didn't mean for that to happen. Y'see, that was the carrot. It's much nicer than the stick." I picked a golf umbrella up from the bin, giving it a test swing, like a baseball bat. "The stick's worse."

"What are you going to do? Trash my store?"

"I'm thinking about using your back room as a pinata. I'll just whack away until some goodies fall out. Then I'll call my old pals at the OIO and tell them what I found."

"You'd really do that?" He kept a shotgun behind the counter, but he wasn't stupid enough to reach for it. The last time we played this little game, he'd nearly gotten his head blown off.

"You help me out, and in the future, if someone needs some work done, I'll send them your way. We both win. No one has to know you squealed. Like I said, Knox is dead. Not figuratively, but rotting in the morgue, doornail dead."

Barry got up, flipped the lock on the door, and changed the sign to closed. "Follow me, and leave the umbrella out here."

I put it back in the bin and followed him through the back room. He unlocked a hidden door and led me into the room where he actually worked. Between the amount of paper and ink, business must have been booming.

"You're not printing money, are you?" I felt the paper, but it didn't feel cottony.

"No." He looked up from his computer screen. "For the record, I wouldn't tell you if I was." He hit a few keys. "Thomas Gunn. Phil Namath. Jerry Marino. And Dan Rice."

"Did you pick those names?"

"No, but they were easy enough. And he paid extra to customize. He said since he'd become one of these people, he should get to choose what his name would be. I couldn't exactly argue with that."

"He was a football fan."

Barry studied the names. "Guess so."

Reaching into my wallet, I pulled out a few c-notes and put them on the desk beside me. "Thanks."

"Hey, Alex," he called after me, "let's not meet like this again."

I shrugged. "No promises."

TWENTY-SIX

Every one of Knox's aliases linked to offshore bank accounts with hundreds of thousands of dollars each, but most of the accounts had gone dormant roughly eight years ago. According to passport records, Knox had flown out of the country the day he disappeared under the alias Dan Rice. Rice had traveled to Fiji, where Phil Namath caught a flight to Vanuatu. Talk about multiple personalities.

Knox had gone to great lengths to cover his tracks. When he returned to the country, it wasn't under either of those names. Jerry Marino returned to the city roughly six weeks later.

According to the timeline, that would have been three weeks after Cross went to Vanuatu, and one week after he returned from Nevada. The police would claim this gave Cross the opportunity to kill Knox since they were both in the city at the same time. So I dug deeper.

Phil Namath had booked a flight to Fiji for the ninth but never got on the plane. Since Knox flew into the city on the seventh, more than likely, that two-day window was when he was killed.

Letting out a breath, I checked Cross's records for those dates. According to his calendar, he was in town and met with several corporate clients. That wouldn't exonerate him.

I resisted the urge to call his old clients to ask about his demeanor, but no one in his right mind would remember something like that. Digging through Cross's credit card statement, I found several charges for KC's. But none during that timeframe. Cross could have paid cash, but I couldn't prove it. I doubted Jim Harrelson held on to bar receipts from eight years ago, but I jotted down a note to ask, if all else failed. Cross's cop pals might be willing to alibi him out if it came down to it. But Cross wouldn't like it.

I went back to examining Knox's alter egos. The addresses, phone numbers, and histories appeared to be nothing but bogus, fictitious details created by Barry to match birth certificates, credit cards, and whatever other items Knox requested.

The overseas banks wouldn't give me the time of day, so I called Mark and asked for another favor.

"The OIO isn't your personal research assistant," he reminded me.

"I'll owe you."

"Anything I want?"

"Name it."

"I want you to forgive yourself for what happened. I'm okay. Lucca's okay. And quite frankly, he's a bit miffed you've been ducking his calls. You owe him dinner."

"You want me to pay you back by taking Eddie Lucca to dinner?"

"He was your partner, Alex. Just because things change, it doesn't mean that bond goes away."

"Now you sound like Cal."

"Who?"

I shook my head, even though he couldn't see it. "Never mind."

"You want this done, so I'll do it. But you have to stop staring at me with those big sad eyes of yours every time you see me. You're breaking my heart. I could barely get my steak down at lunch."

"It didn't seem that way to me."

"Alex," he warned.

"Fine. You're fine. Lucca's fine. We're all fucking fine. Now will you look into those bank accounts, or do I have to sing a song and do a dance?"

"No song, but don't forget to ask Lucca when he and his wife are free. You and Martin can take them out."

I ground my teeth. "Fine."

"All right. I'll call you when I know something. What are you doing in the meantime?"

"I'll dig deeper into Cross's affairs and see who he pissed off. It's possible they may have an enemy who overlaps, but Cross didn't think so. Even I think it's a stretch, but if I come across a name that matches one from Knox's list, I should recognize it."

"Just one last question."

"Now what?"

"Why didn't you call Kate Hartley and ask her to do this?"

"She's out of the office this week."

Mark chuckled. "I wondered if you knew that."

"Goodbye." I hung up and went down the hall to speak to Renner.

Almeada hadn't called me today, so he must be busy. But since he gave me a pass to do whatever I thought would be in Cross's best interest, I figured Renner might be able to shed some light on things.

"Enter," he said when I knocked.

"Hey."

He smiled. "Checking up on the progress I've made on the assignment you dumped in my lap?"

"No. I...uh...thought I'd see if you remembered anything else about eight years ago. Do you remember Cross having a beef with anyone? You knew he'd been in a fight. Did you ever pursue that?"

"We didn't find anything. We retraced his steps, but he never got in any bar fights or drunken brawls. He could have been hurt on the job. But we didn't have access to his case files, so that would have been a dead end. Why? What's going on?"

"I just wondered if he had any enemies. We're pretty

sure he must have pissed off the Russians when he called in the tip."

"If they even knew, which is a big if," Renner said.

"Did you ever cross paths with Joe Gallo?"

"Beat cop?"

I nodded.

Renner rubbed his eyes. "Moretti and I spoke to him after Knox disappeared. Wasn't that in the notes I gave you?"

"It was. I just wondered if you ever had any other dealings with him."

"To be honest, I wasn't the type who paid much attention to what the grunts were doing."

From what I'd heard, Renner had been a hotshot detective who didn't necessarily listen to the officers around him. It's how he'd gotten hurt and why Detective O'Connell had warned me to be careful around him when he first learned we were working together. "Do you think you could ask your friends about Gallo?"

He pushed away from his desk, his notes forgotten. "Yeah, I can do that. Do you want to tell me what you're hoping to find?"

"I just want to know if Gallo's a straight-shooter."

"Give me a sec." He picked up the phone and dialed. After asking a few questions, he hung up. "Aside from a few civilian complaints for minor things, his record's clean. No write-ups or commendations. His arrest rate is on par. My buddy says he's just a cop who clocks in and clocks out. No muss or fuss. He doesn't go above and beyond, but he's not parked behind the donut shop for half his shift either."

"What about the civilian complaints?"

"No beat cop serves as long as Gallo without catching a complaint or two. They were investigated."

"What were they for?"

"Unprofessional behavior." Renner shrugged. "Basically, he was rude."

"I might have witnessed a little of that myself."

"Pot meet kettle," Renner teased, earning the opportunity to glimpse my withering stare. "Hey, I'm just stating the obvious." He blew out a breath. "I happened to spot your car on my way in. Does that have anything to do with Cross's case?"

"Yep."

He tried to hide his grin. "That's great."

"Do you want to pay for a new windshield and paint job?"

"No, that part sucks, but it's a lead, right?"

"The guy had his face covered and avoided area surveillance cameras. It's another dead end."

"Maybe not. I took the liberty of checking it out myself. Embedded in one of the scratches was this sparkly thing. I thought it was glitter, so I asked the guys upstairs to take a look. I hope you don't mind."

"It's a waste of time. FBI techs already gave it the once-over."

"Amir found something the FBI missed. He just e-mailed me. Do you want to go upstairs and see what he found?"

"Lead the way."

Renner ushered me out of his office and to the elevator. My gut said this was a waste, but it shouldn't take long. After this, I'd get back to scouring Cross's history for any names that overlapped with Trey Knox or his known aliases.

When we entered the lab, Amir held up a pair of tweezers. "This fragment was embedded in your car door. It appears to have broken off a piece of jewelry. I'd guess a ring."

To the naked eye, it looked like a speck. Amir placed it on a tray and handed me a magnifying glass.

"Is that a diamond?" I narrowed my eyes at the sparkly crystal, which couldn't have been much larger than a grain of salt.

"It's a cubic zirconia." He nodded to Renner. "We never would have seen it if you hadn't pointed out the shine to us."

"The light just happened to catch it right," Renner said.

"Let me get this straight." I peered down at the crystal and glanced at the mass spec report Amir had run on the scrapings from my door where he'd dug out the stone.

Aside from the basic composition of the paint, Amir had found trace amounts of sterling silver. "Someone used jewelry to key my car?"

"Basically." Amir picked up the report. "We didn't find anything else. No prints. No other unusual trace elements. No tracking devices."

"I know. The FBI went over it."

"They missed this." Renner picked up the cubic zirconia chip. "They could have missed more. Though, I can see why this was overlooked."

Most men I knew didn't wear ornate jewelry. "Do any of the guys around here wear rings with stones?"

"No, just wedding bands," Renner said. "Plain, simple. Nothing with gemstones."

Aside from the occasional earring or gold chain, that was the extent of the jewelry I saw around here. Cops didn't wear fake diamond jewelry either, unless they were undercover.

"Any idea what kind of ring it was?" I asked.

"Something like this, with a small accent stone." Amir keyed in some specifications and rows of various styles of class rings popped up.

"What about sports rings?" An image of Knox's prized championship ring popped into my head. The details on the ring had been made with tiny diamond chips.

"Let's see." Amir entered new search parameters, and the screen filled with plenty of options. "It could be a knockoff of one of these."

The fact that the threat had been carved with a ring similar to the one found on Knox's body caused me to shiver. I considered all the possibilities, but Renner hadn't attacked me. I would have recognized his limp. He just happened to be an astute observer. "Did you find anything else, Amir?"

"No, sorry."

"Thanks for trying. And thanks for noticing." Pulling out my phone, I headed for the stairs. When Heathcliff answered, I asked if the police had any special rings for graduating or retiring.

"They look like class rings mostly or a stamp."

"A stamp?"

"With the badge or department insignia stamped onto the ring."

"Anything with cubic zirconia?"

"Not that I've seen. Then again, the women do have more blinged out options, so it's possible."

"But nothing for the men?"

"I'd have to check. Why?"

I updated him on the situation with my car. "Assuming a ring is how the unsub scratched the warning in my door, I'd say he's probably not a cop or working for Cross. They're too macho to wear stuff like that."

"I'd agree." Heathcliff let out a breath. "I don't like that he might have used a ring to do that. It elevates the threat to another level. You need to be careful."

"For my sanity, would you mind checking to see if Knox's championship ring is still in evidence and that the stones in the ring are genuine diamonds?"

"You don't think someone took it out of evidence just to threaten you."

"No, but I want to be sure."

"I'll call you back in a few minutes."

I'd just delved into Cross's client list from eight years ago when my phone rang. "What's the verdict?"

"Knox's ring is here and intact. As far as the techs can tell, the diamonds are real."

"All right."

"You sound disappointed."

If Knox's ring was a fake or had disappeared from evidence, it'd be easier to cast doubt on Cross's guilt and further investigate the possibility a corrupt cop was behind the attack at the precinct. Instead, I had to keep digging. "Do you think another collector could be to blame for Knox's murder? Collectors obsess over these pieces, especially limited edition, championship memorabilia."

"I'll run this up the flagpole and make some inquiries."

"Careful, Detective. It sounds like you're not sure Cross is the killer."

"Whoever attacked you yesterday morning sure as shit wasn't Cross. I'd like to know who it was and what he has to do with any of this before I make a decision."

"It sounds like you have your hands full. Maybe we should skip the meeting tonight."

"Alex, you're making progress. You shouldn't skip out just because things get crazy. That becomes a slippery slope."

"I'll buy some skis."

"I saw the look on your face yesterday. You were playing the what if game. Didn't Cal warn us about doing that?"

"You don't know that's what I was doing."

"We're going to the meeting, but given the circumstances, I don't think I should pick you up at Cross Security. Will you meet me there?"

I let out a sigh. He'd issue a BOLO if I didn't show. "Fine."

"Promise me you'll go."

"I promise."

"Good." I could hear the smile in his voice. "I'll see you later. Let me know if anything comes up."

"Yeah, and you let me know what you find."

"I'll fill you in tonight."

TWENTY-SEVEN

"One of Knox's accounts is still active," Mark Jablonsky said when I answered my phone.

"Which one?" My research into Cross's past didn't turn up any connection to Knox's known aliases.

"Phil Namath's." He gave me the bank information and account number. "Money comes out every month like clockwork. I'm guessing Knox had automatic bill pay set on that account."

"Where's the money going?"

"To a real estate holdings company." He gave me the information. "Aside from that, there have been a few wire transfers. I kicked that over to the boys and girls in financial crimes to analyze."

"Thanks."

"Look, just give me a few days. We have to do this right."

"With court orders and a task force? Cross doesn't have that kind of time."

"He'll get bailed out. Then you'll have plenty of time. Just wait."

"Okay." But I had no intention of waiting. Phil Namath must be paying rent for something. After a lengthy search,

I discovered Knox had rented an apartment under the alias. The lease had been signed eight years ago, on the seventh, the same day Knox arrived back in the city.

Scribbling down the address, I set out for Knox's apartment. I had no idea what I hoped to find. Maybe I'd stumble upon the crime scene. After all, Knox had been killed elsewhere, his body wrapped and dumped at the field near the airport. But I wondered why a man with a house and mortgage would rent an apartment under a pseudonym. He must have been afraid to return to his normal life. That meant he knew the threat remained. The safe deposit box must have figured into it, somehow. If he was that scared, would he risk returning home to retrieve his ring?

The apartment was situated in a seedy neighborhood. My vandalized car fit in perfectly with the graffiti and broken windows. Leaving it parked on the corner, I made my way through the overgrown weeds and around the cracked sidewalk to the apartment complex.

Phil Namath rented unit 3C. Given what I knew about Knox, I couldn't picture the wealthy professional spending any time in this place. This was the exact opposite of the gated community where his alter ego lived.

As I made my way up the concrete steps, a shiver traveled down my spine. Stopping, I looked around. The place was abandoned, like the scene out of some post-apocalyptic zombie flick. Somewhere above me, the staticky electric buzz from a bug zapper sounded. Not even the flies survived around here.

The concrete on the second floor landing had been tagged by several graffiti artists. The skull with the snake coming out of its eye socket stared up at me. Who needs a welcome mat when you have that? The window in apartment 2E had spiderweb cracks in it. The muffled sound of a radio played inside.

Giving the stairs below me another look, I continued upward. The railing creaked under the pressure from my gloved hand, so I pulled away, watching bits of the wall crumble as the rusted joint quivered against the loose nail. The third floor landing had scorch marks on it, like someone had thrown a Molotov cocktail onto the concrete. What kind of place was this?

Again, I peered below me, but no one was around. I stepped onto the third floor. To my left were four apartments. A tricycle with two missing wheels sat outside 3F. 3C was to my right.

I knocked on the door, standing close to the wall in case my interruption was met by gunfire. But no shots rang out. I tried again, but as I suspected, no one was home. After glancing around to make sure there were no security cameras, I reached for my lock picks.

I'd just inserted the tension tool when footfalls sounded behind me. As I shoved the picks back into my pocket, the handrail let out the same whine, followed by a loud thunk which echoed against the concrete floors and walls.

I kept my eyes on the stairwell while I casually unzipped my purse and tucked my gun into my bag, so I could keep my hand on it without being obvious. People lived here, but the graffiti and decay had made me nervous.

The footsteps grew louder as the man made his way toward me. The stairwell kept him in shadow, but as soon as he emerged, I recognized him.

"What are you doing here?" Detective Heathcliff asked, appearing just as jumpy.

"I'm working. Why are you here? Did Mark call you?"

"No." He glanced around. "The unsub who attacked you escaped in a white sedan. We finished scrubbing the DOT footage. We lost track of the car somewhere in this neighborhood. I've been knocking on doors in the hopes someone might recognize the car."

"I just came up the stairs. I didn't see you."

"I'm on my way down." He eyed the door behind me. "What's so special about this apartment?"

"I'm not sure."

But he didn't believe me. "Is anyone home?"

"I knocked, but there was no answer."

Heathcliff moved toward the door, forcing me to stand behind him while he listened for sounds coming from within. When he didn't hear anything, he knocked again.

"Did you run the VIN? Is the car still here?" I asked.

"I couldn't find the car. By the time I got here, it was gone. I must have just missed it. I called dispatch. Patrol will keep an eye out. Meanwhile, officers will scan the current DOT feed to see if they can figure out where he's going now."

"This would be easier if we had a plate."

"No kidding."

Again, I shivered. Normally, things like this didn't bother me, but this case had me on edge. Ever since I arrived, I'd felt eyes on me, which was ridiculous since no one was around. Maybe it was the threats or fear of what I'd find inside the apartment that was messing with my head.

"Who's the apartment registered to?"

"Phil Namath."

"Is that name supposed to mean something?" Heathcliff peered into one of the windows, but he couldn't see anything through the blinds. "You never told me why you're here. How did you find this place?"

"Knox had several aliases, each with overseas accounts. One of them remained active. Apparently, the rent is automatically drafted from his account. I didn't find any mention of a car though."

"You're sure Trey Knox and Phil Namath are the same guy?"

"Positive."

"How does a dead guy, whose body is in the morgue, key your car and drive away?"

"That's a very good question." A door slammed somewhere below us. "The better question is where's the guy who keyed my car. You said he came here after attacking me. Does he live around here?"

Heathcliff pressed a finger to his lips and edged toward the stairs, peering down them. "Someone's below us. Stay here. I'll be right back."

I moved half a step forward, but Heathcliff gave me a warning look. "Parker, do not make me cuff you to the railing."

Holding my breath, I strained to hear what was going on. Every cell in my body wanted to go with him, to help if he encountered a problem, but he told me to stay. A moment later, I heard him announce himself.

"Excuse me, ma'am, I'm looking for a man who drives a white sedan." He described the car.

"I don't know who that is."

"What about the man who lives in apartment 3C?"

"I've never seen him," she said. "I don't know what he drives. Why are you asking?"

While they were talking, I went back to work on the lock. Thirty seconds later, the knob twisted. After stowing my picks, I removed my gun. Since the man who attacked me had come to this neighborhood, I had to be careful. He wouldn't surprise me again.

The door creaked. Great, so much for a stealthy entrance. The room was too dark to see inside. Feeling along the wall, I flipped the light switch. A lamp turned on in the corner, illuminating a large display case which took up the entire side wall. Glass doors protected the items inside. Signed jerseys, game balls, baseball cards, and other collectibles were on display for the world to see.

This had to be the right place. Trey Knox was an avid collector. This must have been whatever he salvaged from the break-in or bought to replace his lost collectibles.

Carefully, I checked the rest of the apartment. The one-bedroom had plenty of square footage. A leather couch, wood table, and giant flatscreen TV filled what remained of the main area, making up the living room and dining room. The bedroom had a king-sized bed, silk sheets, and a matching dresser set.

Tucked in the top drawer, beneath a row of neatly folded tighty whities, was a jewelry box. It reminded me of the case which housed Martin's watches and rings. I opened the box. Six championship rings, similar to the one found on Knox's body, glistened up at me. Did all of this belong to Knox?

The rings had different years stamped on them. Each looked slightly different than the previous one, but they were similar enough. How many of these did he have? Why would he risk retrieving the one from his house when he had others?

Closing the box, I moved into the bathroom. The cracked tiles reminded me this wasn't a high-end apartment. Water dripped at a slow, steady pace from the faucet. Drip. Drip. Drip. The utilities must be included in the rent.

I opened the medicine cabinet, finding the basics. Oddly enough, none of the toiletries had expired. Replacing the shaving cream bottle, I closed the cabinet, noticing some gunk around the side of the sink.

Returning to the bedroom, I opened the closet door. No clothing hung inside. Instead, I found surveillance photos of Lucien Cross plastered to a giant corkboard. Notes hung beside the photos with dates and times listed. What was this?

I scanned the board, finding photos of my boss with sunglasses, his nose taped. Another photo showed Cross, his eyes surrounded by sickly yellowish-green skin as he left the hospital.

The dates didn't include the year, but the photos must have been taken eight years ago. The one in the top right corner showed Cross getting behind the wheel of an unfamiliar car. It wasn't his Porsche, but he didn't drive that eight years ago.

The next row of photos caught Cross as he exited KC's bar. I checked the date and time. Assuming I had the year right, that would have been taken the day after Knox returned to town. Did Knox take these photos?

Based on his pseudonym's travel itinerary, Knox wasn't around when the first three photos were taken. Or was he? I crouched down to get a better look at the bottom row. The one in the middle showed Cross leaving the bank where Knox opened a safe deposit box. Was that taken this past Monday? I couldn't find a corresponding note to go with the photo.

My blood ran cold when I saw the final image tacked on the end. It was taken at the construction site where Knox's body had been found. Cross wasn't in the picture. I was.

Knox couldn't have taken these photos, at least not the last two. But this apartment was leased to one of his aliases. The sports items appeared to be part of Knox's collection. What was going on here? Who was using this apartment? Who even knew about it?

The doorknob twisted, and the floorboard creaked. "Parker?" Heathcliff hissed. "Are you in here?"

I emerged from the bedroom, finding him standing in the doorway. "You have to see what I found."

Heathcliff surveyed the apartment, refusing to cross the threshold. "How did you get inside?"

"The door was unlocked."

He gave me a look. "I can't enter without a search warrant."

"So wait there." I moved into the kitchen and opened the fridge. "The milk hasn't expired." This didn't make any sense. "Someone's living here. There are photos in the closet of Cross and one of me. That's how recent they are."

"Out." Heathcliff jerked his thumb backward.

I shut the fridge and checked the cabinets. Lots of canned and packaged meals lined the shelves. Whoever was using this apartment had made himself at home. "The man who keyed my car must be staying here. Do you think he assumed Knox's fake identity? Could he have killed Knox? Maybe he's framing Lucien."

"Even more reason to do this properly."

"The photos mean something. You need to see them." Going around the counter, I tripped on the edge of the area rug, catching myself before I faceplanted. I bent down to straighten the upturned corner. Beneath the fringe, a large stain covered the cheap flooring.

I rolled back more of the area rug, revealing an orangey-pink stain. It covered several feet in a roughly oval shape. The center had the darkest hue, the stain growing lighter at the edges. Since the floor was a beige linoleum, the rug was the only way to hide it. "I think Trey Knox was murdered here."

Heathcliff put his hand on the outer edge of the doorframe and leaned forward as far as he could, hoping to see what I'd found. "Are you sure?"

"The floor's been scrubbed, but this looks like blood to me."

"That doesn't mean it's Knox's."

"No, but he rented this apartment. The display case is full of sports memorabilia. And based on the lack of blood at the scene and the way Knox's body had been wrapped in a tarp, we know he wasn't killed at the airport."

"Parker, move your ass. I'm not telling you again." Heathcliff straightened and stepped away from the door.

Unsure if someone was coming, I flopped the rug back into place and met Heathcliff outside the apartment, shutting the door with my gloved hand. He walked the length of the exterior corridor, making sure no one had been spying on us. Once he was certain the coast was clear, he called the precinct. Pointing to me, he said, "Get Jablonsky to forward the details to Moretti. I want everything you've got on Phil Namath and this apartment."

I was certain Mark had already done it, but despite that, I obediently made the call. "Now what?"

"Until the ink dries, we'll hang out here." He glared at me. "You should know better. You could have compromised the scene and the integrity of the case."

"I didn't do anything. The door was unlocked."

"What happens if I search you? What will I find?"

"I'm not a cop, Derek. I don't have to play by the rules."

"When I'm around, you do."

"It's not like I removed evidence or tampered with the scene."

He let out an exasperated grunt. "Tell me about the photographs."

"In the closet, there's an array. They have notes with month and day, even the time, but no year. Except the last few. Those don't have any notes, and they're recent."

"You said he took one of you."

"At the field by the airport. It was focused on the construction site, but I'm in the corner of the shot, talking to the guys who dug up the body."

"That's the same day the note was left on your car. I don't like this."

"Neither do I, but it might prove Cross is innocent."

TWENTY-EIGHT

A patrol car arrived. One of the officers grabbed the roll of yellow police tape from the trunk while the other headed up the stairs to meet us. Heathcliff's badge hung from the chain around his neck.

"Did you call for a warrant?" Officer Swenson asked.

"Yes." While Heathcliff went over the situation with the officer, another patrol car pulled up. Two more officers got out of the car. "Is the mobile crime scene unit on the way?"

"They'll be here. They're just wrapping up a homicide." Officer Swenson handed him the paperwork. "You want us to work crowd control?" Swenson glanced over the railing at the ground below. Aside from the woman Heathcliff spoke to earlier, only three other people had entered or left the apartment building while we'd been waiting.

"Keep your eyes peeled for a white sedan." Heathcliff gave him the specifications on the car and described the suspect.

Before he finished, Swenson's partner came up the steps with the roll of police tape looped around his forearm. "You again?"

With his uniform and sunglasses on, I didn't recognize him at first. "Officer Gallo?" His presence made me twitchy. "What are you doing here?"

"My job." He tucked the stem of his glasses into his collar, the sunlight catching on his ring. Last night, I'd barely glimpsed it and had mistakenly assumed it was a wedding band since he wore it on his left hand. I hadn't noticed the piece of onyx in the center or the small crystal pieces in the corners of the signet ring.

"Nice ring."

Gallo resisted the urge to hide his hand away. "Uh-huh."

Heathcliff turned toward us, glancing at Gallo's left hand. "That is nice. I'd be afraid it'd get damaged on the job."

"I'm not too worried," Gallo said.

Heathcliff continued to eye it. "Is the stone cracked?"

Gallo laughed it off, palming the tape and wrapping his hands around it to hide the ring from our view. "That's why I'm not worried. It's been like this for years."

"How'd it happen?" I asked.

"I cracked it against a handrail while chasing a suspect down some stairs." He glanced at the stairwell he'd just ascended.

Heathcliff scanned the search warrant. "How do you two know one another?"

"We met at a bar," I said. "It turns out Officer Gallo knows Lucien."

"Small world." Gallo eyed me, annoyed that I'd let the cat out of the bag. "I've worked with Commissioner Cross on a few occasions."

"Really? So you're a family friend?" I asked.

Gallo's look could have hardened the melting icecaps. "Detective, how wide do you want the perimeter?"

"I just need to search the apartment, so you can station yourself out here and make sure no one interferes. Should anyone exhibit an unhealthy fascination with what's going on inside, get a name and contact information." Heathcliff tucked the paperwork into his pocket. "I'll perform a walkthrough while we wait for CSU."

"Not a problem." Gallo gave me another look, making his disdain known. I hadn't realized just how much I'd pissed him off the previous night. "Is she staying?"

"No, she's not." Heathcliff's eyes communicated more than enough. "This is police business. Alex isn't a cop. She knows she can't enter a potential crime scene."

"What is she doing here, anyway?" Gallo asked.

"Don't worry about it," Heathcliff said. Since I knew him so well, I noticed the shift before he grinned. "I'll see you later, babe." He kissed my cheek. "Don't forget we have plans tonight."

"How could I forget? You won't let me."

On my way back to the car, I wondered if Heathcliff would have let me stay if Gallo hadn't shown up. Gallo's presence made me uneasy. He made his dislike for me obvious, but that wasn't the problem. It was the damn ring on his finger. I didn't notice it was damaged, but Heathcliff did. Could Gallo be the man who attacked me? The one who took off in the white sedan? He showed up at the crime scene, and he knew Knox and Cross. Could he be operating out of the apartment?

Renner's police pals didn't have anything negative to say about Gallo, but walking the beat and patrolling the neighborhoods for over a decade could take a toll. I'd have to do a deep dive on him. I hadn't bothered to do much digging since I'd been busy with other things, but Gallo checked one too many boxes. Idly, I wondered what Jade would have to say about him.

Another thought came to mind. Since Gallo tipped Cross about the discovery of Knox's body and the safe deposit box key, Gallo must have known Cross would go to the bank. He might have been the only person who knew he'd do that. Did Gallo take the photos? Was all of this an elaborate setup to frame my boss?

Reaching for my phone, I called Mr. Almeada's office, but his secretary said he was in court. I didn't know if that had anything to do with the arraignment or bail hearing, so I asked her to have him call me back.

When I'd spoken to Cross, the only cop he named as a friend was Sgt. Rostokowski, and he'd warned me not to do anything that would harm her or her career. Since Cross trusted her, maybe I could too. Unfortunately, her shift ended early this morning.

By the time I reached my car, I decided I'd just have to dig up whatever dirt I could find on Gallo by myself. Justin said they traded favors. Perhaps Gallo would tip off Cross Security on occasion just to keep tabs on Lucien, in case my boss ever reopened the Knox investigation. But all of this was conjecture. Still, it was the first time in days I had a lead, even if it pointed a finger at a cop. Luckily, Heathcliff had caught on to the oddities too. Moretti wouldn't be able to dismiss my theory so easily with Heathcliff backing me.

I'd just opened my car door when I noticed a folded piece of paper on my seat. Picking it up, I read the message. *Since you came to see me at home, I should return the favor.*

I looked around, but I didn't see anyone nearby. Heathcliff said the white sedan had been tracked to the area, but he didn't spot it. Maybe he overlooked it. Or maybe Gallo was the creep who left the note. I'd seen him pull up, but he took his sweet time meeting us upstairs. Did he have time to leave the note, or could his partner be involved?

Keeping my head on a swivel, I checked every cross street and nearby garage, but I didn't see a white sedan that fit the description. The unsub didn't bother with the theatrics this time. But the note on my seat had done more to freak me out than anything else. It had to be the message. Now, this was personal.

Considering how long Heathcliff and I had remained outside the apartment, anyone could have left it. But my money was on Gallo. I hated to think one of the cops who showed up to help was responsible, but it fit.

On my way back to the office, I stopped by the OIO to have the note fingerprinted, but it was clean. After that, I checked Gallo's schedule. He'd just gotten off shift the night Cross was attacked. That gave him enough time to get changed, grab the lieutenant's credentials, and storm the holding cells. Before sullying a man's good name, I had to be sure. So I found Gallo's address and went to check out his place.

*　　*　　*

Gallo's apartment would put Oscar Madison to shame. Dirty clothes, abandoned dishes, receipts, mail, and various takeout containers cluttered every visible surface. This looked nothing like the organized and maintained apartment I'd just left.

Inside the gym bag next to the pile of laundry and discarded dumbbells, I found body armor—vest and helmet. Is this what the unsub wore when he stormed the precinct? After taking a few photographs, I searched for smoke grenades but didn't find any. I'd need something more than body armor if I wanted to prove Gallo had something to do with Knox's murder. Even if Gallo didn't kill Knox, he had everything at his disposal to frame Cross.

Murder would be a harder sell when it came to convincing Moretti or the DA's office, but if Gallo confessed to setting Cross up, my boss could go free. But aside from finding the same popular brand of shaving cream and toothpaste in Gallo's bathroom that I'd found in Knox's secret apartment, I had nothing else connecting the two besides the body armor.

Maybe Amir could link the cubic zirconia chip stuck in my door to the cracked stone on Gallo's ring, but to do that, we'd need a warrant. To get that, I had to convince someone Gallo was guilty. The way Heathcliff acted before I left Knox's apartment told me he might be on board, but we'd still need proof.

After leaving Gallo's apartment, I went back to Cross Security and spoke to Justin. He didn't know anything else about Joe Gallo besides what he'd already told me. I would have asked Renner what he thought, but he was out of the office, taking care of the security assessment I'd originally been assigned. Luckily, I had two e-mails waiting for me.

I quickly scanned the names, hoping to find Joe Gallo on the list Jade had sent. She'd ranked the names in order from those closest to Scott, from his former partners to his training officers to his best friends. Near the bottom, I found Gallo's name. He and Scott had gone to the academy together.

Rocking back in my chair, I wasn't sure what to do with

this tidbit of information. I'd need Gallo's records. Renner might be able to pull some strings and get them for me, or I'd ask Heathcliff. This could prove motive, at least for the frame job. I wasn't convinced a cop killed Knox, but if he had, that would explain how the murder weapon ended up inside Cross's SUV. Was Gallo a liar and a killer?

My head spun, my thoughts branching off in every direction. The second e-mail came from an unfamiliar address. After clicking the tab, I realized it was from Sara Rostokowski. She apologized for her unhelpfulness, said she was sure Lucien was innocent, and wanted to know if there was anything she could do.

Since she was the only cop Lucien said he trusted, I asked her for Gallo's work schedule and to find out where he'd been patrolling when the notes and vandalism had occurred. My gut said he had to be in the area, just like today. But I couldn't prove it yet. Hopefully, that would change.

Before I hit send, I stared at the screen, wondering if creating an electronic trail was a good idea. I wasn't doing anything illegal, but what I was asking Rostokowski to do could get her in trouble. Cross would not be pleased. But he'd be free, which meant he could give her a job if things went south. "Forgive me," I muttered, clicking the button.

She wouldn't have offered if she didn't want to help. Still, a pang of guilt gnawed at my insides. This is why it wasn't safe for people to be around me or to help me. I was toxic.

As if reading my mind, Heathcliff called. "I saw the photos. CSU is bagging and tagging everything. They think the stain beneath the rug is blood. But due to the amount of bleach, other cleaning agents, and the time that has elapsed, they can't pull DNA from it."

"I'm not surprised." But I wished for better news. "Did they find anything else?"

"They dusted the place for prints, but everything's been polished and shined, even the TV remote. The toiletries have been confiscated. If we get lucky, we might get DNA from them."

"What about hair clippings? I saw shaving cream."

"Yeah, maybe. The bedding is also a possibility. They'll let me know. But DNA will take time unless we have something to compare it to."

"How about starting with Joe Gallo?"

"Parker, let me handle it."

"You saw his ring. Don't you think—"

"I do. I got this." He sighed. "Did you know Cross had gone to the bank the day before we opened Knox's safe deposit box?"

I didn't say anything.

"Dammit. That's important."

I swallowed. "Gallo tipped him that Knox's body had been discovered."

"How? We checked phone records."

"Gallo called Justin with the news."

"Cross's assistant?"

"Yeah."

Heathcliff cursed. "Is there anything else you haven't told me? Anything at all?"

"Gallo has body armor. I can send you a photo. I don't know if it's the same as what the unsub wore, but—"

"Send it, and don't tell me what you had to do to find this out."

"But you just said to tell you—"

"What else?"

"That's all I know."

"Are you sure?"

"More or less."

"Fine." But it didn't sound that way. "We'll talk about your creative approach to crime-solving tonight, after our meeting. And I'll fill you in on what CSU's found."

"What are you going to do about the photos?"

"Cross will be brought to the precinct to answer more questions once we determine where and when they were taken. He has some explaining to do about the bank. If someone is setting him up," Heathcliff wouldn't say Gallo's name when other cops were around, "the more forthcoming he is, the better our chances will be of investigating that claim further. Understand?"

"Yep. Oh, there's one other thing."

"What now?"

"The bastard left another note." I told Heathcliff all about it and promised I'd be careful. As soon as we hung up, I tried Almeada's cell phone. When he answered, I told him everything.

TWENTY-NINE

The last thing I wanted to do was go to a meeting, but Heathcliff said we'd talk afterward. So I'd go. Identifying the man who attacked Cross and threatened me wouldn't prove my boss's innocence, but it'd reopen the investigation to other possibilities. Almeada had strategies in mind. I'd let him deal with the legal issues. I wanted to find the truth, preferably before the unidentified bastard decided he should pay me another visit.

Before leaving the office, I removed the bandage from my face and caked on some concealer and foundation. According to Cal, getting into altercations could be a trigger or symptom of the emotional turmoil caused by grief. The way I saw it, a scrape was just a scrape, especially under these circumstances, but I didn't want to deal with the pointed stares silently nudging me to share with everyone else.

I hated these meetings, but I had to do something. Until things had devolved to a point where I couldn't tell my nightmares from reality, I never would have admitted I had a problem. Then again, admitting there was a problem was the first step to recovery. So I guess I was making progress.

When I arrived, I didn't see Heathcliff's car. I checked

my messages, but he hadn't sent any texts or made any calls. Since I was early, I waited. Heathcliff might have parked elsewhere. But wouldn't he wait for me at the doors? We should have come up with a better plan.

My phone buzzed. *Heathcliff.*

"Where are you?" I asked.

"I can't make it. There's too much going on with the apartment and the things you said."

"That's fine." I stuck the key back in the ignition. "I'll meet you at the precinct."

"No, this is police business. You can't be here. You work for Cross, remember?" The bitterness crept into his tone. He was angry I hadn't told him everything sooner. "We have to get the evidence processed, and I have to check into a few things and hammer down this timeline. We'll discuss everything tomorrow, once I know more of what's going on."

"What about Gallo?"

"I'm looking into him. Just keep your head down and stay out of trouble. Do you think you can do that?"

"You know me."

"Which is why reinforcements are on the way."

"What does that mean?"

"You'll see. Now suck it up and go inside. You promised."

I put my phone on silent, checked my face in the mirror, and took a deep breath. A part of me wanted to escape. This was the first time I had the option without someone forcing me to go in. I could leave. It was my choice, but those two words stuck in my head. *You promised.*

I stood near the door while I debated with myself, knowing how ridiculous I was acting. This was good for me, even though it hurt. And it did, more than almost anything else.

Surely, my time would be better spent tracking Gallo and figuring out how he set up Cross. My thoughts went to dark places. A twig snapped nearby, and I spun, expecting to find Gallo sneaking up behind me.

"Sweetheart, whoa. It's okay. I didn't mean to startle you." Martin rubbed his hands gently up and down my sides, careful to avoid my bruises. "You look like you've seen a ghost."

"What are you doing here?" This must have been what Heathcliff meant by reinforcements. "Did Derek call you?"

"Don't be mad. I offered to fill in for him tonight. I didn't get to see much of you yesterday."

"I can't believe he did this. Shouldn't you be at work?"

"We'll talk about that later." Martin gently enveloped me in his arms and kissed my temple. "Come on. We're going to be late."

"But—"

"I'm here, beautiful. You don't have to face this alone." He ran his thumb along my cheek, frowning at the powder covering his fingertips.

I let him lead me down the stairs and through the door. By the time we set foot inside the room, the meeting had already started. Martin ushered me into one of the chairs against the wall and sat beside me. Obviously, he and the detective had discussed strategy. I didn't like this. I felt like a cow being herded to slaughter.

Martin gripped my hand, and I stared at the floor in front of Cal's feet, where he stood beside the podium welcoming the new faces in the crowd, sharing his story, and explaining the focus of today's session. For the first forty minutes, I kept my mind on Cross's case. I didn't want Martin to see how much these meetings affected me. So distractions were good.

Would it be dark enough when the meeting let out that Martin wouldn't notice the threat etched into the side of my car? Maybe we could go out a different door. How many doors were in this place?

The sound of strangled sobs drew me from my thoughts. My insides clenched, and I gripped the side of my chair. "I just miss him so much," the woman said. "Every day I can't help but think if I'd gone around back, he'd still be here with his family. I should have died. Not him. I wish I could tell him I'm sorry. That it's my fault."

Those words ripped through me. I'd thought them so many times.

"Do you think that's what he would want? Do you think

he blames you?" Cal asked.

The woman stared at him. "Why wouldn't he?"

"Would you blame him if your roles were reversed?"

"No," she let out a shaky breath, "but it's my fault."

"He was your partner. Do you think he sees it that way?" Cal looked around the room. "Does anyone have anything to add or offer?"

A younger guy who had never spoken before told her that he'd felt the same way when his convoy had been attacked during a supply run, but he realized his friends wouldn't have blamed him. He just blamed himself. Several others chimed in, offering up their own struggles in support. She didn't need her partner's forgiveness. She needed to forgive herself.

Based on experience, it was never that easy. Frankly, I preferred holding on to the anger, but that wasn't healthy. Admittedly, most things I did weren't healthy. So I went back to the tried and true technique of avoidance and shifted my focus to wondering if any of the exits would prevent Martin from seeing my car. The last thing I needed tonight was explaining the threat scratched in the paint.

"We have a few more minutes. Would anyone else like to share? This is a safe space." As usual, Cal's gaze stopped on me.

I tilted my head, so I could stare at the wall, uncomfortable with the scrutiny. Martin lifted my hand to his lips and kissed my knuckles. Then he released my hand and stood up. I reached out to tug him back into his seat, but Cal had already seen him.

"Step right up." Cal surrendered the podium.

"This is the first time I've been to one of these," Martin said. "I'm not sure if this is appropriate, but I'd like to say something." He stared at me. "The last words I ever said to my father were out of anger." His face contorted, and he swallowed. "Two weeks later, his car went off the road. It had been raining that day, and he'd been drinking. The police said he probably passed out behind the wheel. There were no tire marks. He never tried to brake." Martin licked his lips, his voice low and pained. The few times he'd spoken about his parents, he always sounded like that.

"When the autopsy report came back, it showed he was barely above the legal limit." He let out an ugly laugh. "My father knew how to drink. He could hold his liquor. He didn't pass out. It wasn't late at night. It was the middle of the fucking day, so it's not like he fell asleep."

His jaw clenched, and he tore his eyes off of me and stared at the wall behind my head. I wanted nothing more than to wrap my arms around him and hold him. After a few seconds, he found my eyes, as if staring into my soul.

"No report will ever say this because of who he was, but he killed himself. And I spent a long time believing that was my fault. I blamed him for not being around when my mom died. I was so angry at him for all the things he did and didn't do. I wanted him to suffer. I didn't realize until after he was gone that he had been suffering. He avoided dealing with her illness and the reality of it to protect himself. I understand building walls and distancing yourself. I get that. But it's okay to ask for help. It's okay to grieve. You don't have to do it alone. That's what he did, and it destroyed him. It almost destroyed me too."

"Martin," I mouthed.

"The guilt ate at me for a long time. I hid from it with work and booze and women. Anything to distract me from it. Eventually, I realized the truth. It wasn't my fault. But that didn't lessen the loss. Time helps, but it never completely goes away. I worry about history repeating itself. I'll do anything to make sure it doesn't."

"It won't," I whispered, knowing he'd understand even though he couldn't hear me.

Martin cleared his throat. "Yeah, that's what I came here to say."

Cal thanked him, and Martin retook his seat. My heart ached, physically ached. These stories always broke me, but now I couldn't tell what was my pain and what was his. When he hurt, so did I. My insides were trapped in a vise. He gave me a reassuring smile, even though it looked sad, which only made me want to cry.

I didn't notice the meeting had broken up until Cal clapped Martin on the shoulder. "Thanks for sharing, sir. Some of the folks want a quick fix, a magic formula that will make everything better. It helps to hear how others have persevered. Are you still struggling? Is that why you sought us out?"

"Actually, I came to support someone else but felt inspired, given tonight's topic."

"You're welcome to join us again, anytime." Cal offered his hand, and I pulled mine free from Martin's grasp so the men could shake. Cal nodded to me. "Tell Derek we missed him tonight."

"Yep," I said, finding the pattern on the floor fascinating.

After Cal moved on to speak to someone else, Martin buttoned his jacket. "Would you mind if we skipped the bar tonight? I have to catch a flight to L.A. early in the morning."

"After that, you're leaving?" The walls were closing in, so I jerked my head toward the door and stepped out of the room. As soon as we got outside, I sucked in some deep breaths. "Does your need to take off to L.A. have to do with Cross?"

"That why I wanted to spend some time alone with you. We didn't get to talk last night. I wanted to tell you about my trip." Martin stopped beside the passenger side of my car. "Alex, your car."

"Yeah, I know." I didn't care. Right now, my internal organs were being crushed. "It doesn't matter." I wasn't sure L.A. mattered either. What he said inside the meeting was the only thing I could think about.

Before I could articulate my thoughts, he asked, "Who did this?"

"I have an idea, but I'm not sure."

"Are you in danger?"

"No." Maybe.

He took the keys from my trembling hand. Marcal had parked the town car a few spaces away. Martin's bodyguard, Bruiser, had come along for the ride since this wasn't necessarily the best neighborhood. "Jones," Martin said, "would you mind taking Alex's car back to the apartment?"

"Sure thing." Bruiser eyed me. "Ms. Parker, are you all

right?"

"Ask me tomorrow." I pulled open the back door of the town car and slid inside.

Martin gave Marcal our destination and joined me in the back seat. He put up the privacy window. "I hate to spring this trip on you. If there was any way I could get out of it, I would. But I'm looking for new backers. Papers were drawn up today, severing Martin Tech's relationship with Cross Security due to ethics violations on Cross's behalf. They aren't signed, but it's best to be prepared. I have to find another partner as soon as possible if there's any hope of salvaging the project and the research."

"Martin, what you said in there..."

He brushed my hair out of my face. "I know. I shouldn't have. But you never listen. I wanted you to hear what I had to say. You're not alone. You don't have to confide in the detective if you don't want to. You have me." He stroked my cheek. "Drop everything and come to L.A."

"I can't."

"Sure, you can."

I wrapped my arms around him, relieved when he returned the embrace without wincing. At least his shoulder didn't hurt. "Stop." Tears welled in my eyes, but they weren't for me. They were for him. "I can't do this right now. Not after that."

"L.A.?"

"Martin, you just dropped a bomb on me. You wanted to talk, so talk. I'm listening."

He worked the muscles in his jaw. "I said what I had to. It's over. We don't have to talk about it ever again."

Clearly, I hadn't cornered the market on noncommunication. "I'm sorry about your dad, that you had to go through that." It explained so much about his work ethic, drive, and sexual history. That was why he worried so much about me. "I'll never leave you, not like that. I promise. I never meant to make you think that. I'm not suicidal. You can read my psych evals."

"I know." But he didn't, or he wouldn't have stood up in front of a room full of strangers and said what he did. A few minutes later, the car lurched to a stop. Martin peered out the window. "We're here."

"Where?" Maybe he changed his mind about getting a drink. I could crawl into a bottle right about now.

He brushed a stray tear off my cheek. "You'll see." He opened the car door, and I stepped out and stared at the sign.

"Tell me they serve liquor."

"Nope. Just ice cream."

On autopilot, I followed Martin inside. The bright colors and sweet scent did nothing to cheer me up. From what I could tell, the vibrant atmosphere had only made Martin sadder. When we made it to the front of the line, he ordered a jumbo banana split with chocolate sprinkles and extra maraschino cherries. Then we took a seat at a tiny booth in the back corner.

Even though we'd made fun of couples who sat on the same side of the table, he sat beside me and put his arm around my shoulders.

"Why did you bring us here?" I asked.

"When I was a kid, my parents used to take me here whenever I had a bad day. We'd get a banana split to share and talk about whatever had me bummed—a bad test grade, not winning a swim competition, a girl turning me down for the school dance."

"That last one never happened."

"It did. Vanessa Hamilton, seventh grade." He stared across the room, seeing it the way he had as a child.

"Tell me about them. Or him. You rarely talk about him."

"Y'know, I've never told anyone about my dad before. My lawyers advised me not to discuss it or question the findings. The life insurance wouldn't have paid out, and it would have turned into tabloid fodder if it was ruled a suicide."

"Is that why you felt compelled to share it with a room full of strangers?"

"I wasn't telling them what happened." Martin turned in the booth to face me. "The only person I was talking to was you." He toyed with a strand of my hair. "I understand a little of what you're going through. You shouldn't blame yourself, but you have to reach that conclusion on your own. So I'll pick you up after meetings or go with you or hold you while you cry yourself to sleep. Whatever you need me to do. I just wanted you to know that."

That's when the tears fell, and I buried my face in his shirt, hoping he hadn't noticed. "Damn you."

When the waitress came, he thanked her. After offering me a spoon, which I declined, he took a few bites. "Is the person who keyed your car the same one who put the bruises on your back?"

"I fell down the stairs," I said. "I didn't lie about that. But someone pushed me. Well, kicked me. Maybe that's why my chest hurts so much. I'm not sure if it's the same guy, but everything indicates it is." I'd have to remember to tell building security to notify us if any cops showed up.

"And this connects to Lucien?"

"Yes. I found some things today which indicate he's being framed."

"By the person who said he warned you?"

"Probably."

Martin finished another spoonful and asked for a container so we could take the rest home. "Is that why Heathcliff couldn't make the meeting?" She came back with four cardboard cartons, and he handed her a hefty tip for her trouble.

"Uh-huh."

"Okay." That eased Martin's nerves. "Let's go home."

By the time we arrived, I'd come to several conclusions. Martin was suffering too. He had been the entire time.

"The reason you worry about me not coming home is because of your dad. That's why you went through that rough patch after I'd been abducted," I said. "It all stems from that."

Martin popped open one of the lids and grabbed a spoon, letting me know he didn't want to discuss this topic any further. "Probably."

"Why didn't you tell me this before?"

He dug out a piece of banana. "Because you'd say you'd never hurt yourself."

"I wouldn't."

"Not intentionally, but we both know you run into danger, not away from it. And when shit goes wrong, you run faster." He stuck the spoon in the container and pushed it toward me. He tugged the wedding band off his finger and read the inscription. "But you'll always find your way back, so I'm not worried."

"Then what was tonight about?"

He didn't say anything, but his green eyes spoke volumes. He'd done it for a reason. I just wasn't sure what that was. "You should have some of this. It's really good."

"That's it? End of discussion?"

"Yep."

"Remember this moment the next time you badger me about not telling you something."

"Like how someone keyed your car?"

Grabbing the container, I scooped up a spoonful of ice cream and took a bite. It wasn't vodka or rum, but it dulled the ache in my chest. Perhaps the cold would numb my insides completely if I ate enough of it. After a few more bites, I put the container down. It wasn't working. "Are you mad at me?"

"No." He studied my face carefully. "Were you in a fight?"

"A minor altercation with a garbage man. The police, FBI, and Cross Security are all over this. It's being handled." As if to prove my point, I took off my shoulder holster and gun and placed them on the counter. "What time's your flight?"

"Six a.m." He exhaled. "Do you need to pack?"

"I can't go with you."

"Why not?"

"You know why." I nipped at his earlobe. "You have work to do, and so do I."

"We agreed work doesn't come first."

"It doesn't." I looped my arms around his neck.

"Will you be okay while I'm gone?"

"Yes." I licked the ice cream off his spoon before kissing him. "Y'know, the ice cream was a good idea, but I know something else that'll make us feel better. Are you game?"

Passion ignited in his eyes. "I didn't think you'd be in

the mood."

"It's either that or we can work our way through your liquor cabinet. I'll let you decide."

THIRTY

Martin nuzzled my shoulder, causing me to giggle. "Are you okay?"

"Shouldn't you have asked me that an hour ago?" I pulled the covers up, turning around in order to kiss him.

He pulled back, a satisfied smile on his face. "We were too busy for words an hour ago. I meant are you okay with me leaving?"

"It's work. You have to go. I have plenty of things to keep me busy." Thoughts of Cross behind bars came to mind. "Cross is the one you should worry about."

"Let's not discuss him right now." He kissed along my collarbone and up the column of my neck.

Closing my eyes, I snuggled closer to him. He pressed his lips against mine before shifting away from me. "Where are you going, handsome?"

"I have to get ready. Marcal will be here in forty-five minutes to pick me up."

The clock taunted me from the nightstand. "What time are you meeting your potential new partner?"

"Noon, L.A. time."

"With a six hour flight—"

"It's more like seven."

"But with the time difference, it's only four. That means you don't have to leave until eight." I traced the lines of his ribs and gave him my best bedroom eyes. "It's your jet. It leaves when you want."

"Temptress." He hovered over me, supporting his weight on his forearms and brushing my hair out of my face. "Are you sure you can't come with me?"

"You know I can't."

He touched the tip of his nose to mine. "I'll call you tonight, once I get settled at the hotel."

"You're not going there first?" I reluctantly allowed him to pull away and climb out of bed.

"It depends on what time I land. I have to stop by the L.A. branch of MT before meeting the potential investor for lunch. The sales director set this up, so I'd like him to brief me on the situation and go over tactics. I don't want to walk into the negotiation cold."

"In that case, come back to bed. It's nice and warm right here."

He laughed, watching my eyelids flutter. "I love you. Now get some sleep."

"But you're leaving."

"I'll wake you up before I go."

Closing my eyes, I rolled over onto his pillow and fell into oblivion. The floor beside the bed creaked as Martin dragged his suitcase behind him. He left it outside our bedroom before coming back to kiss me goodbye.

"Be careful," I said.

"You too, sweetheart. Stay away from the crazies."

"I'll try."

"After Marcal takes me to the airport, he'll go grocery shopping. I'll tell him to be quiet and not to wake you. Would you like him to take your car to the body shop?"

"No, I'll do that myself."

We said our goodbyes, and Martin headed for the door. I was asleep before he even left.

A little while later, I heard a noise in the kitchen. *Marcal,* I thought. The cabinets opened and closed, followed by the fridge. The coffeemaker beeped, indicating it'd just been turned on. Marcal didn't normally make coffee. But it had been an early morning. He might have needed the pick-me-up.

But his footsteps didn't sound quite right. The soft thuds on the hardwood floors could only be made by designer Italian leather. Perhaps Martin forgot something or decided to take a later flight. The scent of freshly brewed coffee wafted into the bedroom. I smiled, wondering if Martin's lunch meeting got pushed to dinner instead. Either way, I should get up and find out what was going on.

Pulling on his shirt, which had been draped over a chair, I stepped out of the bedroom and headed for the kitchenette. I just turned the corner when the barrel of my gun stopped me in my tracks.

Lucien Cross sat at the counter, the gun aimed in my direction while he checked the sights. "I was wondering when you'd wake up."

"How did you get in here?" I took half a step back, my hands at shoulder height. "Building security should have notified me."

"Take it easy." Cross concentrated on lining the shot up perfectly. My backup was in the nightstand. I wouldn't make it to the bedroom before he shot me.

"Are you freaking insane? The neighbors will report gunfire."

Cross lowered the gun. "I'm not going to shoot you, Alex. Jeez. You act like I broke in to kill you. Building security let me in."

"Why? No one's allowed in or out without being on the list, and even then, the doorman will call up to the apartment to announce a visitor." Cross wasn't on the list. He shouldn't be here.

"You're forgetting something." He loaded my gun, then changed his mind, ejected the magazine, and cleared the chamber. "After that incident with the arsonist, Cross Security signed a contract with the building manager to assess risks and safety. I told him I stopped by this morning to perform an equipment check."

"That doesn't explain how you got into my apartment or why you're here."

"Isn't it obvious?"

I edged backward, aware of the gun at his hip. Even if my nine millimeter was unloaded, his wasn't. He'd been pissed about Jade. Was he really going to make good on that threat? Or had I read the entire situation wrong? Was Lucien Cross a killer? "You were in desperate need of caffeine and every shop and store in the city ran out of coffee?"

"You could use better locks. And your sights are off. A hair to the right, I'd say."

"I'll get right on that."

"There are more important things for you to get on, like finding Knox's killer." Reaching over, he picked up a scrap of paper. "But apparently you were too busy getting on something else last night."

My face flushed, realizing Martin had left me a note. "That is none of your business." A sick thought wormed its way through me. "Where's Martin?"

He cocked a surprised eyebrow at me. "I was about to ask you the same thing." He flipped the note over. "It doesn't say. But he refers to you as a goddess. Want to see?" I remained frozen in place, aware of his right hand, resting inches from his holster. He glanced down; vicious amusement danced in his eyes. "Are you afraid of me?"

"You threatened me."

"Do you honestly think I came here to kill you and decided to make myself some coffee while I waited?" Slowly, he removed the gun from his hip and placed it on the counter beside mine. He held up his palms. "I won't hurt you, Alex. It wounds me to learn you think so little of me. From what Lt. Moretti said earlier this morning, I thought you finally believed me. You found photos indicating someone's framing me, or have you forgotten?"

Moving closer, I snatched his gun off the counter, unloaded it, and placed it out of reach. "You broke in and pointed a gun at me. What do you expect?"

He ignored the question. "The cops trashed my place. They tore everything apart. I'm surprised they didn't slash my mattress while they were at it. The office isn't much better. Almeada warned me to stay away from there. That bastard Knox really fucked up my life. It's a good thing he's dead, or I'd kill him."

"And you wonder why I'm nervous around you."

"I didn't do it," he snapped. "I take it you told the cops about my trip to the bank."

"I didn't have a choice. They found a photo in Knox's apartment. We have a lot to discuss."

"That's why I'm here." He turned his gaze to the fridge. "Do you mind if I eat while we talk? I haven't had anything in days."

"They didn't feed you?"

"Poison probably." He stared at the box of cereal on the counter. "May I?"

"Help yourself."

He opened a few of the cabinets until he found a bowl, poured some cereal into it, and opened the fridge. "Do you have anything besides creamer and 2%?"

"No."

"It'll do." He poured the milk into the bowl and grabbed a spoon from the dish rack. His eyes raked up and down my body. "You must have worked up an appetite. Want to join me?" He chomped down on the cereal, polishing off the entire bowl in a matter of seconds before going back for more. "James never struck me as a chocolatey marshmallow cereal guy."

"The cereal's mine."

Lucien shoveled a spoonful into his mouth. "That makes sense. He strikes me as more of a bran flakes or shredded wheat kind of guy." He eyed the boxes of sugary cereals lined up on the counter, which Marcal had bought for me. "Do you do the grocery shopping? Is that what makes you a goddess?"

It was a good thing he unloaded my gun, or I would have shot him. Picking up the note Martin left, I blushed a little at what he'd written. "This is private. You had no right."

"Like you calling Jade?"

"I get it. You wanted to embarrass me. Congratulations, mission accomplished. Are we even now?"

"I suppose." He continued to wolf down the cereal. When he finished, he picked up the bowl and drank the chocolate milk. After wiping his mouth with the back of his hand, he sighed. "Before coming here, I spoke to Justin. Do you have any idea who attacked you?"

"The techs pulled a cubic zirconia chip out of one of the deeper scratches. It could have broken off of someone's ring."

"The asshole's sending a message by using a ring to threaten you."

"Lucien—" I stopped myself, unsure if I should continue.

He scrutinized me and cleared his throat, his gaze resting on the tops of my thighs, reminding me I was wearing nothing but one of Martin's shirts. "You have every reason to be nervous, Alex. You were shot not that long ago. I shouldn't have barged in here and startled you. For that, I apologize. I'm just not sure what to do. The cops found an apartment that belonged to Knox. Someone's been staying there. They've ruled me out since I've never been there, but they still don't know who it could be. Do you?"

"I'm not sure."

"What do you mean you're not sure?" He snorted. "Oh, I get it. You're not sure if you should trust me."

"I saw the look on your face when the police came to arrest you. That's the look of a guilty man."

"Hardly." Cross inhaled an uneasy breath. "I'll say it one last time. I didn't kill Knox."

"Did you hire someone to do it for you?"

He pressed his lips together, his hand going through his hair. "No, I did not."

"The gun that killed him was found in your armored SUV. You let the security teams use that for high risk clients. The gun could belong to one of them, if it's not yours."

"Cross Security does not offer wet work as one of our many services." He fought to remain calm. "I find it troubling the gun was found in that SUV. Only someone with access to vehicle registrations would know that's my car, not the company's. How exactly does a murder weapon find its way into my trunk? Knox's killer has to be close, unless the police are doctoring evidence. Have you verified the ballistics reports yet?"

"I haven't seen them."

"That'll be one of the first things Almeada asks for." He reached for his phone and sent a text. "Someone's framing me. Don't the photos prove it? The same person must know you're looking into it. That's why he threatened you too."

"Not many people fit that bill."

"Do you have a suspect in mind?"

I tugged on the hem of my shirt, growing increasingly uncomfortable. "Joe Gallo."

"Go get dressed. We have plenty to discuss."

THIRTY-ONE

I went over every aspect of my investigation with Cross. He rubbed furiously at the stubble on his chin while I spoke, as if the friction alone would make the hair disappear. When I was finished, he helped himself to another cup of coffee.

"That explains a lot," he muttered.

"Is it possible Gallo's setting you up?"

"Anything's possible. He's a cop. I wouldn't put it past him. Did Sara e-mail you his schedule yet?"

Opening my laptop, I logged in to find it waiting. "He was on duty the morning I was attacked. If he did it, his partner would have to be involved too."

"That would give Gallo a perfect alibi."

"It could be circumstantial." I gnawed on my bottom lip, wondering what Heathcliff had uncovered. "Isn't Joe Gallo your friend?"

"That's far too generous a designation. We trade in favors." Cross shook his head. "Not even. He just calls us with tips if a client gets arrested or finds himself in a sticky situation. Gallo even throws work our way, on occasion. None of that is reciprocated."

"Why do you think he does it?"

"Out of some kind of misguided loyalty to my father." A

dark cloud formed over his head. "Gallo worked the original break-in. He had this weird fascination with Knox. It's like the man never dealt with an unsolved case before. He's a career patrolman. He doesn't work investigations, so I don't know why he obsessed over that one. The only thing I can think of is because I was involved. He must have figured it'd ingratiate him to the commissioner."

"Do you think that's all it was?"

"I'm just calling it like I see it. You don't know what it's like to carry around this name."

"Do you think Gallo could have followed you out of the country and made the recording of you and Knox?"

"No, I'm guessing Knox filmed that himself."

"Would Gallo have killed Knox to protect you?"

He squinted at me. "Protect me from what?"

"Knox mentioned your involvement with the Russians. You still haven't told me what that's about. You said once you were out, you'd tell me whatever I wanted to know. I want to know this."

"I'll answer on one condition."

I knew I wouldn't like it. "What's that?"

"Nothing I say leaves this room. It's for your ears only."

"Fine."

"I'm serious." His eyes smoldered, warning me not to mess with him.

"What did you do?"

"What had to be done." He cleared his throat and ran a hand through his hair. "Knox fucked with some scary people. A woman was killed as a warning to me. If I'd realized what was going on, maybe I could have saved her. But by the time I found out who Knox had pissed off, it was too late. She was dead, and I was next. I did what I had to in order to survive."

"You killed Vasili Petrov."

"Not directly. A gang killed Petrov in a drug deal gone wrong." Cross put his bowl in the sink, ignoring my questioning gaze. "It's possible I may have set those events in motion."

I knew it but refrained from shouting it out. "Could the gang have anything to do with Knox's murder?"

"No."

"Why not?"

"Knox didn't do business with them. His contacts were overseas. He used Petrov's network to create his own smuggling empire. I can prove it."

"How?"

"Like I mentioned before, Knox kept a ledger. He used to keep it in his office. Before he disappeared, he had his assistant deliver it to his house. He couldn't leave without that. His entire business was in that book. I just don't know where it is. If we find it, we'll probably find the killer."

"Is that why you went to the bank? You thought he had it in his safe deposit box?"

"I didn't know what he had in there. We didn't end things on good terms. You heard what I said to him. I thought he might have tried to implicate me, fabricate evidence, create a bullshit theory that I worked for Vasili. I knew as soon as his body was discovered, the police would come knocking. I had to know what he had on me."

"So you broke into his safe deposit box?"

"Obviously not," he growled. "Gallo told me they found a key on the body. When he described it, I knew what it was. I went to the bank as soon as my meeting ended, but I couldn't get the lock open."

"Did anyone else know you were going to the bank?"

"No one knew. I didn't mention it to anyone before I went. Afterward, when I realized my mistake, I spoke to Mr. Rathbone about keeping sensitive materials locked in a bank vault via a safe deposit box. I told him I'd do some checking and let him know what I found. But that was after, not before."

"Gallo knew you'd go. He fed you the intel. He must have taken the surveillance photo of you, unless you told someone else about the key."

"Only Justin, but he wouldn't do this."

"You used car service to get there."

"I always use car service for meetings. It gives me time to prep and adds some class to the operation."

"When did you tell your driver you were going to the bank?"

"Right before we went to the bank. He didn't photograph me, Alex. I would have noticed."

"What about the rest of Cross Security? You hire and train the best. The techs routinely ping phones and monitor a vehicle's GPS data."

"An employee isn't behind this."

Everything about the situation pointed to Officer Gallo. I knew it last night, and that hadn't changed. But I wanted to be careful. Cross's biases would get in the way of rational thought. "This takes us back to my previous question. Do you think Gallo could have killed Knox?" I asked.

"I don't know. Since Knox made his money moving product, I always figured it was a matter of time before he ripped someone else off and got a bullet to the back of the head because of it."

"Instead, he got four to the chest, his fingertips and molars removed, and his skull crushed with a brick."

"Clearly, he pissed someone off."

"Someone who didn't want his body identified but who was stupid enough to leave Knox's most prized possession with the remains. How does that make sense?"

"It doesn't," Cross said. "Just like the murder weapon turning up in my car."

"Could Gallo be on the take?"

"It wouldn't surprise me."

"Do you think he'd frame you after he spent the last eight years kissing your ass?"

Cross laughed. "From what you've told me, Gallo makes the most sense. But if it's not him, it has to be another cop. Someone he knows. Someone who could feed him the information to give to me. It's the only explanation for the gun found in my SUV. One of them planted it. The police found the key in Knox's shoe. They're the only ones who could have put the bank under surveillance before they opened the box."

Despite the fact I'd reached the same conclusion, I couldn't help but play devil's advocate. "The police aren't the only ones who would have known. You're forgetting about the killer. He would have known what was going on. The airport construction's been highly publicized. He couldn't move the body, but he could wait and see what would happen and then alter the evidence."

"He'd have to know the key was in Knox's shoe. If he knew that, why would he leave it there?" Cross asked a good question; one I couldn't answer. He pointed a finger in my face. "See, you can't argue with my point."

"Then how did the murder weapon get inside your car?"

"Isn't it obvious? The police must have found it, held on to it, and once they connected it to Knox's murder, one of them planted it in my car."

"Yes, and Area 51 houses little green men."

"They're grey. And who's to say it doesn't?"

"You can't just say shit like that. You need proof. We have to find something irrefutable or help the police realize they have a corrupt cop among them. But that's infinitely harder since you admitted to wanting Knox dead on camera."

"That's not a crime. Had I known what would happen, maybe I would have killed him. At the very least, I would have paid more attention to the enemies he was making."

"You knew someone would come for him."

"Anyone who ever met Trey Knox knew that. He was a greedy, selfish prick with a gambling problem and a sports addiction. It was just a matter of time before he ended up underwater because of his wagers or because he scammed someone else. Petrov would have killed him." Cross's cheek twitched. "I should have let him."

I scowled. "So much for wishful thinking."

We spent the next few hours going over my notes and running checks on each of Knox's known aliases. Since Cross knew the man, the little things might mean more to him than they did to me, but he seemed just as clueless. Everything hinged on the apartment Knox had rented. But Heathcliff had yet to call with an update. I wasn't sure if it was because he was mad or busy, but I didn't like waiting.

"You've done a lot of work on this," Cross said.

"That's what you pay me for. By the way, I'm billing you for my windshield and a paint job." Going to the fridge, I pulled out the leftover box of pizza, placed it on a pan, and put it in the oven to reheat. Since it was already noon, I reached for the phone. "Give me a few minutes to see what kind of progress has been made on Knox's bank accounts."

Cross nodded, wrapped up in studying the evidence against him.

Mark promised he'd call once he had some info on the bank accounts, but it had been twenty-four hours. I should have heard from him by now.

When he answered, he sounded tired. "Namath's cash transfers went to betting sites. He must have put the cash into an online account reserved for gambling. Other than that, the only money that went out of the account was to pay the rent. Based on the cash transfers, they look like they might have been automatically drafted too, but it's hard to tell. Financial crimes is looking into it. I passed it along to Moretti. They'll need court orders to gain access to the gambling site's account information."

"Do you have any idea where Knox's aliases amassed their wealth? The accounts he had in his name were never touched and remained until his sister emptied them."

"The transfers into the accounts came from all over the place. Always substantial figures, and always from numbered accounts. Several of them are Swiss. Others trace back to the Cayman's. Two of them link back to the Mexican cartel. This Knox guy had connections to everything."

"Including the Russians?" I asked.

"Uh-huh."

"What about other crime families?"

"We're still deciphering it. Since Knox's other accounts have been dormant for so long, a lot of the numbered accounts closed years ago. So far, we've positively identified a few transfers from the Irish mob. But the intel's too old. A lot of the players involved are no longer breathing or in prison."

"Any transfers to or from local accounts? Maybe something linking Knox to Joe Gallo?"

"Moretti told me about your theory. They're investigating. You need to stay out of it. I'll let them know what I find."

"All right. Keep me looped in."

Mark grumbled. "What you meant to say is you've done your part and you're going to stay out of it, so the professionals can handle it."

"If that's what you need to tell yourself."

When I hung up, Cross looked up at me. "Anything?"

"Not yet, but the aliases I found for Knox might be the tip of the iceberg. The OIO found other accounts with equally suspicious names attached to them. The money transfers into the accounts came from several organized crime families and the cartels."

"Sounds like Knox had quite the business." Cross removed the pan from the oven and put it on the counter, helping himself to a slice. I'd never seen him eat so much. In fact, I wasn't sure I'd ever seen him eat before. "Do you think this will lead to anything?"

"I wouldn't count on it."

Cross chewed thoughtfully. "Where did you find the photos? Detective Heathcliff said you brought them to his attention, but he didn't elaborate. They were in the apartment, right?"

"Hidden in a closet."

"How did the place look?"

"Tidy. Minimalist, except for the large display case in the living room. It took up an entire wall. It had backlighting and everything."

"What was in it?"

"Sports memorabilia."

"That sounds like Knox. It even sounds like the way his house was decorated." Cross squinted. "The killer must have been afraid to sell off the collection for fear someone would link it back to Knox."

"Maybe." Before I could say anything else, the intercom buzzed. I went to the wall and pressed the button.

"Derek Heathcliff is here to see you," the doorman said.

"Send him up."

Cross picked up my files and notes and tucked them beneath the couch cushion. He flipped the whiteboard around and scanned the room for anything else the police might be able to use against him.

"Relax. Derek's here to help," I said.

"When this is over, you and I will have a long discussion about your naiveté. In the meantime, excuse me while I make myself scarce. Call Almeada when you're done playing cops and robbers. He'll let you know where I am."

"What about your phone?"

"I'm not using my phone, and given how you've failed to listen to any of my requests, I'm not trusting you with the number to my burner."

"Fine, but you should stick around. You might possess vital intel."

"I'll chance it." He loaded and holstered his gun. Then he grabbed another slice of pizza for the road. Just as he opened the door, the elevator arrived on the twenty-first floor. Heathcliff stepped out, uncomfortable to see Cross leaving my apartment.

"Do I want to know?" the detective asked when I ushered him inside, watching Cross as he stepped into the waiting elevator and pressed the button.

"Probably not."

He cocked an eyebrow at me. "Is everything okay?"

"I woke up to Cross in my kitchen, so not really. On top of that, Martin left for Los Angeles this morning, and I'm still pissed about last night."

"Martin said he'd fill in."

"Oh boy, did he ever." I waved off his question. "Right now, I don't have the mental or emotional capacity to deal with that. Tell me what you found in the apartment that was so important it kept you from our support group meeting."

THIRTY-TWO

"You know I can't do that."

"Derek," I wheedled, "you wouldn't have found the apartment without me."

He took a seat at the counter and rubbed his eyes. "Did Cross say anything to you about the photographs?"

"Just that he's not sure who took them. We ran through the possibilities on the one of him exiting the bank. He's certain Gallo's the only person who could have done it."

"Okay."

"What do you think?"

"Gallo was on patrol when your car was vandalized and you were attacked. He and his partner weren't on a call and didn't respond to any during that timeframe. However, nearby security cams can't place him, his partner, or the patrol car in the area. According to dispatch, they were parked fifteen blocks away."

"Doing what?"

"Getting breakfast."

"Do you buy that?"

"I don't know. I spoke to Officer Swenson. He said Gallo's been acting secretive lately. Gallo had something to take care of that morning. Swenson didn't know what that entailed. But Gallo stepped away to use the john, and he didn't come back for forty-five minutes. He could have made the trek to the bank to find you."

"What about the white sedan? Could he have driven away, ditched the car, and backtracked to Swenson in that short amount of time?"

"See, this is why I'm not sure what to think of Gallo. Without a plate or VIN, we don't have much to go on. DOT cams never saw the driver exit the vehicle. He drove it into a blind spot. The area around that apartment doesn't have a lot of traffic or security cams in the area. It's easy for someone to disappear if he knows where the blind spots are."

"Do you know if Gallo has access to a white sedan?"

"He drives a red SUV. But anything's possible."

"What about the body armor?"

Heathcliff stared at the counter, barely nodding. "It matches."

"That's something."

"Maybe."

"And the ring?"

"I got a better look at it after you left. It's missing two CZs from opposite corners. There's supposed to be four total that punctuate the corners of the rectangle. The rest of his ring is pretty banged up. Tons of scratches."

"Did you notice any paint transfer from my car on it?"

"No, CSU would have to find that. And I wasn't about to ask him to hand it over. We're not ready to tip him off yet."

"We? Did Moretti go to IA with this?"

"They know what we suspect. They're looking into the possibility."

"Does that mean the charges against Cross will be dropped?"

"Not yet."

"But shouldn't this clear him?"

Heathcliff stared into my eyes. "Why?" I opened my mouth, but Heathcliff held up his hand. "The murder weapon was in Cross's SUV." He had me there. "Consider this. Cross and Gallo cross paths after the break-in at Trey Knox's house. They find out Knox is involved in criminal activities, possibly organized crime. Instead of turning Knox in, Cross does something stupid. Knox threatens to blackmail him. Cross kills him and gets Gallo to keep tabs on the case. As soon as Knox's body is found, Gallo contacts Cross. But Gallo grows a conscience or he's afraid Cross is going to cut him out of whatever arrangement they have, so Gallo keeps an eye on Cross and makes sure we have enough evidence to take Cross down if it comes to it."

"Why threaten me?"

"He didn't want you to learn the truth."

"That's your theory?"

"Isn't it possible?" Heathcliff asked. "Depending on how we twist the evidence, it could fit. Until we learn more about Cross's connection to Gallo or until we positively identify Knox's killer, Cross can't be cleared. The suspicion remains. The murder weapon was in his possession."

"There has to be some sort of explanation for that. Every member of Cross Security who accessed that SUV swore there was no gun in the truck. How did it get there?"

"That's your job to figure out."

"Fine, so why is Cross walking around free if you think he's so dangerous?"

"His father made sure the bail hearing got pushed up. He was released last night."

"I bet he was thrilled when you picked him up this morning to answer more questions." That explained why Cross ate breakfast here. "Did he cooperate?"

"More than I expected. He must see this as the light at the end of the tunnel. He wants to put this behind him. But he's cagey. He's hiding something. I know it."

"What he's hiding isn't relevant."

"Let me be the judge of that."

I shook my head. "What do you need from Cross in order to make this go away?"

"We have his bank records. If he paid Gallo, we'll know about it."

"Cut the crap, Derek. There are too many of these weird coincidences. Someone on the force is framing Cross. You know it. I know it. Moretti knows it. Why are we still playing this game? If I were the one accused, this wouldn't be a discussion. You'd set me free and assign a detail to watch my ass."

"It's possible someone on the force is sabotaging our case against Cross. At this point, I could argue either way." He glanced at the whiteboard flipped to the blank side.

"Is that really what you believe?"

He sighed. "The evidence is inconclusive. Yes, I think someone wants Cross to get caught for murdering Knox. Lucien is not stupid enough to leave evidence, like the ring, with the body, but at the same time, I'm not convinced he didn't kill Knox, clean up the mess, and someone else went behind him and planted evidence."

"Wow, and people think I'm a conspiracy theorist. You and Lucien have a lot more in common than I thought."

He rolled his eyes. "What you fail to realize is things are complicated when it comes to Lucien Cross. His father is the police commissioner. And in order to avoid scandal, the law has to come down harder on Lucien than anyone else. His son won't get the benefit of the doubt. The commissioner wants proof of his innocence before we kick him."

"What if you don't find it? This goes to trial and Cross gets sentenced for something he didn't do?"

"If we're this conflicted, the jury will be too."

"Derek, at that point, he'll lose everything."

"He'll maintain his freedom."

"At what cost? Cross Security would no longer exist. Clients wouldn't trust their security to a suspected murderer, specifically one accused of killing a client. We can't let it come to that, not unless we're sure."

"Do you want to share your progress with me?"

"I've told you everything I know."

"Cross was here. He must have said something to you."

"He's innocent."

"Is that you talking? Or him?" He gratefully accepted the coffee I poured for him and took a sip, giving it a funny look. "Is this a different roast?" He peered into the cup.

"I don't think so."

"It's smoother, like the way Martin makes it. His always comes out like the fancy café on the corner. Yours tastes more like it'll keep me up for the next seventy-two hours. This is a little bit of both. Did Cross make it?"

"It's not poisoned. I've already had three cups."

"Should I ask why you need so much caffeine this morning?"

I turned my head, hoping he wouldn't see me blush. At least I'd hidden Martin's note before the detective could read it too. "Martin's flight left at six a.m. We didn't get much sleep."

"What time did you leave the bar?"

"We didn't."

"No wonder you didn't get much sleep."

"No," I laughed, "we didn't go. We got ice cream instead." I opened the freezer, finding the four take-home pints. "Would you like some? He ordered this jumbo banana split that was meant to feed the entire table."

"No, I should head back soon." He assessed me, watching curiously as I opened the lid and took a spoon out of the drawer. "Did you go to the meeting?"

"We went." I swallowed. "Cal said to say he missed you."

Heathcliff smiled. "Sounds like Cal, so you spoke to him?"

"Briefly, just as we were leaving." I ate a spoonful, wondering how Martin was. He hadn't wanted to talk about what he said in group after we left, but he took me for ice cream. He must have wanted to talk more about it, but after his brief reminiscence down memory lane, he dropped the subject entirely. And he said I avoided things. He flew across the country to avoid this.

Getting up, Heathcliff crossed the room and lifted the couch cushion. "What's this?"

"My notes and files."

He skimmed them, but I told him everything I thought was relevant. "Gallo graduated from the police academy the same year Scott Renwin did. Renwin's the cop who died in that shooting involving Cross."

"Yes, but the records are sealed on that. Scott's ex-girlfriend gave me that connection. It's not much, but it could be motive. Then again, Gallo's been sucking up to Cross for years. He could be eyeing a promotion or hoping to get into the commissioner's good graces. Like you said, it reads either way."

He moved beside me. "Listen to me. None of the evidence adds up. You know it, and I know it. The department has a problem. The simplest solution is to take Cross down for Knox's murder and pretend everything is fine. But it isn't. Moretti and I are working to figure out what's going on and who's pulling the strings. But we can't do that unless we have the whole picture. Get Cross on board. Tell him he has to cooperate. Get him to come clean on whatever it is he's hiding."

"He's helping, Derek. You just don't see it, but he is. He wants to know who killed Knox just as badly as you do."

He pointed at the files Cross had hidden in the couch. "That is not helping. Helping would be staying here to discuss matters."

"I'll keep you updated."

"Like you did with the apartment? Or Gallo tipping off Cross? Or the bank?"

"I told you eventually."

"Tell me first next time."

"Will you do the same?"

"I can't," he said.

Neither could I. "Any idea who left the most recent note in my car? My money's still on Gallo."

"We saw them arrive. I'm not sure he had a chance to do it."

"Maybe he did it before they parked in front of the apartment complex. But I take it there weren't any cameras around."

"That'd be correct."

"Has CSU finished with the apartment?" I asked.

"More or less. We have a surveillance team keeping eyes on it. Since it appears someone's been staying there, we'll catch him if he returns."

"Yeah, if he doesn't already know you're staking out the place."

Heathcliff studied me. "You really think it's Gallo?"

"I don't know who else it could be."

THIRTY-THREE

My stomach was in knots. The sooner I figured out what was going on, the sooner everything could get back to normal. I just hoped everything would be okay when the dust cleared, and I wouldn't lose any friends over this.

When I arrived at Almeada's law firm, I found Cross sprawled out on the sofa with his eyes closed. He'd taken the time to shave. "What did the detective have to say?" he asked.

"Not much."

"I'm shocked," he deadpanned, pulling himself into a seated position. "Let's pay Gallo a visit."

"Are you insane?"

Cross cocked his head to the side. "He's the logical choice. No other cop knows that much about me and my involvement with Trey Knox."

"Are you sure? What about Moretti and Renner?"

He laughed. "You want to go after Dominic Moretti?"

"No, that's not—"

"That's exactly what you said."

"I was making a point."

"Not a very good one." He went to the mini bar and filled a glass with soda water. "And we both know it's not

Renner."

"Renner didn't attack me, but he could have hidden the gun in your SUV."

Cross drained the glass and put it down on a coaster. "Bennett wouldn't do that. Hurting me would only hurt him. One of the assholes who served the warrant planted the gun. Did you ask Detective Heathcliff if Officer Gallo was involved in the search?" Cross waited, but I didn't say anything. "That's what I thought, which is why I took the liberty of pulling our security feed. Gallo was there. He did this."

"You're sure?"

"Damn near."

"I still don't understand why he'd frame you or wait so long to do it." But everything indicated Gallo threatened me. I couldn't fathom why he'd tip off Cross only to knife him in the back. "Where would he even have gotten the gun? Are you saying he killed Knox?"

"Have you checked his alibi?"

"We don't have a TOD."

"But it's reasonable to assume it happened during that two-day window. Gallo was around. I remember seeing him at KC's bar one of those nights. As I recall, he'd been giddy about something."

I narrowed my eyes. "You really remember that?"

"Sure, why not?"

But I didn't buy it. "Lucien, pointing fingers isn't going to clear you. We need proof."

"Gallo kept tabs on Knox's house. Knox was buried with his championship ring. The only way he got that was by going home. Moretti had to divert resources to other cases. The police were no longer staking out Knox's place. As far as they were concerned, Knox was a nobody. But Gallo had that sick fascination. He kept tabs. I know he did."

"Can you prove it?"

"After I returned from my trip to see Knox, I ran into Gallo at the bar. He told me he was monitoring Knox's house. He hadn't stopped investigating. He wanted to find out what happened to the man. That's when I said he shouldn't worry about it anymore."

"Gallo never mentioned that part to me."

"Why would he?"

The more I thought about it, the less sense everything made. "Fine, so Gallo spotted Knox sneaking into his house. He followed him to the apartment Knox rented under an alias. Then what?"

"Gallo confronts Knox. Knox freaks. They get into a scuffle, and Gallo shoots him. It could have been self-defense."

"Four times in the chest?"

Cross shrugged.

"Where'd he get the gun? He didn't use his service piece. If it was an accident or self-defense, why wouldn't Gallo report it?" I asked.

"How do you think it'd look?"

"It's more than that. What aren't you telling me, Lucien?"

"After I left your apartment, I dropped by the office to pull the surveillance footage. That's how I found out Gallo had stopped by Cross Security to execute the search warrant, except according to Sara, Gallo wasn't assigned to do that. That got me thinking. So I went home and checked my security system. Gallo paid me a visit too. But by the time he went to my apartment, the police had already finished clearing the place."

"That was the same morning I was attacked outside the bank."

"The way I see it, Gallo dropped by Cross Security, overheard you on the phone with Almeada, and went to stop you. That delayed him from getting to my apartment, especially since he was on shift and had to make an appearance with his partner in order to keep his alibi solid." Cross sunk into Almeada's office chair and clicked the mouse a few times. "Check this out."

I stared at the screen, watching Cross's front door open. It was Gallo. He wore his uniform, hat, and sunglasses, just like he had when I ran into him at the apartment. According to the timestamp, this happened late in the afternoon, approximately around the time he took his dinner break.

"Watch." Cross let the footage play, pointing to the screen when Gallo unbuttoned his uniform shirt and pulled a leather-bound portfolio out. He glanced around the apartment, went to the bookcase, and laid it flat on the top shelf. "He just planted evidence."

"What is that?"

"Knox's ledger."

"How did Gallo get it?"

"I'm guessing he's had it ever since he confronted and killed Knox."

"Where is it now?"

Cross jerked his chin toward the door. "I gave it to Mr. Almeada, along with a copy of the security footage from my apartment. Building security can verify it, along with nearby CCTV feeds. He's presenting it to the authorities."

I stared at Cross, making the conscious effort to keep my jaw from hanging. "Why didn't you start there?"

"I don't think it's enough," Cross said. "That's why I want to confront Gallo before the police give him a chance to talk his way out of this. He's a fucking liar. My involvement with Knox is well known. It's a cold case, which remained open. I was the prime suspect. Hell, I might have been the only suspect. When Knox's body was found, Gallo saw an opportunity to use it to his advantage to set me up."

"Why?"

"Cops want revenge on me. In case you haven't noticed, I'm a troublemaker. You read Jade's e-mail." He didn't bother concealing his annoyance. "Gallo and Renwin went to the academy together. He probably figured he'd get close to me and wait for an opportunity to present itself. The police and their misguided loyalty. My history and involvement with Knox fit perfectly into his plan. That's why the setup is also perfect."

"How would Gallo have gotten access to the surveillance footage of you threatening Knox?"

"It could have been an accident. It must have already been in the safe deposit box. Bank records show the box hadn't been accessed since it was opened. Knox must have done it. We didn't end things on good terms. Gallo got lucky there. But like I told you, Gallo tipped me to the bank. Only he could have known I'd go there. Even if the box turned out to be a dead end, he had photos of me entering and leaving the bank. He could have said I stole the evidence. That only feeds into this bullshit conspiracy theory and forwards this ridiculous narrative. Gallo's done everything in his power to make me look damn suspicious."

"You chose to go to the bank," I pointed out.

He exited the paused surveillance footage. "Do you know what else I found when scrubbing the security feeds?"

"What?"

"The white sedan. It's gone to the same places Gallo has." He stared at me. "Now can we go see him? The police should be knocking on his door as soon as Mr. Almeada finishes with show and tell. I'd like to stop Gallo before he makes more evidence disappear or finds creative places to put it. I can't afford more marks against me."

"What evidence? What else is there?"

"The ledger contained a list of account numbers. Most were for Knox's clients, but Knox used so many aliases and so many accounts, he jotted down who paid which of his aliases and which account it went to. Two of those accounts were emptied." He met my eyes as he pushed away from the desk. "You didn't find them all, but you found a few. Two that you missed were transferred to offshore holdings belonging to an LLC which was created by Joe Gallo seven years ago, right before he popped back up to offer me help with troublesome clients and pass work my way. He thought I might be on to him. That was his misguided attempt to keep tabs on me."

My boss loved the conjecture, but this was the evidence we needed. Gallo had a lot of explaining to do. "All right. Let's go." Grabbing a pen and the pad of stationery off Almeada's desk, I jotted down a note of where we'd be, folded the paper, wrote Almeada's name on the front, and tucked it beneath his keyboard. In the event things went south and the police arrested us for interfering or worse, Cross's attorney would have some idea of what happened.

"I told Justin to pull all the footage from the office and

garage, dating back as far as we can go. Gallo didn't usually drop by. He knows I have a no tolerance policy when it comes to cops snooping around, but he must have been by to perform some recon. That's probably how he determined where I kept the SUV parked. For him to sneak in the gun while the police were conducting a search, he had to know exactly where to hide it in order to get in and out without arousing suspicion."

"You make this sound like a spy movie."

"Isn't it?"

Again with the theatrics. "Didn't the police take the footage and logs with them?" I asked. "Even the servers were pulled. Shouldn't they already have whatever they need?"

"If they bother to look. This will speed up the process and ensure they don't miss anything. Didn't you say I should help the investigation in any way possible? I handed over a crucial piece of evidence. Video footage will be icing on the cake, assuming we can't convince Gallo to fess up once we confront him."

"What exactly is the plan?"

"We find Gallo. The rest will fall into place."

I didn't like this plan. It wasn't a plan so much as wishful thinking. But the look on Lucien's face made me wonder how many lines he'd cross in order to get the cop to confess. And after what I'd recently learned about him, I wasn't sure if there were any lines he wouldn't cross.

"Is this about payback?" I asked.

He let out an exhale. "That's probably what the douchebag's counting on. So no, we're going to do this civilly. I didn't become one of the country's top security consultants by breaking laws or bones, if I can avoid it."

THIRTY-FOUR

We found Gallo sitting on a bench near a food truck. His partner, Officer Swenson, had just gone into the café to get a couple of coffees when we arrived. Gallo finished his chicken sandwich, wiped his mouth, and tossed the napkin into the bag.

"Hey, man, I see they finally let you out. It's about damn time," Gallo said. Even though I couldn't see his eyes behind his mirrored shades, I knew he was looking at me. "How are you doing, Lucien?"

"I've been better." Cross took a seat on the bench beside him. "Do you want to tell me what's going on?"

Gallo swiped his tongue against his front teeth, making a sucking sound. "What do you mean?" He glanced at me.

"It's safe to speak in front of her," Cross said.

Gallo snorted. "I doubt that. She's dating one of the detectives who's trying to stick it to you."

"Answer my question."

"How would I know what's going on?"

"You set me up. I want to know why."

"What are you talking about?"

"The photos that surfaced of me visiting the bank, those came from you."

"I didn't take them. I didn't know anything about them until yesterday."

Cross's voice went deadly. "You sure about that?"

"Shit, of course, I'm sure. I'd know."

"What about the ledger you left in my apartment?"

Gallo turned to make sure Swenson wasn't on his way back from the coffee shop, then he looked down to make sure his bodycam was turned off. "I'm glad you found it. I thought you'd find it useful."

"Useful?" Cross's tone remained neutral, but his hands balled into fists. "Why are you planting evidence on me?"

"That's not what I'm doing. I'm helping you. I've been keeping up with the murder investigation. Someone's framing you. I don't know who. I'm guessing it could be Detective Heathcliff." Again, his gaze went to me. "He's Moretti's lapdog, and you remember how badly Moretti wanted to put you in bracelets eight years ago."

"Where'd you get the ledger?" I asked.

"I found it," Gallo said.

"Where?" Cross asked.

"At Knox's house. After he disappeared, I performed another walkthrough before we released the house to his half-sister. When I opened it, I knew it must be his, but I couldn't make heads or tails out of it."

"Why didn't you hand it over to the detectives working the disappearance?" I asked.

"It was Knox's property. We didn't have grounds. Nothing inside the ledger told us where he'd gone or if he'd been abducted, but I held on to it anyway, thinking I could decipher it. But I never could. It was just a bunch of random numbers and letters. Everything was coded. I would have given it to you to look at years ago, but you told me to let it go." Gallo adjusted his glasses, his gaze fixed on Cross. "Now that his body surfaced, I thought you might be able to use it to clear your name."

Cross gave him a wicked grin. "I intend to."

"Good." Gallo moved to stand, but Cross grabbed his shoulder and shoved him back onto the bench.

"We're not done yet. What can you tell me about the murder weapon?"

"It's a forty-five. The serial number's been filed off. The gun itself is in bad shape. It's starting to rust. I'm surprised the lab was able to get it to test fire. The thing looks like it might have been in the ground too."

"How'd it end up inside one of Cross Security's armored vehicles?" Cross asked.

"Beats me."

"That's your answer for everything, isn't it?" I asked.

"What do you want from me?" Gallo snapped. "I have nothing to do with this. I'm just doing my pal a favor, and you," he pointed an accusatory finger at me, "keep trying to jam me up over it."

Lucien cleared his throat. His tone friendlier, more conversational. "Did you kill Trey Knox?"

Gallo jumped up. "You're insane."

Cross climbed to his feet. His nose practically touching Gallo's. "Cross Security isn't just a name. It's my specialty. I have cameras hidden everywhere. I know you slipped the gun into the armored vehicle when no one was looking, just like I know you broke into my apartment and hid the ledger on the top shelf. As we speak, my attorney is presenting the evidence to several key figures in the police department and the district attorney's office. We'll see what they have to say. I suggest you provide them with better answers."

"How could you?" Gallo took a step back. "I stuck my neck out for you. I called your assistant with the news, and you turn around and do this to me. I'm your friend. Doesn't that mean anything?"

"How fucking stupid do you think I am? You tried to choke me out inside a holding cell."

"I never did that," Gallo insisted.

"What's a matter, Joe? You didn't have the balls to kill me? Or did Alex scare you off before you could work up the nerve?"

"You're fucking crazy." He glanced at me. "The both of you are lunatics."

By then, Officer Swenson had returned empty-handed. From the way he kept his hand poised near his holster, I figured his partner's behavior regarding our presence had made him nervous to the point he thought he should intervene.

"Lucien," I hissed, "we should go."

Officer Swenson maneuvered around me, allowing his back to face me. "Joe, what's going on here?"

"Nothing," Gallo sighed, "these two need to get their facts straight."

"What facts?" Swenson took a cautious step forward.

"It doesn't matter. You ready to roll?" Gallo gave my boss another hard look.

"The watch commander called. He says we should head back to the precinct. We need to get some things straightened out," Swenson said.

Gallo edged backward, the jitters starting. He'd run. I'd seen this behavior before.

"Take it easy, Joe. This isn't a big deal," Swenson said. "We'll just get back in the car and see what the brass wants. It's only the two of us. No one else needs to get involved, right?"

"You did this." Gallo lunged at Lucien, knocking him into the bench and over the back. Cross grabbed for him, but Gallo shrugged out of his grip and took off down the sidewalk.

Swenson keyed his radio as he raced after his partner, requesting backup, and giving his location.

"You good?" I waited for Cross's affirmative before taking off after the two men. I'd only gone half a block when gunshots rang out in front of me. From my position, I couldn't tell who had fired. "Dammit."

Palming my gun, I ran faster. Flashes of my recent altercation played through my mind. Gallo grabbed a homeless man's shopping cart and tipped it over as he ran, spewing cans and the man's other possessions all over the sidewalk. Swenson got tripped up in the mess, but I zipped around it, catching a glimpse of Gallo darting down a staircase to the subway.

"Watch out." I pushed my way through the crowd. Gallo fired one shot, above my head. Everyone on the stairs ducked. A few screamed. But he kept moving.

With the crowd suddenly at a standstill, I watched him

descend the final few steps and hurry toward the turnstiles. He'd be gone in seconds.

"Move." But the frightened masses remained. I zigzagged down a few steps, but I couldn't get through the crowd, so I pressed against the railing and slid down, gasping when I reached the bottom and was jettisoned off the edge.

In a stumbling run, I shoved my way through the turnstile, searching in every direction for Joe Gallo. The police uniform should stick out, so I searched for the dark blue. Halfway down the platform, the crowds parted like the Red Sea. That had to be Gallo.

"Where'd he go?" Swenson asked, running up beside me.

"There." I pointed.

He gave me a wary look, noticing the gun in my hand. "Stay here and wait for help to arrive." He moved forward at a fast clip, scrambling from one cover position to another. Since waiting wasn't in my vocabulary, I went after them.

When Gallo reached the end of the platform, Swenson called out to him, "End of the line, Joe. Don't make this harder than it has to be."

"I didn't do it," Gallo called back.

"I'm sure you didn't. We just need to clear this up. Put your weapon down. We'll take this nice and easy, okay?"

Gallo nodded. "I'm putting it down." He held his gun out to the side, the barrel facing away from Swenson. Gallo crouched down, as if to put the gun on the ground. "See? I'm doing what you said."

Swenson kept a bead on his partner, waiting. "The last thing I want to do is hurt you. Let's just get this over with. Maybe we'll get home in time for dinner. All right?"

"What are you having tonight?" Gallo asked.

"Meatloaf, I think. Why? You having something better? Want to invite me over?"

"Maybe next time." Gallo turned his firearm upward and fired a shot at the ceiling, immediately dropped the gun, and ran for the tunnel.

A collective scream echoed and died as everyone waiting

on the platform scattered in fear. In her haste to escape, a woman kicked Gallo's discarded gun, causing it to discharge a second time through the crowd.

Swenson dove to retrieve it, just as Gallo escaped into the darkness. "He's heading through here," I yelled as I zigzagged through the crowd and along the narrow ledge that led into the tunnel.

Gallo had jumped down to the path beside the tracks, but he only made it a few feet before I was on him. We crashed to the ground. He tried to roll me off of his back, but I yanked one of his arms behind him. Before I could get my cuffs on him, he reared back, knocking me against the elbow-high concrete wall. Every nerve ending ignited where my back had collided with the precinct stairs. But I didn't let go.

I wrapped my leg around his and pulled backward, opening my hips. He toppled backward, and I swung my body around, keeping a firm grip on his wrist as my legs pinned him down. He'd been through the same type of training, but I caught him off guard.

Sitting up, I tugged harder on his wrist, jerking him forward and kicking him in the jaw. His head lolled. While he was dazed, I flipped him over. But before I could cuff him, the ground beneath me began to vibrate. A blinding light headed directly for us.

"The train," Gallo gasped.

The vibrations grew stronger, my teeth rattling. "Quick, get up." I hauled him to his feet and practically shoved him onto the narrow ledge before scrambling up after him. The light was blinding, everything turned a yellowy-white.

Pressing my sore back against the wall, I couldn't tell if I was shaking or if that was the ground. A horn blared, deafening me to everything but the rattling shriek. Turning away from the light, I stared at Gallo. Would he push me in front of the oncoming train?

My handcuffs remained in my hands, so I clicked one bracelet around his wrist and the other around mine. Then I pressed my back harder against the wall. If he slipped, so would I.

Squeezing my eyes closed, I held my breath as the hot,

humid air whipped around me. The force made me slide a few inches closer to Gallo. He gripped my forearm as the train barreled past us. The light from the cars strobed in front of us as one car passed, followed by another, and another.

When it was over, he released my arm and sunk to the ledge. I sucked in a breath, lightheaded and dizzy. Cautiously, I unhooked the handcuff from my wrist. "Are you done?"

Gallo nodded. "I didn't mean for any of this to happen. I'm a police officer. I never hurt anyone. I would never hurt anyone."

"The bruises on my back say otherwise." I clicked the other bracelet into place. "On your feet. Let's go."

By the time I dragged him out of the tunnel and back to the platform, Swenson and two other cops were waiting for us.

"You wanted him gift wrapped, right?" I shoved Gallo toward the waiting officers who took over.

Swenson spoke to me while the other officers took his partner into custody. "You were with Detective Heathcliff last night outside the apartment."

"Is that a crime?"

"No, ma'am." He led me up the stairs and back to the daylight. "Mind telling me why I got a phone call from the watch commander asking if I could bring my partner in for questioning? Does this have anything to do with that?"

"It's not my story to tell." When we made it to the surface, I spotted Cross waiting near my car. "Someone mentioned you noticed Gallo had been acting strangely lately. Would you mind elaborating on that?"

Swenson hesitated. "He's my partner. We're friends. He's always had my back, until now. I shouldn't say anything. He deserves the benefit of the doubt."

"How long have you two worked together?"

"Almost three years."

"Has he ever behaved erratically before this?"

Swenson shook his head. "I don't understand what's going on. This has to be a mistake."

"One Gallo made." Cross moved beside us. "Alex, give

me your keys. I'll call Almeada. We'll meet you at the precinct."

After handing Cross the car keys, I turned to Swenson. "Looks like you're my ride."

THIRTY-FIVE

Lt. Moretti hadn't said a word to me since I arrived at the precinct. Instead, he remained behind his desk, reading my statement and grunting every few seconds. Whether that was disapproval was anyone's guess. Finally, he signed off on the report and closed the folder.

"This is a shitfest. You realize the optics aren't good, no matter the outcome." He rocked back in his chair. "You work for Lucien Cross and you helped apprehend the cop who you and your boss have accused of framing him."

"Gallo didn't just frame Cross. He attacked me. He tampered with evidence. He violated chain of custody."

"I'm sorry. Is this your office?" He held up his nameplate and glared daggers at me. "I didn't think so."

"Sorry, sir," I muttered.

"Then shut up. I don't want to hear it. I'm aware of the situation. The brass and IA have been riding my ass so hard, I have bruises." He sighed. "I know you didn't make this mess. I'm not sure who did. However, you're the reason we're sitting here right now, so don't think you're in the clear either."

"No, sir."

"Cross's attorney presented us with surveillance footage

which paints Gallo in a less than professional light. Detective Heathcliff has already spoken to me about his suspicions and yours. But Joe Gallo's been on the force for a good fifteen years. He drove the commissioner around when his regular driver was on vacation. You understand why I'm having problems believing a man like that would take police insignia out of a superior's car, raid my precinct, and assault a man he claims is one of his friends, let alone the commissioner's son."

"I don't suppose you expected him to open fire in a subway station either."

Moretti growled at me. "To be fair, he didn't fire on Swenson or any civilian. He didn't even shoot at Lucien, which is why I'm having a difficult time believing he tried to kill him."

"Off the record, maybe Gallo didn't want to kill him. Maybe he just wanted to scare him. Cross's profession, along with his last name, makes him easy prey. The attack in the holding cell ensured the bail hearing was moved up and encouraged the judge to sign off on it. Given Lucien's capabilities and wealth, I'm surprised he didn't get placed under house arrest with an ankle monitor instead."

"You think Gallo was doing him a favor?"

"Not exactly, but I don't think Gallo wants Cross dead. Honestly, I'm not sure he wants me dead either. I've fought him twice. He didn't pull his punches, but he didn't go in for the kill either. He could have."

Moretti stared at me. "Spit it out, Parker."

"I don't think Gallo killed Trey Knox."

"Do you think Cross did?"

"No."

"Fuck." Moretti scrubbed a hand over his face. "The entire reason this is happening is because I'm investigating Trey Knox's murder. Now you're telling me that despite the evidence and circumstances, we're back to square one."

"I'm not telling you anything. What I said is my opinion, and it was off the record. As you've pointed out a dozen times, Cross hired me. He didn't kill Knox. We know Gallo broke into Cross's apartment and planted the ledger. We also know Gallo went to Cross Security while the warrant was being served. Surveillance footage doesn't show him planting the weapon, but Cross confronted him about that. If you push, I'm sure Gallo will admit to hiding the gun in Cross's SUV. I don't know where he got the murder weapon. Logic would dictate since it had been in his possession, he's the killer."

"But you're not convinced."

I shrugged. "What do I know?"

Moretti rolled his eyes and jerked his chin at the door. "Get out of my office. I have work to do."

"What about Cross? Are the charges dropped?"

"That'll depend on what Gallo says." Moretti let out a huff. "But since the ledger points to Gallo emptying two of Knox's bank accounts and you think we can get him to confess to planting the gun, it'd take a hell of a lot of evidence to shift the focus of the investigation back to Cross."

"Thank you."

"Yeah, yeah," he pointed at the door, "now get out."

When I stepped out of Moretti's office, Heathcliff looked up at me. "Now what did you do?"

"Nothing."

"I don't buy it." He nodded down at my arm. The tussle on the train tracks had reopened the wound, and blood had soaked through my sleeve. "Sit down." He pushed a chair out with his foot while he pulled the first aid kit out of his drawer.

I sat, mostly so I could read the intel covering his desk. "Do you watch anything on TV besides doctor shows?"

"The only other thing to watch is cop shows, and I get enough of that at work." He rolled up my sleeve, peeled the used bandage off, tossed it in the trash, and wrapped a fresh one around my arm, making sure it was tight enough before tucking in the end and taping it.

"You need to broaden your horizons. Comedies. Cartoons. Alien invasions. Cooking shows."

"Those make me hungry."

I laughed.

"You must be feeling pretty good since you got another man off the hook for murder," Heathcliff said.

"I guess." Chewing on my bottom lip, I sifted through the photos of the murder weapon. Gallo was right. It hadn't been kept up. The forty-five showed patches of what looked like dirt, but could have been rust, in most of the nooks and crannies. "Did CSU test this residue?" I pointed to the brown specks.

"It was dried mud and sediment." He slid the report over to me. "The killer must have dropped the weapon when he was burying the body."

"Do you think it was buried with the body?"

"The construction workers who found the body didn't report finding a gun. The responding officers didn't have any information on it in their reports. As far as I know, no one had seen this weapon prior to its discovery at Cross Security."

"Did Gallo report to the scene the night Knox's body was discovered?"

"He was off duty."

"That doesn't mean he didn't show up. He might have heard the call."

Heathcliff picked up the file and stood. "Give me a few minutes."

While he was gone, I slid into his chair to compare the timeline with Gallo's work schedule. Yesterday, Heathcliff pointed out a few discrepancies. I wanted to see what they were.

I already knew Gallo had allegedly been with his partner when I'd been attacked, but now that I knew he'd gone to Cross Security earlier that morning, I wondered just how much Swenson was covering for him. So I clicked a few keys and brought up Officer Swenson's personnel file.

Like Gallo, he appeared clean. He had one civilian complaint two years ago, which IAD had cleared him from, involving the amount of force used to break up a domestic dispute. Those were messy, so I was willing to give him the benefit of the doubt. He also had a citation for bravery for entering a burning building to save a child when the fire department was delayed. From what I'd witnessed today, Swenson appeared to be a good cop, uninvolved in whatever mess Gallo had gotten himself into. But I couldn't be sure. Appearances were deceiving. Still, he brought Gallo in. That had to mean something.

The police would have to look into alibis, but since Swenson had a family, as indicated by the photo clipped to the visor of his cruiser, it should be simple to ascertain his whereabouts. Gallo, on the other hand, was a bit trickier.

Gallo had been off duty when Knox's body was dug up, but my gut said he'd shown up to the scene anyway. Surely, one of his fellow officers could place him there. That must have been what Heathcliff went to check on. Maybe that's when Gallo found the murder weapon, if he didn't already possess it. But why would he take it and plant it in Lucien's SUV? That didn't make any sense unless he wanted to ensure Cross took the fall for Knox's murder.

Confused, I shifted my attention to what Heathcliff found inside the apartment. Since he didn't answer any of my questions earlier today, I'd just have to read the reports myself.

Most of the items in the display cases matched the inventory list taken at Knox's residence at the time of his disappearance. He must have gone home, packed the rest of his stuff, and left. That's probably how the killer found him, followed him to the apartment, and killed him.

Keying in another search, I checked to see if any 9-1-1 calls had been placed during the two-day window we believed to be when Knox was murdered. Two calls had been placed from the apartment complex on the eighth, the day after Knox flew back to town. The callers reported hearing gunshots. Police arrived on scene twenty minutes later, did not find anything suspicious, and determined the sound must have been firecrackers since they found burn marks on the third floor landing.

I grabbed the sticky notes from the corner of Heathcliff's desk and scribbled down the date and time. That's when Knox was murdered. I was sure of it.

I made a copy and stuck it to the edge of the detective's monitor. He better appreciate me. I'd just determined TOD. For that, I should be deputized.

Now that I knew when Knox was killed, I moved on to the other things the police found in the apartment. The

DNA from the toiletries found in the bathroom had yet to match anyone in the database. Flipping pages, I wondered if any samples inside the apartment matched Knox.

"Get out of my chair," Heathcliff said.

"That's Thompson's line." I glanced over at the other detective's desk while I switched chairs, but Detectives Thompson and O'Connell had been embroiled in a stakeout for the past week which kept them out of my destructive path. "Did you find any of Knox's DNA at the apartment?"

"No."

"Not even on the collectibles?"

"CSU swabbed everything. They believe all the samples belong to the same person, but they don't think he's in the system."

"Is Gallo's DNA in the system?"

"Yes, we keep it on file in order to rule him out for possible scene contamination. I'm wondering now if that had been a mistake on any of his other cases."

"On the bright side, you know the sample CSU found doesn't match Lucien." He'd been arrested enough times that the police had everything they'd ever need on him. But that got me thinking. "Trey Knox didn't have a record. Why was his DNA in the system? How'd you get a sample to compare it to? Or are you using a familial match from his half-sister?"

"We had Knox's DNA." Heathcliff plucked the note off his monitor and stared at it. "When he disappeared, we searched his house. CSU found blood in his shower drain. They used a sample of hair from his hairbrush to see if the blood matched."

"Did it?"

"Yes, not that it matters, since he didn't die there." He put the note down. "How'd you figure out TOD?"

So I told him. "You're slipping. You need a refresher course on detecting."

He narrowed his eyes at me. "I would have gotten to it eventually. I haven't exactly had time with everything else coming in. Ledgers, account numbers, suspects, you bleeding all over the place."

I looked at my arm. "I am not."

"Be that as it may, I have to sort through this shit. But seeing as how your boss is no longer our prime suspect, you can stay and watch me work."

"You just want me to stick around, so I can share more pointers."

"No, it's so I can make sure you stay out of trouble. Plus, when we interrogate Gallo, we might need your input. I doubt Cross will come back to share his insights."

"He might if you ask nicely."

"Phhtt." Heathcliff snorted. "We are talking about the Lucien Cross who tried to hide your files from me by sticking them under the couch cushion. He's prided himself on not helping the police. That's not about to change, especially after these last few days."

THIRTY-SIX

"He won't confess," Heathcliff said when he returned from the interrogation room.

"I didn't think he would. What happens now?"

"The murder weapon's the clincher. Gallo admitted to placing it in Cross's SUV. Apparently, Cross already convinced him we knew this, which helps strengthen our case. Your boss is good."

"I know." That's why I questioned every action he took. He always had an ulterior motive. "Did Gallo say where he got the murder weapon or where he kept it?"

"He says he got it from Knox. He didn't say much more than that. His lawyers have advised him not to talk until they have time to work out a strategy."

"Gallo's already said too much. He'll have to find a way to control the narrative."

"Like Cross did?" Heathcliff asked. "I can already tell you how it'll go. Gallo continued to investigate the Knox disappearance. When Knox returned to the city under a false name, Gallo spotted him, probably at the house. He followed him back to the apartment and confronted him. Given the details the OIO has uncovered and the additional evidence contained in the ledger, Knox must have had the weapon for protection. He probably drew on Gallo, a fight ensued, and Gallo got a hold of Knox's gun."

"That doesn't explain shooting him in the chest four times."

"In the heat of the moment, with emotions running high and potentially fearing for his life, I can see it happening," Heathcliff said. "After that, Gallo freaked, wrapped up the body, and found a place to hide it. He probably buried the gun too, figuring he'd be less likely to get caught."

"Until the airport decided to clear the field in order to expand the parking lot."

"Yep."

"Okay, so why frame Lucien?"

Heathcliff hid his snicker in a cough. "It couldn't happen to a nicer person."

I gave his arm a shove. "I'm serious. Why? Gallo's been sucking up to the Cross family for years. Not just Lucien, but his dad too."

"Maybe that's why. Lucien never shook off the suspicion of his involvement in Knox's disappearance, but nothing ever became of it because of his father. Gallo must have figured Cross was Teflon. It'd be safe to frame him."

Given what I'd seen regarding Cross's treatment in this case, I had problems believing that. "Really?"

Heathcliff shrugged. "Honestly, the commissioner is more concerned about optics—appearing tough on crime and coming off as fair and just—than his own son's well-being. He ordered Moretti to crack down hard on the murderer. If that was Gallo's plan, it backfired. Lucien was being railroaded, but you didn't hear that from me."

"I saw it with my own two eyes."

"Still, we had evidence. Everything lined up. You know it."

To a certain extent, it still did. Cross and Gallo could be working together, given the evidence. But I wouldn't dare suggest it. "Gallo told me he never hurt anyone."

"He insists he didn't shoot Knox. He says we have it wrong."

"Did he say who killed Trey Knox?"

Heathcliff shook his head. "I'd say the more we dig up regarding Gallo's whereabouts over these last few days, the more apt he'll be to talk. Right now, he still has the opportunity to claim self-defense. He could plead down."

"A cop in lockup doesn't bode well. Cross proved it, and he isn't even a cop."

"We'll do our best to keep Gallo safe," Heathcliff promised. "I'm surprised you care so much. He tried to kill you."

"No, he didn't. He could have pushed me in front of the train. Frankly, I thought he might, which is why I handcuffed the two of us together."

"And you hate handcuffs."

"But he didn't, just like he didn't fire at anyone in the train station."

"He kicked you down the stairs. He choked out Cross. Those are violent tendencies. Maybe he has anger management issues or something."

"What about the apartment?"

"Patrol's been showing his photo around the neighborhood and asking if anyone's seen him. Luckily, they had better luck finding people to talk to than I did. Three different people said they've seen Gallo entering or leaving the apartment on more than one occasion over the last two weeks. He's probably been staying there. From what I hear, he might have needed to escape the mess of his apartment."

"Yeah, that would explain stocking the same brands of toothpaste and shaving cream at both places. But what about the DNA? You already said it wasn't Gallo's. Someone else must have been using the apartment. Who's Gallo protecting?"

"I don't know, but I will find out."

"Do you think it's Swenson or another cop?"

"Doubtful," Heathcliff said. "We'd have their DNA on file too. I'm guessing Gallo asked someone to stay at the apartment to make sure no one came snooping around. He couldn't risk a break-in, and in that neighborhood, it'd be a matter of time. Gallo wouldn't want the stain on the floor or what's left of Knox's collection to be discovered or stolen. If any of it surfaced in a pawn shop, that would have led to more trouble. He probably told whoever it was to take off as soon as the body was discovered. I'm guessing Gallo gave him the keys to the white sedan and told him to leave town."

"Did the neighbors ever see anyone else at the apartment besides Gallo?"

"I'm not sure, but we'll figure it out. Agent Jablonsky's offered to help us look into the accounts. The BOLO is still in effect on the car. With the FBI getting involved, whoever's working with Gallo won't get far. The federal government has a lot more resources at its disposal than we do." Heathcliff nodded toward the double doors. "Do you think Cross Security might want to help out?"

"The department would question anything we found," I said, catching a glimpse of Cross and Almeada as they spoke to an ADA and a police captain I didn't recognize. "Until the charges are dropped and an apology is issued, Cross won't have anything to do with the department."

"I can't blame him." Heathcliff studied me. "One of these days, you're going to tell me what he did that convinced you he was guilty."

"He didn't do anything."

"We both know that's a lie, Parker. We've spent too much time undercover together. I know your tells, just like you know mine."

"He didn't kill Knox. That's the beginning and end of it."

"I guess we'll have to agree to disagree, but he's your boss. So I get it. I'm sure if he posed a danger to society, you'd let me know."

"Absolutely."

The police captain and ADA walked away, and Cross waved me over.

"He's beckoning," Heathcliff said. "You better go."

"Will you let me know what shakes loose?"

"Are you still worried some prick is going to show up at your house? Because you shouldn't be. Gallo's in custody. Our case is solid."

"You said that before. But someone's in the wind. Until you find the sedan and whoever's been staying in the apartment, I'm going to keep one eye open."

"I'll send a few extra patrols your way just to be on the

safe side, but I don't think you have anything to worry about." Heathcliff jerked his chin toward the door. "Get going. I have to finish up the paperwork and get everything squared away before your boss gets that apology."

*   *   *

The rest of the day flew by. Cross, Almeada, and I went over everything. Afterward, I headed home and waited for Martin's call. But my mind wouldn't turn off. I couldn't fathom why Officer Gallo would kill Trey Knox. If it had been in self-defense, like Heathcliff suggested, Knox wouldn't have four holes in his chest. I didn't think Gallo would have had the stomach to remove the man's fingertips, molars, and bash in his skull, but I might have misjudged him.

The man I ran down in the subway tunnel had given up gracefully. Someone who'd go to those extremes to hide a body wouldn't surrender that easily. I was missing something.

After speaking to Martin, I crawled into bed. Maybe a good night's sleep would clear my mind and give me a fresh perspective. Right now, nothing made sense.

An unfamiliar chirp woke me. Rolling over, I pulled my nine millimeter from where it'd been hidden beneath Martin's pillow and aimed at the doorway. I waited, listening. The neon glow of the clock read 1:43.

It was too late for visitors. Cross wouldn't be stopping by at this hour. But I heard something. I just didn't know what it was.

Silently, I crept out of bed. After this morning, I had the foresight to sleep in pajama shorts and an oversized t-shirt. A glance at my phone didn't show any missed calls or texts, so that wasn't the source of the sound.

Without turning on the lights, I edged toward the doorway and peered into the living room. Everything appeared as I'd left it. Once I made it to the kitchen, I hit the light switch and ducked behind the island. No shots rang out.

"All right, Parker, you're losing it." Perhaps I'd been

dreaming. But to be on the safe side, I cleared the apartment, searching every room, closet, and hiding place. Bolstering my nerves, I pulled the curtain to the balcony. But no one was outside.

Leaving the lights on, I went back to bed. But I couldn't sleep. Instead, I stared at the ceiling, listening to every creak and pop. The apartment building wasn't as quiet as Martin's estate. The noises were eerie and unfamiliar.

When I couldn't take it anymore, I put on a pair of jeans and checked the hallway. At this time of night, no one was around. I took the elevator down to the lobby, figuring a quick chat with building security would make me feel better.

I'd just exited when the doorman smiled sheepishly at me. "I'm sorry. I didn't mean to disturb you. That's why I didn't buzz the intercom that long."

"What?" Had that been the source of the sound?

"He thought I wanted to come up," Heathcliff said.

I spun, surprised to find him in one of the armchairs. "What are you doing here? What's going on?"

He held up his palm. "Relax, everything's fine."

"If that were true, you wouldn't be camped out in my apartment building at two o'clock in the morning."

The doorman did his best to ignore us, but from the look on his face, he found our exchange entertaining. He glanced at the detective, as if to say *I told you so*, and went back to working on a crossword puzzle.

"Did something happen?" I asked.

"No, I just..." Heathcliff rubbed the scruff on his jaw. "You were right about Cross and Gallo, which made me wonder what else you might be right about."

I blinked, confused. "What?"

"Go back to bed. Everything's fine. I'm just going to hang out here and make sure it stays that way."

I sighed. "Come upstairs."

"No. I'm good here."

"Derek, we're not having this discussion down here. Come upstairs." I pressed the button for the elevator and stepped into the car the moment the doors opened. He got up from his spot, placed the magazine back on the table, nodded to the doorman, and joined me. "Are you okay?" I asked.

"I'm fine."

"Fine doesn't show up at your doorstep at two a.m."

"I got here a little after 1:30."

"Did you find the sedan? Has the threat level increased?"

"No, nothing like that."

"So this is about you." I gave him a pointed look. "You hate it when I try to protect other people. Who said you could protect me?" I cracked a smile and nudged him, so he'd know I wasn't mad. "Is this what happens when you skip a meeting? You should see if you can find another one to go to tomorrow to make up for it."

"It's not about that."

The elevator opened on the twenty-first floor, and I led the way to my apartment and unlocked the door. "What is it about?"

"We don't know who killed Knox. We don't know who's been staying in the apartment. Gallo hasn't given up anything useful, but I'm not convinced he did it."

"I pointed this out earlier today."

"You did, and I said you shouldn't worry about it." He stared at the refrigerator to avoid eye contact.

"But it got to you too. Annoying, isn't it?"

"Look, I'll go. This building is secure. You should be safe. We're fairly certain Gallo left the threatening messages on your car, and he's in custody. You should be fine. I just wanted to hang around in case the guy who disappeared in the white sedan was the one who planned to make good on said threat. But he should be running for the hills by now."

"Don't you think, even if Gallo didn't leave the last note on my car, that whoever this unknown third man is, he has no reason to want to hurt me? It's too late. We have Gallo. Cross is cleared. I'm done." That made me wonder again why someone had been so adamant to have me back off the investigation. "Did you ask Gallo if he left the threats?"

"He denies it, but he denies everything."

"What about handwriting samples?"

"The techs aren't sure. Handwriting analysis isn't an exact science, but the letter formation looks similar."

"See, no reason to worry."

"Which is why every light in your apartment is turned on, the closet doors are open, and your nine millimeter is tucked beneath that oversized shirt I can only imagine you were sleeping in."

"Since you're such a brilliant detective, what am I going to say next?"

Heathcliff smirked. "The extra pillows and blankets are in the closet. I'll be on the couch if you need me."

"Thanks, Derek."

THIRTY-SEVEN

The phone rang, and I rolled over. Grabbing the device, I blindly hit answer and held it to my ear. "Hello?"

Nothing.

"Hello?"

Pulling it away from my face, I blinked the blurriness from my eyes and stared at the home screen. From the living room, I heard muffled grunts. *Heathcliff's phone.* I moved to the doorway and combed my fingers through my tangled hair.

"What happened to him?" He paused. "Shit. Are you sure?" He shook his head a few times. "All right. I'll be there soon." He hung up and blew out a breath while he stretched.

"What's going on?" I asked.

Heathcliff turned to look at me. "State police spotted a white sedan with stolen plates. They tried to pull the car over, but the driver freaked and drove off. He lost control and wrapped his car around a tree. He's dead."

"Shit."

"Yeah," Heathcliff said sullenly. "The staties identified the driver as Paco Campos."

The name rang a bell. "Mexican cartel?"

"He's in the ledger." Heathcliff clipped his holster and badge onto his belt. "I have to go. But since Campos connects to Knox, I'm guessing he's the man we've been hunting."

"Why would Gallo protect him?"

"I don't know." He shrugged into his jacket and bent over to pull on his shoes. "But I plan to find out."

After he left, I checked the time and phoned Jablonsky. It was just after seven, but that wasn't too early. He'd be awake or getting ready to wake up. I gave him the details, itching to shadow the police to see what was going on, but I couldn't. I worked for Cross. Until the charges were officially dropped, he wasn't in the clear, which meant I had to be careful not to overstep. But this was driving me crazy. So I got dressed and headed to the office.

For the next few hours, I dug up everything I could on Paco Campos and Trey Knox. Campos worked for one of the cartels and had made several payments to one of Knox's offshore accounts. The last payment had been made three days before Knox was killed.

The DEA had credited at least a dozen and a half kills to Campos. He'd burned and mutilated several of the bodies, but none of those murders had happened on U.S. soil. And since Campos paid off the federalis, nothing ever became of his violent streak. I could see him murdering Knox, especially if Knox had skimmed some product off the top when working import/export for the cartel soldier. But why would Gallo protect him?

When I couldn't wait any longer, I called Heathcliff. Gallo still wouldn't talk. He insisted he didn't kill Knox and had nothing to do with the attack on the precinct. Without evidence as proof, it'd be hard to make a case. However, when asked about Campos, Gallo still wouldn't say anything.

"That was his chance. I don't see why he won't talk," Heathcliff said.

"Could he be working for the cartel?" I asked.

"I doubt it. We've ripped apart his life and financials, just like the Bureau's done. Aside from the two offshore accounts which were funded entirely by Knox, we haven't found anything else."

"Did we know Campos was in the city?"

"No. His passport would have been flagged. He must have snuck in. If he was staying at Knox's apartment, who knows how long he's been here."

"What about DNA?"

"The lab will run it as soon as they can." Based on his wording, I didn't think this was a priority.

"What about Cross?" I asked.

"We'll do another deep dive into his connections, but if he doesn't have anything to do with Campos, he'll be cleared."

"All right." I headed upstairs to share the good news with my boss. Maybe he'd feel more like celebrating. I was too confused to see this as a win, even if it wrapped everything up into a nice neat bow.

Cross listened to the updates. "What's going to happen to Gallo?"

"He admitted to planting the gun in your car and the ledger at your apartment," I said. "That's something."

"It's nothing. The cops were gung-ho to solve Knox's murder when they had me in custody. Now, it's just an afterthought. Funny how they wanted to take me down, but when it comes to punishing one of their own, they change their tune."

"That's not true."

"Isn't it?"

"These things take time. Is there anything about Paco Campos or the cartel I should know?"

"Nothing." He stared at me. "I'm not a criminal. Knox was, and apparently, so is Gallo. The money in Gallo's offshore accounts came directly out of Knox's account. The ledger opens a lot of that up. No one can deny Knox was involved with some scary people. More than likely, he ripped them off, just like he did the Russians, figuring he'd get paid and retain some product to sell on the side. Gallo might have caught on, so Knox paid him to keep quiet. Knox was a cheap asshole, but he learned one thing from his time with Vasili. It was best to pay off your enemies than to piss them off." Cross stuffed his hands in his pockets. "What about the murder weapon?"

"Gallo says he found it. He won't say where, but the dirt and sediment pulled from the crevices are the same composition as the dirt at the dig site."

"Do you think Gallo buried Knox?"

"I did until a cartel soldier wound up dead."

"Gallo must have been tailing Knox. He saw him get killed and where he got buried. But he couldn't do anything about it because he'd be implicated for taking a payoff. That's probably why he held on to the ledger, to make sure no one else could find it."

"Do you think Gallo was telling the truth when he said he gave you those things in order to clear your name?"

Cross mulled it over for a few moments. "Knowing that shit-for-brains, he must have thought I'd help him out."

"How?" I asked.

"I don't know. Why don't you ask Gallo?"

"He's not talking."

"That's the first smart thing he's done." Cross snorted. "At least I'm finally in the clear."

"Well, once the police and FBI make certain you don't have any ties to the cartel or Campos."

"I don't." Cross went to the wet bar, cursing when he found his liquor was gone. "Dammit. This is ridiculous. The police storm in here, upend my business, and still can't get shit done. This is why I tell you they are incompetent and corrupt." He pressed the intercom. "Justin, where'd you hide the liquor bottles from my bar cart?"

"I moved them to the supply closet," Justin said.

"I'll get them myself." Cross released the intercom button. "Now what am I supposed to do?"

"I guess you carry the gin back into your office."

He glared at me. "I haven't been cleared yet. My trial date is looming. Are they going to finish this investigation before then?"

"Probably." A small part of me enjoyed watching him sweat, but the worry that etched his face was beyond reasonable. "Why are you in such a rush? What are you afraid they'll find?"

Cross inhaled, closing his eyes briefly and pausing. "I'm

concerned this will circle back around and the police will dig deeper into Knox's ties to the Russian mafia. There are a few things I'd like to keep secret regarding my involvement with Vasili Petrov."

"Are you afraid Gallo knows something about what happened to him?"

"No, but Knox made that recording. Who knows what other traps he might have set for me?"

"Do you think Gallo knows anything?"

"No." Cross looked around his office, unhappy with the disarray. "Have you found anything else out? I hear Detective Heathcliff spent the night at your apartment. Is there any particular reason for that?"

It was my turn to glare. "That's my business, but if you must know, I was concerned about the threat left on my car. So was the detective."

For the first time today, Cross looked contrite. "I'm sorry to have put you at risk again. I can arrange for security teams to follow you."

"No, until I know more about how Gallo gained access to this building and your apartment, I'm not sure how much I trust the security specialists you hired."

"But you trust the police? That's ass-backward."

"I didn't say I trust the cops, but I trust Heathcliff."

Cross let out a displeased grunt. "Where's James? He didn't come home last night. Is there any credence to Gallo's claim that you're dating the detective?"

"Now you're stalking me? Do I need to remind you about boundaries?"

"I'm just curious."

"You're not fooling me. You're curious about the status of your partnership with Martin Technologies."

"In-house counsel informed me paperwork has been drawn up to dissolve our partnership. Due to the contract terms, I don't have much recourse. But nothing's been signed yet. Do you know what's going on? Is our venture dead in the water?"

"You should speak to Martin about that."

"He isn't in the office. His people said he's out of town. Is he hoping to save the project by pitching it to other investors? Or did he take off because you're stepping out on him?" Cross narrowed his eyes at me. "That seems unlikely given your goddess status."

"That's the last time you get to say that before I bury you in an abandoned field. Do I make myself clear?"

He smiled, infuriating me. It'd be a lot easier to help him if he didn't push my buttons, especially when he got such a perverse joy out of it.

But despite my irritation, something he said had sent my radar buzzing. I had to learn more about Officer Joe Gallo. And I knew just where to start. "I have work to do. I'll see you later."

"Tell James that App-med would be interested in the research."

"Why would you want to help a competitor?"

"We aren't competitors. I want to explore security and protection applications. They want to use biotextiles for tissue engineering and medical applications. Neither is necessarily in line with Martin Tech's original R&D, but I'm guessing they'd still pay to have access to the research since MT's focus is on increasing production and finding alternative sources, which will be useful for all of us."

"I'll let him know."

THIRTY-EIGHT

I went back to KC's bar in the hopes of gaining some intel on Joe Gallo. How deep was his connection to Trey Knox? Did the police officer do Knox's bidding? Did he have ties to the cartels? Maybe he assisted narcotics on a bust at some point. Is that why he hadn't given up Campos? Or was he afraid of the cartel soldier?

Or was Heathcliff right? Did Gallo track Knox from his home to the apartment, confront him, and end up in a struggle that resulted in Knox's demise? Maybe Campos helped him dispose of the body, and that's why Gallo hadn't come clean. But I had no way of knowing any of these things.

I didn't know much about Gallo or how he operated. Our previous interactions made me believe he had a conscience. He didn't want to hurt people, but the road to hell was paved with good intentions. So it was time I did some digging.

"What are you doing back here?" Jim Harrelson asked when I entered KC's. "Lucien's out on bail. I'm not sure there's anything else I can do to help."

"You got him a bail hearing?"

"No," Jim hefted the box onto the counter and began

pulling bottles out and placing them on the shelves behind him, "I called his pops and let him handle it."

"I'm sure Lucien's grateful."

"He'll cuss me out for getting his father involved." He shoved the new bottles behind the open ones and made sure everything lined up neatly. "So don't tell him. Let's just keep this between us."

I looked around, but it was too early for anyone to be here. "I'll keep your secret on one condition."

"What's that?" Jim wiped his hands on his pants and hefted a second box onto the bar. With a box cutter, he sliced through the tape, folded over the edges, and went back to stocking the shelves.

"You tell me everything you know about Officer Joe Gallo."

"Why is that important?" He didn't turn around, but he watched me through the reflection in the mirror. "Does Gallo have something to do with Lucien getting framed?"

"You haven't heard?"

"I'm not a cop, remember?"

"Neither am I." But Jim didn't let anything slip. Maybe he really didn't know what was going on, so I kept my mouth shut about Gallo's arrest. If he didn't know, he'd be less likely to censor his responses. "When we spoke last time, you remembered Lucien interacting with Gallo. And since you had a mojito ready for the man, you must know him rather well."

"He comes here to drink and only orders one of two things. Mojitos and beer. It doesn't take a genius to remember that."

"Still, that's something. How long has he been coming here?"

"Since I took over the place, possibly before, but I couldn't tell you that."

"Did you ever work with him?"

"Nope."

"Gallo says he's driven the commissioner around before."

"As a temp." Jim finished with the shelves and turned around to face me. "Gallo caught some kind of case when he first became a patrolman. I can't remember what it was about, but it was something high-profile. A politician had gotten into trouble for something. Y'know, the usual."

"Did Gallo ever work any cases that linked back to the cartel?"

Jim stopped stocking the shelf. "Probably. Anything specific?"

"I don't know."

"Drugs and violence go hand in hand. A lot of cases we worked involved one or the other. I'm sure Gallo's encountered someone or something cartel related. I'm sure every cop has."

"Okay." That didn't help me any. "What was that high-profile case about? Why was the commissioner involved?"

"Someone did something they shouldn't have in a hotel room. Senators and congressmen have pull. That's how Gallo got on the commissioner's radar. And since he did such a good job, Gallo got rewarded." The words appeared to leave a bad taste in Jim's mouth.

"I see. Did it involve anything nefarious?"

"You got a dictionary. I might have to look that one up."

I stared at him, not buying the act for a second. "Any chance Gallo could be on the take?"

"If he is, he should pay off his bar tab." Jim shrugged. "I don't know. He comes here a lot. Always alone. He table surfs. He knows a lot of cops, but I don't think any of them are particularly close to him. Your best bet would be talking to his partner. He'd know the guy better than anyone else. He could answer your questions better than I can."

"Does Swenson drink here?"

"Nope. He only comes in for promotions, memorials, and retirements. Club soda and lime, every single time. Maybe he's into that clean living shit, or he's a recovering alcoholic. Doesn't make a difference to me. But you're not gonna catch him here unless the department's throwing some kind of party."

"I've already spoken to him."

"Well, there ya go."

"Is Gallo married?"

"Nah, he used to be, but he had a wandering eye. Nowadays, he takes someone home about once a month. They'll be hot and heavy for a couple of weeks, and then it usually results in a slap to the face. A few weeks later, it's just rinse and repeat."

"Are he and Lucien close?"

Jim laughed, hiding his mouth behind his hand. "Geographically, sure. But that's about it."

"Gallo acted like Lucien was his best friend, that they traded favors and exchanged secrets."

"I wouldn't know about any of that." Jim nodded to the door. "I'd suggest you ask him about it."

I turned to find Cross entering the bar. He looked around the room, relieved to find it empty except for a waitress refilling the napkin dispensers. His eyes homed in on me, the dark cloud settling again.

"What are you doing here, Alex?" he asked, joining me at the bar.

"Digging up intel on Gallo. What are you doing here?"

"I wanted a drink."

"Go somewhere else," Jim muttered. "I don't have any of your fancy gin in stock."

"I see three bottles right there." Cross pointed to the top shelf.

"Then you need to get your eyes checked, son," Jim said.

"I'm not your son." Cross went behind the bar and grabbed one of the bottles. He pulled a glass from beneath the bar and poured. After taking a sip, he turned toward Jim, who stared incredulously at him. "I know you called my father."

"Someone had to."

"You shouldn't have bothered. He knew where I was all along, but he couldn't have cared less." Cross downed the rest of his drink and poured another one.

"Yeah, well, it was about damn time someone got him off his ass and reminded him about doing the right thing."

Cross almost smiled. "Thanks." Jim looked shocked as Cross clapped him on the shoulder and went around the bar to take a seat beside me. "Will you do me another favor?"

"Depends. Is hell going to freeze over?"

"Don't bust my balls," Cross said. "I need to know everything about Joe Gallo."

"Does anyone else hear an echo?" Jim jerked his chin at me. "I'm not repeating myself. Ask her to fill you in."

"Did you leave anything out?" Cross asked.

"Nope."

"What about surveillance footage? I'd like to see who Gallo's been talking to lately." Cross spun on the stool, pointing out the security cameras as he went.

"The system's in back. Help yourself," Jim said.

Cross snickered. "I see you're on your best behavior."

"It wouldn't be nice to tell you to fuck off in front of a lady."

"She's no lady," Cross said. "She's a goddess."

I leaned in close. "Lucien, you're dead."

Cross grinned. "Thanks for proving my point. Didn't I say people make threats like that all the time?"

"It's not a threat."

He continued to smile. "We'll see. In the meantime, let's get to work."

Three hours into scanning KC's security footage for Gallo's unknown accomplice, my phone rang. It was Heathcliff.

"What's up?" I asked. "Did Gallo give anything up?"

"He's weaving quite a tale. You're not going to believe what he's saying now." Heathcliff snorted. "He's claiming the guy who lives in the apartment stole police credentials and attacked Cross inside the precinct. He also said that's the man who left the threatening note in your car."

"What about the other two threats?"

"He admitted to the first two—the one on your windshield and scratching up your paint job. He says he did that because he didn't want Cross to get into any more trouble."

"What's that supposed to mean?"

"I don't know," Heathcliff said.

"It sounds like Gallo's talking a lot about the guy in the apartment. Did he give you a name?"

"Gallo won't give it up, unless he gets immunity. It has

to be Campos. I can't imagine why he'd want immunity otherwise."

"He shouldn't ask for immunity. He should ask for witness protection."

"That would require him to admit too much. Gallo's close to breaking, but he's not there yet. I'll get him there."

"Have you confronted him with Campos's death?"

"I have, but it didn't faze him in the least. He didn't react to the name at all."

"That's odd." Gallo must have a better poker face than I imagined. "Have you found anything in Gallo's accounts or in his phone records to connect him to the cartel?"

"No. I'll save you a phone call. Neither has Jablonsky. The staties found a burner on Campos's body. The techs are analyzing it now. We'll just have to see where that leads, but Moretti went ahead and moved things along. You can tell your boss the charges have been dropped. He should be getting a written apology delivered in the morning."

"Lucien will be glad to hear it." After we disconnected, I shared the good news.

THIRTY-NINE

"This was an utter waste." Cross warily made his way through the bar. During our time spent in the back room, the place had filled up. "At least I don't have to worry about any of this shit. We're done." He held the door, gesturing for me to exit.

The sun had just set. The high humidity, growing darkness, and remaining heat felt oppressive. My shirt stuck to my back the moment I stepped out of the air conditioning. The parking lot had filled up, but I didn't spot Cross's car. "Do you need a ride?" I asked, scowling at my busted windshield. Maybe I'd take it to the body shop tomorrow.

"No, I'm around the corner. I didn't want to give an off duty cop any funny ideas."

"You still think they're out to get you?"

"They always will be."

"Why?" I asked.

He shook his head, staring up at the sky. "Too much history."

"I'm sorry."

He cocked his head and eyed me. "That's just how it is." He turned his gaze to my car. "Is that thing safe to drive like that? I could barely see out the cracked windshield."

"I'll make an appointment in the morning."

"Just drop it off at the office. I'll have someone take care of it. After all, it's my fault. I'll pay for it, like you insisted." He headed for the sidewalk, turning when he got to the end of the property. "It's back to business as usual. I'll see you at the morning meeting. Eight a.m. Conference room B."

"I might be late."

He pointed a finger at me. "Tomorrow morning. Don't be late."

I chuckled. "Night, Lucien."

He disappeared around the corner, and I got behind the wheel. It wasn't that late. Heathcliff might still be at work. Maybe I'd see if he wanted some assistance now that Lucien Cross was no longer on anyone's radar. I was halfway through dialing when a fireball lit up my rearview mirror. The resounding boom shook the ground, followed by a cacophony of alarms.

Jumping out of the car, I hurried to the edge of the parking lot and turned in the direction of the explosion. A couple of people had already congregated on the other side of the street, giving the flaming Porsche a wide berth. I ran toward it. My heart in my throat.

"Lucien," I screamed. *No, not again.* "Lucien!"

I found him on the ground, eight feet from the burning car. Kneeling down, I felt for a pulse. He opened his eyes, dazed and confused.

"Are you okay?" I asked.

He blinked a few times. His skin pink from the heat of the blast, and his eyebrows singed. Blood dribbled down the side of his neck. I gave the injury a more thorough exam, but he hadn't caught shrapnel. His eardrum might have burst. I couldn't tell.

I held a few fingers in front of his face. "How many fingers am I holding up?"

He didn't answer. His eyebrows furrowed as he stared at something in the distance.

"Lucien?" I turned, shouting to the person across the street. "Call 9-1-1. We need an ambulance." Reaching for my phone, I realized I'd left it in my car. How could I be so stupid? "Can you hear me?" I grabbed for my keys, using the flashlight to check his pupils. They reacted normally to the light.

"Is he okay?" someone asked from behind.

"I don't know. Is help on the way?"

Cross's eyes went wide. "Alex, watch out."

But it was too late. The jolt started at the small of my back, simultaneously moving down my legs and up my spine. My nerve endings lit on fire, locking my muscles in place. The world tipped sideways. Cross grabbed for his gun, but the figure moved forward from behind me and kicked him in the jaw. The man zapped me again when I forced my hand to move toward my weapon. The crackling noise signaled the fate that awaited me.

The second jolt put me flat on the ground. He leaned over me, pressing the business end against the exposed skin at the base of my neck. I would have screamed, but the world went black before that could happen.

*   *   *

When I came to, I didn't immediately recall what had happened. My arms tingled painfully. I tried to shake some blood back into them, and that's when I realized I couldn't move. Blinking my eyes open, I stared at the dirty concrete floor beneath me. Oil stains and tire marks covered most of the painted surface.

I rocked a few times on my shoulder, hoping to roll myself up, but my hands were bound behind my back to something heavy. When my fingers came into contact with someone else's hand, I screamed.

"Alex, are you okay?" Cross asked.

"I think so."

"Alex?" He brushed his fingers against mine, and I latched onto his hand. "Are you okay?" he repeated.

"I'm fine," I said louder. "Are you?"

"Aside from this damn ringing in my ears and this fucking headache, I am too."

"All right. Let's see if we can sit up." It took a few tries to coordinate our movements, but we pulled ourselves up. He leaned against me, his back against mine. "Are you sure you're okay?" I asked.

"A little dizzy, but nothing to worry about."

I waited for him to get his bearings while I scanned the room. We appeared to be in a garage, possibly a small hangar. I couldn't tell what it was. Open cardboard boxes, rags, and a workbench with some tools lined the walls. I couldn't see behind me, so I had no idea how large of a place this was. A roll-up metal door stood in front of me. I didn't see any other way in or out. No windows.

"Do you remember what happened?" I asked.

"I clicked the unlock on my key fob and the blast knocked me back." He made a humming sound and cleared his throat. "I swear, I thought I saw Trey Knox."

"Knox?"

"Yeah, I know. Insane, right?"

Using my heels, I maneuvered myself around as far as I could. Behind us, the room continued to spread out beneath a domed ceiling. We weren't dead. "Do you know where we are?"

"An airport, maybe. I thought I saw a propellor blade over there."

"How long was I out?"

"Not long." He shifted. "Let's stand up."

With our backs together, I got my heels beneath me and pushed against his back while he pushed against mine. Slowly, we brought ourselves off the ground. All right, this was progress. He released the hold he had on my hands and shifted his right arm forward, which tugged mine backward.

Taking a step away from him, as far as our bindings would allow, I angled my head, feeling the ache in my neck from the taser burn. Whoever abducted us had used my handcuffs and Cross's to bind us together in a diagonal pattern, right wrist to right wrist and left wrist to left wrist.

"I don't suppose you have a handcuff key handy," I said.

"I don't think so. If I do, it's in my front pocket. I can't exactly reach it."

"Hang on." I stepped backward, turning as far as I could to give him the most reach. "What about now?"

"Other pocket." I shifted around, and he brought his

fingertips to his pocket. "It's gone."

"So's my gun."

"What about your phone?" he asked.

"I left it behind. Yours?"

"Cracked."

Giving the boxes and tools another look, I sidestepped toward them. "There has to be something around here we can use."

Performing an awkward dance, we got to the side of the room and peered into the boxes. I didn't spot anything small enough to pick the lock. Cross stepped unexpectedly forward, making me stumble backward. "This might work, but I need some give," he said. I moved my arm across my back, and he snatched a pair of needle-nose pliers from the table. "This would be easier if I could see what I'm doing."

"Sorry, I'm not a contortionist. If I were, I'd pop my shoulder joint out of place so we'd be facing one another."

"Feel free to give it a try," he mumbled, frustrated as he tried to work the narrow end into the release.

"Do you have any idea who took us or why?" While he worked, I eyed a wrench. We'd need to escape, and we'd need weapons.

"I don't know. The bastard nearly blew me to kingdom come. Quite frankly, our brains should be splattered on the sidewalk. I don't know why we're alive. It would have been quicker and cleaner to kill us and escape." The pliers fell to the floor with a clang. "Dammit."

"Let me try." Crouching down, I waited for Cross to squat down so I could grab the pliers off the floor. He lost his balance and crashed into me, knocking us both to the ground. We hit the table, causing the toolbox on the end to tumble over the edge. The noise echoed off the concrete surfaces, and a door opened. That was our way out.

Quickly, I grabbed the pliers and pressed against Cross to conceal them from whoever just entered. Footsteps sounded at the far end of the room. A hooded figure loomed beneath the light. His features concealed from view.

No one moved. The figure remained for a full minute, doing nothing but watching. Then he went back to the door. When it opened, I glimpsed the night sky. I hadn't been unconscious that long. We couldn't be too far from KC's bar.

Once the door slammed, Cross relaxed. "Hurry before he comes back."

"I'm trying." I fidgeting with the pliers, hearing him hiss in pain when I adjusted my grip and stabbed him in the hand. "Sorry."

"Me too." He shifted to give me as much slack as possible.

After what felt like an eternity, the bracelet on his left wrist loosened. He tugged his hand free and flopped onto his back and closed his eyes.

"Stay with me, Cross. Keep those eyes open," I said.

"Don't worry. I'm fine."

But, after that kick to the jaw, I didn't think he was. However, arguing would waste precious time. "All right." I switched hands, hoping to use my left to open the right set of cuffs, but the pliers kept slipping. After slicing the outside of my wrist, I finally got the end of the pliers into the key hole and forced the cuffs to release.

Cross pulled his hand away from mine, glad to be free. "Let's get out of here."

"He couldn't have taken us that far. I don't think we were out that long. He must have had a car waiting." I thought about the vehicles near the explosion. One of them had its lights on, but I couldn't remember any details about it. "We weren't far from KC's. I heard the blast from my car. The cops inside must have heard something. I left my phone and door open. Someone's going to notice that. They'll know we're missing. People must be looking for us by now."

"Are you sure that's a good thing?" Cross eyed me, his eyes a little unfocused. He didn't have a concussion before, but I wasn't sure that was true now.

"Who do you think took us?" I asked, getting up to search for weapons.

"I don't know, but this has to do with Knox's murder investigation. You said the police found a cartel soldier. He must have been working with Gallo."

"You think the cartel abducted us?" The thought made the knot in my stomach tighten.

"They'll torture us for information. They must want the ledger and Knox's account numbers. Maybe that's why Gallo gave me the ledger in the first place." Cross used the table to pull himself to his feet. "This looks like a hangar at a private airfield. It'd be easy for them to fly out once they get the answers they want."

"I don't know about you, but I have no intention of sticking around and waiting for any of that to happen. We have to get out of here." I picked up a wrench the length of my forearm and handed it to him. "I'd prefer to avoid the door if we can."

"Agreed." He scouted the far side of the room while I grabbed a heavy metal tool that looked like a horseshoe attached to two long handles. It had something to do with rivets. Then I moved along the wall, checking for any openings, hidden doors, or windows. "Maybe we can roll this up," I suggested when I reached the back wall.

"If he's outside, he'll notice."

"Not if he's around back," I said.

Cross knelt down, testing the door. "Once we open this, we'll lose all cover. We don't know how many guys are out there. We could be overrun in seconds."

"Do you think they have an army outside?"

"I don't know. But they might."

I crouched beside him, but we couldn't get it to budge. It was locked, and I couldn't figure out how to open it.

"It looks like we're back to door number one," Cross said.

"I don't like it. We know someone is outside guarding it. He came in when we made a noise. If we try to go out, he'll notice."

"Does it matter?" Cross asked. "We don't know what the terrain looks like on either side. We'll be just as exposed and in close proximity to the enemy no matter what door we use. At least we know that opens."

"Does it?" I moved to the other end, but there was no way to see outside. Raising the riveting tool in preparation to strike, I reached out and gently tried the handle, but the door didn't budge. "We're locked in."

"Guess we'll just have to lure him inside."

Before I could protest, Cross banged his wrench against the aluminum wall, leaving a dent and making the entire hangar rattle.

FORTY

The door pulled out, and the man with the hood stood just out of striking distance with a gun in his hand. He aimed it at me. "Back up," he ordered. From the way his finger tensed over the trigger, he meant business.

"Take it easy," I said. "What do you want from us?" Edging backward, I moved to the side and placed the riveting tool down on the table.

"I don't want anything from you. This is about him." The man entered the hangar, leaving the door open.

I made myself as small and unintimidating as possible. If he didn't see me as a threat, we'd have a chance. "Please don't hurt me." I knelt on the floor at the end of the table, taking cover behind it. I had to find a way to edge around and get behind the guy. If Cross had just waited instead of being so impetuous, we could have come up with a reasonable plan.

"I can't guarantee that." He snickered, turning his attention to Cross who stood a few feet away. "Hi, Lucien. How's tricks?"

Cross stiffened, the large wrench hanging by his side. "You've got to be shitting me. You're supposed to be dead."

The man laughed. "You're right. This is the afterlife.

Welcome to hell."

Cross took a step forward, and the man aimed right at his chest. "If I'm already dead, you can't hurt me," Cross said.

"I forgot how stubborn and self-righteous you are." The man gestured at the wrench. "Drop that, unless you want to see what the next life is really like."

Cross let the wrench clatter to the floor. "What do you want? I told you never to come back here, Trey."

"I wanted my ring. I asked you to bring it to me, but you refused. You left me no choice."

While the men spoke, I searched for another cover position, but I didn't see any. The table was too heavy to move, but if I could get underneath it, I might be able to edge closer without the man noticing. Cross called the man Trey, but Trey Knox was dead. DNA proved it. How was he standing here, holding us at gunpoint?

"What are you going to do now?" Cross asked.

Knox laughed. "Well, I'm going to kill you and your friend. I'm thinking burying you in an empty field's a good plan. That should suffice for the next eight years or so. But the police might keep looking for your bodies, so I'm thinking of staging something spectacular." He reached behind his back and pulled out my gun. "I can shoot her with this gun," he said, indicating the one in his right, "and then shoot you with this one." He raised the one in his left. "The cops will think you shot her because she found something juicy on you, something irrefutable that would put you behind bars for the rest of your life. But she manages to shoot you in the process. It's a murder-murder thing. But I'm not sure if anyone will buy it. What do you think?"

"I see you're still a delusional, self-aggrandized prick," Cross said.

Knox tucked my gun behind his back. "The only other option is a murder-suicide. Do you think that's more believable?" Knox used his free hand to scratch his eyebrow. "I pop you both and put the gun in your hand. That should paint enough of a story, right?"

"That won't explain my Porsche," Cross said.

Knox nodded a few times. "You're right. I guess I'll just put you in the ground and not worry about the rest. Like you said, I'm dead. No one's going to look for me because a dead man can't be a killer. Plus, a friend of mine is supposed to be meeting me here soon. We're going to Mexico."

Apparently, Knox didn't know Campos was dead, and I wasn't about to tell him.

"What happened to you?" Cross asked. "The last time I saw you, you were a sniveling, fraidy cat. When did your balls finally descend?"

"Funny story, really. Things went downhill pretty fast on the island, so I came back home to get my ring and figure some things out. Since most of the police force had lost interest in finding me, I used an alias to set up a safe house, so I could resume doing business in the city. The best sports conventions are always here. I didn't want to miss those. You'll be happy to know I've attended every single one. But I digress." Knox grinned. "Anyway, one of my problems followed me back to the states. A client of mine broke in to my apartment wanting revenge. By some miracle, he tripped over one of my moving boxes. His gun slid right to me. I picked it up, shot him, and kept shooting until he went down." Knox's eyes went wide. "I don't know how many it took, but it seemed like a lot. Then I asked myself what would Lucien do, and I did that." He chuckled. "Hiring you actually came in handy. I really should have paid you."

While Knox reminisced, I slid beneath the table, hoping he'd stay lost in his story. Cross spotted me crawling toward Knox and moved to his left, forcing Knox to angle himself away from me. The table would end in another two feet. Then I had to clear a ten foot expanse before he could turn and shoot me. Still, I didn't see any other alternative. *Keep him talking*, I thought, hoping Cross could read my mind.

"Who was the dead guy? Your twin? His DNA matched yours. The police ran it based off your hairbrush. Hell, I ran a comparison to your toothbrush. How did you fake that?" Cross asked.

Knox laughed. "I'm brilliant. I had to be to pull everything off. And I got away with it, just like I got away with cultivating my business right under a Russian kingpin's nose. I'm not a moron, even though you treated me like one. Damn, I've missed you. I forgot how much fun you are. You really fell for my act. I'm not some pathetic bastard, Lucien. I'm a certified genius."

Narcissistic asshole would be more accurate, I thought.

"Come on, tell me. How'd you pull it off?" Cross asked. Since Knox wanted to talk, it wasn't hard to keep him going. I just didn't know if it'd be enough of a distraction.

"When I wasn't sure you'd be able to solve my Russian problem, I decided to stage my death and move on. Except, that's hard to do without a body. One of my clients had some experience with such things and offered up a bag of blood and the toiletries to match. He promised me he had the same blood type, so the authorities would be convinced it was my DNA. They had no reason to doubt it. I packed up my stuff, scrubbed my house from top to bottom, and replaced it with his stuff."

"But the DNA in your house matched the body."

"I'm getting to that," Knox said. "Don't be so impatient. It's been eight years. Let's have a little foreplay before we get down and dirty, all right?"

Cross grunted, his knuckles turning white. If I didn't make a move soon, he'd run at Knox and get blown away in the process.

"The client who helped me fake my death was the same one who helped me set up shop in Vanuatu. But we had a falling out after I arrived. He thought I owed him and should only work for him. But I didn't go through all that trouble just to become someone else's bitch. That's how Vasili treated me, and I wasn't going to do that again. Lesson learned."

"So you fled, again," Cross said. "I always knew you'd screw someone else over and they'd try to kill you."

"The joke's on him. He's the problem that followed me back to the states and to the apartment I rented, and that's when I realized I could solve my own problems. After that, I didn't worry so much about my enemies. Since I was believed to be dead, I could function without worry. My DNA and prints weren't in the system. And my enemies thought I was long gone. I had saved enough money over the years, so I could be picky about clients. I even got someone to help me out with protection."

"Officer Gallo," Cross said. "You bought a cop."

"Well, he kept snooping around. One day, he recognized me. He wanted to bring me in, but I told him I needed protection, that the Russians were still after me, and gave him a cut in order to keep an eye out for me. It was cute. He thought he was filling in for you. I didn't realize you had groupies."

"Gallo knows you're alive?" Cross asked.

"He thinks I'm in witness protection or some privately created version of it. He might even think you created it."

"He bought that?"

"For enough money, people will believe anything you tell them." Knox smiled, satisfied to share his triumph. "Anyway, it was nice catching up with you."

The story was over. I had to make my move now. Knox had realized he hadn't been paying enough attention to me and turned just as I broke from cover. He aimed, firing two shots while I ran straight for him. The bullets ripped past me, missing by mere millimeters. I swung the riveting tool at him. It connected with his shoulder, knocking him to the ground.

I pulled the tool backward, prepared to swing again, when Knox rolled over, kicking off the floor and sliding on his back to put some distance between us, while firing. I dove to the side, dropping my weapon in my haste.

Cross tried to tackle the already downed Knox, but due to his injuries, Knox tossed him aside. "Run," Cross yelled, tripping as he got his feet beneath him. "I'm right behind you."

Knox was outnumbered, but he had guns. We didn't, so I ran for the door with Cross at my heels. We made it through as three more shots echoed. One hit the doorframe just to the right of my head. The other ricocheted off the frame above us, and the third sailed past.

Cross shoved me to the side, just as we made it out the

door. He'd been right. We were at a private airfield. The surrounding area was completely empty except for the tall fence lining the perimeter. The chain-link was too high to climb. We'd have to circle around the front.

"This way," I said, pointing as I ran around the side. But when we reached the front, we found the gate had been locked.

Knox rounded the corner, firing shot after shot in our direction. Cross and I split up, running in opposite directions. Knox cursed, ejecting the magazine and shoving another one inside. Cross must have had an extra magazine. I didn't since I wasn't expecting trouble. For once, it was good I hadn't been prepared.

A thought came to mind as I scrambled to find a defensible position. What happened to Knox's taser?

Bullets rang out, and I continued running around the hangar. Parked on the far side, I found Knox's car—a white sedan. The bullet struck the window, knocking a few shards of glass backward from the force of the impact. Shielding my eyes, I continued to run, the bullets getting closer and closer.

Sliding across the hood, I landed and rolled on the opposite side. I gasped, hoping to catch my breath. Where was Lucien? Did Knox shoot him?

I moved along the car, toward the back, and peered around the trunk. Cross was down. From here, I couldn't tell the extent of his injuries, but since Knox didn't seem concerned with him, I assumed the worst. *No, this couldn't be happening. It had to be a nightmare.*

"Come out, come out, where ever you are," Knox sang out.

Every cell in my body wanted to charge him, knock him to the ground, and rip him to shreds. But from my count, he had several more bullets in that gun. I'd be dead before I cleared the car. I had to come up with a better plan. I needed a weapon.

Deciding to risk it, I moved to the middle of the car and sat up on my haunches, peering inside. Another two shots rang out. Immediately, I dropped down and rolled beneath the car. Knox, came around the front, and I rolled out from beneath the car and tugged on the door handle while he searched the other side for me. The front door opened, and I grabbed the taser off the seat.

He spun, firing through the passenger side window. The sting cut through my arm. I didn't know if it was glass or a bullet. Frankly, it didn't matter. I slid beneath the car again, my belt snagging on the undercarriage, but I stretched my hand out as far as I could and pressed the button.

The taser didn't have much juice left in it, but the staticky click sounded, and Knox crashed to the ground. Backing out from beneath the car, I went around and gave him another jolt, pressing the button until the taser was dead. Knox lay on the ground, limp.

Where was the gun? I couldn't find it. Searching his pockets, I found a cell phone and dialed 9-1-1 while I ran to Lucien.

I gave the 9-1-1 operator all the information I had, hoping she'd be able to determine our location. Only one private airfield was close to KC's. We had to be there. It was the only logical choice.

"Lucien?" His shirt was damp. There wasn't enough light to see if it was blood. But what else could it be? "Cross, wake up." I rolled him over. "Come on, open your eyes. Don't be a pain in my ass."

A wet stain had formed along his side. He'd been shot. Before I could check his pulse, he jerked upright, grabbing for my throat.

"It's me," I choked out.

He shook himself, releasing his hold on my neck. "Where is he?" He frantically searched the surrounding field, his breath coming in ragged gasps that matched my own.

"He's down."

"Down? Not dead?" Cross got onto his hands and knees and hoisted himself off the dewy grass. Clutching his side, he and I headed back to the car. But Knox was gone. Bending over, Cross picked up the gun that had fallen behind the front tire. He checked the magazine. Two shots left. "Alex." He wobbled, and I grabbed for him, hoping to steady him, but it was too late. I did my best to slow his descent as he crashed to the ground.

That's when I felt the barrel of a gun press into the back of my head. "This one's fully loaded," Knox said.

"Lucien," I whispered, "I could use some help." He'd collapsed on top of the gun. I'd never get it before Knox wasted us both. Biting my lip, I thought about Martin. "You can run," I said, swallowing my fear. "Everyone thinks you're dead. The police pulled over a drug dealer in a white sedan. They think that's who did this. But you have to go now. The police are on the way. They'll see your car. If you kill us, they'll keep hunting you. You should escape while you still can."

"That puts a chink in my plans. I'm tired of running. I don't have the resources left to run."

"I have your ledger. Your accounts. I can get it all back to you, even your championship ring collection. I'll take you to it, but we have to go now."

"Can you do that?" Knox asked.

"I'm a consultant. I have access to everything."

The barrel of the gun no longer pressed into my skull, and I cautioned a glance over my shoulder. Knox had stepped back far enough so I couldn't take the gun from him. He wasn't a helpless idiot, but he was no genius either. "Tell me where everything is, or I'll kill you." He steadied the gun in both hands.

"The ledger? Or your rings?" I asked, hoping to buy time.

"Both."

"Right, but which one do you want to know about first. They're in different places."

"Let's start with my rings."

Everyone had said this guy had a skewed sense of his priorities. On autopilot, I launched into a long-winded lie, wondering how long it'd take for the authorities to arrive. They had to be ten minutes out. And since we were on one of the smaller runways at the private airfield, it'd take them longer to find us. Knox would surely hear the sirens and see the lights before they got close enough to take him out. So I couldn't wait for help to arrive.

"And the ledger?" he asked. "I need access to my accounts. Didn't the police freeze them?"

"No, and they won't. Once they determine what's what, they'll relinquish everything to Emily, your half-sister."

"Emily? What does she have to do with any of this?"

"She's living in your house, the one where you allegedly died. She has all your things. Well, everything you didn't take with you. If you pay her a visit, I'm sure she'd give it all back."

Knox stared at me for the longest time. Then he laughed. "Do you expect me to believe that?"

It was now or never. "No." I lunged forward.

The gunshot deafened me as I collided with him, the force knocking both of us to the ground. Blood coated my shirt, hot and sticky. I yanked the gun in his hand up and away from us, and it went off again. He kicked me in the stomach, knocking me off of him. Then a third shot rang out.

I gasped, hoping to get my lungs working, as I stared into the dark night sky.

FORTY-ONE

Cross pulled himself to his feet, tossing the empty gun to the ground. He kicked the gun out of Knox's hand, almost collapsing in the process. "You son of a bitch." He sneered at him.

After several failed attempts to breathe, my lungs filled. Yanking up my shirt, I felt around my chest, but I hadn't been shot. The bruises on my back and sternum had made me think otherwise. So who fired the shots?

Cross teetered, and I slipped beneath his arm before he could fall. Unlike me, he'd been hit at least once. In the dark, I couldn't tell how many more bullet wounds he sustained, but he remained upright, leaning against the car for support as police cars and an ambulance arrived. The adrenaline would keep him going for a few more minutes.

Picking up the gun, I found it empty. "You killed Knox," I said. "Do you think the police are going to charge you again?"

"I wouldn't put it past them." He swayed, just as police cleared the area and allowed the paramedics to enter. "Why did you call 9-1-1? Our mobile medical unit is better equipped."

"You're welcome," I said.

Police clustered around, and I did what I could to answer their questions while my focus remained on Cross and what the paramedics were saying. They got him onto a backboard and carried him to the ambulance. Once he was in the rig, I got a better look at his injuries. He'd caught a graze, which had sliced across the side and front of his torso, but the bruises beneath it worried me far more. I'd only seen bruises like that once before.

Images of another explosion that claimed the life of my partner came to mind. My mouth tasted metallic, and everything dimmed. My heart pounded in my ears.

"You can't let him die," I said. Ignoring the police officers who'd been questioning me, I climbed into the rig beside the paramedics. "His car exploded. I'm not sure how close he was to the blast. But it threw him backward. He said his ears were ringing, and he had trouble hearing. That asshole kicked him in the jaw."

"It's all right, ma'am. We got this." The paramedic checked the monitors. "He looks stable. We'll get him to the hospital. A trauma team will check him out. Do you want to ride along?"

The last time I did, it had been catastrophic, but Cross stared at me with a helpless look I'd never seen before. "I'll stay with him."

"We'll meet you there," the police officer said, slamming the door and tapping it twice.

*   *   *

"You missed the morning meeting," Cross said when I entered his hospital room. "You'll do absolutely anything to avoid those, won't you?"

"Shut up." I put the drink carrier down on the tray table, watching as he tugged on a shirt. "I thought they wanted to keep you another day for observation."

"If I need someone to observe me, I'll handpick who's going to do it."

"You're such a control freak."

He stared at me from the corner of his eye. "And you're not?"

"I brought you coffee with a shot of espresso. Justin called in the order, so it should be to your liking." I looked around the room. "I'm surprised he's not here."

Cross picked up the cup and took a sip, carefully holding his side with his free hand. "Unlike you, he's actually doing his job."

"What do you want me to do? You had me pass my cases off. Renner's handling them. And now that Knox is dead, Almeada asked me to stay on top of things at the police department."

"Is there a problem?" Cross asked. "What did you say when you gave your statement?"

"The truth."

"What the hell's taking them so long? It's been two days since the shooting. Knox is dead. My actions were reasonable. The case should be closed."

"They had everything wrong. The victim. The crime. The suspects. Everything. They have to mop up the mess. That takes time."

"And you're helping?"

"Trying to," I said.

"More like annoying us," Heathcliff said, knocking gently against the door. "Glad to see you're up and about. I heard you're getting discharged. How are you feeling, Mr. Cross?"

"Fine, but I prefer hospitals when I'm not the patient," Cross said. My boss did his best not to scowl at the detective. "Are you hoping to arrest me now that I've actually killed Knox?"

"No," Heathcliff looked at me, but I picked up my coffee and sipped it slowly, "Alex corroborated everything you said that happened. And Officer Gallo has come forward regarding his knowledge of Knox's illegal actions."

"How'd you get that sycophant to talk?" Cross asked.

"We promised leniency for his crimes and the cover-up in exchange for details. Knox smuggled product in and out of the country for a lot of big players. Gallo's intel helped us crack the ledger. We finally have names and dates. A lot of cases are moving forward. We have evidence on key players that we've never had before." Heathcliff looked at me. "We're coordinating with the OIO, FBI, DEA, and ATF on a lot of this."

"Jablonsky told me," I said.

Heathcliff nodded, turning his focus back to Cross. "None of that would have been possible without you. The commissioner wants to honor you."

"He can go fuck himself," Cross muttered.

Heathcliff snorted. "He's right outside. I'll let you tell him that. We'll give you some privacy." The detective stared at me. "Ms. Parker, I believe you have a prior commitment."

"Don't remind me." But Heathcliff wouldn't leave without me. "Do you need anything, Lucien?" Hopefully, he'd need me to stay.

Cross shook his head. "Tomorrow, I expect to see you at the morning meeting."

"You're going to work?"

"Yes. I'll be there tomorrow to address everyone and answer questions. You better be there too. That's an order."

"Yes, sir." I followed Heathcliff to the door, telling him to give me a minute. "Hey, Lucien, thanks for not dying."

He gave me an odd look. "I wasn't planning on it."

"I don't think most people I know do, but it happens anyway."

His expression softened. "Thanks for having my back."

"Always."

Heathcliff waited for me at the end of the hall. We went down the stairs, avoiding the elevator so he wouldn't have to face an awkward encounter with the police commissioner. We didn't speak about what happened. We'd already gone over every detail and every part of Knox's confession ad nauseam.

He parked in front of the church and opened the car door. "Is Martin meeting us at the bar afterward?"

"No, he's still in L.A. He should be getting home late tonight."

"Did you tell him what happened?"

"I told him enough."

"And he's still pulling out of the deal with Cross Security?"

"I'm not sure. He wants more financing. Whether that means Cross is out and someone else is in, I don't know. Why? You planning on buying stock or something?"

Heathcliff chuckled. "No."

We went down the stairs, and I entered the room where the support group met. I didn't have the energy to fight against it. I already hurt, but it was different. Cross didn't die, and that had shifted things in my mind. It was like a do-over. Maybe Heathcliff, Cal, and everyone else were right. It wasn't about the ones we lost; it was about the ones we saved.

Halfway through the session, the door in the back opened. I turned, surprised to find Martin sneaking inside. From the way he was dressed, he'd come straight from the airport. He smiled at me and found a seat near the door.

"Does anyone else want to share?" Cal asked.

The lull remained. Taking a shaky breath, I glanced back at Martin and stood up. It was time. "I want to say something."

Past Crimes

Don't miss *Sinister Secret*, the next book in the Alexis Parker series:

A woman's secret could be Alexis Parker's undoing...

When Eddie Lucca, Alex's former partner, asks for a favor, she can't say no. But as soon as Alex meets with the client, she knows this is a mistake.

Years ago, Daria Waylon barely survived a brutal attack which left her with permanent brain damage. Now, Daria's claiming she's being hunted by the man who almost killed her. There's just one problem. He's dead.

Unsure how to help, Alex agrees to investigate Daria's claims and provide the woman with some peace of mind, if for no other reason than to pay back Lucca. After all, Alex owes him her life, so she'll do whatever he asks. But in this instance, Alex knows she should have said no.

Available in print and ebook.

Past Crimes

ABOUT THE AUTHOR

G.K. Parks is the author of the Alexis Parker series. The first novel, *Likely Suspects,* tells the story of Alexis' first foray into the private sector.

G.K. Parks received a Bachelor of Arts in Political Science and History. After spending some time in law school, G.K. changed paths and earned a Master of Arts in Criminology/Criminal Justice. Now all that education is being put to use creating a fictional world based upon years of study and research.

You can find additional information on G.K. Parks and the Alexis Parker series by visiting our website at
www.alexisparkerseries.com

Made in United States
North Haven, CT
06 May 2023

36290913R00189